Then There Were Giants

A novel by
Nicky Heymans

PUBLISHING

First published 2023 by

malcolm down
PUBLISHING

www.malcolmdown.co.uk

27 26 25 24 23 7 6 5 4 3 2 1

British Library Cataloguing in Publication Data

A catalogue record for this book is available from the British Library.

ISBN 978-1-915046-78-9

Cover design by Esther Kotecha
Art direction by Sarah Grace
Printed in the UK

Typeset using Atomik ePublisher from Easypress Technologies

Dedication

This book is dedicated to my father, Reg Lawton,
whose support and belief in my writing ability made
the publishing of this book possible.
Dad, thank you so much. I love you.

Acknowledgements

Anyone who has authored a book knows the amount of hard work that goes into the process of writing, rewriting and editing in order to make a book publishable. They also know that it is not a one-man (or one-woman) job. There is always a team around the author who support and advise and, without their help, the book would likely not be published.

My family are, without a doubt, my greatest support team. To my children, David, Caleb, Talitha and Leanne: thank you for your encouragement and affirmation, and for your helpful feedback. It means so much to me. To my husband, Kingsley: thank you from the bottom of my heart for your faith in my writing ability. Thank you for being willing to invest in my books, both financially and practically. Thank you for giving me the time and space I need in order to write, especially for noticing when I'm in my 'happy place' or am 'on a roll'. Your patient endurance is so appreciated!

To Mark Stibbe, my writing coach: once again, your creative input and firm but gracious challenges have inspired me to hone my skills as a writer. I am so thankful to have a mentor who believes in me, and who shares my passion for a deep relationship with Yahweh and His Word. You inspire me and motivate me, and I look forward to continuing to learn from you in the years to come.

To Malcolm Down, my publisher: it has been such a pleasure getting to know you over the last couple of years. You are a wonderful human being! Thank you for being a guiding hand and support to me, and especially for your advice to me as a new writer.

Note from the Author

Writing this novel has been an absolute joy! However, it also presented me with a significant challenge, one that I hadn't encountered when writing my first book in the *Wilderness Trilogy*.

The beginning and end of the Israelites' journey through the wilderness are well documented in the Bible. My first novel, *Into the Wilderness*, covered the first two years of their wandering, including their leaving Egypt, the parting of the Red Sea, Yahweh's presence with them in the form of the cloud and pillar of fire, the miracles of manna, water flowing from a rock and a rather bizarre battle strategy that involved Moses holding his staff above his head! During those two years, the Israelites turned to idolatry and worshipped a golden calf, were given the Ten Commandments and laws by Yahweh, and they refused to go into their promised land of Canaan, which resulted in their being sentenced to wander in the wilderness for forty years.

You get the picture: a lot happened in those two years!

The Bible also documents the period of time at the end of the Israelites' forty years of sojourning, much of which will be covered in the third book in this trilogy. It records how the Israelites prepared to enter the promised land of Canaan, how Moses was forbidden to enter the land because of an act of disobedience, and how Joshua was chosen to take over leadership of the nation of Israel when Moses died. That period of time includes incredible events such as the crossing of the Jordan River, the sun standing still at Joshua's command, the iconic story of the destruction of Jericho, and how Joshua led his people to victory against a seemingly never-ending barrage of enemies in the land of Canaan.

Then There Were Giants covers a span of approximately thirty-seven years, starting from when the Israelites were sentenced to wander in the wilderness, up until they were preparing to leave the wilderness and enter Canaan. Unlike the beginning and end of their journey, the Bible tells us *absolutely nothing* about what happened in this 'middle section', apart from giving us a list of locations where they camped, and a couple of references to Yahweh's faithfulness in providing for them. It's an 'almost blank' canvas. Although that was an exciting prospect for a storyteller like me, because it left so much scope for the imagination, it also presented me with a very real challenge. Thirty-seven years is a long time; a lot must have taken place. But what? What did life look like for these ex-slaves wandering around in a wilderness, year after year?

I chose to tell the Israelites' story through the eyes of Joshua ben Nun. In the biblical account, we're told very little about him as a person, apart from his skills as a warrior leader and the fact that he was Moses' manservant. There are a couple of 'clues' in Scripture, such as the verse in Exodus 33:11 which tells how Moses returned to the camp, but Joshua stayed at the Tent of Meeting. That, to me, shows how important Yahweh's presence must have been to Joshua, and I referred to that fact often in *Into the Wilderness*. The other clue, I believe, is found in the fact that Yahweh told Joshua at least three times to be 'strong and courageous', and also frequently reassured him that He would be with him.

I believe that no one becomes a great leader without going through some significant challenges of one kind or another, because overcoming difficulties is what builds strength of character in us. Why did Yahweh keep telling Joshua to be strong and courageous? Because He knew that Joshua needed to hear it. Because, to do what Yahweh had called him to do, Joshua would need to be both strong and courageous. Possibly because Joshua *didn't* feel he was strong or courageous. The *Wilderness Trilogy* outlines many of the battles that Joshua fought; the physical battles and wars that took place but, more importantly, the internal battles that raged within him. In *Then There Were Giants*, a lot of these centre around his fear of facing the giants of Canaan, and of not being able to defeat them or protect his family from them. Most of us grapple with issues around the pertinent questions of 'Who am I?' and 'Am I enough?' and I believe Joshua was no different.

On the subject of giants, again, the Bible does not give us much in the way of a description of their appearance, apart from mentioning their size and stature. I have chosen to portray the giants in what might be thought of as a slightly unusual way. This portrayal, again, is entirely fictitious, although their size and stature are based on biblical references.

Although there are various theories around the subject of Joshua's family, the Bible does not record Joshua as having married, and there is no record of him having fathered children. For the purpose of this trilogy, I have chosen to align with that mode of thought and, instead, have given Joshua an adopted family. While many of the characters in the books are real people, as mentioned in the Bible (such as Moses, Aaron, Caleb and Eleazar), many are fictitious, including the members of Joshua's adopted family.

It is important to note that a large proportion of this second book in the trilogy is fictitious, due to the previously mentioned lack of information given to us about this period of time. I have endeavoured to present an informed picture of what the Israelites, and more specifically, Joshua, might have been through, while staying true to the biblical narrative. However, please bear in mind that the stories that take place within the first two-thirds of this book are a work of fiction.

My prayer is that, in reading about his struggles and successes, you will be provoked to ponder your own life and that, just like Joshua, you will be filled with a growing, deep desire to know and love Yahweh, and to press into all that He has for you.

For more information, or to email the author, please go to
www.nickyheymansauthor.com.

Contents

1

Man-god

The hairs on the back of my neck bristled. My heart started pounding, my body trembled. A shiver ran down my spine; something was behind me. Everything in me screamed, *'Don't turn around!'*

I did.

Crouching low, I swivelled in slow motion and saw what looked like two tree trunks. The tree trunks moved. Not tree trunks – legs! I stared at them with morbid fascination, tracing the sinewy contours of calf muscles. Gazing upward, my eyes lit upon the flawless features of a being so arresting, he took my breath away. He was uncommonly tall and his robe, tied with a long leather cord, did little to mask his powerful, athletic build. Every part of his anatomy, from the broad set of his shoulders to his sculpted facial features, was perfect.

I felt mesmerised, powerless, drawn to his terrible beauty. Fighting the urge to bow down in homage, I wondered who he was. A messenger from Yahweh? His great stature and formidable physique were like the celestial messengers I had encountered before, but my instincts told me this creature had not come from Yahweh. He exuded a coldness, a sense of suppressed malevolence, as he studied me with disdain from his lofty heights. The lift of his head was arrogant and aloof, as if he knew how magnificent a specimen he was.

Then he smiled.

In truth, it was more of a sneer than a smile. His eyes narrowed and one corner of his mouth lifted. In a flash, his seductive beauty transformed into predatory treachery. His gaze darkened and he snarled, lifting his arm to reveal a huge mace with a hefty metal head, covered in spikes. The titan stepped towards me, brandishing the mace. My hair wafted in the current; I dropped to the ground on all-fours. Scrambling backwards, I managed to clamber to my feet, reaching for my sword, but my hand found an empty scabbard; I was defence-less. The giant sneered at my obvious horror. Gasping in shock, one thought outstripped all others.

'*Ruuuun!*'

I took off, sprinting as fast as I could across the desert terrain. He gave chase, half-laughing, half-roaring at this unexpected opportunity for sport. The ground shook from the impact of his footsteps as he pounded after me. Glancing behind me, I tripped over a rock and hurtled to the ground, skidding face-first on the stony earth. I wiped the blood out of my eyes and turned over but, before I could hoist myself to a standing position, an enormous sandal-clad foot shoved me back down. I stared up into the snarling face of the man-god looming over me.

'You thought you could outrun me?' the giant's smooth tone was like honeyed slime. I gasped for breath and pushed against his foot, to no avail. My hands were like those of a child against the mass of his foot. The giant laughed at my pitiful attempts to free myself, tossed his mace to the ground, and crossed his arms with a condescending smirk. The mace landed with a thud a mere finger's breadth away from my face. I began to feel light-headed, my sight blurred. From a scabbard attached to his leather belt, the giant drew a dagger which he held to my neck, taunting me.

'You are a weak, pathetic creature,' he growled, dark evil gleaming in his eyes. Lifting his dagger, he gave a mighty roar, and brought it down on my neck.

'*Aagh!!!*' I uttered a strangled cry and sat bolt upright. My heart thumped wildly; my body was covered with perspiration. I panted, trembling with fear, and looked around me.

'A dream? No! It cannot be,' I muttered to myself. I brushed strands of sweaty hair out of my eyes and slumped over, exhausted. Judging from the state of my bed roll, I must have been thrashing around in my sleep. I wondered if I had made a lot of noise; the thought of my family in the nearby tents hearing me was embarrassing. A sense of panic still lay heavily on me; I felt groggy and disorientated.

Freeing myself from the tangle of bedclothes that had wrapped themselves around my body, I stood up and walked to the entrance of the tent. I drew back the flap and peered out.

Everything was still.

Apart from the scuffling of nearby sheep and a baby's cry, the camp seemed bizarrely peaceful. A breeze ruffled my hair. I closed my eyes, relishing the effect of the cool night air on my hot, clammy body, but no sooner had I closed them then the snarling face of the giant loomed in front of me. I gasped and opened my eyes with a start, stumbling backwards while grasping for my sword. It wasn't there. Of course it wasn't – I was still wearing the robe I slept in, no belt, no sword.

'*Oysh!*' I whispered, heart pounding again. 'You hunt me even in my waking hours?' Realising there would be no more sleep for me that night, I went back inside my tent, washed, and put on my outer robe. There was only one thing that could calm my racing heart: Yahweh's presence. I drew my cloak around me and hurried through the camp, past the countless tents that littered the desert floor, until I arrived at the Tabernacle, our holy place of worship.

On the day that our God led us out of captivity in Egypt, His presence had gone before us in the form of a cloud. However, this was no ordinary cloud; it was breathtakingly beautiful, undulating constantly, glimmers of iridescent colours flickering within its form. One section of the cloud flowed down to form a billowing pillar that moved, leading our new-born nation when we travelled by day. The pillar of cloud transformed each evening into a glowing pillar of fire which kept us warm, providing light and protection by night.

My heartrate slowed in response to the fire that towered over me, like a glowing sentinel, outside the entrance to the Tabernacle. Flickering tongues of fire surrounded the pillar, dancing in exquisite partnership around glowing embers. I entered the Tabernacle courtyard and sank down on my knees, drinking in the soul-quenching magnificence of Yahweh's presence.

'Lord my God,' I whispered, hands pressed to my chest. 'My soul longs for You, like the parched desert lands before the early rains.'

The giant's leering face began to fade from my consciousness.

15

'I thirst for You, Holy One. My spirit makes diligent search for You.'

I closed my eyes, listening to the cracking sounds that emanated from the roaring blaze of His fire.

'You are near to those who call upon Your name.'

I reached out my arms to the heavens. Peace settled upon me like warm sheep's wool, purging the giant's venomous words from my mind.

'You, Lord, are my salvation; I will trust and not be afraid.'

I opened my eyes and turned to gaze upon the pillar of fire. Faint outlines of blazing-winged creatures flew in the midst of the embers, spiralling upwards then plummeting down, their outstretched wings tinged with glistening hues of gold, bronze and crimson.

I cried out, 'My heart exults in the Lord who hears the cries of His people.'

Strength flooded my being.

Faith replaced fear as I worshipped the Lord God of Israel throughout the last watch of the night, until the faint glow of dawn appeared on the horizon. Hearing the familiar chirp of desert sparrows as they woke to greet the new day, I stood up to watch the shimmering outline of a glowing orb appear on the rocky horizon. The desert sparrows went quiet; silence fell for a few moments of hushed anticipation. I held my breath, mesmerised by the sight of that regal sphere as it rose, drawing in its wake a majestic train of rippling light. Flickering fingers of sunlight stretched out over the landscape as the veil of night started to lift, eclipsed by the blinding light of the desert sunrise.

I started out, reluctant to leave the Tabernacle, but confident that the giant of my dream had been dethroned.

My confidence was misplaced.

As I walked away from the Tabernacle, the mocking face of the treacherous titan reappeared. The further I walked, the louder I heard the relentlessness call of his contemptuous voice, repeating over and over again that cursed mantra: *'You are a weak, pathetic creature.'*

2

Desert Wanderers

With the dawning of the new day, families all around me started to emerge from their tents, like a colony of termites spilling out of the ground after a heavy rainstorm. Bustling here and there, the sound of their chattering filled the air, competing with the twittering of the sparrows, as the camp burst into life.

By the time I arrived home, my family were all awake, some yawning and rubbing their eyes, others already setting their hands to the morning's chores. The family I lived with were not my blood family; my kinfolk had all passed away while we were still in Egypt. My father, Nun, was the last of my family to die shortly before we escaped from Egypt. In our culture, family was everything. To be alone, without family, was to be utterly bereft. So, before he went the way of the earth, my father joined my hands with those of his closest friend, Jesher, in an oath. Jesher took me into his heart and, from that time onward, he became my father. His family became my family and I grew to love them as if they had been my own blood kin. To be thrust into the middle of Jesher's diverse, vibrant family was a joy to me – an unexpected, often baffling and sometimes rather overwhelming, joy!

'*Shalom*, Joshua,' a loud voice greeted me as I arrived home. Mesha, the brother of my heart and Jesher's youngest born, stumbled out of his tent, arms outstretched, mouth wide open in a strenuous yawn.

I clasped him by the arms, kissing him on each cheek. '*Shalom*, Mesha. Did you sleep well?'

'Always, brother, always.' He grinned at me, scratched his head, and tried to smooth down his tousled mop of dark hair. 'Not much disturbs my sleep, *nu?*[1] I grunted, wishing I could have said the same. I set about clearing the ashes of last night's fire but, before I could lay a new one, a familiar voice interrupted my labour.

'*Shalom*, my lord.'

'Melech?' I dropped my bundle of sticks and stood up. '*Shalom, shalom*,' I greeted him. Melech was newly married and very young to have been given the responsibility of a watchman. However, his keen eyesight and unusual sense of responsibility for one so young had made a way for him, and he had proven his worth over the last few months. But the watchmen usually made their report to Moses each morning, so why was he here, and so early? A sense of foreboding rose up strongly; the image of that malicious giant from my dream flashed before me again. I could feel my breath quickening. 'What is it?' I asked him. 'What have you seen?'

'Nothing, my lord,' he panted. 'Except... the traders, they have sent word to you. They will be arriving shortly at the east side of the camp.'

Relief filled my heart. I breathed out, releasing the tension in my shoulders. This was welcome news indeed. When Arab merchants first arrived at our camp, our people were suspicious of them and treated them with indifference or mistrust. However, as time had gone by and the traders continued to visit us, despite the cool reception they received, the level of scepticism in the camp lessened. Nowadays, they were welcomed with open arms and, as soon as they heard of the arrival of the traders, our people would flock to see what they had brought with them. I admired the traders' resilience in returning to us time and time again, despite the initially poor welcome, although I was not naïve enough to think it was purely out of love for our people that they had persevered. For a company of merchants, a multitude such as ours presented great opportunity for prosperous trading!

Their leader was a man named Asad, of a similar age to me. Asad and I had built up a unique friendship over the past few years and our relationship had developed into more than that of a typical trader and customer.

---

1   *Nu* is a Hebrew expression.

He was burly, strong of frame and quick of eye. I had noticed the weapon he carried – the curved sword that his people were famed for – and believed him to be a warrior. It seemed he deduced the same about me, especially when he saw the ornate sword and scabbard I carried, which had been given to me by Moses' father-in-law, Jethro. One day, he unsheathed his scimitar and pretended to attack me, smiling and lifting his eyebrows. His challenge did not go unanswered. We sparred together and were soon surrounded by a circle of spectators who gathered to cheer us on. I was right, he did have some skill with the sword. Each time he and his caravan came to our camp, after we had finished trading, he would tap his scimitar with his hand, eyebrows raised expectantly.

'Eh?' he would say, his bright eyes fixed on mine. 'Eh?'

Sparring together had become our ritual, one that we both looked forward to. Over the years, I watched how Asad treated his fellow traders and I saw the way they honoured him in return. A mutual respect formed between us and I had grown to love this man, even though he was not one of our people.

Asad and his company usually pitched their tents a little way from our camp, far enough to maintain their privacy, but close enough to encourage prospective customers. He always invited me to break bread with his company at their camp in the evening, and I spent many a pleasant night with them. Bartering was accomplished by using basic gestures, counting on our fingers, showing what we had to offer and pointing to the items we wanted, while nodding or shaking our heads, displaying the relevant expression of delight or disdain. Asking them questions of a more complex nature or having a meaningful discussion, however, was far more difficult. Over time, Asad and I had learned a few words of each other's tongues and could now hold a very basic conversation using our rudimentary grasp of each other's languages. We used gestures and facial expressions to portray our meaning, but a lot of our communication took place without any words being spoken.

I knew from looking into his eyes how much his family meant to him, and how seriously he took his responsibility of leading and protecting them. I knew how much respect he had for warriors who fought well and trained hard. I knew of his love of bartering, how he thrived on the ancient game of haggling and wrangling over the value of a product. I also knew that he could easily spot a customer who was trying to defraud him or trick him into buying substandard goods. I realised that he had learned to value the smaller, seemingly inconsequential things in life, when I saw the look of wonder on his face as he watched a flaming sunset stretching across the horizon, or the birth of a new lamb. I knew he had a heart of compassion when I saw his eyes fill with concern for a child who fell and scraped their knees.

Even though conversation was very limited, I always looked forward to our times together and relished the opportunity to learn about their culture and laugh with them. The food they offered was simple – their womenfolk did not travel with them when they journeyed far into the desert to trade – but delicious, and I sampled the delights of their cuisine over the years.

'Yusha!' they would shout at regular intervals throughout the evening, raising their goblets in my direction. 'Yusha!'[2]

In turn, I would raise my goblet and shout, 'Asad!' and their whole company would erupt into cheers of agreement, honouring their leader.

Because Asad and his fellow traders drew great crowds in such a short time, of late he had started sending a messenger ahead of them to give me warning of their arrival, so that I and my family could get first pick of their goods. Their arrival was a carefully guarded secret among us and, whenever we received word of their imminent arrival, plans were put into motion with near military precision. This was one such time.

'That is good news, thank you for coming so quickly, Melech. I will make haste to meet them. But perhaps... uh ... do not share this information with anyone else until the traders have arrived, *nu?*' I said with a smile, lowering my voice and raising my eyebrows. Melech's face broke into a knowing smile.

---

2   The Arabic form of the name 'Joshua'.

'Yes, my lord,' he said, giving me a quick nod and walking back the way he had come.

'Traders, mmm?' Mesha gave me a mischievous grin. 'I'll let everyone know.'

3

Trading

'*Yusha!*' Asad shouted, a wide smile plastered all over his face. Pulling me close, he embraced me once, twice and yet again on my arrival at their trading outpost. I returned his embrace with gusto and he immediately set about asking after my family and my health. By the time we had finished reporting on the state of our families (which didn't take very long, bearing in mind our limited shared vocabulary), my family had started to arrive.

'Mesha! Helah! *As-salaam alykum*,'[3] Asad greeted my adopted brother and his petite wife, his bright eyes alighting on the large bundles they were carrying. He gestured to them, eyebrows raised in expectation. 'What... this...? Hmm?'

They unwrapped the bundles and laid their wares out, ready for inspection. We knew the process well. Once Asad or one of his fellow traders had examined what we had to offer and confirmed that they were interested in trading for it, we perused their wares until we found something that caught our attention. Then the game began! We learned very quickly the foolishness of offering a reasonable, competitive price at the beginning of the negotiations. The process of bartering was based upon the premise that a respectable amount of haggling backwards and forwards had to take place before goods could exchange hands. It was therefore expected that the initial offer would be much higher than the price that would eventually be agreed upon, to allow for some vigorous negotiations to take place. The whole process took quite some time and was entered into with great fervour by all concerned.

---

3   An Arabic saying meaning 'peace be upon you'.

Asad looked at the prepared goat hides that Mesha had brought, turning them over and examining them closely for defects. He could find none; the skins had been de-haired, bated,[4] cured, soaked and limed with great precision. Asad raised his eyebrows, trying unsuccessfully to hide the fact that he was impressed with the quality of the skins. They would make a handsome tent or covering.

'Good, yes?' Mesha asked, grinning and nodding at Asad.

Asad didn't answer. No experienced trader would ever openly admit to being impressed with the quality of the goods he was examining. Much deliberation and discussion had to take place before he would deign to give his approval. He turned to the woven reed goods that Helah unwrapped, fingering the mats and baskets, noting their complex patterns and neat workmanship.

'Good, yes?' Mesha asked, again, receiving a non-committal glance from Asad in response. I laughed and slapped them both on the shoulder, moving on to see what else my Arab friends had brought with them. Mesha loved to haggle as much as Asad; it would take a long time for these negotiations to be concluded!

'Is this not a beautiful piece?'

'It is beautiful, but I have no need of it.'

I turned to see Eglah, Jesher and Shira's second-born. Although I would never have admitted it, Eglah was a family favourite of mine. She and her husband, Hareph, had not been blessed with children, and were unlikely to have any now, as she was no longer a young woman. She bore her pain well. I never heard her complain, although I knew how desperately she wanted a child; I had seen the longing in her eyes many times when she tended her nephews and nieces. But, instead of letting bitterness fester in her heart, she focused her attention on ministering to her husband and helping to look after her brothers' children.

'It looks so beautiful against your skin, Eglah,' Hareph protested, holding a beaded necklace up near her chin. 'Come, let me buy this for you.'

'You are kind, husband, and I love you for it,' she whispered, 'but I

4   Softening the skin by pounding it.

do not need trinkets like this – I would not feel comfortable wearing it. Do not waste your money, *nu?* Let us look for something that would be useful for the home.' Hareph sighed, but nodded his agreement.

Just then, Eglah's niece and nephew ran up to her, pulling at her skirts to get her attention.

'Ephah! Ethan! What is it?' she said, bending down to embrace them. 'Have you seen something you like?'

'Yes! Yes!' they responded with enthusiastic cries. 'Come! Come and see!' Eglah allowed them to pull her over to a large mat where some children's toys were displayed. Hareph glanced at me and shrugged. I smiled; we both knew what was about to happen. We followed behind them and watched as the twins, Ephah and Ethan, pointed to a small leather ball stuffed with seeds, pleading with their auntie to buy it for them. Eglah turned to Hareph.

'Can we? The children would love this. It would make them so happy, yes?'

Hareph didn't even bother to protest. We all knew the tenderness of Eglah's heart when it came to her nephews and nieces – there would be no argument broached over this purchase. Leaving them to haggle over the price, I moved on to where Jesher, my adopted father, stood studying a pile of rugs, cushions, and bolts of fabric. Jesher was not a man given to the accumulation of possessions. Issues of the heart were far more important to him then worldly goods so, more often than not, he would buy something from the traders not for himself, but to give to his family.

'*Abba?*' I said, putting my arm around his shoulders. 'What have you found?'

'Cushions!' he replied, gazing up at me with a look of great satisfaction. The love in my heart for this man was such that he could have been my blood relative. I still missed my blood father, Nun, and not a day passed when I did not think of him and wish he could be with me. But Jesher had embraced me as a son in a way that I never thought could be possible. I had learned much from his wisdom and sound judgement, and my heart flourished under his care.

'Yes?' I replied. 'Which one does your heart desire?'

'All of them,' he said, chuckling to himself. Wrinkling his nose, he smacked his lips and looked up at me. 'I would like to buy them all for my family, but I think it would be wise for me to choose one for each of my children, and perhaps one for Shira and I, *nu*? Which one would you like, my son?' he asked me, and set about trying to decide which cushion would suit which of his children.

He was soon joined by his wife, Shira, who came bustling up to us the minute she saw what he was doing.

'If you must buy from these... traders,' she sniffed, peering at them with a look of suspicion, 'then at least ensure the quality is sufficient for our needs, yes?' Ripping a cream-coloured bolster out of Jesher's hands, she muttered, 'This will not do. No, not at all. The material is far too coarse, and how do you expect us to keep it clean, in this dusty wilderness? No, we need darker colours like this.' She picked up a luxurious crimson cushion with a thick weave that looked far more suited to a palatial mansion than a simple sojourner's tent. 'Or this one', she said, choosing a dark grey cushion with deep blue threads running through it. She pursed her lips, frowning in concentration.

I stepped back, giving them space to finalise their choices. Looking up, I saw Asad standing a short distance away, watching us. He caught my eye. He never said it in so many words, but I knew he saw my love for my father, and the pain that ripped into my heart when Shira scorned or dishonoured him, as she so often did. The look in his eyes told me it angered him also. Honour was a quintessential part of his people's culture. I held his gaze for a moment, then he turned away and I continued browsing.

Azriel, Jesher's first-born son, was already deep in negotiations with Asad's uncle, around the value of some dishes, platters and pitchers that he had brought to trade for supplies. Azriel had become a skilled potter and the items he produced, although not as intricately decorated as Jesher's had been in his days as a potter, were sturdy and well-formed. Azriel took the responsibility of being Jesher's first-born, and now head of the family trade, very seriously. He bartered not so much for sport, as did Mesha, who treated each bartering sessions like a potential jousting match against a worthy opponent. For Azriel, it was about the importance of knowing he had secured a good price for his labour.

By now, Jesher had moved on, leaving Shira to decide which cushions they should purchase. He strolled up to his grandson, Joel, and Joel's wife, Alya, who had just bought a rattle for their baby girl.

Alya had never known what it was to be loved and nurtured in a family environment. Her mother had died in childbirth and her father was a cruel man. When she and Joel married, she found herself part of a family that not only accepted her, but truly embraced her. She warmed to Azriel and his wife, Leora, straight away, and found much joy in the loving relationship she had with her new in-laws. But it was Jesher who won her heart. Her new grandfather opened his heart and his arms to her and she, in turn, was always attentive to his needs and helped him whenever she could. Joel and Alya named their little girl Sadie.[5] She was Jesher's first great-grandchild, and she was a source of great joy to him.

'And how is my precious little one this morning?' Jesher asked, stroking Sadie's cheek.

'She is well, *Saba*,'[6] Alya replied, smiling up at Jesher with a look of adoration. 'It will not be long now before she takes her first steps, I am sure.'

'Aah, she is thriving, *nu*? Our little princess is growing so quickly,' he replied, patting Alya on the back and giving her a peck on the cheek before heading back to Shira to help finalise the negotiations for the cushions... not that Shira needed any help with haggling over prices.

Joel left Alya and wandered over to me. 'Joshua, have you found nothing that stirs your heart?' he asked.

'No. I have all that I need,' I said, looking around at my family. 'Although I must ask Asad about the dried fruits and grains he promised to bring. It would be good to share them around our table, *nu*?' As I made my way over to where Asad was standing, I noticed Mesha's son, Yoram, looking longingly at a dagger which lay among an impressive array of weaponry. The trader standing by the display of weaponry

---

5   Sadie means 'princess' in Hebrew.

6   Hebrew word for 'grandfather'.

was the oldest of their company, much advanced in years. His gnarled hands and leathery skin had obviously seen many years of exposure to the harsh desert sun and his sharp features told me that, in his time, he must have wielded these weapons with great skill. He gave Yoram an inviting smile and babbled something in his Arab tongue. Picking the dagger up, he took it out of its sheath and offered it to Yoram to examine.

Yoram shook his head and gestured with his hands, refusing to accept it. 'Thank you, but I cannot take it,' he said, staring at the gleaming blade.

'You have keen eyes, Yori,' I said, coming to stand by him. 'This is a fine blade.' I took the dagger from the old man and ran my finger along its edge. 'It has been skilfully crafted. Any man would be proud to have this in his possession.'

'Will you buy it?' Yoram asked, eyes wide with anticipation.

'Yes,' I replied. 'But not for me. I have no need of another blade – this is all I need,' I said, patting the ornate scabbard that hung on my belt. 'No.' I turned to face him. 'I will buy it for you.'

'F... for me?' he stammered. 'No! You cannot do that, Yoshi. I cannot accept such a costly gift.'

'You will have no choice,' I said, grinning at him. 'You could not refuse a gift from your favourite uncle, surely?'

'But... I didn't ...'

I put my hand on his shoulder. 'Yori, you have nearly reached your twentieth year. You will be starting army training soon, and you will have need of a good blade. This will be yours. It is a gift. I want you to have it. Please, accept it.' The old man grinned at us, clearly anticipating a lively bartering session over the price of such a costly blade. He got what he expected. It was a delicate balance, knowing how long to barter, and when to yield to the seller's demands. Holding on too long or belittling the desired purchase in an effort to knock the price down could result in the merchant feeling dishonoured, and perhaps refusing to sell, whereas giving up too soon was seen as a sign that you did not value the item enough to really fight for it.

This dagger was no ordinary blade, and I knew it would require lengthy negotiations before we reached the right price. Yoram stood by my side while we argued back and forth, the old man pointing out the finer points of the dagger one by one, while I refuted the exorbitant price he wanted for it. They knew I had nothing to trade, and that I paid for my acquisitions with treasures that I brought out of Egypt. In their estimation, it was worth holding out for! After a while, the rest of the family, as well as some new onlookers, gathered round to witness the final agreement, and a cheer went up when the negotiations were concluded.

People were starting to spill out of the camp now, making their way towards the traders.

It was time!

Asad turned to me and tapped his scimitar. 'Eh?' he said, cocking his head. 'Eh?'

I accepted his challenge and we moved into a clear space. The crowd formed around us; no more trading would take place until the contest was over. We both drew our swords, readied ourselves, and Asad lunged first. The contest continued for quite a while. We were evenly matched, both competent warriors, dodging and weaving, thrusting and blocking, until finally, as Asad lunged for me, I swung round, grasped him from behind, and held my sword up to his neck.

He shouted out in frustration at having been beaten by me, then acquiesced. I released my hold on him and we sheathed our weapons. Bowing to the crowds gathered around, we laughed and grabbed each other in a fierce embrace, slapping each other on the back.

That night, after sharing their evening meal, I sat with Asad's family around their fire. The jingle of the camel's harnesses merged with their excited chattering as they shared stories of the day's trading. Although I couldn't understand their conversations, I did get the general gist of what was being said, and laughed with them when they mimicked some of their customers' antics. I turned to Asad and asked in my limited vocabulary how their journey to our camp had been.

'Your travels...' I said, acting out a man riding a camel over the dunes. 'Were they good? Good travels?'

'Good,' Asad replied, mimicking my actions. 'Tra... tra...vels. Yes,' he nodded. He glanced away and I saw his countenance fall. Concern masked his smile.

'What is it?' I asked, grasping his arm. 'What?' I gestured. 'Good travels? Or not good?'

He looked at me as if unsure whether or how to tell me what concerned him. Leaning in closer, he lowered his voice and muttered some unintelligible words, at the same time using gestures to explain what he was trying to communicate. He pointed to his eyes and then far away in the distance to indicate something he had seen far off.

'You saw something? What? What did you see?' I asked.

He looked at me, searching for any signs of mockery or scorn. He found none. I wanted to know what could have brought such unease to a seasoned warrior such as he. Looking around the fire, seeing the rest of his company laughing and talking among themselves, Asad turned back to me and whispered some more words in Arabic, while acting out a huge, aggressive being.

'Leopard?' I asked, knowing how feared these desert creatures were, who preyed on our livestock in the dead of night and attacked those foolish enough to stand in their way. I bared my teeth and acted out a leopard attacking. 'You saw a leopard?'

Asad frowned in frustration at the limitations of our conversation and shook his hands in denial.

'No, no,' he said. He put one hand on his chest and then on mine, then lifted his hand high above his head to indicate a huge being... muttering the same words over and over again. He tried several times to explain to me the vast proportions of the creature he had seen.

Embarrassed by what obviously now felt like foolishness to him, he mumbled something and gave a wry laugh, as if to say, 'It was nothing.' He turned to reach for more food, signalling the end of our conversation. It was nothing. Nothing to worry about.

But I knew it was not nothing.

He had seen something.

Something dangerous.

Something unusual.

Something that caused fear to rise, even in the heart of a brave warrior such as Asad.

The same sense of fear that had shrouded me since my dream engulfed me once again. My heart started thumping faster and I heard the mocking voice of the giant echoing in my mind as he accused me, again and again, *'You are a weak, pathetic creature.'*

4

Betrothal

'Joshua! Joshua!'

'What?' I stopped dead in my tracks and swung round to see Mesha running towards me. 'What is it?'

'It's Yoram!'

'Yoram? What about him? Is he unwell?' Mesha stopped. Bent over double, with his hands on his knees, he didn't respond. '*Mesha*! Is it well with him?' I urged.

'Yes, yes, he is well.' He panted, trying to catch his breath.

'Then what are you shouting for?' I asked, confused.

Mesha stood up and swung his arms wide open. 'He is betrothed! My first-born son will soon be married!'

My face broke into a huge smile. 'That is wonderful! Yahweh be praised!' I pulled my friend into a bear hug; we slapped each other on the back and laughed. 'His bride to be – is it Samina?'

'Oh yes. There has never been another for Yoram. We went to see her *abba*[7] this morning; it is all agreed and the bride price is confirmed.' Samina's family were from the same tribe as Mesha, the tribe of Benjamin. Mesha told me that, although they were not considered wealthy, her father, Yosef, was a herdsman, so livestock would form much of the bride price. Our family had a few goats and lambs, but it would be good to increase the size of our herd. Mesha had made a business agreement: Yosef would supply him with pelts and hides for his tentmaking, and Mesha would, in turn, give him a percentage of the profits from his tentmaking trade.

I raised my eyebrows. 'That is a good contract. Was it of your making, or Yosef's?'

---

7   Hebrew word for father, more informally, 'Daddy'.

'Mine.' Mesha saw my surprised expression and frowned. 'I am not a fool, Joshua. A bit crazy at times, maybe, but not a fool – especially when it comes to business!'

We laughed and I slapped him on the back.

'My heart rejoices for you, my friend – and for Yoram. Is he contented?'

'He is like a lamb in springtime! He cannot sit still or concentrate for more than a few minutes; I have never seen him like this before. He pricked his hands so many times this morning that he was getting blood on the pelts, so I sent him away. Yahmal will not want a tent splattered with blood now, will he?'

I grimaced, and asked, 'Has the wedding date been set?'

'Yes. They will be married on the fifth full moon.'

'That is soon.'

'Yes, but Yoram has had sheep's eyes for Samina for over a year, so we have known for a while.'

I shook my head. 'Yori getting married! My mind cannot conceive it.'

Mesha nodded. 'I can still remember when the midwife handed me that little bundle, wrapped up tight in his swaddling cloths, just his little face peeping out. Bawling his head off, his face red and wrinkled and *egh*! What a set of lungs he had! Now he is to be wed, and soon he will have his own children!'

We stood in silence for a while, thinking back to the precious moments we had shared through the years. At first, I had been a bit awkward around Yoram, being unused to handling babies, but I soon grew accustomed to his ways and, as he grew into a toddler, I spent many an evening playing with him, telling him stories about our ancestors. As a baby, Yoram could not pronounce my name, so he would call me Yoshi. By the time he entered puberty, we had formed a firm friendship – and he still called me Yoshi. My name of endearment for him, Yori, also stuck fast over the years.

Yoram often turned to me for advice about the many challenges that a young man faces. If the truth be told, Yoram had confided in me about his desire to marry Samina before he had spoken to his parents, but I never told them that, and I never would. It was one of the many secrets that Yoram had shared with me, and I treasured each one of them in my heart as if he had been my own child. I had no children of my own, so instead, I poured out my love on Mesha and Helah's children and became an honorary uncle to them. My heart had been set on marriage in my younger days, but the woman I loved, Merav, had been given in marriage to a family friend, and I had never been able to embrace the thought of marrying another woman. The likelihood of me fathering children was growing smaller and smaller as the years went by, which was why my adopted nieces and nephews meant so much to me.

'You have fathered him well, my friend,' I said, breaking the silence. 'You have brought him up in the ways of the Lord. He will bring much honour to you and Helah.'

'Yes, I believe he will.' Mesha heaved a sigh. 'Well, I must be on my way. Helah is so excited, she keeps talking about all the things that we – or mostly I – must do before the wedding. It is only once in a lifetime that your first-born gets married, yes?'

I nodded. 'I will see you this evening.'

'Yes. Samina and her family are joining us to break bread and Helah wants me to slaughter a goat so we can celebrate together! It starts already, *nu?*' he said, shrugging. '*Shalom*, Joshua. *Shalom!* Don't be late tonight!' Mesha shouted as he ran off, zigzagging through the clusters of tents. Although he was nearing two score years, Mesha was still as young at heart as ever and, more often than not, still ran to wherever he needed to get to, instead of walking. I still thought of him as my unpredictable, boisterous childhood friend, so it seemed somewhat bizarre to think that he was to be a father-in-law and, thereafter, a grandfather. *Mesha, a grandfather? No!* I shook my head and laughed to myself.

The sounds of laughter and celebration reverberated that night as our two families feasted and celebrated Yoram and Samina's forthcoming union.

'Helah, that roasted goat was delicious!' I said, wiping my mouth and leaning back into my cushion. 'I have eaten so much; I cannot eat another bite!'

'We noticed!' Mesha said, grinning at me.

Helah tutted at her husband and turned to me. 'I'm glad you liked it.'

'It really was delicious, Helah – what herbs and spices did you use?' asked Samina's mother.

'Ooh, that is a secret family recipe, Hodiah,' chuckled Helah, 'but, since we're going to be family, I will tell you; and you too, Samina,' she said to her soon-to-be daughter-in-law. 'I'll share my family recipes with you and teach you how to make Yoram's favourite meals, yes?'

Samina blushed and said, 'Thank you,' before glancing quickly at Yoram to see his reaction. He smiled at her, open admiration in his eyes, and she blushed again and lowered her gaze. I watched them, a feeling of quiet satisfaction warming my heart. In our culture, parents chose spouses for their children, and not every couple was lucky enough to start their married life with the stirrings of love already forming. These two young people were clearly devoted to each other, and it filled me with a strange sense of pride as I watched them.

'With your permission,' I said, raising my voice so as to be heard over the babble of conversation, 'I have something I would like to say.'

'You're not going to go on about my wife's wonderful food again, are you?' Mesha joked.

'Mesha! Be quiet!' Helah said, prodding her husband's arm.

'No, as wonderful as your cooking is, Helah, it is not about that.' I turned to Yoram. 'It is about your marriage celebration.' Everyone turned to stare at me. 'I told Moses the good news, and he said it would be his privilege to come to the wedding celebration and bless your covenant, if that is pleasing to you?'

There was a stunned silence. Every eye was on me, mouths open in shock.

'Uh...' I looked around the room in concern, then turned to Jesher. 'Forgive me, *Abba*, should I have spoken to you about this first?'

'*Moses!*' Yoram blurted out. 'Coming to our wedding celebration?'

'Yes. If that pleases you?'

'*If that please me!*' he shouted, turning to Jesher and Mesha. '*Saba! Abba!* Did you hear that? Moses... Moses himself, coming to our celebration!'

Jesher smiled at me, put his hand on his heart and inclined his head, nodding his approval. Mesha, uncharacteristically quiet, just stared at me. The beginnings of tears formed in his eyes and he looked down, blinking them away. Clearing his throat, he looked up at me. 'Thank you. Please tell Moses we would be honoured to have him with us, and for him to pray the covenant blessing.'

The family broke into whoops of excitement and another flurry of conversation erupted. In my ignorance, I had not realised the impact this news would have on my family. Moses was our nation's leader, but he was not a typical leader. He was a prophet, the mouthpiece of Yahweh, and a miracle-worker. He was the man who Yahweh chose to confront Pharaoh and lead His people out of a life of slavery in Egypt, into national freedom. We had seen Moses perform miracles, both in Egypt and here in the wilderness, and those who tried to rebel against his leadership or turn away from the ways of God had received the penalty for their actions not from Moses, but from Yahweh Himself.

My path had crossed with Moses' shortly after we had left Egypt and, just a few months into our wilderness journey, he had asked me to become his manservant. Since that time, I had spent nearly every day in his company and, although my respect for him was still unchanged, I was not as awestruck by him as those who did not know him person- ally. Yes, I had seen the powerful, miracle-working prophet in action, but I had also seen the man; the humble man who hated being the centre of attention, and who struggled with his own shortcomings.

I looked around the family circle, watching the high-spirited conver- sations that were taking place and the joy on everyone's faces; all except one. Helah's face was pale. She turned to me and whispered, 'Joshua, will Zipporah be coming with Moses?'

'Yes, I believe so, and their sons – if it pleases you?' I noted the anxious expression on her face.

She gasped. 'So, I will be cooking for Moses himself, and for his wife and sons too?'

'Yes. But do not fear, Helah. They will love your food,' I reassured her.

'But this is Moses and his family, Joshua. Yahweh help me, what will I cook for them?'

Her reaction baffled me; the answer to her question was obvious.

'The same food that you cook for your family. In fact,' I said, 'I think you should cook exactly what you cooked tonight. It was a feast to please even our father Abraham!'

Yosef, who up until now had been listening and watching, turned to Helah. 'Yes! We will give you a goat to cook for the feast. Two, three – no, *four* goats!' he said with a flourish, glancing across at Mesha. 'If Moses is coming, we will provide a feast fit for a king, *nu?*'

'Yes! We will do the cooking together,' Hodiah said, putting her hand on Samina's arm, giving it a squeeze. 'All of us. My sisters, my aunts, my mother, my daughters – all of us will come and help your women. We will be family together, yes?'

Helah nodded, still dazed at the thought of cooking for Moses and his family. Another buzz of conversation broke out, this time around the topic of food and how many goats would be needed for the wedding feast. I turned to Helah and whispered, 'Helah, Moses is a man of simple tastes. Your food will more than satisfy him. In fact,' a smile flickered across my face and I leaned in towards her, 'you must not speak of this to anyone else, but I happen to know that Zipporah is not a very good cook!'

Helah cocked her head to the side and looked at me with disbelief.

'It is true! Helah, I speak the truth! Your food will taste like nectar in their mouths, compared to what they eat from day to day. But you must never tell anyone I said that, hmm?' I finally coaxed a smile out of her. Lifting my arms, I shouted, 'A blessing on the happy couple. A blessing on your union, Yoram and Samina. May the voice of gladness and joy ever be heard in your tents! May you live a full and bountiful life together, and may your womb be fruitful and your children's children plentiful! Amen!'

'Amen! Amen!'

5

Tentmakers

'Watch the size of those stitches, Yoram,' Mesha said, pointing at the section of tent which Yoram was sewing. 'Make sure you keep them all the same size, and make them tight, yes? No loose strands. No gaps.'

'Yes, *Abba*.'

Father and son sat together outside the family tent, under the cover of an awning made of black goats' hair, especially chosen for its tough, waterproof qualities. Although Jesher had been a skilled potter in his day, Mesha did not have the patience required for moulding clay on the wheel. A strong tent was an absolute essential when journeying in the wilderness, and he'd discovered he had a natural skill for handling the tough animal hides and pelts. Mesha's strong fingers adapted well to working with the bone needles used in tentmaking, and he told me he enjoyed the process of seeing a tent grow day by day under his shaping. His joy was made complete when Yoram joined him as an apprentice tentmaker.

I sat outside my tent, watching father and son work together, side by side.

'*Abba*?' Yoram asked.

'Mmm?'

'I was not aware that we had received an order for a new tent.'

'Mmm.' Mesha concentrated on threading twine around the grooves in a small bone needle. Yoram was right, it was unusual for a completely new tent to be ordered, as a new one required many, many animal pelts. Most of the orders Mesha received were for the patching of rips due to general wear and tear and, more often than not, from the powerful desert winds that tore through the camp.

'So who is this tent for, then?' Yoram asked.

Mesha stopped working and laid his hands in his lap, still holding onto the pelt and bone needle. He looked at his son with tender affection and said, 'It is for you.'

Yoram's head shot up. 'For me?'

'Yes. For you and Samina. We don't have a lot of time, but I am sure we can get it ready before your marriage celebration.'

'But I thought we would just make a dividing curtain and add a section onto our family tent.'

'I know. But your *ima*[8] and I wanted the two of you to have your own tent. You are our first-born, yes? After all, what is the point of being tentmakers if your family can't enjoy the benefits of your labour, hmm?'

Yoram was flabbergasted. 'But... but...' he stuttered, 'all these hides and pelts – they must have cost you a year's wages.'

'Aah, now that is where you are wrong,' Mesha said, grinning from ear to ear. 'You happen to have a future father-in-law who thinks very highly of you, and who loves his daughter dearly – *and* who has a very large flock of goats! He has the skins; I have the skills – it is the perfect match!'

'*Abba*, thank you!' Yoram dropped his hide and flung himself into Mesha's arms, nearly knocking him over in the process.

'Wooooah, hold on,' Mesha said, laughing. 'I don't want to impale you on this bone or damage you before you become a husband!' He put his section of the tent down and stood up, holding out his arms.

'Thank you. Thank you so much, *Abba*,' Yoram whispered as they hugged long and hard. 'I don't know how to thank you enough.'

'You just have, my boy.' Pulling back, Mesha smiled at Yoram and said, 'Now, why don't you go and find that beautiful woman of yours and tell her the news?'

'I will. Thank you! *Thank you!*' Yoram yelled as he bolted off, shouting to me on his way. 'Yoshi! We have a tent! We have a tent! *Wooooh!*'

We laughed together as we watched Yoram's fast disappearing form. I walked over to Mesha. 'He is a very blessed young man, Mesha. You have done a wonderful thing for them. I have not known any newly-weds who began their life together with a new tent.'

---

8 Hebrew word for 'mother'.

'I know, but he is a good son. He works hard and is growing in skill and, who knows, maybe one day he will be able to do the same for his children?'

'I am sure he will. This will be your legacy, *nu*?' I said, grasping Mesha's arm.

'I cannot speak assuredly on that but, like I said, it is only once in your lifetime that your first-born son gets married.'

'True, true! Talking of which, I must go and see Joel. I want to ask him about a gift for me to present to Yoram and Samina at the celebration.'

'What do you want him to make?'

'Aah, now that I cannot say,' I said, turning to leave.

'Joshua!' He put his hand on his chest and peered at me. 'I am the brother of your heart, your closest friend, yes? So you can tell me what it is.'

'I can, yes. But I won't!' I grinned at him. 'You will just have to wait like everyone else, my friend, and find out on the day! *Shalom*!' I said with a cheeky wave, as I strode off to find Joel. The sun had been up for less than an hour, but already the heat was stifling. I found Joel at Bezalel's workshops, sawing a large tree branch into smaller pieces. '*Shalom*, Joel!'

'Joshua! *Shalom*.' We grasped each other by the hand, placing our other hand on top in a strong grip. 'Is something amiss?' he asked.

'No, why?'

'You don't usually come and find me when I am working, especially when I saw you only a short while ago.'

'Ah, yes. I need to talk to you without other ears listening in.'

'About...?'

'Yoram and Samina.'

'Oh.' He looked surprised and not a little mystified. 'Come, sit. It is time for my break.' Joel wiped the sweat off his brow and led me into the shade of a cloth canopy stretched over some timber struts. 'Drink?' he said, pouring me a cup of water from a waterskin that hung from one of the timber struts.

'Thank you.' I accepted the cup and sat down as he poured himself a drink.

'I'm happy for Yoram.' Joel sat next to me. 'Samina is a lovely girl and she will be welcomed in our family. Yoram will make a good husband.' We passed the time discussing Yoram and Samina's forthcoming nuptials, and then I told Joel the reason for my visit.

'I would like to commission you to make a chest out of acacia wood, carved on all four sides and on the lid. It will be my gift for Yoram and Samina at their marriage celebration.'

'A chest? Out of acacia wood?' Joel was clearly astounded. 'Joshua, that is a very costly wood. I will speak to Bezalel. I am sure we can find some, but it would take quite some time to make the chest and carve all its surfaces. Are you sure that is what you want?'

'I am certain. You know I have no children of my own to bless, and Yoram is like a son to me. I want to do this for him and Samina.'

'As you wish. I will talk to Bezalel and – '

'Do not tell him who it's for,' I blurted. 'This must be a surprise! *No one* must know about it, not even your uncle Mesha or any of the family, or even Bezalel, until after the presentation. You must give me your word.'

'You have my word,' said Joel, smiling at my boyish enthusiasm. 'I will start on it this week.'

'You have nearly five moons to craft it – is that enough time?' I asked.

'It will have to be, won't it?' he grinned.

'Good. When you have spoken to Bezalel, please tell me the cost of the acacia wood and I will give you the means to acquire it.' I reached down and drew out of the folds of my robe a leather pouch, which I held out to Joel. 'But for now, this is a payment for your workmanship.'

He frowned and didn't take the pouch from me. 'No, Joshua. We are family, I cannot charge you for making it. I owe you so much – I cannot...'

'You can and you will. I will allow no dispute, Joel. You are a master craftsman and you will be paid at the rate of a master craftsman.' Seeing the concern on Joel's face, I smiled. 'Do not worry, truly. You may or may not remember this but, when we left Egypt, Yahweh instructed us to ask the Egyptians for treasures to take with us. The ones I spoke to were... uh... particularly generous and seemed unusually eager to share their treasures with me. In hindsight I realised it may have had something to do with my size, and... uh... general demeaner at the time!' I chuckled to myself at the memory and then turned my attention back to Joel. 'I have no wife or children to lavish gifts on, and a good workman is worthy of his hire, *nu?* What is the point of having wealth if it just sits in your tent, hidden away? I will not give Yoram and Samina a gift that has cost me nothing. So there it is.'

'I... thank you, Joshua. Thank you for honouring me in this matter.'

'You honour me by accepting this order. I still marvel when I see the carving and sculpting on the furniture you made for the Tabernacle – and Moses' table? Beautiful! This will be good for your business too. The orders will come pouring in when the guests see the chest at the celebration!' I stood up to take my leave. 'But not a word to anyone, yes?' Joel stood with me and nodded. I gave him my empty cup, bade him farewell, and went on my way to meet with Moses.

'Little Yori, betrothed?' I mumbled as I strolled through the camp. I still couldn't believe it.

6

Marriage Celebration

The ceremony took place on the eve of the full moon, under a canopy strewn with stars. A cool breeze wafted through the camp and the buzz of cicadas filled the air, like a festive chorus of rhythmic clicking. The smell of roasting goat meat filled the air, along with the tantalising aroma of fresh herb bread baking on the coals.

Oil lamps had been hung all around the open area near our family tents where the celebration was to be held, creating halos of light as the night drew in, like a glowing circle around the huge stack of logs and dried dung which burned in the deep firepit we had dug in the middle of the clearing. The logs cracked and popped, sending showers of sparks up into the night sky, echoing Yahweh's own fiery display that stood like a burning sentinel near the middle of the camp. Excitement was in the air, further exacerbated when Moses and his family arrived. I stood with Jesher, Shira, Mesha and Helah to welcome the guests and, after the necessary introductions had been made, I showed Moses and his family to their seats of honour and went to check on Yoram. Mesha stood with his son in the family tent, a look of loving pride on his face.

'Mesha, Yori – are you ready? It is time,' I asked.

'I'm ready,' Yoram said, fiddling with the tassels on his head covering.

'Then let us go and fetch your bride, yes?' I stood on one side of him, Mesha on the other, and we led him out through the throng of guests. The male guests cheered and joined our merry troupe, and Joel played a joyful tune on his reed pipe as we snaked in-between the tents, fiery torches in our hands, singing and dancing as we went. We found our way to Samina's family tent, a short distance away, where Yosef and his sons welcomed us. Greetings and embraces were exchanged, then the tent flap opened, and Hodiah brought Samina out to us. A surge of whooping and shouting greeted her as she took her place near Yoram, gazing shyly up at him through her veil. Surrounded by her mother, grandmother, aunts and sisters, we led her to her new home with shouts of jubilation.

When we arrived at the clearing where the rest of the guests waited, Jesher (who was not as mobile as he had been in years past, and had elected to stay behind) rose to his feet, along with Moses, who had stayed with him (probably to try to avoid the crowds). Shouts and cheers welcomed us, more greetings were exchanged, and then we led Yoram and Samina to a canopy bedecked with palm branches, yellow acacia blossoms, and clusters of small white and pink tamarisk flowers.

Yoram looked resplendent in his new robe, and had a noble bearing. He had grown so tall, inheriting his father's rugged good looks. To look at him tonight, no one would have guessed that he came from an ordinary family of lowly birth. He conducted himself as a prince would have, and my heart swelled with pride. If I felt like this, I could only imagine how Mesha and Helah were feeling.

Moses and I joined both sets of parents as they stood with Yoram and Samina under the canopy, and the rest of the family and guests gathered round. Yoram's face lit up as he turned to his bride to declare the words of his covenant with her, vowing to protect her, provide for her in the years to come, and walk steadfastly in the ways of Yahweh. Samina's thick, dark tresses had been braided with golden threads, and the circlet of coins attached to her headdress jingled when she turned to look at him. Helah and Hodesh lifted Samina's veil as the women from both families declared over her the same blessing that had been spoken over Rebekah centuries before, when she travelled to a distant land to marry Isaac.

'Our sister, may you increase to thousands upon thousands; may your offspring possess the cities of their enemies.'[9]

Samina smiled at them, then turned to look at Yoram. With her veil now lifted, she looked so young and innocent. 'That's as it should be,' I thought to myself. A pang of longing filled my heart as I imagined what

---

9   Genesis 24:60.

Merav would have looked like if she had been my bride. As quickly as the thought came, I brushed it away. It was futile to walk down that pathway, today of all days. I focused my attention back on Yoram, as Moses stepped forward to pronounce a blessing on their union.

Recalling Yoram's initial reaction when I told him of Moses' willingness to attend the wedding, I had expected him to be in awe of the prophet, perhaps a bit tongue-tied. He wasn't. In fact, after a quick glance at Moses, Yoram's gaze shifted straight back to his beautiful bride; he only had eyes for her. Moses prayed, blessed the couple and, as soon as he finished, a roar erupted from the crowd, more blessings were pronounced, and everyone gathered round to embrace the newlywed couple.

The musicians started playing and the sounds of celebration filled the air. Jugs of water and cloths for handwashing were brought out, and it wasn't long before the first dishes of food were served to the guests.

'My beloved,' Mesha said, looking at Helah with admiration. 'You have triumphed! Look at all these people enjoying the fruits of your labour. I am the envy of every man here!' Helah smiled up at him and was about to respond when Moses joined in.

'Mesha, Helah, this is a feast fit for a king!' He wiped some meat juices from around his mouth. 'The roasted goat is delicious! I have not tasted anything like it before.'

'Ah well,' Mesha responded, 'my wife prepared the goat herself, and cooked all the food, with the help of our women.' He looked at Helah with great pride and she blushed, all at once looking as young and pretty as a bride herself.

'Is this true?' Zipporah asked, looking at Helah. 'Well then, could I ask... would you teach me how to roast meat like this?'

'It would be my honour,' Helah said. 'I could come to your tent and show you there, if that pleases you?'

'That would be wonderful!' Zipporah replied, before turning to Moses to discuss her thoughts. I chuckled quietly to myself and winked surreptitiously at Helah. She hid a smile and sent me a quick frown before turning her attention back to Moses and Zipporah.

I was pleased to see how easily Mesha and Helah seemed to be talking to them. Helah told me afterwards that Moses and Zipporah were a lot more 'normal' than she expected, and Mesha was surprised to discover that Moses told jokes – and good ones at that!

Hearing the beat of the drums starting, Mesha's face lit up. '*Oysh*! It is time for the dancing! Let's find Yoram and Samina!'

We found the young couple, and the men formed a circle around Yoram, while the women encircled Samina. Linking arms, we danced around them, stamping our feet, gradually picking up the pace until the music culminated in a crescendo of clapping and cheering. I discovered that Caleb, my firm friend and military second-in-command, was similar to Mesha when it came to dancing; both were wild, impulsive and potentially dangerous! I stepped out of the circle after a while and went to stand by Jesher, laughing out loud as I watched them linking arms with Yoram. They clapped and shouted, eventually letting go of each other, their arms flailing wildly in a frenzy of celebration. Hareph, who was not blessed with a natural sense of rhythm, soon joined us, panting, and shortly afterwards, Azriel also left the circle to join our huddle of spectators.

Later that night, the presentation of gifts took place. Yoram and Samina were given everything from chickens, goats and other food items to household furnishings such as rugs, mats, cushions, bowls, pots, and even items of clothing and jewellery, most likely courtesy of our former captives when we left Egypt!

There was one gift, however, that received the greatest applause: my gift to the young couple. As flattering as the recognition of the crowds was, it meant very little to me. My focus was solely on Yoram and his bride. Joel had finished the chest on time, as promised. He had carved their names on the lid of the chest, along with intricate designs of leaves and fruit to symbolise abundance and fruitfulness in their marriage. It was an object of absolute beauty, and I saw tears come to both Yoram and Samina's eyes when it was uncovered.

'Yoshi...' Yoram ran his hands over the engraving on the top of the chest. 'This... this is... thank you. With all my heart, thank you.' He flung himself into my arms and held me tightly. Drawing back after a while, he asked, 'Did Joel...?' I nodded and Yoram turned to find his cousin and closest friend. Joel was standing nearby leaning against a tent pole, his arms crossed, watching Yoram's overwhelmed expression with obvious satisfaction. The two men strode towards each other and hugged fiercely, slapping each other on the back. The guests gathered round to admire the chest and I was right; Joel received many new orders as a result of that chest.

The music started up again and the guests formed circles. I looked up to see Zipporah dancing in the middle of a large circle of women. Helah, Hodiah and Samina were with her, clapping along as they watched Zipporah twisting and weaving her way around the circle of women, her hands flicking in an intricate series of movements. Mesha came to join us and we watched her, fascinated by the movements she was doing.

'Well, it looks like my wife is teaching the women a new dance,' Moses said, his eyes not moving from her undulating form. 'She is a *magnificent* dancer, is she not?'

'She is indeed. I have not seen this kind of dancing before,' Mesha replied.

'No. It is the wedding dance of my wife's people, the Midianites. Very beautiful, hmm?' he asked, tearing his gaze away from her to grin at us. 'I will never forget the night of my own marriage celebration. Zipporah danced for me, and I lost my heart to her all over again.' Moses's smile lit up his face. We watched Zipporah clasp Samina by the hand and pull her into the middle of the circle, encouraging the young woman to copy her movements. Once Samina had learned the dance, Zipporah pulled Helah, protesting and blushing, forward. Mesha whooped his encouragement and, before long, all the women in our two families had been drawn into the circle to join in the new wedding dance. They twirled and spun to the beat of the drums, their menfolk standing nearby, admiring them unashamedly.

Later that night, Mesha revealed the gift that he was giving Yoram and Samina. The crowds burst into spontaneous applause, along with much foot-stomping and cheering. It was almost unheard of for a newlywed couple to have their own tent, and Yoram and Samina were acutely aware of the huge privilege that had been afforded them.

The guests created a pathway for the newlyweds to walk through, leading up to their tent. Blessing after blessing was spoken over them as they walked through the tunnel of people, pausing to wave at the entrance before going in and closing the flap, fastening it from the inside. The guests cheered and clapped, the women ululating, the men shouting out blessings. The music started up again and the dancing resumed. This time, it was mainly the men who danced, stomping to the beat of the pounding drums in a cycle of testosterone-inspired fervour, as the women sat discussing children, marriage and wedding feasts.

I sat with Moses and Jesher watching the dancing, glowing with contentment. Yoram was married. Little Yori was now the husband of a beautiful young wife. Even though I had known for a long time that this day would come, it still seemed quite surreal; my mind could not comprehend it. I stared into the flames that flickered lazily in the huge firepit. Images of Yori flashed through my mind: baby Yori reaching out to take hold of my finger as I held him in my arms, Yori toddling towards me, babbling with delight, when he learned to walk. The innocent expression in his big brown eyes as he tried, without success, to pronounce my name. The way he smiled up at me with such pride when I taught him how to make his first fire. His embarrassment at the raspy, squeaking sounds he made when his voice broke and manhood came upon him. The broad set of his shoulders as he grew from a boy into a man, and the gentle love that radiated from his eyes when he told me about the woman he wanted to marry. And now he had. He was no longer a boy. He was a married man.

We sat for a while, watching the dancing and discussing the finer points of tentmaking, until Moses decided it was time for him to take his leave. Soon after he and his family left, the crowds dissipated and drifted off to their own tents. Mesha went to sit by the dying embers in the firepit. He was unusually quiet and I wondered if he sought solace, or whether I should join him. It seemed wrong to leave him by himself, so I went to sit with him.

'So, it is done,' I said. 'Your first-born is married, and to a beautiful young woman.'

Mesha nodded. 'My little boy, a husband. How can this be?' he murmured.

'I was pondering the same thoughts this evening.'

'Mmm.'

Silence descended. We sat side by side, contemplating the mysteries of love and marriage. I leaned forward, placing my forearms on my thighs. My chin rested on my crossed arms, and my eyes were fixed on the charred remains of the logs in the firepit. I stared at the flickering fingers of flame as they stroked the glowing lumps, finding myself hypnotised by the spluttering sounds of the fire, along with the rhythmic chirping of crickets. My eyes blurred. I let them lull me into a state of mesmerised contentment, blinking in languid satisfaction as the undulating night breezes caused the embers to flare up, then fade away, flare then fade.

I closed my eyes.

All was well.

'Peace, be still,' the fire spluttered to me. 'Rest now,' the cicadas whispered in chorus.

All of a sudden, the fire spat and roared into flame. I started and opened my eyes. There in front of me, shimmering among the flames, was the glaring face of my tormentor, his flaming eyes boring into me.

'*You are a weak, pathetic creature,*' the flames hissed at me. Their damning accusations sounded over and over, fading into ashy darkness shortly before dawn, the giant's sneering scowl dissipating with them.

7

The Night Watches

'Again? Why?' I muttered to myself, wiping the sweat off my brow. I hit the ground with my fist, muffling a groan of frustration. This was too much! Why did these giants continue to haunt my dreams? The horrific nightly encounters were becoming more and more frequent; these days, I dreaded falling asleep, lest they hunt me again in the night watches.

The dreams were usually the same, but tonight's had been much worse, because there was not one giant, but two, and they weren't just hunting me – they were hunting Yoram and Samina as well. My heart thumped in response to the terrifying images that still flashed through my mind; Yoram holding Samina's hand, dragging her behind him as they fled from their pursuers. I heard their screams as they fell, watched the terror on their faces as one of the giants pinned them to the ground. I felt the frantic pounding of my heart as I struggled to get free from the other titan, who held me with just one arm, gagging me with his other. Unable to speak, my muffled cries echoed in the darkness. I watched helplessly as the giant that held Yoram and Samina turned to me and growled the cursed words which I loathed with such passion.

'*You are a weak, pathetic creature.*'

The last thing I heard was the hiss of his sword as it swung down to end their lives.

'No!' I would not think on it. 'You will not oppress me in this way,' I muttered to my unseen tormentors. Lack of sleep over the past few months was affecting me. A deep resentment was growing on the inside of me towards these creatures who had been responsible for our prolonged sojourning in the wilderness, and were now tormenting me each night.

53

When our people escaped Egypt, our path led towards the land which Yahweh had promised us as an inheritance, the same land where our forefather Abraham had dwelt: the land of Canaan – a land of milk and honey, a bountiful, fertile territory where our people could thrive. I was part of a group of twelve men chosen to go and spy out the land. Canaan was everything we had hoped for, but for one thing: there were giants in that land. My companions became so fearful of these god-men that all of them, bar Caleb, rejected the land that Yahweh had promised us and convinced our people not to go into Canaan.

My memories of that day were still as clear as if it had happened yesterday. Grief ripped into my heart as Yahweh's chosen people rejected Him and, as a consequence, received the ultimate punishment. All of our men aged twenty and over who had been numbered in the census, with the exception of Caleb and I, would not enter the promised land of Canaan. Instead, our tribes would wander this wilderness for forty years, one year for every day that we had spied out the land, until that generation of warriors passed from this world. It was a devastating blow, the ramifications of their disobedience far-reaching.

'You did this,' I muttered at the unseen instigators of our misery. 'And still, you wreak havoc on me, in my dreams.'

I rearranged my blanket, lay on my side and closed my eyes, determined not to let these bestial creatures rob me of my sleep. Eventually, I did fall into a fitful slumber, tossing and turning. When I awoke, the sun was well on its way in its journey across the sky, and I could hear the voices of my family. My head throbbed. I sat for a while, rubbing my temple, before dressing and going to join them in the communal clearing outside our tents. The men were sitting around the family circle on large woven mats, while the women cleared away the remnants of the morning meal. Had I slept for that long? Mesha noticed me first.

'Ah, *shalom*, Joshua,' he said. 'Come, join us. We put some manna cakes and fruit aside for you.' I gave my face and hands a quick wash, dried them with the cloth and sat down next to him. Mesha shoved a dish into my hand.

'Thank you,' I said, rubbing my eyes. I squinted at the small crusty mounds. Manna was Yahweh's miraculous provision for us while we were in this inhospitable wilderness. We woke each morning to find pieces of crumbly, wafer-like fragments covering the ground on the outskirts of the camp, and our womenfolk had become accomplished at baking coriander and honey-flavoured cakes, herb bread or raisin cakes with them. They were delicious, especially when eaten warm, straight from the coals, and I would usually have devoured them without a moment's hesitation. Today, however, I had no appetite.

'Joshua, you are not hungry?' Jesher looked at me, concerned. 'You are usually the first to rise in the morning. Are you unwell?'

'No, *Abba*,' I replied, rubbing my temple. 'I am well. I... uh... I have not been sleeping well of late.'

'Why is this, my son?'

I hesitated, embarrassed to speak of the dreams in front of my family. I was supposed to be the strong one – the great warrior, the leader – and I was brought low by mere dreams? By now, however, all the family who were around had stopped what they were doing and were looking at me, waiting to hear my response. I had no choice but to tell them, so I shared a condensed version of the dream, leaving out the part that involved Yoram and Samina, who sat among us.

'*Ech!*' Mesha said when I finished. 'I have had many dreams over the years. They mean nothing. Pay them no heed.'

Azriel nodded his agreement. 'Yes, perhaps it is best to cleanse your mind of those thoughts, hmm?'

'The best way to deal with dreams like that,' Mesha continued, 'is to turn a blind eye. Turn from them until they cease to pursue you, yes?' A smattering of agreement echoed around the family circle. Jesher, however, said nothing. He studied me with his piercing gaze and scratched his beard. Then, out of the midst of the chatter and noise, I heard a quiet, calm voice.

'My lord, I would not discount these dreams.'

8

Yahweh Speaks

Everyone turned to look at Joel's young wife, Alya, who was standing near the entrance to the tent, rocking Sadie to sleep in her arms. Alya blushed and lowered her head. 'Forgive me, I do not mean to speak out of turn, but...' she paused, then lifted her head and met my gaze, 'I believe that Yahweh speaks to us through our dreams.' A smattering of deliberation erupted, along with some scornful responses. Joel got up and went to stand by his wife, putting a protective arm around her as she held little Sadie. I could see he was readying himself to speak out in her defence but, before he could say a word, Jesher held up his hand to silence everyone.

'Alya? Tell us more, child. What has led you to believe this?'

She held little Sadie closer and gulped. 'I believe it to be true, *Saba*, because... because Yahweh speaks to me through dreams.'

A wave of gasps rippled throughout the gathering.

'*Psht!*' Shira scoffed, moving closer to glare at Alya. 'Yahweh does not speak to women.' I could see she was preparing to launch into a long, robust rebuke centred around Alya's audacity in presuming that Yahweh would speak to her, but her sermonising was silenced by Jesher's hand.

He smiled at Alya. Warmth and something akin to curiosity radiated from his kind eyes. 'Please, tell us more.' Shira rolled her eyes and huffed. She was not a woman who believed in, or had time for, mysteries or deep thoughts, and she appeared to despise those who did. Crossing her arms, she stood in front of her grand-daughter-in-law, ready to render judgement as soon as Alya had finished her explanation.

Alya did not appear to be intimidated by Shira. She didn't back down, nor did she resist or retaliate. Watching her now reminded me of the time I first met her. Being aware of her family's dubious reputation, I had expected to find a defiant, rebellious and possibly wanton woman. She was anything but that. The woman I met was modestly dressed; she carried herself with a quiet humility, and had a noble bearing. She had spoken to me with great courage and conviction at our first meeting and, as I looked at her now, I saw the self-same qualities. Alya looked at Shira with her calm, liquid green eyes, then turned to speak to Jesher.

'It started when I was just a girl. I had a dream about an accident. In the dream I saw a pillar of stone crumble and fall on my brother, wounding his leg. I told my *abba* about the dream, but he did not believe me, and I was... punished for my foolishness. A few days later, my brother was brought home from the quarry, his leg torn and bleeding from stones that had collapsed and fallen on him. There were other dreams, but they also were not well received, so I learned not to share them, but to ponder them in my heart and bring them before Yahweh.'

'And you believe my dreams are messages from Yahweh?' I asked her. I heard Shira guffawing and, out of the corner of my eye, I saw her shaking her head at such a foolish notion. I ignored her. So did everyone else. We were all intrigued by Alya's story, curious to know more.

'I would not presume to know whether they are or not, my lord, or what Yahweh might be saying to you through the dreams. I only know that He can and does speak to us in the night watches, and I believe it is wisdom on our part to bring dreams such as these before Him, and not simply discard them.'

Shira huffed again, shook her head and stalked into the tent, muttering to herself. Mesha raised his eyebrows, looking across the circle at Azriel. The women in our company looked at Alya with undisguised admiration before continuing with their chores. Not only had she taken part in a conversation that, according to our cultural norms, should only have been strictly for the men among us, but she had also successfully stood up to Shira – a feat that not many of them had been able to accomplish!

The morning meal now over, we prepared to go our separate ways; Joel to work at Bezalel's workshops, Azriel and Hareph to their potter's wheel, Mesha to a mandatory army training session, and the women to their chores. I walked over to Alya and Joel.

'Alya.'

'My lord, forgive me, I meant no disrespect.'

'Alya, you must not call me "my lord". Please, call me by my name. We are family, *nu?*' This was not the first time I had asked this of her. In fact, over the last few years since she had married Joel, I had asked her several times, but it seemed she could not bring herself to call me Joshua, possibly because she had known me as the commander of Israel's armies before she came to know me as part of her new family. It seemed that that mindset was too deeply engrained in her now to change.

'I will try, my l...' She shook her head and her cheeks flushed. 'I will try... Joshua.'

'Thank you, and thank you for sharing your thoughts about my dreams. I would like to talk to you more about your experiences, if you are willing?'

'You would?' She looked up at Joel, as if seeking his approval. He smiled at her with great pride.

'Yes, very much so,' I replied. 'I must take my leave now, the men will be waiting for me, but perhaps this evening, or during Shabbat, we could talk more?'

'I would like that.' Alya gave Joel a kiss on both cheeks and took little Sadie into the tent for a nap.

We watched her go, then I turned to Joel. 'Did you know about Alya's dreams?'

'Yes. There are no secrets between us. At first she struggled to tell me, but now, whenever she has a notable dream, she shares it with me.' Noting the curiosity on my face, he smiled. 'There is much about my wife that is yet unseen by our family. Her wisdom and insight are like treasures hidden in a deep pool of water, waiting to be discovered.' Joel stared at me for a while, almost daring me to challenge him, then he bade me farewell and went on his way.

My morning was spent at our military training grounds on the west side of the camp, with a large company of men from the tribe of

Benjamin. Part of my duties as commander of the armies of Israel lay in the training of our men in the ways of war. All who were of an age to fight underwent military training on a rotation system and this month, it was the tribe of Benjamin who were scheduled. Caleb, my second-in-command, and I were actively looking for men who showed both skill in battle and leadership potential, so we could appoint captains and put into place a solid structure for each tribe's army.

I watched as Caleb drilled the men in the skills of swordsmanship, archery, spear throwing or hand-to-hand combat, but I struggled to concentrate and did not have the energy to take an active part in their training. My mind and body were so tired that, no matter how hard I tried, I could not focus. Thoughts of the giants, images of Yoram and Samina fleeing, and the desperate question of how to protect my family in an event of an attack, bombarded my mind over and over again.

The morning dragged on and, when the training ended, we dismissed the men. Caleb came to me for our usual discussion about which men had displayed potential of being warrior leaders.

'Is it well with you, Joshua?' he said straight away. Caleb had never been one to sidestep difficult issues. Sometimes I found his forthrightness disconcerting but, for the most part, I welcomed it. At least I always knew what was on his mind, and didn't have to fumble around trying to extract information from him. 'You are not yourself. Has something taken place?' he asked me, crossing his arms in a confrontational pose.

'Forgive me, my friend. You are right, I am not myself.' I knew I owed him a proper explanation, so I told him of my night-time struggles and the detrimental effect the dreams were having on me. I was telling him about what Alya had said that morning, when Mesha walked across and joined us. As one of the Benjaminite men chosen to train this week, he showed great skill as a warrior. He and Caleb were alike in many ways and their personalities, as well as their fighting styles, were so similar, at times it was uncanny.

'*Ech*! Not your dreams again?' he said to me, punching my arm before turning to Caleb. 'I told him, the way to deal with these dreams is to banish them from your mind. Give no thought to them and in time they will go. Yes?'

Caleb didn't seem to agree with Mesha, which was unusual. Most of the time they were of one mind, but not this time. Caleb frowned and asked me, 'How long have these dreams been afflicting you?'

I had to think for a moment. It felt like years, but I knew it couldn't be. 'A few months.'

'And it is the same dream all the time?'

I hesitated, not wanting to mention Yoram and Samina's presence in my last dream in front of Mesha. 'Mostly, yes.' Mesha listened to our discussion, but I knew he was starting to get irritated. He derived great pleasure from discussing the training sessions and their outcomes with us, and was clearly not happy about my dreams stopping these deliberations from taking place, or the fact that Caleb was taking my dreams seriously when he had not.

'And Alya has had many dreams like this, dreams that foretold an event that came to pass?' Caleb asked, obviously intrigued by the notion.

'It seems so. It started when she was a girl, and she still has them now.'

'*Agh*, she is a woman!' Mesha blurted. 'Women have lots of dreams. They are emotional creatures, *nu*? If I paid heed to everything that Helah tells me, *ooph*...' He rolled his eyes.

Neither Caleb nor I responded. Perhaps, years ago, I might have agreed with Mesha. Now I wasn't so sure. Caleb clearly agreed with me because he asked, 'Have you told Moses of these dreams?'

'No. I did not think they warranted bothering him, but now...'

'Talk to him. Tell him all that is in your heart. He is wise. You will glean much from his counsel and sound judgement.'

It seemed strange to be on the receiving end of advice such as this from Caleb – it was usually the other way around – but I knew he was right. Mesha crossed his arms, clearly not impressed by the direction our conversation had taken. 'Mesha...?' I asked, wanting to include him in our decision.

'Go, if you think it necessary,' he muttered, curling his lips and shrugging his shoulders.

I nodded. 'I will go now. Perhaps I can talk to him during the midday rest. *Shalom*, Mesha. *Shalom*, Caleb, and thank you.'

Mesha grunted and stomped off in the opposite direction, throwing one last resentful look at Caleb as I hurried off to find Moses. I was right, he was in his tent resting, and was glad to see me. He was clearly expecting a report on that morning's training and any prospective captains, and was surprised when I asked to talk to him about something personal. We sat in the shade of an awning together and I told him everything, including the details of last night's dream about Yoram and Samina.

Moses listened attentively, nodding, rocking slightly and saying 'mmm' from time to time, as was his way, until I finished. He was not a man who was quick to speak, he was one who listened and thought and prayed and, only then, would he speak. So I waited until he was ready.

'You saw giants when you crossed over into Canaan with the other spies, yes?'

'Yes, but mostly from far off. There were many of them, especially further north, in the land of Ammon and near Hebron. Fearsome creatures, men of immense stature and strength. But even though I saw their size and stature, I did not fear them. I knew that Yahweh was giving us the land and I knew that we could conquer them. So why am I so fearful of these giants that appear in my dreams? My heart pounds when I think of them, even in my waking hours, let alone when I meet them in my dreams. I was not fearful of them then, so why am I so fearful now?'

'Mmm,' he mumbled, then went quiet again for a while. 'We know that Yahweh speaks to us through our dreams, yes? One of our most honoured descendants, Joseph, had dreams which spoke of his own rise to power in Egypt, but do you remember the dreams that Pharoah had, which Joseph interpreted for him?'

'My *abba* told me the stories often, as a boy,' I replied. 'One was about seven healthy cows that were eaten by seven malnourished cows, and the other about seven large heads of grain that were swallowed up by seven thin heads of grain.'

'Yes. Those dreams were a warning to Pharaoh of the seven years of famine to come. Yahweh moved on Joseph, giving him the interpretation of the dreams, and enabling him to rise to power in Egypt and save many in that land from starvation.' Moses thought hard before continuing. 'Yahweh uses dreams to warn us of what is to come.'

'And you believe my dreams are warnings from Yahweh?' I held my breath. My heart started thumping loudly; I wondered if Moses could hear it.

Moses turned to look at me. 'I believe they could be.'

'But what does that mean?' I thought to myself. 'Giants attacking us here, in the wilderness? Or in Canaan? But when? How many? How does one battle such a powerful creature?' I slumped forward and put my head in my hands, rubbing my still-throbbing temples as I recalled the seductive lure of those beautiful predators, and the desire they invoked in me to fall down and worship them. What did it all mean? It did not bode well.

'Master, have you ever encountered one?'

'A giant?'

'Yes. Have you ever come across a giant?'

Moses nodded, but seemed reluctant to talk of it. 'Once, when I was a boy in Pharaoh's court. They captured a giant who had strayed too close to our borders. He was brought before Pharoah manacled, weighed down with heavy chains. Even chained as he was, he was terrifying, and yet so compelling at the same time. I remember staring at him, drawn to his incredible beauty, fascinated by his stature and power. He stood straight-backed and would not speak even one word in response to Pharaoh's questions.' Moses rubbed some dirt off his fingernail. 'They made him work in the quarries, but he refused to labour and became so disruptive that Pharaoh handed him over to the priests and soothsayers. They put him on show outside the temple, publicly humiliating him, torturing him in front of the crowds who came, day after day, to see the spectacle. I was taken every day and made to watch. What they did to him, no man should have to endure, giant or not.'

'What happened to him?'

'He died, eventually. A horrible death. It took days.' Shaking his head as if to erase the memory, Moses sighed and looked at me. 'Bring your dreams before Yahweh, Joshua. Petition Him. Ask Him about their meaning. I will also entreat Him on your behalf. He will speak, of this I am sure.'

'He had better speak to me soon,' I thought to myself as I left Moses. 'I don't know how much longer I can endure these nightly attacks.' I was weary to the point of desperation from trying to rid my mind of the curse that echoed round and round my thoughts in a never-ending cycle of doom.

'You are a weak, pitiful creature.'

9

Languishing

She had been ill for days, languishing in her tent while the women hovered over her, nursing her with gentle touches. Eglah had always been slender but, since this illness had beset her, she had become even thinner. Her body rejected food of any kind; she could not keep down even the smallest mouthful, apart from the vegetable broths that Shira made her, if she sipped them slowly. At first we thought it might have been something she ate that had turned her stomach but, as the days went by and her health did not improve, our thoughts turned to more serious causes.

Hareph was distraught. He hardly slept and would not leave the tent even to take a short walk. I knew he was fond of Eglah, but I felt ashamed to admit that I had wondered in times past if his affection for her was based more on the fact that she looked after him so well, and not so much on the passion in his heart for her. During this time, I began to see more clearly the depth of his love for his wife. He loved Eglah with a fierce devotion, and the fear that she might be taken from him was driving him to distraction. Hareph tended to talk to himself at the best of times, but now, in his present state of anxiety, a consistent stream of mutters trickled out of his mouth. He was unable to keep still; no sooner had he sat down then he would get up again and start pacing, his shoulders twitching continuously in a deranged kind of dance. His eyes, which each tended to drift lazily in their own direction at times, now darted about even more, as if trying to keep pace with his jumbled thoughts.

Shira had to ban Hareph from sitting with Eglah, as he became so distressed when she retched and she, in turn, became anxious about the distress it was causing him. Shira allowed him to come and see her at regular intervals throughout the day, just for a short time, but no more than that, for both their sakes.

We watched Hareph from the side lines, unable to calm him, helpless to ease his suffering. Even Jesher could not keep him still long enough to have a meaningful conversation with him or bring much comfort to his heart. So we waited and watched and entreated Yahweh on his behalf. We all felt the pain of Eglah's malady. Of all the women in the family, she was the one who was usually first to notice when one of us was in need; her kindness and gentle words were a healing balm in our midst (a trait which I believe was passed on to her by Jesher). Now, however, it was she who was in need, and we felt helpless to know how to aid her.

Although I tried not to let them, my thoughts kept wandering, imagining what life would be like without Eglah. Because she was reserved in spirit and did not often make her opinions known, you could be mistaken into thinking that she was of little consequence. Nothing could be further from the truth. I realised how much of a sense of peace and belonging she brought to our family. She had a way of making each one of us feel significant – that what we said or thought was important, and deserving of attention. She was the thread that wove the tapestry of our family life together. Without her, we would flail and unravel.

What about Hareph? How would he fare without Eglah?

A question occurred to me, one that I had never consciously thought of before: Why did Hareph and Eglah live with our family, and not with his family? In our culture, a woman went to live with her husband and his family when she married. Jesher and Shira's third child, Zivah, had left home when she married a man named Seled. Unfortunately, Seled's father had fallen out with Jesher and Shira soon after the marriage celebration. Shira's sharp tongue and uncompromising opinions about the raising of children had created offence which had unfortunately resulted in Seled's family being unwilling to form a close relationship with their daughter-in-law's family. Jesher had never spoken of it in so many words, but I sensed a deep regret and sorrow in him whenever he mentioned Zivah or her children.

Zivah had moved away to live with Seled's family when she married him, so why had Eglah not gone to live with Hareph's family when they married? I asked Mesha and Helah if they knew the reason why.

Mesha chuckled to himself. 'That is a good question, my friend. Hareph was the only son out of five children. By the time he took Eglah to be his wife, all four of his sisters were married and living with their husband's families. When Eglah married him, she went to live with him and his parents. But very soon after they married, Hareph's *abba* was killed in an accident at the quarry.'

'I remember it well,' Helah added. 'Hareph's sorrow was great, being the last in his bloodline, and his *ima* did not bear her grief well. She was brought very low and, when her time of mourning was over, she decided to go and live with one of Hareph's sisters, who had just given birth to twins and already had four children to look after. Hareph and Eglah had no children and her heart yearned for her grandchildren. With his sisters all married and his *ima* now living with one of them, Eglah and Hareph were alone.'

Mesha took over again, telling me how Jesher had asked them if they would like to come and live with his family. It was unusual for a son to leave his family home and join with his wife's family, but not unheard of, and Hareph and Eglah accepted his invitation straight away.

'*Abba* was glad of the opportunity to have Eglah back,' Helah told me, smiling to herself as she recalled that time. 'He told me so himself. He had missed her, her thoughtful ways and kind words. He grew to love his new son-in-law, especially Hareph's passion for the ways of Yahweh.'

'Yes,' I replied. 'There is much kindness in Hareph's heart, and he has a sharp mind.'

Just then, Shira pushed aside the curtain of the women's section of the tent and came outside. As soon as he saw her, Hareph leapt up and blurted, 'This has gone on too long. We must send for a healer. We can delay no longer.' Turning to Jesher, his voice broke as he pleaded, '*Abba*, I beg of you, we must find a healer. We must save her.'

Before Jesher could respond, Shira walked up to Hareph, laid her hand on his arm, and said, 'Your wife has no need of a healer, Hareph.'

Raising her other hand to stop his protestations, she continued, 'But she will have need of a midwife, in time.'

Hareph froze. His shoulders did not twitch, his head was still. Only his eyes moved, darting from side to side as he gazed into his mother-in-law's face. Shira's face broke into a smile – a smile unlike any I had seen on her face before – when looking at her son-in-law. It brought beauty to her countenance. There was compassion in her smile, and joy – even a thread of love for this man who, up until now, she had appeared only to despise.

Hareph stared at her, wide-eyed. 'She will not die?' he whispered.

'No, she will not die,' Shira whispered back.

'She... will live?' he whispered again.

'Yes. She will live.'

Hareph started gasping and panting. Noises started coming out of his mouth; cries of relief, joy, disbelief all tumbled out in a jumble of sounds. Nodding first to Shira, then to himself, he mumbled, 'She will live... she will live. She will not die. She will live.' He shrieked, spun around, and grabbed the person nearest to him, who happened to be Yoram.

'She will live!' he shouted to his nephew, giving him a kiss on each cheek before rushing to the next person. Hareph rushed around the circle, giving each of us a hug and kissing our cheeks, shouting out, 'She will live!' as he did so.

Finding himself back with Shira again, he grasped her tightly to himself, giving her the same treatment as the rest of us. Her eyes shot open as he caught hold of her, then she relaxed and returned his embrace, patting him on the back and laughing at his response. That was the first time I had ever seen them embrace. It warmed my heart.

Releasing Shira, he stepped back, clapping his hands in delight. 'She lives!' he shouted again. The smile froze on his face as he gawped at her. 'But... did you say... midwife? She will have need of a midwife? Eglah? My wife? She is... is she...?'

Shira had obviously been wondering how long it would take him to realise what she had said. She smiled at him, reached out and grasped his shoulders as if to steady him. 'Your wife is with child, Hareph. You are going to be a father.'

'She is...? My Eglah? With child...? I am... I am to be a father?' Shira nodded and Hareph let out a cry of delight. 'A child! She is with child! I am to be a father!' He swung round to face us, laughing uproariously while tears rolled down his cheeks. Rushing around from person to person, he embraced each one of us a second time – in truth, I believe he hugged some of us three or four times, such was his exhilaration, but none of us minded! Some of our neighbours came out of their tents to see what the commotion was about. As soon as he saw them, Hareph shouted out, 'She is with child! I am to be a father!' and rushed over to embrace them as well, to their great surprise.

We laughed at his exuberant, childlike delight and I wondered what kind of a father Hareph would be. One thing was for certain: this child would be undeniably welcome and unequivocally cherished.

As soon as he had finished embracing the neighbours, Hareph rushed back to Shira. 'Can I see her? Can I see my wife? I need to see my wife. I must see her *now*!' he urged.

'Yes – but only for a short while,' Shira replied, trying to look stern, but without success. 'She must rest, *nu?*'

'Yes. She must rest,' Hareph repeated, then rushed over to the tent. He paused at the entrance, seeming to steady himself, then opened the flap and tiptoed inside to see the bearer of this most wondrous miracle.

10

Eimlaqi

The priests were going about their duties, their worship rising like a sweet-smelling fragrance in the Tabernacle courts. Their music calmed my spirit and brought peace to my heart. I knelt with my face to the ground in prayer; it was late in the afternoon and I had come to pray. In truth, I came most afternoons of late, to spend time before Yahweh before going home to break bread with the family. My prayers, more often than not, were cries for help. Why were these treacherous giants still hunting me in my sleep? Why did the dreams keep reoccurring so frequently? What did they mean?

'Speak to me, Lord God,' I prayed. 'Please. Tell me what You would have me do.'

'My lord?' A quiet voice cut through the stillness. I sat up and opened my eyes to see a young man crouching on one knee beside me. I recognised his face – I had seen him often with Abidan, an elder from the tribe of Benjamin. I believed him to be Abidan's grandson.

'Attai?'

'Yes, my lord,' he whispered. 'Forgive me for disturbing you here, but I have been sent to fetch you. You are needed. You must not delay. Please. It is of great importance.'

What was so urgent it could not wait until I had finished praying? The sneering, prideful face of my unseen adversary flashed in my mind. I frowned, frustrated; I had just come to a place of peace, here in Yahweh's Tabernacle, but now it had dissipated. I grunted, rose to my feet, and followed Attai. Once we were away from the confines of the Tabernacle, I stopped and put my hands on my hips. 'What is it that I must attend to?' Attai, however, had taken off at a fast pace, and did not stop or shorten his stride. I ran to catch up with him, annoyed that he had not stopped to accommodate my questions. 'Attai, where are we bound in such haste?'

'To the watchman's tower, my lord, on the north side of the camp.'

'Call me Joshua, please,' I muttered. 'What have the watchmen seen?'

'Traders.'

'Traders? Asad's company?' Attai nodded but didn't slow down. 'What of it? They visit the camp regularly and have never brought danger to us. We have been expecting them for some time – this is good news, surely?'

'This is a day of trouble for them, my lord. They have been grievously attacked.'

'Attacked? By who? Surely not by any of our people? Who would do that? Why?'

'We do not know. None of us speak their language and their hearts are so troubled, they... they are not themselves, my lord. Their wounds... they are unlike anything I have seen before.'

'What do you speak of?'

'They look not to be from the thrust of a sword or the piercing of an arrow. They... they are...' The more Attai tried to explain, the more agitated he seemed to become. I began to wonder what manner of evil awaited me. 'I cannot fathom what could have caused this defilement,' he added by way of explanation. 'Please, you must see for yourself. We must make haste.'

I asked no more questions. Our walking turned into running and, before long, we reached the watchman's post. A large crowd had gathered and I heard a jumbled noise of voices arguing, mingled with cries of anguish. Attai and I pushed our way through the wall of bodies and found four men sprawled on a woven mat on the ground. I recognised two of them – Nadeem, Asad's brother, and his son, Sufian. I greeted them. Nadeem seemed relieved to see me.

'*Yusha*,' he mumbled, clutching onto my arm. '*Yusha*'.

The other two men were not known to me. The arm of the older one hung lifelessly by his side. His sleeve had been ripped off and his arm was covered with what looked like large puncture marks, as if multiple fangs had bitten into him in sequence. Blood oozed from each gash, running down his arm in a steady trickle. He was moaning and rocking in pain, his eyes closed. His younger companion was talking to him, trying to calm him, although he was clearly also in pain. He also had gashes on his body, and one of his legs was bent at an unnatural angle; it looked to be broken.

Nadeem and Sufian seemed to have fared better than their companions. They both had wounds, although Attai was right: these were not the clean-cut wounds of a sword or arrow, they were jagged rips where the flesh had been torn. Their faces had streaks of blood on them, but I could see no lacerations there and, for the most part, their wounds looked to be superficial. I knelt next to Nadeem, desperate to know what had happened.

'Nadeem, who did this to you?' I asked, opening up my hands to try to demonstrate my question. 'This,' I pointed to their wounds. 'Who did this?' I spoke slowly and clearly, all the while knowing that it would make no difference no matter how slowly I talked. Although over the years, Asad had built up a basic vocabulary of words with which to communicate with me, none of the others had done so. Any dialogue between our two peoples had been done through Asad and me. Nadeem and his companions gazed at me, squinting in confusion at my words, then looked at each other and started babbling in their own tongue.

'Was it my people?' I asked, gesturing to the men standing around. 'Were your attackers from here?' I asked, pointing to the middle of the camp and back at their wounds. I pointed to the camp again, and acted out someone attacking them. They seemed to understand. Talking to each other, they shook their heads, and signalled with their hands as if to say 'no'.

'No?' I asked. 'Not my people?' They continued to signal 'no'. Nadeem put his hand on my chest, then on his wounds, and then made the 'no' signal again. 'Then who?' I asked, relieved to hear that their attackers had not come from within our camp. 'Who did this to you?' Nadeem's eyes opened wide and filled with terror. He repeated one word over and over again.

'*Eimlaqi! Eimlaqi!*' He lifted his arm to indicate something very large and tall. '*Eimlaqi! Eimlaqi!*'[10]

A shiver ran down my spine. I looked at Attai, Nosson the watchman and the men gathered around, in the vain hope that someone might understand what they were trying to communicate. Their faces were as blank as mine. Finally, Nadeem leaned over and started drawing in the sand with his finger. He drew the crude outline of a man's body with head, arms and legs. Pointing to himself, then back to his drawing, he said, 'Nadeem.' Using his finger, he started to draw a figure next to the man. I crouched down next to him and watched with a growing sense of dread as the drawing took shape. It was another man, but this man was nearly twice the size of the first one.

'*Eimlaqi!*' he said, pointing to the second drawing. '*Eimlaqi!*'

I stared at his drawing in the sand. Nadeem had drawn a giant, I was sure of it. A giant – or giants – had attacked them. My mind went blank, overcome by the monstrous reality of that revelation. Giants? Here? Near our camp? Just as quickly, my warrior instincts came into force and a primeval urge to protect our people took over.

Standing up, I turned to find some men who I recognised and trusted, and started barking out orders. 'Shaul, make haste and find Caleb ben Jephunneh. Tell him to rally the warriors. We need a troop of two hundred of our strongest, ready to meet with me outside the Tabernacle at sunset. Ask Caleb to meet me at Moses' tent as soon as he can. Then go to Moses, tell him what has happened, and say that I will come and report to him when I am able.' I turned to a young man who I recognised from army training. 'Yakir, run! Summon all the watchmen. Tell them to meet Nosson here without delay. Nosson,' I said, turning to the watchman who had been the first to have sight of the traders, 'I want four watchmen stationed on each side of the camp, spread out along the breadth of the camp; sixteen for each watch, yes?' He nodded. 'They are to stand watch throughout the night and day, with sixteen more in reserve. When one tires, the next will take over. Put your best men on duty. We must be on our guard.'

---

10   An Arabic word for 'giant'.

The four traders were watching me, bewildered and clearly in shock. 'Attai, these men need their wounds tended. They need food and drink, and a tent where they can stay until they heal. Their tent must be near the middle of the camp, not on the outskirts. Can you perform this task?'

He nodded. 'I can, my lord. My grandfather, Abidan, will aid me. But how are we to get them to their tent? The camels they rode on are tethered nearby, but their wounds are great and they have lost much blood; I am not sure they...'

'No. No, they cannot walk or ride on a beast. They must be laid in the back of a cart – two carts. Bariah,' I called to an older man standing nearby, 'we have need of two carts. Can you find them and have them brought here? We will need blankets and sheepskin rugs to lay these men on. I will settle the cost of these later, but we must find some without delay.' Bariah was a wise old man, much loved by his people, and I felt sure he would be able to lay his hands on two carts and the skins within a short space of time. He and Attai left to fulfil their tasks. I needed one more messenger.

Looking around, I saw a leader from the tribe of Naphtali who I knew to be a reliable, trustworthy man. 'Allon,' I called. 'These men need tending to. It would serve us well if you would go and gather some healers. Can you do this?' Allon nodded his head and turned to leave, but I grasped his arm to stop him. 'Explain to them the nature of these men's wounds; tell them to bring everything that they might have need of, and come in haste. As soon as Bariah brings the carts, we will take these men to a tent near the middle of the camp. We will meet the healers there.' Allon muttered his agreement and, after taking one last look at the disturbing sight behind him, he left.

I knelt down next to Nadeem, put my hand on his uninjured shoulder, and said to him, 'We will look after you. Do not fear, Nadeem. We will watch over you.' I knew he could not understand my words, but I hoped that he would hear in my voice the compassion and concern that filled my heart. He did. Tears came to his eyes and he nodded his head, muttering, '*Shkran lak, Yusha. Shkran lak.*'[11]

---

11 Arabic for 'thank you'.

A question had been circling my mind for a while: where was Asad? Had Asad been with them when they were attacked? I needed to know if he was alright.

Making eye contact with Nadeem, I asked, 'Asad – was he with you? Asad?'

Nadeem's face crumpled. He fell into my arms, repeating Asad's name and babbling in his own language, wailing with unrestrained grief. I closed my eyes as if to shut out the pain of what I now knew. I would not look upon Asad's handsome face again or see his bushy eyebrows rise in challenge. I would spar with him no more; his sparring days were over. I held the sorrowing man in my arms until the carts arrived and we could take these injured souls to a safe place where they could heal and rest.

By the time we had got them settled into their tent, washed, fed and watered, the sun had set. Moses and Caleb joined me and we spent time discussing what to do, while the healers tended to the four men. They cleaned their wounds, made poultices to smear on the ugly gashes and bound their wounds. They were not hopeful about the outcome for the older trader whose lifeless arm had been so grotesquely punctured. He passed out when we lifted him into the cart and, when the healers pulled his robe back to wash him, they found similar puncture wounds on his chest. His worst injuries, they believed, were not those that could be seen with the eye, as bad as they were, but the unseen wounds deep inside his body.

The camp had been put on high alert; a troop of warriors had already been positioned at each of the sixteen watchmen's stations, armed and ready. They would sleep there overnight, alert to the call of the watchmen. Messages had been sent out to the elders of the twelve tribes and our people had been told that under no circumstances was anyone to venture outside of the camp boundaries.

We put men on guard outside the traders' tent, mostly to stop curious onlookers from disturbing them, but also to bring word to us of anything the four men might have need of. I felt a strange sense of responsibility for these men; they had become like family to me. I was yet to find out what had happened to Asad, but I vowed to honour his memory by caring for his people to the best of my ability.

'I will stay here with them tonight,' I said, glancing into the tent.

'No,' Moses replied. 'That will not be necessary. Two of the healers will stay with them throughout the night to tend to them. They are safe and warm. Now they must sleep – and so must you. We will have need of you tomorrow, Joshua.'

I was not happy, but I had no choice but to accept Moses' instruction. 'Master, we need to talk to them, find out what happened. If it was giants that attacked them, we must know where they came from, how many there were, and their means of warfare. We must send word throughout the camp to find out if anyone knows their tongue.'

'I will talk with them tomorrow; I speak their tongue.'

'You understand their language?' I said, both astonished at this revelation, and frustrated that Moses had not told me before. 'How is it that you speak their tongue? Why did you not make this known?'

'You did not ask.' He looked at me, his expression clear, without guile. 'Besides, it looked as though you were learning their language quite well in your own time. I learned to speak Arabic as a child in Pharoah's court – I was tutored in many languages from an early age. Although,' he wagged his head from side to side, 'I have not spoken their tongue for a very long time; my words may not flow well. But it will come back to me, I am sure.'

'We must talk to them now, find out what has...'

'Not now, Joshua.'

'But if the giants are st...'

Moses lifted his hands and cut me off. 'Joshua, not now.' He was unyielding; there was no point in persisting. 'These men need to sleep. We all do. This has been a troubling afternoon. The watchmen are at their posts, and the warriors are standing by. If anything happens, you will be the first to be summoned. We will talk to the traders tomorrow.'

I hardly slept at all. The giants were relentless in their attack of me that night; the dream was repeated over and over again but, this time, Asad was with me. I woke, filled not only with fear, but with grief, my face wet with tears. The dawn was still a little while off, but I could stay in my tent no longer. I dressed and made my way to the traders. As I arrived, one of the healers opened the tent flap and came outside. He looked troubled. Staring up at the pillar of fire, he pulled his robe tighter around his body and sighed. When he saw me, he shook his head slowly from side to side in answer to the question I had not yet asked.

Entering the tent, I saw four figures lying on bed rolls on the floor. One lay on his back, covered with a cloth that stretched over his body and face. I turned around to check the other three sleeping forms, breathing a sigh of relief when I saw Nadeem sleeping peacefully. His son, Sufian, slept beside him, and the other young man with the broken leg, who I now knew was called Umar, twitched restlessly on his bed. The older man, Haseeb, had succumbed to his wounds during the night. I sat down next to Nadeem and prayed silently, waiting for the sun to rise.

When the rays of sun started peeping through the seams of the tent flap, Nadeeb stirred. Opening his eyes, he saw me sitting next to him. Initially confused, he wiped his eyes, then sat up, grimacing in pain.

'*Yusha. As-salamu alaykum*,'[12] Nadeem whispered.

'*As-salamu alaykum*, Nadeem,' I whispered in response, hand on my heart, knowing that the dawning of this day would bring anything but peace to him.

He yawned and looked over at his son, smiling when he saw Sufian sleeping peacefully. As he looked to his right and saw the covered form of the older man, his smile faded. A cry of grief spilt out of his mouth as he crawled over to his friend's bedside.

'Forgive us, Nadeem, I beg of you. We did everything we could to save him, but his wounds were too great,' I tried to explain, but Nadeem could not understand me. He was focused on the still form of his friend; I don't think he even heard me. Sufian and Umar woke at the sound of Nadeem's cries and the sound of wailing filled the tent. I didn't want to intrude on their grief, so I stood up, bowed, and left them to mourn in private, closing the tent flap behind me.

Standing outside their tent, I stared off into the distance, my fists

---

12   Arabic greeting meaning 'peace be with you'.

clenched, my heart filled with rage and anguish and a desperate need for revenge.

'I will avenge you and your kin,' I muttered. 'As surely as I live, I swear it; these giants will meet their end by my hand.'

11

Just for Sport

Later that morning, we sat in their tent, away from the prying eyes of those who had heard the stories about the merchants who narrowly escaped death by the hand of giants. Caleb and I watched and listened while Moses had a faltering conversation with Nadeem. He started off asking simple questions and relaying the answers to us. How many giants were there? Two. How many were there in your company? Fifteen men, and two boys, aged eleven and thirteen. Where were you when the giants attacked? By a small oasis, not half a day's journey from our camp.

After a while, however, when they started to talk in more detail about what had happened, Moses stopped asking questions. Nadeem needed no prompting. Anguish poured out of him in an unstoppable torrent of emotion as he told Moses in detail what had taken place. Sufian and Umar did not speak. Sufian sat, tears streaming down his face as he listened to his father. Umar stared at the ground, his eyes wide but unseeing, his hand tapping the ground in a tense rhythm. Moses didn't interrupt but, as he listened, I saw immense pain fill his eyes. He shook his head and grimaced as Nadeem recalled the savage brutality of the previous day, gesticulating, rocking and then wailing, until at last words failed him and he could speak no more.

It was then that Moses drew him close and held him, as a father would. His eyes tightly closed, he did not let go of Nadeem until his wails had diminished, and shudders racked his body. When Nadeem had come to himself, Moses spoke gentle words to him and his companions. All three nodded at him and laid back down on their bed rolls as Moses stood, beckoning us to follow him out of the tent.

We walked to Moses' tent in silence and sat down, but it was some time before he was able to tell us what Nadeem had said. Asad's company had been made up of his brothers, nephews and uncles. He was the eldest of four brothers, Nadeem being the third-born. Moses told us that the older man who had died of his wounds, Haseeb, was Nadeem's uncle.

'In their tongue, the name Haseeb means noble, to be respected.' Moses' voice cracked; he paused to gather himself before continuing. 'It seems Haseeb was such a man.'

Asad's family had been merchants for many generations. Their lives were spent traversing the desert, trading and bartering, usually only returning to their families after many months had passed. They had been travelling for many weeks, and were on their way to our camp with a large caravan of camels laden with goods, when they decided to stop late that morning to rest by an oasis. The giants had come upon them as they slept under the shade of the palm trees; they were taken completely by surprise.

Moses struggled to hold back the tears as he went on to tell us what happened. The attack was brutal, the giants without mercy. Nadeem spoke of their shock and horror at seeing such magnificent-looking creatures turn to utter savagery for no apparent reason. Their youngest boy died first, his neck snapped and his lifeless body thrown aside like an unwanted rag. Asad and his family ran to find their weapons, but the giants were too quick. They tried to defend themselves, but it was pointless. The reach of the giants' arms was so long that they could not get near them to strike. One of the giants grasped a man in each hand and smashed their heads together. They crumpled to the ground, dying instantly, their skulls shattered.

Nadeem told Moses of the weapon wielded by the first giant; a huge metal mace, formed on its end into rusty metal spikes. My heart skipped a beat. I had seen that weapon in my dreams, many times. It was from the injuries inflicted by that same weapon that Haseeb had died, and Nadeem said the giant's mace had only glanced off Haseeb. Asad and Nadeem's younger brother had not been so fortunate; he met the full fury of the giant's mace and was instantly disembowelled.

Moses turned to me. 'Asad gave his life for his kin,' he said, holding my gaze. 'He shouted at Nadeem and the others to run to the camels and escape. Nadeem thought Asad was with them but, as he mounted his camel and turned to look back, he saw that Asad had drawn his scimitar and was facing the second giant, to give them time to flee. Asad's son refused to leave; he stood with his father and Asad could not dissuade him. It all happened so quickly. The titan broke a large branch off an acacia tree and swung it at Asad and his son, killing them both with one blow.'

There were but two giants, but the destruction wrought by their hand was catastrophic for the men in Asad's family. Out of seventeen lives, only four had escaped, fleeing on the backs of camels. Now, only three were alive to tell the tale.

'They laughed as Nadeem and his companions fled.' Moses' voice broke; he could no longer hold back the tears. 'The giants laughed at their fear as they fled,' he said in disbelief, gasping in an effort to control his emotions. 'To die is the end of all men. Death comes to us all; it is not something to be feared. But to die such a death, to face such derision, without honour, is...' Words failed him. He took a while to gather himself. Pouring himself some water out of a jug, he walked over to the entrance and leaned on the tent post, staring out at the distant horizon. 'Nadeem wishes to go back to the oasis, to bury their dead.'

'Is that wise?' Caleb asked. 'The giants may still be there.'

'Whether it is wise or not, he is going. We cannot stop him. He says he cannot leave the bodies of his family there, to be food for wild animals and vultures. He is already in much anguish that they have been left for so long.' Turning to face us, Moses said, 'I have told him that we will send warriors with him, for protection, and to help them bury their dead. He wanted to go today, but it will take a full day and I do not want them lodging by the oasis overnight. They will journey tomorrow.'

I rose to my feet, the thud of my heart as a reverberating alarm within me. 'I will go and make the necessary preparations.'

'No.' Moses glanced at me, probably knowing that I would not like what he was about to say. 'Not you, Joshua. I need you here, with me. We must defend the camp. Caleb,' he said, looking at him, 'you will go in our stead.' Caleb did not flinch, although I saw his jaw clench and his breath quicken. 'Choose one hundred of our best warriors to go with you. You must leave before first light. Nadeem and Sufian will come with you. Umar will stay here – the bones in his leg are broken; he must not be moved for some days. Joshua,' he said, turning back to me, 'take word to the elders. I will meet with them after the midday rest. There is much to discuss.'

We left Moses staring into space in his tent, wiping away his tears. I was angry that he would not let me lead the mission, but I was also grateful. Perhaps he thought to spare me the wretched sight of the decaying bodies of Asad and his kin. I didn't know what his reasoning was, but I could not dwell on it now, it would only bring me anguish.

'I want Mesha with me tomorrow.'

I stopped in my tracks, and my head snapped round to see Caleb, who paused and turned to me. He waited until I responded.

'Why?'

'I must have men with me who I can trust. Mesha is brave and strong, and I trust him.'

My eyes narrowed but I said nothing. After a while I nodded and we walked on in silence.

The rest of the day passed in a whirlwind of meetings, discussions and preparations. I was awake early the following morning and walked with Mesha to the meeting point where the warriors gathered. The mood was sombre and I was grateful for the darkness, which masked the fear on our faces. When it came time for them to leave, I could not speak. The flawless faces of the depraved giants from my dreams flashed in my mind; fear for my friends rose up strongly in me. I clasped first Mesha and then Caleb to my chest, then watched the company move out, melting into the darkness. I lifted my hand in farewell to Nadeem and Sufian, perched on the backs of their camels. Nadeem's eyes were glassy, his face set like flint, but Sufian's eyes betrayed the fear that lurked within his heart.

The day crawled by. I couldn't settle. I couldn't eat. I couldn't be at home and see the fear on Helah's face, or watch my family's fruitless efforts to try to calm her. I was sure Moses knew the battle that raged within me; it was most likely the same one that raged within him. We spent much of the day in the Tabernacle in prayer and worship and, as the afternoon wore on and evening approached, we went to Melech's watchtower on the north side of the camp and waited.

I lost track of how long we waited but, eventually, Melech called out and we saw the vague outline of a caravan of camels and troops drawing near. Everything in me wanted to sprint towards them like an arrow released from a bow, but I made myself stand tall and wait, straining in the deepening twilight to see how many were returning, and who they were.

Then I saw him.

Mesha's tousled mop of hair was blowing in the wind – I would recognise it anywhere. He marched next to Caleb, near the front of the troop, and my heart rejoiced to see them both. I could see no injured among them, and the number of troops looked much like it had when they left. Nadeem and Sufian rode on camels, and a string of camels followed them in steady procession, tied together with woven ropes. The camels were laden with goods and, for a moment, I wondered if I had imagined the attack, or perhaps I had dreamed it? Why were the camels so laden with bags and bundles? They looked like they usually did when they arrived to trade with us, not as though they had endured a deadly attack.

I pushed that thought aside and went to greet Mesha and Caleb, embracing them warmly. Caleb spoke briefly to Moses and me, reporting that they had not encountered any giants and that all had gone well. Then the caravan continued on its way, pushing through the crowds of curious onlookers. A full report would be given in the morning but, for now, everyone was to return to their families, and the traders to their tent to rest and eat.

'Let's get you back home, yes?' I said to Mesha.

'No,' he said. 'Forgive me, brother, but I cannot go back yet. I need time to... I need time.'

I understood why Mesha could not return home yet. I knew the impact it could have on a man, the images that flashed through a man's mind after facing the barbarity of death. It took time to think through what had happened, for the horror of what you had experienced to release its grip on your mind and emotions. Home was a safe place, a place of comfort and warmth. Home was family. It needed to be kept separate from the horrors of warfare, lest it become sullied by it.

'When I need to think, I go to the Tabernacle,' I told him. 'I find great peace from pondering Yahweh's fire and cloud. It is where I find solace. Does it seem good to you to go there now?' He nodded. I turned to find a reliable messenger. Many of the elders had come to wait with us at the watchman's post, Abidan and his grandson, Attai, among them. I called Attai and asked him to take a message to the family telling them that Mesha had returned, unhurt, and that we would return to them in a while.

We walked to the Tabernacle in silence. Mesha was not a man who was comfortable with quietness; he always found something to say to break up the silence. I found it disquieting to see him so solemn, so locked up within himself, but I knew not to entice him to speak. He would talk when he was ready.

We sat in the courtyard of the Tabernacle and listened to the evening worship, gazing at the swirling pillar of fire nearby. Its flickering form brought warmth to our hearts, thawing the numbness that gripped us. From time to time, showers of sparks burst out of the flames. I closed my eyes and listened to the cracking, sputtering sounds they made, and the whooshing noise that occurred when the wind blew. Peace fell. The tension in my shoulders started to loosen. I moved my head round in a circular motion, consciously trying to relax. I focused on the warmth of Yahweh's presence, the sense of stillness that brought such calm to me.

'They took nothing.'

I opened my eyes to see Mesha staring at me. 'The giants. They took nothing. All the traders' supplies, their sacks of food, bolts of cloth, animals, even their weapons, their gold and valuables. It was all still there. They took none of it. Their camels were by the water, untouched. They took no plunder.' He watched me, trying to gauge whether I understood what he was trying to say. 'Yoshi, the giants did not kill to lay their hands on the traders' treasures or livestock. They killed just for sport.'

There it was, out in the open. The naked truth of what had taken place.

I had never seen such raw vulnerability on Mesha's face. Disbelief mixed with anguish. Utter confusion. I didn't know how to respond.

'Even Asad's scimitar – it lay near his body. It is a weapon beautifully crafted, a blade of great price. They did not take it. They slaughtered all those men, to what end? For sport? What manner of beasts are they?' Mesha's voice cracked as he went on. 'There were two boys. Both dead. Not a mark on them, but their necks broken. Why? When I saw them, I could not help but think of Yoram, Arad and Shallum. What would I do if those were my sons? I could not bear it. Yoshi, my heart could not bear it.'

Now that he had started speaking, there was no stopping him. 'There were two men lying side by side. No blade had touched their bodies, but their skulls were crushed, their faces ugly, deformed. What could cause such mutilation?' The story Nadeem told Moses of the giant crushing two men's heads together sprang to mind. I didn't tell Mesha. He didn't need that image in his mind; there was enough horror filling it already.

'The vultures were there. They had been feasting for some time,' Mesha continued, focusing on the ground. 'They gathered mainly around one corpse. The young man's belly had been split open, his innards spilt on the ground. They...' Mesha shook his head. 'Why?' he asked me. 'Why, Yoshi? Why would someone do that, for no good reason? Just for sport? When a man slays another for want of his possessions or to protect his family, I can understand it. I don't like it, but I understand why he would do it. But this? I cannot comprehend it. My heart cannot...' His resolve broke and he slumped over, his body wracked with sobs. I put my arm around his shoulders and held him tight, but didn't answer. What could I say? I had no answers.

After a while, Mesha recovered enough to continue.

'We gathered up the bodies, wrapped them, anointed them, and helped Nadeem and Sufian bury them. Their lament was terrible to behold, Yoshi. It has been many moons since I last heard a man sorrow in that manner. My heart was torn asunder.' Mesha shuddered. 'When Nadeem mounted his camel to return to the camp, I saw him holding something against his chest.' He looked at me. 'It was Asad's scimitar. He clasped it tightly to himself as we journeyed, never once letting it go.'

I nodded. I had no words. There were no words that could heal the lesions that had marked Mesha's heart. In time, perhaps, but not today. We sat there, side by side, for a long time, watching Yahweh's fiery pillar and letting the beauty of His presence dissipate the claws of fear and grief that gripped our hearts.

12

With a Limp

Nadeem, Sufian and Umar stayed with us for many moons. Their bodies needed time to heal but, more important than that, their souls were in great need of restoration. Umar's leg took some time to mend. After a while he was able to hobble around a little with two people aiding him, but the healers told us that he would always walk with a limp. Moses told me that the name Umar meant 'long life'. I thanked Yahweh that Umar had been saved from the giants, and prayed many blessings over him for a long, prosperous life.

In times past, when they had come to the camp to trade with us, they made their own camp a short distance away. This time, however, we kept them with us near the centre of the camp, and it seemed they felt safe in our midst. Before too long, they became a fixture of the camp. Passers-by would nod and greet them and they, in turn, responded with a blessing. Once their time of mourning had passed and they were feeling stronger, the three men displayed some of their wares outside their tent, and started trading. It was good for them; the familiar process of setting out their products and haggling over prices helped to restore their sense of routine and daily rhythm. A steady stream of customers started to gather around their tent, so much so that we had to move them to where there was more space for them to spread out.

Each day on my way to meet with Moses, I stopped off at their tent and spent time with them, examining the various products they had chosen to display that day. Although we could still not speak each other's languages very well, they had learned a few phrases and understood more than they could speak. They laughed at my coarse attempts to speak in their tongue, although I think they were pleased that I made the effort, and I, in turn, teased them for the strange way they pronounced some of our words. Umar never said much. He listened and watched a lot. He reminded me of my father Jesher, who was also a man of few words, but not much escaped his notice. Jesher came with me one evening to meet them, and took a liking to Umar straight away. It seems Umar felt the same; I found it heart-warming to see him smile at Jesher as they shared a joke.

Caleb and I spent many an evening sitting round the firepit outside their tent, sampling their food and, at times, sharing ours with them. Moses joined us when he could; there was always a lot more conversation when he was present. He quickly became accustomed to the role of interpreter as the traders spoke of their traditions and family heritage, and we told them the history of our people, and of our escape from bondage in Egypt. They were particularly fascinated by Yahweh's cloud and fire. Nadeem and Umar had seen the pillar of cloud and fire before, on previous visits, although from much further away. Sufian, however, had not. His first time witnessing the changing of the pillar of cloud into fire was memorable. He pointed at the cloudy pillar and started jabbering away to Nadeem and Umar.

'*Naar! Naar!*'[13]

Sufian watched, transfixed, as handfuls of sparks started to flicker inside the cloudy pillar, multiplying with intense ferocity. He jumped to his feet, his eyes wide with shock, looking at us to check our reaction. We smiled and Nadeem reassured him that this was a 'good fire', as we watched glowing embers form within the belly of the cloud. The embers grew brighter and brighter, finally bursting into a tower of multicoloured flames. Watching the expression on Sufian's face, I recalled the first night we had seen the miraculous transformation of cloud into fire. It was good to see it through his eyes and be reminded of this miracle, which Yahweh wrought for us daily. Thankfully, Moses was with us that night, and was able to explain the phenomena that was Yahweh's glorious presence, and answer their questions.

After that night, whenever one of us was with them in the evening,

---

13   Arabic for 'fire'.

either Nadeem or Sufian would point at the fiery display, turn to us, and mutter with hushed voice, 'Yahweh! Yahweh!'

Our times together were generally quiet, especially when Moses was not able to be with us to translate. It mattered not. We shared a common understanding of the preciousness of life and the pain of loss, and that was enough. Sometimes we played games – the simple games that our children played, throwing stones at a target, or building with sticks – but I never sparred with them, and they never suggested it. We never spoke of the giants again. They had started to move on from the trauma of that day, and to speak of it now would not be helpful.

But the giants never left my thoughts for long. They hovered in the recesses of my mind, like dogs sniffing around a bloody carcass.

The day came when Nadeem told us they had decided to return home to their people. Umar's leg had healed well and he was able to walk and ride a camel with ease, although the healers' prediction had proven true – he would always walk with a limp. There were tears in Nadeem's eyes when he told us of their departure and, when the day arrived, we walked with them to the north side of the camp to say our farewells. Countless blessings were spoken over them by our people as they walked through the throngs, and many embraces shared. When we reached the north watchman's post, Nadeem embraced me, holding me tightly in his arms for a long time. Then, reaching into the folds of his robe, he took something out. Asad's scimitar.

Holding it out, he said, '*Hadha lak.*'[14] I stared at him, confused as to his meaning, but he held it out and said it again, this time more forcefully. '*Hadha lak, Yusha.*'

'No, Nadeem. I cannot take this from you. It is too precious.'

Moses, who was standing nearby, whispered to me, 'Joshua, you must accept it. To refuse would be to dishonour Asad's memory.' I frowned at him and started to protest, but the look on his face stopped me. Turning back to Nadeem, I reached out, and Nadeem placed the scimitar in my upturned hands.

---

14 Arabic for 'this is for you'.

Putting his hand on my shoulder, he nodded and said, 'Asad – Yusha.' He grunted and muttered something unintelligible, then turned his back and mounted his camel.

I did not see Nadeem or his family again for quite some time; it was years before they were able to face the journey across that fateful desert to find us again. But, one day, I received a message: the traders were back and my presence was requested. Our reunion was filled with joy, although bittersweet in many ways, because their number was much reduced. Umar and Sufian were still with Nadeem, and a few other men who I believed to be business partners, not family. There were no boys among them. We traded as usual, and spent time eating together in the evenings, practising speaking each other's languages once again. They came back to trade with us many times over the remaining years of our wandering. Each time they arrived, I still found myself looking for Asad, searching their numbers for his handsome face and burly build.

The last time I saw Nadeem was when we were camped on the plains of Moab, just weeks before we crossed the Jordan River and entered the land of Canaan. I asked him if they would come to see us in Canaan, but he shook his head. 'Old man …' he told me. 'See… much; my days of tra… vel finished. My people not go there; it is land of giants.'

It was with a heavy heart that I bade him farewell one last time. His leathered face was now wrinkled, his eyes dimmer, but his smile had not changed and his embrace was just as strong as it had always been. We held each other tightly, then he stepped back, hand on his chest, and bowed. Pointing up at the pillar of cloud that towered over the centre of the camp, he smiled at me, blinking back his tears, and whispered, 'Yahweh, mmm? Yahweh.'

13

Lineage

'Joshua! Calm yourself!'

I glared at the torturous implement I'd just flung on the ground. Raking my hands through my dishevelled hair, I moaned through clenched teeth, 'Master, I cannot do this.'

'You *can* do it. You are well able, but you must learn patience, *nu?* This cannot be mastered within days, even weeks or months. It takes time... and patience,' he said, his piercing eyes boring into me. I blanched, tugging the neck of my robe to let in some more air. Patience was not something I seemed to possess – not in this context, at any rate.

Days had turned into weeks, and weeks into months, and there had been no more sightings of giants near our camp. Caleb and I took troops out on regular reconnaissance missions, but all were uneventful so, eventually, I ordered the troops stationed on the borders of the camp to stand down, and the sixteen watchmen's posts were reduced to eight and then to four. Nevertheless, I was relieved when Yahweh's cloud started moving one morning, signalling that it was time for us to move on to our next destination. We had been camped at Libnah for well over a year and, for me, that name would always bring to mind the attack on our Arab friends and the looming threat of giants. I was happy to move on from there.

Moses had decided some time before that I should learn how to read and write, and be able to speak the languages of other nations. So, to my great dismay, a portion of my mornings was spent under his tutorship as I struggled to master the necessary skills. Moses seemed to think I had an ear for languages, as I gained a rudimentary ability to converse with him in the tongues of our neighbouring cultures within a relatively short time. I also grasped the concept of reading fairly quickly and learned to enunciate most of his inscriptions, albeit in a clumsy, faltering fashion.

However, my mind balked at the necessity of learning the skills of a scribe.

'I am a warrior, not a scholar!' I thought to myself. 'Why must I waste endless hours copying these words, when I could be training with my men?'

Initially, I used my finger to practise writing the words in the sand, but Moses decided I had improved enough to move on to the meticulous art of writing on parchment. He had been taught in the courts of Pharoah to make ink from a mixture of soot, resin, olive oil and water, and he taught me how to make my own – although mine never seemed as fluid as his and, more often than not, I found lumps in it, which resulted in big blotches splattering on the parchment.

The cane pen was my greatest adversary. My hands were large and calloused, suited to holding a sword or spear, not a delicate reed pen. I lost count of the number of pens that I had broken. My secret hope was that Moses would give up on his quest to teach me the skill of writing, but I should have realised that he would never do that. He was not a man who gave up on anything very easily. Instead, he crafted a larger, stronger cane pen for me to use and I scratched away, hour after torturous hour, trying to copy his beautifully crafted symbols.

'Be careful, Joshua! Gently now!' he would admonish me, his bushy eyebrows meeting in the middle as he frowned at my pitiful efforts. 'Do not stab the parchment. Stroke it, yes? It takes patience to scribe, do not be in such haste.'

I wished I *could* stab the parchment – over and over again with a sharp dagger – so that I wouldn't have to endure this torment. But I couldn't. Parchment was precious and hard to come by, and to abuse it in any way would be frowned upon. I don't know that I ever fully mastered the level of patience that Moses hoped I would, but I did learn to endure.

I couldn't share my frustrations with my family; they were so impressed that I was learning the skills of reading and writing that I couldn't tell them of my passionate dislike for it, or my struggles to master it. It was only many years later that I came to realise the value of those lessons, and appreciated the rare privilege of being able to read and write the laws of God, and scribe the words He spoke to me.

On the days I spent scribing, it was pure joy to put away the grievous implements of writing and escape to my family. They were flourishing; Eglah's belly was growing larger by the day, Samina and Yoram had announced with great excitement that she was pregnant with their first child and, a few months afterwards, Alya told us that she was with child again. There was an air of excitement around our family mat these days that I found both refreshing and energising.

'How do our expectant mothers fare today?' I asked as I arrived home. It had become my habit to ask after our three pregnant women before doing anything else and, although Mesha and Azriel rolled their eyes at me, I believed that secretly, it pleased them.

'All is well,' the three women would reply. Their response would usually be followed by a detailed report from Hareph about Eglah's day; what she had eaten, how she had fared throughout the day and, more recently, how many times the baby had kicked her swollen belly!

Eglah's pregnancy had been much smoother than any of us had thought possible. Being an older first-time mother, we had expected her to find it harder than most to carry a child, but that had not been the case. In my experience, every woman with child had a certain glow about her, but with Eglah it seemed to be magnified five-fold. She was not a beauty in natural terms, but the larger her belly grew, the more beautiful she seemed to become. A smile hovered around her lips, as if she harboured a mysterious secret, and the light and joy in her eyes were entrancing.

Hareph hovered around her continually – so much so that Azriel had taken to asking his son Naim to spin the potter's wheel for him, as Hareph never seemed free to work with him anymore. Naim, who was nearing the age of apprenticeship, was happy to do this, and I watched his relationship with his father deepen over the months as they moulded the clay and fired their creations together.

Hareph would not allow Eglah to exert herself in any way; he waited on her hand and foot and, although it was not part of our culture for a man to do that, none of us had the heart to point that out – including Eglah! Her baby was now moving inside of her, kicking at regular intervals. Hareph insisted on sitting next to her each time she sat down so that, when the baby kicked, he could be the first to place his hand on her belly and feel the bump in her skin. His eyes lit up every time he felt it; he marvelled daily at the miracle of life that Yahweh had given them and, through his eyes, so did we all.

Alya was only just showing, and had some time to go before her second child would be born, but Samina was due to give birth a few weeks after Eglah, and was blossoming like a sheep in springtime.

'This beautiful *ima*-to-be is faring very well,' Yoram told me, standing behind Samina with his arms around her, stroking her growing belly. Samina's appetite had grown significantly since she had fallen pregnant and her once slim frame was now plump and curved, much to Yoram's delight. When she and Yoram first married, I would often hear her humming to herself while she cleaned or cooked. Now that she was with child, her humming had taken on the form of serenading, and the tuneful sound of lullabies to the child in her womb filled our family campsite. When they had first married, Samina was shy and quiet, but pregnancy had developed in her an air of great contentment and, with it, a newfound confidence.

Samina looked up at Yoram and sighed. 'I am as fat and contented as a calving cow.'

Yoram cupped her face in his hands and said, 'You have never been more beautiful, my beloved.' Even though it had been nearly two years since Yoram and Samina had wed, sometimes I still struggled to reconcile the fact that 'little Yori' was a married man, and soon to become a father.

I derived great satisfaction from watching our three pregnant women together. Despite the fact that she was so much younger than Eglah, Alya had taken on the role of supporting Eglah and Samina. Apparently, she had talked at length with Moses' wife, Zipporah, at Yoram and Samina's wedding celebration. Zipporah shared with

Alya her knowledge and experience of childbirth and told her of her people's customs and traditions in that regard. In turn, Alya shared with the others her knowledge about childbearing, as well as the secrets Zipporah told her about the ways of the Midianite women. The older mothers in the family didn't seem to resent Alya and, in fact, although they probably wouldn't have admitted it, I think they found Alya's views on childbirth interesting. Alya had an inquisitive mind and a thirst for knowledge that was rare in the women of our culture.

I was not the only one who enjoyed watching them. Jesher sat outside, hands folded over his belly, beaming with almost smug satisfaction at the women's interactions. My family brought me such joy, helping to distract me from the tedious monotony of learning to scribe, as well as the other weighty issues that lay heavily on my mind. I had not been able to free myself from the dreams of giants, but their frequency had lessened and, by now, I had trained myself to go back to sleep afterwards.

As the time for Eglah's birthing drew near, an air of nervous tension started to grip the family. No one said it in so many words, but I knew that we were all apprehensive about how her birthing would go. Hareph would not leave her, even for a moment, unless Jesher commanded him to go for a walk with one of his brothers, for his own well-being and Eglah's, promising to send word if anything should happen while he was out.

One morning, as I sat in my tent, I overheard Leora voicing her concerns with her daughter-in-law about Eglah's forthcoming birth.

'How will she deliver the child?' she whispered to Alya as they prepared the day's manna cakes. 'Eglah is so slim. I fear for when her time comes.'

'Do not fear, *Ima*. Eglah is stronger than we think, and she is calm, and wise. That will hold her in good stead. I am told that the size of a woman's girth does not determine how she will bear a child. Eglah is a woman of valour, and besides, she has her family to help her. All will be well.'

'Yahweh bless you, Alya. I hope what you say comes to pass.'

Eglah's labour started in the early hours one morning soon after-wards. When we arose to break our fast, we were told there would be no fresh manna cakes that morning. Eglah had need of her sisters and none of them wanted to leave her side. I was torn between the desire to stay at home with the other men, and the need to fulfil my respon-sibility to the warriors I was due to meet with that morning. I spoke to Helah when she came outside to fetch more water and she told me that Eglah's baby would be a long time coming.

'Go, Yoshi. It will not help for you to sit here idle. Go and fulfil your duties. We will send word to you if anything happens, *nu?*'

I did as she suggested, although my meeting was fruitless; I could not concentrate. My thoughts were consumed with images of Eglah labouring to bring forth her child, and thoughts of my own mother, who had died in childbirth along with my stillborn brother. Fear welled up in me. Eglah could not die. She must not die. *Yahweh, deliver her,* I cried out silently, while my men, knowing that something was wrong, felt unable to ask me what it was. In the end, I agreed to meet with them another day, and dismissed them.

Arriving back home, everything was as I expected: Hareph was pacing up and down by the firepit, wringing his hands and muttering to himself, while the men tried to calm him. The women came out at regular intervals to give Hareph an update and, each time, the message was the same: Eglah was strong and her labour was progressing well. My knowledge of childbirth was sparse, but I did know that there was usually much noise and travail. I could hear none of the wailing and groaning that was typical of our birthing mothers. In fact, I couldn't hear Eglah at all. All I could hear were the muffled voices of the other women. It unnerved me. I didn't know if that was a good sign or a bad one.

'Why is she so quiet?' I whispered to Mesha, seated next to me on the mat. 'Is it well with her?' He frowned and shrugged. 'Helah bore you five children; do you not remember how it was? Was she quiet or did she cry out?'

Mesha glanced at me. 'I don't know. I just remember the waiting.'

We had to endure another few hours of tarrying before we heard the sounds of guttural grunting, deep groanings, and then our women talking all at once. Instinctively, we stood to our feet and gathered round Hareph, who had gone pale and looked like he might collapse.

Then we heard it.

The angry wail of a newborn babe. We erupted into shouts of celebration (and relief!) and, a few minutes afterwards, Shira came outside holding a little form wrapped in cloth. The child had not been cleaned and was still covered with the creamy, waxy coating of birth, mixed with smudges of blood. Helah told me later that they decided not to make Hareph wait until they had cleaned the child properly before bringing him out to meet his father.

Shira walked towards Hareph. Smiling, she held the little bundle out. 'Hareph, you have a son.'

Hareph stared at the bundle. He reached out to take the child from her, gazing at his son in wonder and what looked like awe. I waited for the tears to fall – Hareph was prone to emotional outbursts – but they didn't. Not this time. He stroked his baby's cheeks then caressed his wet, waxy hair. We gathered around him like silent watchmen. Something miraculous was happening, something too precious for words. I felt Yahweh's presence in our midst.

I felt His pleasure.

Tears formed in my eyes, not Hareph's and, after a while, Hareph turned to face us. 'I have a son. My line is not broken,' he said, looking at us one by one. 'This is my son. This is Davi ben Hareph. My son. He will continue my lineage. My son. Davi.' Hareph stood tall and his shoulders were no longer stooped. There was a look in his countenance that I had not seen before. It was the look of a man who has found his purpose in life. It was as if he was transforming right in front of us; the second miracle I had witnessed in just a matter of minutes.

Alya told me the following day why Eglah made very little noise during her travail. She said Eglah had breathed with closed eyes, as if unwilling to engage with life outside of her own body, so focused was she on bearing her child safely. Even during the hot stretching of her flesh when she pushed her son out into the world, she did not scream or panic, like so many women did. Once again, Eglah had won the respect of those around her. The reward for her labour lay in her arms and nuzzled at her breast.

She was a mother.

Finally, she was a mother in Israel.

14

The Cycle of Life

A few short weeks after little Davi was born, Samina went into labour, and our family was once again gripped with the tension that comes with the birthing of a first-born child. This time, I didn't leave. No matter how long this labour took, I would not leave. I sent a message to Moses and sat with Yoram to wait out the birth of his first child.

Yoram didn't pace up and down like Hareph, but I could tell that he was no less anxious. Mesha, whose approach to most things in life was to talk or take action, tried to get his son to speak, without success. He then proceeded to bring out some of the goatskins that he and Yoram had been preparing for their next job, and started scudding them, scraping the hair off with a dull knife.

'We must keep busy – that is our way, *nu?*' he told Yoram, who joined his father for a short while. However, each time he heard Samina cry out, he flinched and looked up. After cutting himself several times, succeeding only in getting blood on the hairy skins, he gave up.

The hours dragged on.

Hareph was holding little Davi, who dozed in his arms. I noticed him watching Yoram. In his eyes was the compassion of one who truly knows what another is going through. He didn't talk, which was unusual; the incessant chatter which had been Hareph's default for as long as I had known him had reduced significantly since he had become a father. He was still the same deep thinking, sensitive man that he had always been, but now seemed less restless and much more contented.

Hareph stood up and walked towards Yoram. He placed little Davi in Yoram's arms and, without saying a word, went back and sat down. Yoram, taken by surprise, held his nephew and glanced at me, asking for an explanation. I smiled at him as if to say, 'You will soon be holding your own child in your arms.' Holding Davi seemed to calm him. He stared down at the beautiful little boy, studying his features and stroking his head. Hareph glanced at me over the flames that flickered in the firepit and smiled. Davi slept in Yoram's arms for a long time; only when he stirred and cried out for feeding did Yoram relinquish him to Eglah.

Before the new day dawned, Yoram held his own child in his arms; a little girl who they named Miriam. Yoram turned to thank Helah and Shira for helping to deliver her. 'We are not the ones you need to thank, Yoram,' Helah responded. He frowned in bewilderment. She gestured to the other side of the clearing. 'Alya is the one who helped Samina birth your child.' Hearing her name, Alya turned to face them.

'Alya?' Yoram said.

'Yes,' Shira interjected. 'Alya has a unique understanding of how a woman's body functions. Samina's baby became twisted and she was too tired to push. It was Alya who helped deliver her.' Shira stared at her granddaughter-in-law with what looked like reluctant admiration. 'You have the skills needed to become an excellent midwife. I believe you will help many of our women to deliver safely, in the days to come.'

Shira was right. A few months later, Alya gave birth to her second child, a boy this time: Joash. After that, she started to assist and learn from the midwives who served at the births of women in the camp, and the stories of her skill, as well as her knowledge of herbal remedies, spread. When Eleazar's wife, Bathshua, fell pregnant, he shared with me their fears of losing the child. Bathshua had miscarried and lost their first child, and it had taken years for her to conceive again. Alya went to see Bathshua, helped calm her fears, made herbal remedies for her throughout her pregnancy and safely delivered her child when her time came. Eleazar had the son he had always longed for, and Bathshua was among the mothers in Israel.

Life at our new camp, Rissah, was simple, but not unpleasant. It was mostly rocky terrain, but the hills that surrounded our camp provided some relief from the sun, plentiful dew in the early morning and fresh streams to water our people. We had been camped there for nearly two years and I was grateful not to have to break camp and move on so often. It felt good to put down roots for a while.

There was another reason why I was thankful that we were staying at Rissah for a longer time. Jesher was advanced in years and, although he never complained about it, I could hear the breathlessness in his voice when he walked even a few paces. He no longer attended elders' meetings, not being able to walk the distance to the Tent of Meeting.

'These old bones are not what they once were,' he mumbled with a gentle smile.

He was usually last to arise in the mornings; indeed, the older he grew, the more he relished his sleep. However, although his body was wearing out, there was nothing wrong with his mind! Jesher was a man of few words, but there was little that escaped the notice of his dusky blue eyes. He loved to spend his days sitting in the shade under the awning of his tent, watching the world go by. Jesher was a watcher. He had always been a watcher more than a talker; I think he was far more insightful than any of us gave him credit for.

One afternoon some weeks after Miriam's birth, the family were all preparing for Shabbat; there were goats to be milked, food to be prepared and fuel to be collected for the fire. I was busy cleaning the firepit and laying a new fire. Eglah sat with Jesher watching little Davi, who had been able to stand for a while now, and looked about ready to take his first steps. Jesher smiled as Davi stood up, clapped his hands and giggled in delight. He glanced at his daughter.

'It has been the longing of my heart for so long to witness you bear a child. My heart rejoices that I have lived to see you become a mother before I leave this earth.'

Eglah glanced at Jesher, but her smile faded as she realised what he was trying to tell her. Her eyes filled with tears and she reached out to take her father's hand in hers. Unlike Mesha, who brushed aside any mention of Jesher's age or frailty with glib comments, she looked at him and, with a quiet strength, faced the pain of what she now knew was coming. She lifted Jesher's hand to her lips and kissed it, then held it in her lap. She didn't speak. She and Jesher were so alike, they needed no words to express their hearts to one another.

My heart constricted at the vulnerability on both their faces; the poignancy of the moment brought tears to my own eyes. I brushed them away, pretending to be busy with the fire. It was almost impossible to find an opportunity to speak to someone in confidence while living in the camp; we learned early on in our wilderness travels that nothing is private in the life of a nomad. However, Jesher had obviously decided that now was as good a time as any, because he called me over and patted the ground next to him. Eglah picked Davi up and moved away to give us space. I wished she wouldn't. I hoped the family would arrive at that moment, so I wouldn't have to hear the words I knew Jesher was about to say.

He peered at me from under his bushy grey eyebrows. 'Joshua.' He waited for me to look at him before continuing. 'My son, I am not long for this world.' I knew better than to patronise him or feign ignorance, so I said nothing. I shivered, all of a sudden feeling cold. 'I am old and full of days, and I have no regrets. But, before I go, there is something I must ask you.'

'Anything, *Abba*. You can ask me anything.' My voice was thin, straining to hold back the torrent of emotion rising in my chest.

He paused before whispering, 'Will you watch over my family when I am gone?' I couldn't speak. I nodded. 'Azriel is a good son and I believe he will make wise decisions... but it may take some time before he is fully able to take on the mantle of leading our family.' He looked down. 'He would benefit from someone like you to stand by his side and give him wise counsel. Will you do that for me?'

I nodded. Both of us stared off into the distance as Jesher continued to speak in a low tone. 'Mesha will be brought low when I am gone. You know him well – he does not always know his own heart, and he is not ready for me to leave. He is not ready to face this. My passing will lie heavily on him but, after some time, he will heal and find his strength again. You will help him do that.'

I nodded again.

'I have one more request, but I fear this one will not be easy for you. It concerns Shira.' I glanced at him, puzzled. He sighed. 'I know she has not embraced you like I hoped she would – or like you deserved.

She has not been an *ima* to you. Her contempt of you has brought me much anguish over the years, although you have borne it well. But Shira is my wife and she has served me all these years. She raised our children and kept a good home. I do not know how she will be, when I am gone.' He gave a throaty chuckle. 'In truth, most of the time I cannot fathom her at all! But I wish no harm to come to her and, even though it may pain you, Joshua, I must ask you: will you watch over her in her old age?'

I cleared my throat. 'I will, *Abba*. You have my word, ' I rasped.

'Thank you, my son. Thank you,' he whispered. Gazing off into the distance again, he mumbled, 'I could have loved her, if she had but let me...'

We sat in silence for a little while longer, then Jesher turned to face me. 'Joshua. You may not be of my flesh, but you are of my heart. You are the son of my heart. You *are* my son.' His voice broke and he could not continue. Instead, he grasped my hand in both of his, nodding his head over and over as tears filled his eyes. He didn't release my hand. I looked down at my large, rough-skinned fingers, enfolded in his small, leathery, wrinkled hands and thought to myself, 'This is what love looks like. The love of a father and son.'

Soon afterwards, the family came back from their errands and the routine of washing in readiness for Shabbat began. When Alya brought a dish of water to Jesher and helped him to wash, I escaped into my tent. Kneeling on my bed roll, I buried my face in my blanket, panting in my efforts to try to stop the flood of grief from pouring out of me. I was grateful for the noise of conversation and laughter outside. It masked my muffled sobs.

Later that night, after our Shabbat meal, Jesher called the children together to tell them a story. They rushed to sit in front of him, already requesting their favourite stories.

Ethan and Ephah, the twins, spoke first. '*Saba*, tell us about Abraham.'

'No!' little Sadie cried, tugging at his arm. 'I want to hear about Noah. Please tell us about the ami... aminals, *Saba*,' she said with a wide-eyed, earnest smile. Sadie's little brother, Joash, who always copied everything she did, joined in.

'Es! Es, *Saba*! Aminals!'

'What about Jacob?' Davi argued. 'We are descended from him, his story is important. Tell us about Jacob, how Yahweh changed his name to Israel, and how our twelve tribes came to be.'

'These are all good stories, my children,' Jesher said, holding up his arms to silence their arguments. 'But tonight, I am going to tell you a very special story: the story of our family, how Yahweh brought us out of captivity with a mighty outstretched arm, how He split the waters of the Red Sea and provided water for us from a rock, and manna for food, so you will know how Yahweh has led us to where we are.' He motioned to Joash, who climbed into his lap, pouting. Looking around the circle of faces, Jesher added, 'Next Shabbat, I will tell you about Jacob or Noah, *nu*? But tonight, I will tell you about our story.'

Jesher didn't get to tell them the story of Jacob or Noah.

His storytelling days were over; he didn't live to see another Shabbat.

The following morning, I carried him outside and placed him on a soft sheepskin rug in his favourite position, propped up under the shade of his tent awning, supported by bolsters of rolled-up cloth. 'Come... tarry with me... a while,' he mumbled breathlessly. He smiled and patted the ground next to him. I sat down and we soaked up the warmth of the morning sun together. When I turned to him a short while later, his eyes were closed and a gentle smile caressed his face. He had breathed his last and slipped away, doing what he loved to do most: watching the world go by.

15

Lost

We were lost without him. All of us. Lost.

Jesher had never been a loud or particularly dynamic person. He had never demanded respect or desired to be the centre of attention. In fact, the opposite was true – he avoided it. The authority he carried, and the reach of his influence, were based not upon how often or how loudly his voice was heard. They were based upon the quiet strength that lay hidden in his heart, and the extraordinary love he carried for his family and his God. He had been the bedrock of our family, of our lives, for so long, and I had always known his passing would affect us greatly... but I never expected to feel so utterly bereft without him.

I don't think any of us did.

I found myself going to the place where Jesher had been laid to rest, outside the borders of the camp. At first it was once every few days, but my visits increased in frequency until I could not let a day pass by without going to his grave. I talked to him there, just as I would have if he had still been with us. I told him how we were faring, how the babies were growing, and of my nightmares, which had increased in number since his passing. I wrestled with giants nearly every night and I was never alone in my dreams; there was always at least one other family member with me, being hunted by those cold-hearted monsters. Each time, I strove to protect them from the giants' attack and, each time, I failed. I could not protect my family from the brutality of a gruesome death by the hand of those entrancing assassins.

My heart despaired of ever being free of them, just as I despaired of knowing what to do if – or when – I faced them in this life. I knew that day would come. I would have to face them; if not now, then when we crossed over the Jordan River and entered Canaan. The giants we saw in Canaan were every bit as intimidating as the vile creatures in my dreams, but I had not feared them.

'Why?' I muttered, asking the same question I repeated each time I came before Yahweh in prayer. 'Why do I fear them in my dreams and yet I did not fear them when I saw them with my own eyes? Yahweh, speak to me. Please. Tell me what I must do.'

Whenever I found myself in need of someone to talk to, with no threat of interruption or fear of misunderstanding, I sought out Eleazar. He and I had been friends since we started our desert wanderings, nearly nine years before. As Moses' nephew, and son of the high priest, Aaron, he spent a lot of time with Moses. Moses often sent us out together to relay messages or gather information for him, and a friendship had formed. Our friendship deepened significantly when we discovered that we shared a mutual passion for Yahweh's presence, for His cloud and fire. When I first knew him, Eleazar had been a timid, somewhat clumsy and largely misunderstood young man who lacked confidence. That all changed when he encountered Yahweh in the Tabernacle we built for Him. That encounter transformed Eleazar, and a spirit of wisdom now rested on him, along with an unfathomable peace. It was to that man that I now hurried.

We greeted each other and I asked after his son, Phinehas.

'He is a strong boy; he has passed his first year and has started talking,' Eleazar told me, glowing with pride. 'I will always be grateful to Alya for the help she gave Bathshua when she carried him. Without her, I don't know whether I would be a father today.' Knowing there would be a reason why I had sought him out, Eleazar changed the conversation.

'How is your family, since Jesher's passing?' he asked.

'They are... they...' I sighed. 'We are brought low, Eleazar. Very low. It is as though the lifeblood has drained from our midst, and I know not what to do to make it right.' As was his way, Eleazar did not interrupt, but listened while I unburdened myself. I told him of Azriel's struggle to step into the role of patriarch. From time to time, when Jesher had still been with us, I had seen frustration and, at times, even disdain on Azriel's countenance. It was usually as a result of a decision that Jesher had made which Azriel disagreed with but, more often than not, it was because of an action Jesher had *not* taken. Azriel honoured his father and never contradicted him in front of the family, but it seemed to me that he believed Jesher was lacking in his leadership of our family. I saw ambition in him, a desire to take charge of the family and lead us a different way.

I glanced at Eleazar. 'I see that in him no longer. Azriel's zeal to lead has melted away with Jesher's passing. He questions himself; his footsteps are not sure any more. There was a time when I believe he even wished Jesher gone, so he could take his place. But no longer.'

'It will take time for him to find his way,' Eleazar reassured me, 'but he will. He will find the path that is right for him. I have seen it many times. Azriel is a good man and he will be a good leader, but he needs time. Encourage him to become the leader that Yahweh would have *him* be, not the leader that his *abba* was, *nu*? How is Shira?' he asked next. 'How has she fared since Jesher's passing?'

'She is much changed,' I told him. 'More than I ever thought possible.'

'Is the change a good one?' Eleazar asked.

I thought for a moment. 'Yes and no.' He waited while I tried to find the words to explain what I meant. 'She has softened. It is as though she no longer has the need, or the desire, to be right all the time, or to be in control of the family. She is much quieter. Her sharp tongue has found a gentleness.'

'That is good, yes?'

'Yes, it is. But... Eleazar, she is lost, so lost without him.'

'Truly?' The surprise on Eleazar's face was almost comical. I would have smiled, had it not been for the concern in my heart.

'Truly. She grows older and more frail with each day that passes, as if the life is slowly leaving her. She no longer takes the girls to collect water from the stream, and does not put her hand to cooking or cleaning much at all. She doesn't shout at the children when they are noisy, and she has even stopped reproaching us when we tread dirt into the tent!'

Eleazar stifled a smile and looked down. 'That does not sound like Shira at all.'

'No. It is not the Shira I know – or that any of us know. It is as though she has lost her way. Yes, assuredly, she is lost. But then, I think we all feel lost without Jesher. Leora has taken charge of the home now, alongside Azriel, and she is doing well, but I find it disquieting seeing Shira like this'.

We pondered for a while, then Eleazar asked, 'What of Mesha?'

I glanced at Eleazar and grimaced. 'He is also much changed – but not for the better.'

'How so?'

I explained to Eleazar the changes I had seen in Mesha in the last few weeks since Jesher's death; his shock at discovering his father's passing, his grief at not having been able to say goodbye and his anger at feeling totally unprepared for Jesher's death.

'He is so angry, all the time,' I explained. 'You know Mesha – it is not in his nature to be aggressive, but when he realised that some of us in the family knew that Jesher's time was coming and he did not, his rage was terrible to behold. He railed at me, wanting to know why *Abba* did not tell him. I explained that Jesher had tried to tell him, but it only made him angrier.' I turned to Eleazar. 'Jesher knew this would happen. He told me himself, the day before his death. He knew that Mesha would walk a dark path after his passing. I don't know this Mesha. I don't know how to talk to him; everything I say seems to make him angry.' I made a helpless gesture and slumped back. 'There is much discord in our tents of late. It is not a peaceful place to dwell.'

Eleazar nodded his head. 'And what of you, my friend? How is it with you?'

'I fear I am much the same as Shira; I am lost without him. I lost my *abba* before we left Egypt. That broke me, but my grief was made bearable because I had Jesher to stand with me. He helped me through it. To lose one father is a cruel affliction... but to lose two...

I... Eleazar, I cannot let him go!' I blurted, feeling the same cold, heavy lump in my stomach. 'Since his passing, no tears have fallen from my eyes. I cannot mourn his passing. I am stuck fast. I am lost.'

I saw the concern in Eleazar's gaze as I told him of my daily trips to Jesher's grave, and of how I talked to him there. 'No one else knows I go there. There is no one I can tell,' I said, embarrassed.

'Joshua, you must release your *abba*. You must let him go.'

'I know this, but how?' Frustration welled up in me. 'My heart is like a river whose waters have been held back. I am imprisoned, ensnared by my own grief. What must I do?'

Eleazar remained silent for a while. He closed his eyes, and his body rocked gently backwards and forwards. He always rocked when he prayed, a habit I believe he had acquired from Moses. I unclenched my fists and examined my fingers, thinking of the last time Jesher's hands had enclosed mine, longing to feel the warm touch of his fingers on mine again.

'What will happen when we move on from Rissah?' Eleazar asked me. 'We cannot stay here indefinitely; we will break camp and move on, one day, when Yahweh's cloud moves. You will have to leave him then, Joshua. Jesher will rest here, but you must go on. Have you thought on this?'

'I have. Many times. But I cannot do it. He was always there for me. If I let him go, I am alone again.'

'Joshua,' Eleazar grasped my arm. 'You are not alone. Permit me to help you.' I stared at him; my fear met his strength head-on. His strength won.

We went together to Jesher's grave and I found my long-awaited release. The dam that had held back the waters of my heart finally broke, and my faithful friend sat with me until I was done, holding me in his arms while I wept for not one, but two fathers. Grief for the father of my blood, Nun, and the father of my heart, Jesher, poured out of me and, in its stead, peace came, bringing with it the stirrings of hope. It would take some time for hope to fully anchor itself within me but, in time, it did, just as Jesher knew that it would.

Jesher's passing caused our family to cleave together and, as the weeks passed, we gradually found a new rhythm – a new way of doing life without him. We missed him no less, but were able to move on, discovering who we were as a family without him.

All except Mesha.

His wrath was not appeased by the passing of time. He seemed to cling to it; it shrouded him like the stench of rotting rags on a corpse. I tried to talk to him on several occasions, to no avail. His resentment towards me because I had known of Jesher's imminent passing, and the fact that I had been with him when he died, hindered him from receiving any help from me. Mesha resented Azriel for taking Jesher's place, and would not take counsel from any within our family, wrongly supposing that we had made a pact to exclude him. His insight was clouded and I was considering asking for help from an elder such as Abidan, or perhaps Eleazar, when something unusual happened that changed everything.

It was in the last watches of the night. I had woken from another nightmare and couldn't get back to sleep. My thoughts dwelt on Mesha and would give me no rest, so I went outside to look upon Yahweh's pillar of fire. I was not alone. Sitting by the dying embers of the firepit I found Shira. She started when she saw me. 'Joshua! Does sleep evade you too?' she whispered.

'It does,' I replied, sitting down near her. 'But whenever I am disquieted, my soul finds peace gazing on Yahweh's presence.'

'Mmm. What has troubled you?'

I glanced at her, wondering whether to trust her, but something in her countenance – a humility, an openness previously unseen – made me decide in her favour. 'Mesha,' I whispered. 'Grief for him lies heavy on my heart. He is much changed since Jesher's passing. I have never known him to be so full of wrath. I have tried talking to him, but he will not hear me. I cannot reach him... he is not himself.'

'No, he is not,' Shira responded, frowning. 'But then, none of us are. Everything has changed since Jesher left us.' She studied the embers and shivered, pulling her scarf closer around her thin shoulders. I picked up a small branch and poked the embers, blowing on them until a tiny flame flared up. Placing some tumbleweed on the flame,

I added some kindling and blew some more. When the kindling blazed, I added some dried dung and, only when a hearty fire was burning did I sit down again. We sat in uncommonly peaceful silence together for a while, before I decided to ask, 'Is it well with you, since Jesher's passing?'

She turned to look at me, staring into my eyes as if searching for something. I had never seen such a look of raw vulnerability on Shira's face before. I was confounded by it, even more so when she spoke. 'No,' she whispered. 'It is not well with me, Joshua. I have never felt more alone, more anguished in spirit, then I do now. Without Jesher... I no longer feel fully alive.'

I stared at her in shock. I didn't know what to say, so I said nothing. Shira turned back to the fire. 'I never saw it... never realised... Why is it only now that he is gone that I realise who he was? I lived with him, bore his children, shared his bed for nearly three score years, but I never knew him. Why?' she whispered. Tears started rolling down her cheeks. I had never seen Shira cry before. 'How could I not have seen the goodness in him – the strength that lay in his heart? Was I the only one who could not see it?' She turned to me, but did not wait for me to answer. I was relieved. That was not a question I wanted to answer. Many times over the years I had wondered how Shira could be so blind as not to see the wisdom and goodness that ran through Jesher's soul. It was like a gold thread woven into a wedding garment, but she had not seen it. Until now.

Turning back to the firepit, she wiped the tears away and continued, 'My soul accuses me constantly for the way I treated him... it is torment. Knowing how I dishonoured and disregarded him when there was so much I could have shared with him, given to him... how I could have loved him. How could I not have seen it? Was I so blind?' This time, she waited for an answer.

'Jesher was everything you say and more. It was my great privilege to call him *Abba*.'

'He loved you as a son, withholding nothing of his heart or his love from you,' she mumbled. 'That is something I have not done. You called him *Abba*, but you never called me *Ima*.'

'Forgive me, I – ' I started to explain, but Shira put her hand out and cut me off.

'No. I will hear no apology from you, for no guilt can be laid at your feet. The fault is mine, all mine.' She glanced at me and tears rolled down her cheeks again. 'How could you call me *Ima* when I have not been an *ima* to you? I have treated you with such disdain and for this, I beg your forgiveness. I was blind, but now I see. I see so much now, but it is too late. Would that I had seen it before.'

I reached out and took her thin hand in mine. 'It is never too late.'

'Perhaps not.' We sat for a while, her hand in mine, content to gaze at the pillar of fire as it crackled and sparkled in the distance. I thought about the miraculous transformation in Shira, and was smiling to myself at the thought of Jesher's pleasure in knowing that we were finally reconciled, when I heard Shira speak in a calm, low tone. 'I will talk to Mesha.'

'Yes?'

'Yes. There is much I need to share with him. I will talk to him. All will be well.'

'Very well. Do according to all that is in your heart.'

She did. I don't know what she said to Mesha – I didn't ask either of them what had happened. That knowledge was not mine to know. What I do know is that a few days later, when we sat down to share our evening meal, he was changed. He was not the Mesha I had known before, and perhaps never would be now, but the fury that had lain coiled within him like a cobra ready to strike, was gone. He smiled and talked, mostly to Shira, who sat next to him that evening. The bond between them had changed; where before, there had been pride and striving, there was now peace and understanding. It was heart-warming, beautiful.

That same night, I called Shira '*Ima*' for the first time. It was not a conscious decision, but an intuitive response to an indefinable shift that had taken place in our relationship. As we sat around the mat, she passed me a bowl of figs, and I said, 'Thank you, *Ima*.' I only realised what I had said when I saw Shira's head shoot up. She stared at me, unblinking, only looking away when tears filled her eyes. Laughter filled the air and the conversation continued without missing a beat. No one else noticed, save one: Eglah. The warmth in her gaze as she watched our interaction reminded me so much of Jesher. It was as though he was with us, watching and noticing as he had always done, only this time, through the eyes of his daughter.

16

To Slay a Giant

The time had come. We woke one morning to find that Yahweh's cloud no longer hovered at the entrance to the Tabernacle, but had started to move towards the outskirts of the camp. It was time to move again. We had been at Rissah for well over two years, and I had been dreading leaving there. When it came to it, however, I was surprised at how easy I found it. It seemed the discussions I had with Eleazar about Jesher had enabled me to move on more than I had realised.

There was always a huge amount of work to do when we broke camp, especially when we had been camped at the same place for a long time, as was the case with Rissah. Although we followed a set pattern given to us by Yahweh regarding the order in which our twelve tribes travelled, disputes and arguments were unavoidable at times like this, so my days were largely spent resolving conflicts and problem solving. It was only when the last tribes of Dan, Asher and Naphtali had broken camp and started out, and we were well on our way, that I realised I had not had time to go to Jesher's graveside one last time to bid him farewell. I stopped in my tracks and turned to look back at Rissah.

'We must continue on our journey, *Abba*. It is time for us to move. Yahweh's cloud has moved on and we must follow. But I will carry you in my heart. You are always with me, *nu?*' I whispered, placing my hand on my heart. 'Peace be upon you. Rest with your fathers.' For a brief moment, I imagined my two fathers sitting together, reunited again, perhaps watching the world go by. It made me smile. I turned to re-join our company of sojourners, and never looked back.

Our next camp was just a few days' travel from Rissah and, when Yahweh's cloud stopped, I was relieved to see that the same stream that had watered us at Rissah ran through our new campsite. Moses named the place Kehelathah which, in our tongue, meant 'Gathering' or 'Assembly', and rightly so: we were now a large gathering. Our people were multiplying and our camp stretched as far as the eye could see.

As soon as the Tabernacle was set up in the middle of our new site, I assembled the captains and organised a new rota for guard duty around the perimeter of the camp. I always felt on edge when we moved to a new location, much more so since the giants' attack on the traders. Caleb led some scouting parties to scour the land around us, but found no sign of adversaries, giants or otherwise. For the moment, it seemed we were safe, but I could not rest. As long as those gruesome titans ruled my dreams, I was unable to let down my guard. I set about training the men with renewed vigour.

Mesha had been promoted to the rank of captain over a troop of one hundred warriors long ago, and trained with them regularly. Yoram and Joel had also both served in the Benjaminite army for some years, and attended training sessions together. Both were physically strong and had skill in combat but, whereas Joel's passion lay in using his strength to craft with wood, Yoram seemed to have a natural inclination towards warfare.

Caleb and I stood watching the Benjaminite warriors as they practised hand-to-hand combat in the training grounds just outside the camp. Azriel had done the basic army training, but no longer attended, due to his years and his responsibilities within the family. Hareph had also done basic training, but was relieved of duty early on when we discovered that he could be more of a danger to himself and his fellow warriors than he would ever be to the enemy! He and Azriel concentrated on their work at the potter's wheel while Mesha, Yoram and Joel represented our family in the Benjaminite army. They fought together now against three other opponents, swords in hand. They were well matched.

'Yoram has much skill with a sword.' Caleb was watching him with great interest. 'He is strong, but also fast. See how he dodges, shifting his weight all the time?' he said with undisguised admiration. 'His sword is an extension of his arm, as if cleaved to him. I have not often seen that in a warrior.'

'Yes. He has the makings of a captain,' I replied, glad that Caleb had pointed it out first. I had noticed Yoram's skill quite a while ago, but wasn't sure if my esteem for his swordsmanship was influenced by my close relationship with him, so I had chosen to remain silent.

'You speak truth,' Caleb replied, not looking away from Yoram, who was sparring with a much larger, heavier-set man. 'He is young but his skills rival those of our older, more experienced warriors. Look at how he dances around Eliab! Eliab cannot match him for speed or skill.'

'Yoram has the mind of a warrior,' I said, trying unsuccessfully to hide my pride in him. 'Strength and skill are essential, and he has both, but he is also shrewd. He has the ability to see beyond the warrior in front of him, to the scope of the battle around him. His thoughts stretch not only to his own needs, but to those of the men he fights alongside. That is the mind of a captain.'

When I heard no response, I tore my eyes away from Yoram and glanced at Caleb. He stood with his arms folded, grinning at me.

I shrugged. 'Is it not true?' I asked him, feigning disinterest.

'It is. You are right in what you say – and you are right to be proud of him.' Before I could retaliate, Caleb pretended to draw his sword and jab me in my side, then walked off to observe some of the other men.

I frowned and crossed my arms, still watching Yoram, Mesha and Joel face off against their rivals. I didn't like it when Caleb teased me. He knew what Yoram meant to me and how proud I was of him; I could not deny it. But at least he could also see Yoram's potential as a leader; that was gratifying. I continued staring at the men as they trained, while my mind started wandering. I was thinking about how soon we could promote Yoram to the rank of captain when, out of my peripheral vision, I saw a form appear a short distance away from me.

'No!' I thought. My heart skipped a beat, then started pounding. 'It cannot be!' The form took on shape. Standing there, in broad daylight, was the giant that had first haunted me in my dreams. I drew my sword, glancing towards the men training, but they seemed not to have seen him.

'How is it they cannot see him?' I asked myself. The creature was massive – even bigger in real life than in my dreams – how could they disregard him? I knew I had to draw his attention away from them, so I readied myself and was about to charge when two more forms appeared a few feet in front of me. These were not giants – at least, not in manner or bearing. They were easily as tall as the giant but, whereas the giant was contemptuous and treacherous, these men displayed a noble bearing and calm air of confidence.

I knew who they were. I had seen them before.

These were the shining men!

My mind recalled the time I first saw them, nearly eight years ago, when Moses had been confronted by a huge mob of rebels set on taking over leadership of our nation of Israel. Yahweh fought for His chosen leader that day. Jets of fiery flames had burst out of His glory cloud, consuming the rebels in an instant, but the innocent bystanders among them had been protected by a company of 'shining men' who had appeared out of nowhere. The shining men were remarkably tall and broad-shouldered, robed in white and fully armed. They had moved with inexplicable speed, shielding the innocents from harm.

No one had seen them but me.

Everyone I talked to, when that terrible day was over, denied seeing them. Even Moses himself, Caleb and Aaron... all they saw was smoke or cloud. But I knew I had seen them – and now they were back! The two men who stood before me were just as glorious as I remembered. One was dark-skinned with short, dark-brown hair and handsome, sharp features. The other had blond hair and olive skin, with eyes of burnished bronze. Both were muscular, armed with swords and either a spear or bow and arrow. Either would have been more than a match for the giant.

The fear that had strangled my heart for so many moons lifted off me. Their presence filled me with courage and confidence, so I raised my sword, focusing on the beguiling titan that stood a short distance away. I *would* take him down. I would slay the spawn of darkness this very day and be done with him! Before I could move, however, the dark-haired shining man stepped forward and held out his arm to stop me. He did not speak, but I knew by his expression that I was not to take action. Unwilling to sheath my sword, I gripped it still, resisting the urge to wield it. He and his companion walked up to the giant, who sneered at them with a malevolent glint in his eye, but seemed unable to move.

Looking back at me to make sure he had my attention, the dark-haired shining man unsheathed his sword and used it to point to the back of the giants knees, first one, then the other. While the golden-haired man lifted the giant's arms out to the side, his comrade then put the tip of his sword in the giant's armpits, again pointing first to one, then to the other. The giant seethed but complied; he seemed unable to resist. Last of all, both shining men raised their swords and pointed them at the giant's throat.

One of the shining men walked towards me, stared at me to make sure he had my full attention, then gestured towards the giant. The darker of the two nodded at his companion and drew his sword. Turning to the giant, he swooped down and sliced the back of the giant's knees. The giant staggered, crying out in pain and shock but, within seconds, his heavenly opponent had crouched down low and plunged his sword into the giant's right armpit. The giant howled and clutched his wounded arm, lurching unsteadily. The blond shining man by my side drew an arrow from the quiver on his back, and loosed it from a large, ornate bow. The arrow flew like a flash of lightning and pierced the giant's throat, protruding from the back of his neck. The giant staggered again, stunned by the speed of their attack. The shining men watched with an air of calm satisfaction as he toppled over backwards, falling to the ground with a mighty thud.

The toppling of the giant took a matter of seconds; I was awestruck by their faultless attack, executed with grace and agility. The shining men sheathed their swords and stood, staring at me with a deliberate gaze. Then, with a hint of a smile and an imperceptible lift of their eyebrows, they were gone, their incapacitated victim disappearing with them.

I stood, as if frozen in time, until a voice shook me out of my stupor. 'Joshua? Joshua!'

'Hmm?' I couldn't tear my eyes away from where they had just stood.

'Joshua? What are you staring at?' Caleb asked, looking first at me, then to the clearing ahead of me.

'They... there were...' I gestured to the clearing and glanced at him, then looked back at where the shining men had stood. 'Did you see them?'

'Who?'

'Uh... wa... warriors,' I stammered, all at once feeling breathless.

'No.' Caleb's look of curiosity changed into concern. 'Not there. Did you?'

'Yes.' By now, Mesha had walked over to join us, and looked at us in turn, seeking an explanation.

'Did you see anyone there?' Caleb asked him.

'Where?'

'Over there,' Caleb pointed to the area where the shining men had stood.

'No. Why?'

'Joshua saw someone.'

'Oh.' The two men looked at each other, and then at me. The haze in my mind was starting to clear; realisation flooded me and I stuttered, 'I think... they... they were showing me how to...' Looking down, I saw my sword still clenched firmly in my hand. I slid it into its scabbard. 'I must speak with Moses.'

'Moses?'

'Yes. I believe they...' I felt a growing sense of excitement. 'They were showing me how to slay them. They...'

'Who?' Mesha asked, clearly getting frustrated with my lack of clarity.

'The shi...' I grunted and shook my head. 'I will explain to you later. I must speak to Moses about this without delay.'

'Shall I come with you?' Mesha asked.

'No. Finish your training, I will see you this evening. Caleb,' I said, turning to him, 'Come.' I headed off in the direction of Moses' tent, Caleb following close behind me. It was only much later that I recalled the look on Mesha's face as he watched us leave; a look of aggrievement which turned to cold, hard resentment.

17

Honour Denied

Moses and Caleb listened, astonished, as I told them about my vision of the shining men and the giant. Only when I had finished did Moses ask questions.

'These... shining men... they are the same ones you saw at the rebellion of Korah?'

'Yes.'

'And they slew the giant in front of you?'

'Yes. But before they slew him, they showed me how to do it. They pointed out what I believe to be the giant's weak points.'

'Mmm,' Moses rubbed his beard, then chuckled. 'It seems that Yahweh has sent warrior messengers to you, to aid you in your plan to slay the giants, yes? This is what you have petitioned Him for. Yahweh has heard your cries, Joshua. He has answered you.' Moses and I were astounded by the uniqueness of this great honour afforded me. Caleb, however, dived straight into action without pausing for breath.

'We cannot match these giants strength for strength, we know that, but we can outwit them by targeting their weaknesses. That is what these shining men revealed to you! We must go low, attack them from the ground – the backs of their knees first, yes?' Without waiting for our response, Caleb continued his narrative. 'That can be accomplished by skilled swordsmanship – or perhaps by archers? The pits of their arms could be reached by long swords, if we can get close enough to them to take aim, but perhaps spears would be more effective, to avoid the reach of their arm? Once they are felled and brought low, we end them by cutting their throats, just as the shining men showed you, yes?'

'There is much to discuss,' I responded, still slightly dazed by the details of the vision and its ramifications.

'We must train our men in this art of giant warfare – but not all of them,' Caleb looked at me, then at Moses, then back at me. 'This training cannot be for all our warriors. We must choose a small group of men; they must be strong and brave, but fleet of foot and quick of eye. Speed and agility will be most important, yes?' His eyes glistened with excitement as he announced, 'They will be the giant slayers!'

Moses and I smiled at Caleb. It was hard not to get swept up in his passion once he got an idea in his head, but I knew we would need to think this through carefully. 'There is much to discuss, my friend, but yes, this training would be best accomplished by choosing a select group of warriors – perhaps one hundred of our finest soldiers?' I said, turning to Moses to see his reaction. He nodded, so I continued. 'We will assemble all those with the rank of captain and have them battle each other, test their skills with the sword, the bow and the spear. Then we...'

'Joshua.'

'Yes, Master?' I was surprised; it was unusual for Moses to interrupt.

'The choice of who is to be part of this troop is an important one. We must be far-sighted in this regard. Many of our captains are seasoned men.'

'Assuredly. Is that not what we seek? Seasoned men who have skill in warfare?'

'No,' he said, looking at both of us with a solemn countenance. 'The men you train will face the giants that dwell in the land of Canaan, when we cross over to take that land which the Lord God has given us.'

'Yes.' I didn't follow his line of thinking. Why wouldn't we put our best men in this troop of elite warriors? We would be fools not to.

'We have been wandering this wilderness for a little over ten years now. All our warriors aged thirty years or more will not enter Canaan.' He paused, staring at our faces to see whether we understood his meaning. We didn't. He continued, 'The men you choose to be giant slayers must have seen less than thirty winters. They are the ones who will live to see the land promised to us. They are the ones who will face the giants of Canaan.'

There was a stunned silence. Caleb and I stared at him, unblinking.

He was right. Of course he was right. But... my thoughts scattered like chaff on a threshing floor, blown in every direction by a fierce wind. A jumble of faces flashed through my mind; faces of the captains who served under me. Good men. Loyal men. Brave men. Men who would not bear the honour of being called a giant slayer, simply because they would not live to see the land of Canaan.

Something within me broke at the thought of having to tell them that they would be denied this honour. Their faces continued to flash through my consciousness – faces filled with anger and pain – but one face loomed in my mind above all the others.

Mesha.

18

Giant Slayers

We sat with Moses in his tent late into the night, going through the lists of soldiers to be tested for their suitability to be trained as giant slayers. Caleb and I did most of the talking, discussing potential training strategies alongside the capabilities of the men. Moses didn't say much, except when we asked his opinion about certain individuals, but I saw his concern and I knew he sensed the conflict within me. We had entered the second watch of the night when he stood up and stretched, yawning loudly.

'The hour is late. We have accomplished much this night, but now it is time to rest our bodies and our minds. Go home to your beds – we will meet again in the morning, *nu?*'

Caleb and I bade him goodnight and left. The towering pillar of fire cast shadows in our path as we wound our way through the jumble of tents, whispering among ourselves, until it was time to go our separate ways. All was dark and quiet when I arrived back at my tent. The embers of the fire were only a faint glimmer in the pit and my family were nowhere to be seen. I was relieved. Much though I loved them, I didn't have the capacity or desire to talk through what had happened that day. I was exhausted. I washed, disrobed, and lay down on my bed. Closing my eyes, I steeled myself to meet the giants once again in my dreams.

They never came.

My sleep was restless, not because they pursued me, but because thoughts of how to tell Mesha the news ran through my mind throughout the night. I woke in the morning to hear the noise of the family preparing to break fast, and the tuneful singing of Samina as she tended to

Miriam. I had overslept. I hastened to wash and dress before taking my place around the mat. Azriel pronounced the blessing, we gave thanks to Yahweh for the food He had provided for us, then the dishes were handed around. My thoughts were still very scattered and I was preoccupied, thinking on my vision of the shining men, when I heard Mesha's voice.

'So? Where were you last night?'

Realising that he was talking to me, I replied, 'I was with Moses and Caleb. Our meeting took much time.'

'You were with Caleb. Of course you were.' Mesha said. I thought I heard a sourness in his tone, but perhaps I was mistaken. I wasn't sure how to respond, so I lowered my face and bit into a fig, hoping his attention would shift onto someone else. 'You told me you would see me later and explain what happened. I waited.' I looked up to see him staring at me, challenging me to refute what he had said. I realised I had become so caught up in conversation with Moses and Caleb, I had totally forgotten my words to him. That must be why his tone seemed sharp.

'Forgive me, brother. My thoughts were so many, I must have put it out my mind.'

'Clearly.' He smiled at me, but his tone was clipped. The rest of the family sitting around the mat stopped talking, realising that something was amiss.

'Of what do you talk?' Azriel asked Mesha. 'What took place yesterday?'

'I know nothing,' he responded, shrugging and pulling a face. Looking back at me, he continued, 'That is why I waited up last night, so Joshua could tell me what happened.' The smile had evaporated, leaving behind a cold stare.

'Brother, I did not mean to slight you. Forgive me, I beg of you.' Mesha studied me for a while, then gave a small smile and looked away, reaching for more manna cakes.

'Yoshi, what happened yesterday?' Yoram asked, obviously trying to break the tension that hung in the air. The last thing I felt like doing at that moment was trying to explain to my family how two celestial glowing men and a giant apparition had appeared to me in a vision while I stood on the training grounds, unseen by everyone else, but I had no choice. Refusing to tell them now would only make things worse, so I gave them a brief, factual version of the events that had taken place, purposefully leaving out any mention of our plans to form a special troop of 'giant slayers'.

Reactions from the family ranged from astonishment to excitement, on the part of the men, at least. Most of the women looked anxious at the very mention of battling giants, all except Alya. She said nothing, but I knew by the expression on her face that she must have had a similar kind of encounter in days past. I made a mental note to find a way to talk with her privately; I wanted to hear her insight on the subject of visions.

'Does this mean we will be trained in the ways of warring giants?' Yoram asked, his face aglow with passion.

'We... Caleb and I are...' I hesitated, not wanting to say anything more. I could not trust myself to speak. My mind was in turmoil and I knew I would probably say the wrong thing, or say too much. 'There is much to discuss, and many plans to be made, which is why, with your permission,' I said, glancing at the family members seated around, 'I must take my leave of you. Moses and Caleb will be waiting for me.' Without pausing further, I clambered to my feet and said my farewells. The last thing I saw as I left was Mesha's face, his eyes narrowed in suspicion as he watched me make my escape.

Moses, Caleb and I spent most of the day strategising over training methods, and going through the final list of potential giant slayers. Yoram's name was mentioned within the first few minutes, but not by me. Caleb insisted that he be included. It looked as though Yoram would be promoted to the rank of captain sooner than I had expected; my heart sang. Towards the end of the afternoon, Moses drew our meeting to a close, then asked me to stay behind. He knew me so well. Not bothering to waste time giving me an opportunity to bring the subject up myself, he went straight to the heart of the matter.

'This will not sit well with Mesha, will it?' he asked.

'No. Being told that he cannot be a giant slayer will be injurious to him. He is an esteemed warrior, and his pride in his fighting skills and captaincy is great. But hearing that his son is to be among the chosen when he is not...' I glanced at my feet to avoid the concern I saw in Moses' eyes. 'He was much changed after Jesher's passing, and has only recently come to himself. I fear what this will do to him.'

'Mmm. Would you withhold this honour from Yoram to ease Mesha's pain?'

'I cannot do that!' I blurted. 'Must a son be held back from honour because of a misfortune that has beset his father?' I exhaled in frustration and shook my head, trying to clear the debris that littered my thoughts. 'No. Yoram has earned his place among the giant slayers. He is not of my choosing alone,' I said. 'Caleb has also noticed his skill with the sword. He sees that Yoram is strong, and brave, and fleet of foot – but he is more than that. His thoughts are measured and he does not flounder in the face of attack. He is not reckless. He does not run swiftly into battle without first giving thought to what will take place. He will make a great captain, and could be among the best of our giant slayers. I cannot withhold that from him.'

'So be it, then,' Moses said. 'When will you start the trials to choose your hundred?'

'Two days hence,' I said. 'We will send messengers to summon the contenders tomorrow. The trials will start the following morning.'

'Mmm.' Moses nodded his head, as he always did when pondering important matters. 'Joshua?' He waited until I looked at him. 'You must tell Mesha without delay. The longer you wait, the harder it will become.'

I agreed and said my farewell. My feet felt heavy laden as I trudged home that evening. I considered going to the Tabernacle to spend the evening in prayer, but knew I could not miss breaking bread with the family two nights in a row. That would not ease the situation with Mesha, much though I longed to escape. My mind sifted through various scenarios, trying to find a legitimate reason why I could avoid going home. I couldn't think of a single one – at least, none that would justify offending Mesha further. The family were already gathering around the mat when I arrived home and the women were bringing out woven baskets of bread and clay dishes of vegetable stew. I sat next to Eglah and Hareph, little Davi sitting between them, bouncing up and down on his bottom, giggling as he waited for the rest of the family to join us.

Mesha emerged from his tent. I saw him glance at those of us gathered on the mat, then he went and sat next to Shira, on the same side of the mat as me, but further up. I wondered if he had done that on purpose, to avoid having to look at me during the meal. Whatever his reason, I was ashamed to say that I was glad he had done so. I fielded more questions from the family about the shining men and our giant slaying plans, answering as ambiguously as I could, grateful that I didn't have to look at Mesha as I spoke. He didn't participate in the discussion, but I resolved to speak to him as soon as we had finished eating, perhaps suggest a walk. The women cleared away after the evening meal and went to settle the children, leaving us men to sit around the fire and discuss the day's events. I sat by the fire and waited for Mesha to join us, but he didn't come. When I asked her, Helah said he was weary and had gone to lie down. It seemed our talk would have to wait until the morning.

Another restless night passed but, thankfully, again no dreams of giants. I wondered if this would continue. Perhaps my encounter with the shining men had banished the giants from my dreams. Would that they could banish my anxious thoughts about Mesha. I woke, determined to speak to him as soon as we had broken our fast but, when I sat down to eat, he was not among us.

'Where is Mesha?' I asked Yoram.

'He has gone to collect the new batch of skins from Yosef.'

'Now? Why so early in the morning?' I queried.

Yoram shrugged. 'He said he needed them straight away, for the repairs we are making to Elisa's tent.'

He was clearly avoiding me. Initially, I was relieved that we had some distance from each other, but my relief was starting to turn into frustration and, with it, anger. I needed to talk to him, and soon. The trials were due to start the following morning. That evening, before the meal had ended, I seized the opportunity. Leaning forward to get Mesha's attention, I asked him to walk with me after breaking bread.

'Aah, I cannot, not tonight. I am going to see Elisa, he will be waiting for me.'

'He would meet with you tonight? Can you not meet him tomorrow?'

'No, he will be waiting. There is much to discuss about the design of his new tent. It is a big job and will take quite some time. I will only be home much later. But perhaps tomorrow.' Without waiting for a response, he leaned back and turned to talk to Helah, who was seated on his left. As soon as the meal had ended, he left. I knew I would not have time to speak to him before the trials now, as I had to leave early the following morning. I would tell Moses that my failure to talk to Mesha was not for lack of trying.

The sun had only just risen when I made my way to the training grounds, but already beads of sweat were forming on my forehead. A sultry wind blew across the desert plains, blowing tufts of tumbleweed across my path. It was going to be a scorching day. Caleb waited for me with his son Iru who would also take part in the trials. Our young warriors started arriving and stood in groups, chattering with excitement, eager to be pitted against each other. I marvelled as I watched their eagerness to take on the challenge of facing giants, oblivious to the horrors that might await those who were chosen. The passion of youth displayed in all its glory... and all its ignorance. An uncomfortable feeling shrouded me; I felt something I had not felt before. I felt old. Shaking if off, I squared my shoulders and walked towards Yoram and Iru, who stood together discussing the trials. Iru was a few years younger than Yoram, and not yet married, but he had his father's skill in warfare, and his accuracy with a bow and arrow was undisputable.

'It's time! Shall we begin?' Caleb asked, looking with great satisfaction at the selection of strong young warriors assembled before us. Looking over my shoulder, he frowned and muttered, 'What is he doing here?' I turned to see Mesha making his way towards us, his sword buckled to his leather belt. '*Shalom*, Mesha,' Caleb said. 'Have you come to watch the trials?'

'*Shalom, shalom*,' Mesha replied. 'No, I have not come to watch, but to take part. Set me against your best.' He drew his sword from its scabbard and brandished it aloft. 'I will vanquish them!'

Caleb and I looked at each other, then back at Mesha. Neither of us said a word. Mesha noticed the consternation on our faces. 'What is it?' he said, frowning. 'Have I come at the wrong time? Are the trials not today?'

'Yes, they are.' My heart started beating faster. How had he found out about the trials? Who had told him? Yoram. It must have been Yoram. 'Ech, what does it matter now?' I thought to myself, irritated at my desire to try to work out how he knew. He was here now, so pointless to ask why or how. I berated myself for not speaking with him yesterday. I should have been more insistent, made him speak with me.

Mesha was clearly confounded by the witless expressions on our faces. 'So...? Shall we begin?' Caleb glanced at me, clearly unwilling to be the one to tell him. I took a deep breath.

'Mesha... the trials... only a select number of warriors have been chosen to take part.'

'Assuredly. We must choose our best warriors if we are to slay these giants, *nu*?' Thinking he understood the reason for our hesitation, he held up his hand and said, 'I ask for no favours; I will compete and prove myself like the rest of the warriors.'

I glanced at Caleb, silently begging him to intervene. He didn't. I could prevaricate no longer. 'Mesha, you are not among the men chosen to do the trials.'

Mesha's glance darted at Caleb and I in turn. He frowned and rubbed his nose. 'But I am a captain, a seasoned warrior. Are captains not among your...?'

'There are some taking part in the trials, but...'

'But not me?' His eyes narrowed; his lips tightened. 'I have served for many years, fought by your side, and attained the rank of captain, but I am not worthy to be a giant slayer?'

'Mesha...' Caleb, stepped forward and put his hand on Mesha's arm.

He shook it off. 'Was this your decision?' he asked Caleb. 'You would rob me not only of my closest friend, but of my honour as a warrior as well?'

'Wh... what do you speak of?' Caleb stuttered in confusion.

All the bitterness that must have been festering in Mesha's heart now rose up and spilled out, like vomit spewing out of his mouth. 'I know what you've been doing,' he said, pointing his finger in Caleb's face. 'Coming alongside my brother, turning his heart away from me, speaking evil of me to him. You have maligned me. That's why you are always at his side, isn't it? To stop him joining his heart with mine. You have stolen him from me. What have I done to deserve such evil?'

'Mesha, stop!' I urged him, aware that some of the younger men were watching with great curiosity. 'This is madness! What you speak of is not true. You are one of our bravest, most loyal warriors. Caleb knows that, as do I. You not being chosen for the trials has nothing to do with your ability as a warrior. Would that you could compete, but it cannot be so.'

'Why so?' he said, clenching his free hand at his side.

'We cannot train warriors who have seen more than thirty winters.'

'Why? These young pups know nothing of the experience of battle. Why would you choose them over men like me?'

'Because...' I gulped to try to get rid of the huge lump in my throat. 'Because we can only train those who will live to cross over into Canaan and battle the giants.'

Mesha froze, his eyes wide and unblinking. He could not have looked more shocked if I had plunged a sword into his gut. I saw anger, confusion, and something far worse: raw vulnerability. We stood still, none of us willing to break the silence; none of us knowing what to say.

After a few moments, he gave one curt nod, turned and walked off, his sword dangling from his hand, trailing behind him in the dust.

19

Troubled

The weeks that followed were troubled, and the weather reflected the atmosphere in our homes. We were well into the hottest season of the year, waiting with growing impatience for the first rains to fall, bringing with them some relief from the oppressive humidity that overshadowed both our days and our nights. We tied up the sides of our tents to allow what little breeze there was to blow through our homes, though it was of scant help. The wind itself was so warm, it did little to dispel the sticky heat that hovered over us, stealing our breath and our joy. We lay on our bed rolls at night, slick with sweat, longing for the morning when we could wash the foetid stench of clamminess off our bodies.

The heat made everyone irritable. Even mild-mannered Eglah snapped at Hareph when he complained yet again about the heat, and Samina's songs were few and far between. We saved up our energy for doing essential duties; our waterskins were our most cherished possessions.

After some discussion, Caleb and I had decided to forego the start of training with the giant slaying troop until the weather broke. After a few days of trials, the troop of 100 men had been selected. I shared with them the details of my vision of the shining men, we discussed the strategy that we planned to follow, and we introduced them to the type of training that they would be doing. However, the sweltering heat sapped our strength and made it almost impossible for us to concentrate on anything, whether mental or physical, for any length of time. We released the men back to their families, with instructions to gather the day after the rains came.

Home was no longer a place of joy or peace for me. It saddened me greatly when I remembered how it had been when Jesher was still with us – the lifegiving discussions we would have at mealtimes, the laughter that filled the air and the stories he told the children, which the adults loved just as much as the little ones! Azriel was growing into the role of patriarch, but he was not Jesher. Whereas Jesher had been a dreamer and a watcher, Azriel was more of a doer and a talker. There was a grace and an ease about Jesher which Azriel did not have, although, as Eleazar kept telling me, he just needed time to find who he was as the new leader of our family.

'It is hard to walk a pathway that another has trodden for so long,' Eleazar said as we sat outside his tent one day, resting in the midday heat. It was the desert wanderers' way to rest at midday when the sun was at its highest, but our resting time had increased significantly in this sultry season, giving us even more time to think and talk.

'Mmm.' I stared into the distance at the hills that surrounded our camp, masked by a shimmering heat haze. 'He is not a bad leader,' I explained. 'It's just that he is not Jesher. Yes, I know,' I said, smiling at Eleazar. 'We must give him time – and we will. We are.' I sighed. 'But Jesher would have known how to help Mesha, what to say to him. Azriel cannot reach him.'

'How is it with Mesha?' Eleazar asked. 'Has he found peace yet?' I had told Eleazar some time ago what had happened when Mesha arrived on the day of the trials. He was my confidant; there was not much about my life or my heart that he did not know. Caleb had also become a close friend; he was a man of like passion who I greatly admired. He made me laugh and I profited much from our conversations about warfare and the ways of men. But his impetuosity and hot-headedness meant that I could not always share with him the leanings of my heart. Eleazar was the one I sought when I had need of wisdom or a listening ear.

I grimaced. 'In truth, it is hard to know how Mesha is. He has...' I hesitated, trying to find the words to explain what had happened to Mesha since the day of the trials. 'He has withdrawn inside himself. The anger that raged within him has gone. He talks and smiles, but it is as though he is not there. Not fully. I sense much disquiet in him, but it hides behind a thick veil and will not reveal itself.'

'Is there anyone else who can draw him out of that place? Anyone he trusts who he can share his heart with?' Eleazar asked.

I thought for a while. 'Helah. She loves him fiercely and has some understanding of the conflict in his heart, but she has only been able to draw him out so far. She does not condemn me for what happened with the trials, she understands why he and the other captains were set aside. But Mesha has always been so strong and confident, he has never been spurned before. He loves Helah and has fathered their children so well – he would battle a giant without a moment's hesitation to protect his family from harm. He is a man of great courage. But it seems that over these years of our sojourning, he has brushed aside, or perhaps buried, the words that Moses declared over the men who will die before we enter Canaan. I fear that our dispute with him on the day of the trials reminded him that he is not indestructible; that he will die and will not live to see Canaan.' I winced as I remembered the look on Mesha's face that day. It had haunted me ever since. Turning to Eleazar, I said, 'It was as if the death sentence had been spoken over him once again, but this time not by Moses, but by me.'

Eleazar nodded. 'That is bitter wine to swallow for any man, let alone a man as strong and unwavering as Mesha.'

'Helah says he will not talk of it, but his greatest conflict is that which concerns Yoram. His pride in his son is great, but it is now coupled with a fierce jealousy, because Yoram has been given what he himself cannot have. Mesha cannot forgive himself for that. He hates himself for the envy that stains his heart towards his son.'

'Has he told you this?'

I snorted. 'No. He tells me nothing of the issues of his heart now. He has told only Helah, and that only once, briefly. She says the shame in his heart clouds his thinking; he will not talk of it any more.'

'Does Yoram know if it?'

'According to Helah, Mesha has not spoken of it to him. He will not speak of it, he is too ashamed, and Helah has not told Yoram. But he knows. I have seen it when he looks at Mesha. There is a wisdom in Yoram that belies his years; he has discerned the cause of the conflict within his *abba*.'

'Yoram is much like you, isn't he?' Eleazar smiled at me – a gentle, warm smile, one devoid of expectation. His smiles brought peace to my soul, as did our conversations. As long and draining as the heat of that sultry season was, it proved fruitful for me, because it gave me much time to talk through the issues of my heart with my friend.

The first rains fell some days later. The heavens opened and we all stood up to greet the first rains. Head coverings were removed and we lifted our faces to the sky in relief, savouring the sensation of cool water trickling down our faces. All around us, neighbours were doing the same thing; the camp was littered with bodies standing under the spout of the waters of heaven, faces upturned, mouths open and arms raised in gratitude.

Those first rains seemed to wash away far more than the dust and dirt that had clung to us during the long, hot months. Their cleansing showers also washed away the tension that had hovered over our family, bring with them a freshness, a contentment. Work was resumed with renewed vigour, our training with the giant slayers recommenced and the women set about preparing for the winter that would soon be upon us. The months passed, winter came and went, and peace was restored.

For a while, at least.

20

Alone

I arrived home one evening to find Mesha and Helah standing in the clearing by the firepit, in the throes of a robust argument. They were surrounded by the family, all of whom looked either confused or concerned. Mesha and Helah's daughter Serah was crying and her older brother, Arad, stood with his arm around her, trying to comfort her. Yoram came over to me as I arrived, and told me what had taken place. Caleb and his brother had come to see Mesha and Azriel that afternoon to seek permission for Serah to be betrothed to Caleb's eldest son, Iru. Mesha had said no.

'I have told you why: Iru is not of our tribe. His family are from the tribe of Judah,' Mesha told Helah, ignoring the rest of the family gathered round.

'But why should this stop them from being wed?' she asked. 'Shua's husband was not a Benjaminite but you did not stop her from marrying him.'

'No, but I should have. I would like at least one of our daughters to marry into our own tribe. Serah must marry a man from the tribe of Benjamin.' Serah burst into a fresh bout of crying at his words. She was a young woman with a gentle spirit and, usually when she was in distress, Mesha indulged her and comforted her. Not today. He didn't even look at her.

'But Mesha, Serah and Iru have known each other for some time. They are well suited. It is a good match,' Helah continued.

'It is not a good match, because he is not a Benjaminite. Besides,' he interjected before Helah could protest, 'Serah is not old enough to be married. She must stay here with her family for a while longer.'

'Not old enough...?' Helah looked at him in bewilderment. 'She has been a woman for more than a year, Mesha. You know this. It is time for her to marry and Iru has an upright heart. Caleb's family is well respected and they will be good to Serah. It is a good match.'

'It is *not a good match*,' Mesha shouted. 'I have made my decision and my decision is *no*.' Pointing his finger in Helah's face, he raved, 'You are my wife, and you will *obey me*.'

Helah gaped at him in shock.

Mesha's eyebrows furrowed, his chest heaving with emotion.

We all held our breath.

In all the years I had known them, I had never heard Mesha speak to his wife like that. They had had disagreements over the years, like all couples, but they were usually able to discuss the matter and agree what to do. There had always been a mutual respect between them; this was the first time I had seen Mesha attack Helah in that manner. Arad, his arm still around his sister, turned to me, and asked, 'Joshua, what do you say about this matter?'

It was the worst possible thing he could have said.

'Why do you ask Joshua?' Mesha glared at his son. 'He is not the head of this family. Azriel is the leader of our family. Joshua does not make the decisions around here. I will decide who my daughter marries, not Joshua. Caleb has taken my friend from me, and now he wants my daughter as well? He will not have her. I will not allow it.'

There it was.

The truth had slithered out of Mesha's lips and into the light, as truth has a habit of doing. The real reason for Caleb's denial of the betrothal was laid bare for all to see. There was a stunned silence; even Azriel said nothing, his eyes just darted between me and Mesha.

Turning to Arad, I spoke quietly and calmly. 'Your *abba* is right, Arad. This decision is not mine to make. Azriel is the leader of this family. He and your *abba* will take counsel together.'

Azriel, jolted out of a daze by my words, cleared his throat. 'This is not a matter to be decided quickly. Let us take counsel and talk about it tomorrow, yes?' Before Mesha could retaliate, he looked around and said, 'Come, let us wash and sit down to share our evening meal, hmm?' The family dispersed, somewhat subdued, and I watched Azriel smile at some of the little ones, guiding them towards the clay basin to wash. For a moment, it was just as if Jesher was there. I saw Jesher in Azriel; that's just what he would have done. Jesher would have brought the same sense of calm and order that Azriel had just brought. I realised something.

The family was in safe hands.

Mesha's outburst made it clear that the peace which had reigned for the past few months was only a thin veneer, masking a raging storm of resentment. Mesha's grievances were not resolved, they had just been suppressed. I think I'd known that all along, but hadn't wanted to believe it. Now I had to. I knew what I had to do. It was time for me to go. The following morning I went for a walk with Azriel before going to see Moses. I told him that I felt it was time I moved away from the family.

'No! You cannot do that!' he blurted, his face fired with determination. 'You are part of this family – you belong here with us. If this is because of what Mesha said yesterday, I beg of you, just give him time. He did not know what he was saying. Mesha is your brother, Joshua.' His face clouded over and I thought I saw tears come to his eyes. 'As am I,' he mumbled, looking down. 'You place is with us... with your family.'

I was touched by his fervour. Azriel was not a man who was comfortable with open displays of emotion; I had not expected him to be so ardent in his disagreement of my plan. I stopped walking and turned to face him. Placing my hand on his shoulder, I said, 'Azriel, Mesha will always be my brother, as will you. In moving away, I do not seek revenge. As the Lord lives, there is no bitterness in my heart towards him. You must believe me.'

He hesitated, then whispered, 'I do.'

'Moses asked me some time ago to move my tent nearer to his, to enable me to serve him better, but it was not long after Jesher's passing and I did not feel it was the right time. Something happened yesterday which made me realise that the time has come. It is time for me to move on.'

'What do you speak of?'

We continued walking. 'It was you, Azriel. The words you said after Mesha's outburst, the way you spoke to him, how you guided our family. The peace and wisdom in your manner reminded me of *Abba*. I saw him in you. You are the leader of our family, and Yahweh's hand is upon you to take on this mantle fully.'

He flushed. Glancing at me, he lifted one eyebrow and gave me a gentle smile. 'So you reward me by leaving?'

I smiled back. 'I may be moving my tent away but, if it pleases you, I would still like to join you for the evening meal when possible.'

'Our home will still be your home, Joshua. You will be welcome around our mat at any time and there will always be a sleeping roll ready for you. You need not send word.'

I put my hand on my heart and bowed my head slightly. 'You honour me, Azriel, thank you. Please, let my going out and coming in be good in your sight.' He responded in like manner, bowing his head to me, and we continued on our way.

'When do you seek to move?' he asked me.

'Tomorrow, if that pleases you. I see no merit in waiting longer.'

'Mmm.' He scratched his beard thoughtfully. I concealed a smile; he was even starting to display Jesher's mannerisms. 'I will tell the family tonight when we break bread, yes?'

The mood was more sombre than usual around the mat that night, and became even more so when Azriel told everyone of my imminent move. Mesha didn't look at me, but muttered, 'It is probably for the best.'

'How could this be for the best?' Helah said, her eyes openly accusing him. 'Joshua is part of our family. He is your brother and he belongs here with us. Joshua,' she said, turning to me, 'you cannot move away. Please, stay with us. All will be well.' I opened my mouth to respond but, before I could say a word, I heard Azriel speak.

'The decision has been made, Helah, and we must honour it, *nu*? Moses asked Joshua to move his tent near to his own tent some time ago, so he can serve him better. The time has come for that to take place. But,' he said, smiling around at the family, 'Joshua will be joining us to break bread as often as he can, and he will spend Shabbat with us too, so we will still see much of him. The Lord bless you and keep you, Joshua, as you continue to serve Moses.' Dipping his bread into the remaining sauce in the clay dish, he smiled at Shira and said, 'This is delicious, *Ima*, how did you make it?'

Just like that, it was done. Azriel had done exactly what Jesher had always been so adept at doing; he had stopped any more conversation around that topic from taking place, shifting our focus effortlessly in an entirely different direction. It was as if Jesher had been sitting there. The conversation picked up again and the dish was passed around so that the last of the sauce could be mopped up with the remaining bread. Azriel glanced at me; I smiled at him and inclined my head, silently thanking him for easing my transition. He lifted his cup and nodded back before drinking deeply.

The following morning, Yoram helped me pack down my tent and sort out my belongings. I was a simple man with simple needs; there was not much to pack. As soon as we had broken fast, I stood up to leave, but Helah came to me, holding me tightly before stepping back. With tears glistening in her eyes, she said, 'You make sure you eat enough, *nu*? I know what Moses is like, he forgets to eat, and you and I know that Zipporah's food is... not what you are accustomed to. You come back home as often as you can and we will feed you, yes?'

I smiled at her, gave her one last embrace, and kissed her forehead. I had no desire to prolong my departure so, after glancing at Azriel and giving him a quick nod, Yoram and I set off, carrying my tent and belongings between us. As I rounded the corner, Mesha stood before me. He hesitated when he saw me, crossed his arms, and lowered his head. I glanced at Yoram, who muttered, 'I'll walk on ahead.'

I stood before Mesha, willing him to look at me. 'Is your heart right towards me, as my heart is towards you, my brother?' I asked him.

He sighed, uncrossed his arms, and studied my face. 'You are my brother.'

'And you will always be the brother of my heart,' I replied, reaching out to place my hand on his arm before moving on to join Yoram.

We spoke very little on the way. Yoram and I were so alike, we didn't need a lot of words to convey the issues of our hearts. He helped me erect my tent, moved my belongings inside, then gave me a tight embrace before walking back the way he had come.

I stood and watched him until he disappeared from sight. My heart ached with an unexpected feeling of abandonment and ruin.

I had never felt more alone in my life as I did at that moment.

21

Regrets

My soul longed to see them, but I purposed in my heart to wait a while before going back. I needed to give the ache in my heart time to heal first.

Eleazar and his wife, Bathshua, were good to me during my time of transition, inviting me to break bread with them at their tent each evening. Their tent was very near to where mine was now pitched, so it made visiting much easier. I enjoyed their company and found them easy to be with. They never expected me to sit and make conversation long after the evening meal was over, but they also made it clear that I was welcome to stay, if I chose to. I knew I had made the right decision in moving away from my adopted family, but I had lived with them for so long that being separate from them was a wrench – far more so than I had anticipated. Eleazar and Bathshua's home was a much-needed place of comfort for me, and healing.

I felt apprehensive the first time I went back home. The closer I got to the Benjaminite camping grounds, the more my stomach churned, but I need not have worried; I was welcomed with open arms. Strangely enough, it was Shira who was the first to welcome me. She was sitting outside her tent in the shade. I couldn't recall ever seeing Shira just sitting down, resting; she was usually busy, cleaning or cooking, or looking after her grandchildren. To see her just sitting there was such a rarity, it took me by surprise. Her face broke into a smile when she saw me and, although she didn't rise to her feet (her joints had grown stiff and she struggled to move about as she used to), she held out her arms to me and gave me a warm embrace.

'Joshua! *Shalom, shalom!* You have come back to us! My heart rejoices to see you.'

The rest of the family gathered round and I was welcomed with great excitement. We sat around the same woven mat; I ate the same food that I had eaten for years, with the same people. Nothing had changed. But everything had changed. Although I knew it was not intentional and no one meant to treat me any differently, they did. It was a subtle, unintentional shift; I was now a visitor. I was given special attention and was treated differently to how I used to be. They were still my family – that would never change – but I was not part of their daily lives now, and that had altered the dynamic of our relationship. I realised that I had crossed a line and wouldn't be able to go back.

Over the next week or so I visited them as often as I could, and spent Shabbat with them. Mesha was amenable enough; quiet and somewhat detached, but not unfriendly. Helah told me that Mesha had relented and given his permission for Serah to be betrothed to Iru – although he had insisted on a betrothal of at least one year.

'In truth?' I asked her, amazed at the news. After Mesha's outburst that day, I was convinced he would never give in. 'How did you get him to relent?'

'I didn't,' she replied. 'Shira did.'

'Shira? How? What did she say to him?'

'I don't know. She did not say, and Mesha has not told me what took place. Perhaps he will one day, but not yet. I will wait until he is ready to tell me.'

I sat with Shira as she rested that afternoon. My curiosity got the better of me, so I asked her if what Helah had said was true. Had she been the one to change Mesha's mind about Serah's betrothal to Iru? She nodded and gave me a gentle smile. '*Ima*, how did you get him to change his mind? What did you say to him?' I whispered.

'It makes my heart glad to hear you call me that,' she replied, pausing to think before answering. 'I shared with him what has happened to me since Jesher's passing. I spoke to him of my regrets, of all the opportunities I missed, all the blessings I could have received – and given.' Shira gave a forlorn sigh. 'I said so many cruel things which can never be unsaid. I cannot erase them now; they are in the past. I cannot change the past; neither can Mesha. We cannot take back the harmful words we have spoken, but we can look to the path ahead of us. We can choose to walk a good path for the rest of our days.'

She hesitated, staring at the ground. 'I told him not to let the pain inside his own heart cause him to inflict anguish on his kinfolk.' She glanced at me. 'I did that for so long, Joshua... so long. I took the pain from my youth and I let it harden me.' Shira noticed my quizzical expression. 'I was not favoured by my *ima*, or my *abba*. My younger sister was the delight of their heart; everything she did was wondrous in their eyes. I worked so hard to try to earn their love, cooking and cleaning and serving, but nothing I did made any difference. She was their joy and pride; I was just the other daughter. I stored up pain inside my heart, and took it into my marriage to Jesher. I could not let it go. I didn't know how to.'

Pointing towards a couple of shrubs that were growing side by side in the nearby scrub, she spoke in a low tone. 'I showed Mesha these plants. See how one is thriving, its leaves thick and green, while the other is thin and sickly? One represents our past, the other our future. We must choose which one to water and nurture, and which one to leave alone. I told him not to water the plant of his past, not to focus his gaze on his past failures or regrets. That bush must shrivel up and die; it is in the past, it has had its time. He must water the plant that represents his future, tending it so that it grows strong and true.'

I was astonished at what I saw. A lump caught in my throat. I whispered, '*Ima*, there is much wisdom in you.'

'Perhaps I did learn a little from Jesher after all, *nu?*' she said, giving a little chuckle and squeezing my arm. To me, at that moment, Shira had never looked more beautiful. A lump formed in my throat. I wished Jesher could have been there to see her, to see the transformation that had taken place in his wife's heart.

Serah and Iru were betrothed for just over a year before being joined in marriage. Serah moved away to live with Iru, Caleb and Johanna, and their family, in the tribe of Judah's camping grounds. Iru was given a year off army training when he married her, but I saw him often when I visited Caleb and Johanna. He and Serah seemed happy, and it was not too long before they shared the joyous news that she was with child. Although he never spoke of it, I felt sure that Mesha's struggles to let her go to Caleb's family had never fully abated, as he asked me often of her well-being. My response was usually the same: it was well with her, she was well looked after, Iru was a kind husband, and she said of her parents-in-law: 'There is much love in their hearts for me.'

However, although Mesha was always glad to receive the news that Serah was well and happy, I couldn't help but notice that his jaw clenched whenever we spoke of her love for her in-laws and theirs for her.

22

Treacherous Beauty

Training sessions for the giant slayers' troop had been underway for many moons and Caleb and I were pleased with the progress we had made so far. We realised very quickly that our initial focus would not need to be on training the men physically, so much as challenging their thinking. Training to battle a giant was fundamentally different to the training applied when fighting a normal-sized man.

Our warriors were used to fighting face-to-face with their opponents, but that was impossible with giants, as they were so much taller than us. The emphasis in normal warfare was usually on the strength of a man's arm but, when fighting a giant, agility and fleetness of foot were more important. Brute strength was pointless when challenging a giant, while a well-thought-out strategy and a quick mind were essential. Hand-to-hand combat must be avoided at all costs, as the reach of the titans' arms was so long. Our warriors had to learn how to attack from the ground, to strike from underneath, rather than face-off against their adversary. They had to learn to move and think with the cunning of a cobra, rather than the strength of a bear.

Initially, their frustration was evident and we spent much time repeating the same mantras.

'Strike from underneath.'

'Fleet of foot, not heavy of hand.'

'Stealth, not strength.'

We designed armour specifically for the giant slayers, armour that was lighter in weight and allowed them flexibility of movement. The more heavy-set of our warriors struggled with the new form of training, and took much longer to grasp the new concepts than the lither young men in the troop. Yoram and Iru were both lean, and able to adapt more quickly than most to the new regime, although it took a long time for the new ways of fighting to become instinctive, even for them. We made the decision to pull the giant slayers out of the normal rota for army training, as the two methods of fighting were so opposed, to enable them to focus their attention solely on learning the tactics of giant warfare.

During the first few months, we trained the warriors in three different areas of weaponry: swordsmanship, archery and spear-throwing. By the time three months had passed, each man specialised in one of these areas, although each of them had to be proficient in all three. We drilled them over and over – it was not enough for them to hit their target, their weapon had to pierce the exact spot on the giant's frame to make the necessary impact. Timing and accuracy were vital. The men were organised into units of three; each unit had one warrior from each specialism in it, one of whom was appointed captain over the three.

Yoram, who was renowned for his skill with the sword, was chosen as captain of his unit. With him was a sturdy young man named Erez, strong of arm and an expert spear thrower, and Caleb's son Iru who was a master archer.

We made life-sized representations of giants for the warriors to practise on. The images were stuffed with straw and sown into thick hides, armour was fastened on each of them, and they were mounted on long poles so that they could be moved – our giant slayers had to learn to battle moving targets. Initially, our troop of one hundred were disconcerted by how large the giant images were, but Caleb declared to them that the bigger the giants were, the more there was to aim for, and the easier they would be to hit! We worked on different combinations of attack with the units to provide them with a few options to choose from when facing their giant. So far, it was working, and we noticed their attitudes were starting to change from frustration to satisfaction.

Being the only one who had seen the giants close up, albeit only in my dreams or the daytime vision, I was acutely aware of their terrifying ability to bewitch using their external beauty. I put it off for quite a while, but knew the time had come for me to have an honest discussion with the troop about what happened when I first encountered the giant in the night watches.

'Think not that the giant's size and strength is all you must contend with,' I said to the group of men gathered around. 'Your greatest test as a giant slayer may not be in your skill as a warrior, but in your ability to resist the excellence of their form.'

I watched as confusion filled most of the men's faces. Some of them looked around to see if others felt the same, and muttered among themselves as to my meaning.

'The creatures that Yahweh revealed to me are...' I hesitated. How could I possibly hope to explain to these young men the power of the titans' flawless form, or their terrifying hold on their victims? 'Yahweh, help me,' I prayed silently. I leaned forward on the rock I was perched on and made eye contact with the men individually. 'Their form is unblemished; every aspect of their body as if sculpted from the finest marble, their limbs well-knit and defined, their countenance akin to perfection.'

No one muttered now. All eyes were fixed on me, waiting for me to explain myself.

'Do not get drawn aside by their appearance – their beauty is but a guise, a ploy to beguile you. They entice you to come closer, to gaze upon them and marvel at their form – and that is how they ensnare you.' I pointed to the bemused faces of the young men before me and admonished them, 'Remember my words well! Write them on the tablets of your heart. Do not be ensnared by the giants' beauty, for it is as treacherous as the venom of a cobra when it strikes to kill.'

'Commander?' one of our younger warriors spoke up.

'Speak, Erez.'

'Were you... entranced by the creature you saw in your dream?'

'I was.'

'What did you do?'

This was no time for false heroics. I had to prepare these men for the reality of what they might face, even if I was lessened in their estimation because of it. 'I was bewitched by him and my heart deceived me. It urged me to bow down and worship at the titan's feet.'

Gasps rippled throughout the throng. Erez's eyebrows furrowed, meeting in the middle. He asked the question they all wanted to know the answer to. 'And did you?'

'Did I what?'

'Did you worship the creature?'

My face broke into a smile. 'No, Erez. I worship Yahweh, and Him alone. I will worship no false god – and neither will you, when you face these creatures. But do not be deceived! Their power is great. Hear my words! The beauty of their form will entrance you, but it is fleeting and turns with the blink of an eye into treachery. Even while you gaze upon them, they will strike suddenly and without mercy.'

My thoughts turned to the horrifying stories that Nadeem had shared with Moses about the giants' attack on his family. Skulls crushed, young boys' necks snapped, men decapitated or disembowelled. No, mercy was not in their nature and I would have none of my warriors taken by them. The mood at the end of our discussion was sober, but I didn't attempt to lighten it. I could not water down the reality of what these men would face; they must be ready when the time came. I cautioned them to refrain from telling others what I had shared with them that afternoon; that information was for them alone.

Yoram thrived on the training and talked about it whenever he got the opportunity, but I never heard him speak to any of the family about what I told them that day. Anger and suppressed tension seemed to fill the atmosphere whenever giant slaying, or Caleb's skill as a warrior and trainer, were mentioned. Yoram's regular recounting of what happened each day at training only served to exacerbate Mesha's resentment and I could not risk alienating my brother any more. Our relationship was hanging by a hair and the slightest provocation could snap the tenuous thread that held us together. I must not lose him. I could not endure that.

23

The Giant Within

Truthfully, although I was proud of the giant slayers' achievements and pleased with how the training was going, I welcomed the opportunity to turn my attention to something else. My life was overtaken with thoughts of battling giants, and it wearied me. Every day, except for Shabbat, was spent training the troops. I did little else. I no longer spent time with Moses, reading and learning to scribe. The hours that I usually spent with him in the Tabernacle were now taken up with training and, because I was no longer conveying messages or speaking to people on Moses's behalf, I felt out of touch with the life of the camp. I missed it.

I missed talking with families as I walked through the camp.

I missed seeing how fast a new mother's baby was growing, or hearing the news of a betrothal.

I missed spending time with Moses and learning from him.

I missed our times of prayer and worship before Yahweh.

I even missed learning to scribe, although, in truth, I never imagined I would yearn for that! My life just seemed to be one long training session.

One day as I was standing at the training grounds watching the men compete in pairs, I saw Moses walking towards me. '*Shalom*, Master!' I greeted him. 'Is it well with you? Do you have need of me?'

'No, no, all is well,' he said, smiling at me. 'It was in my heart to visit you here and see how our giant slayers are progressing.' Studying them with great interest, he asked, 'Are you pleased with them? Are your efforts bearing fruit?'

'I believe so, Master. The men train hard every day and we…'

'Every day?'

'Yes. Except Shabbat, of course. They have developed skills in specific weapons, and we have divided them into units of three.' I went on to explain the strategy behind our training regime, pointing out various warriors who excelled, while showing Moses the methods we used to train them.

'This is good, Joshua, very good,' he muttered, nodding his head. Then, turning to me, he said, 'Come, walk with me.'

'Uh... now, Master?'

'Yes, now,' he said, with a benevolent smile, as though talking to a child.

'As you wish.' I motioned to Caleb that I was leaving and we set off, trundling along the path that wound its way through the camp.

'Joshua, you and Caleb have done well. The training these men have received is deserving of praise; I am confident in their readiness for battle, when the day comes.'

'Thank you, Master.'

'Tell me, do the giants still pursue you in your dreams?'

His question took me by surprise. 'No. Not since the day I encountered the shining men.'

'Aah, that is good. My heart rejoices to hear that,' he said, scratching his beard. He stopped and swung round to face me. 'So, why are you driving these men so hard?'

I stopped. Another question I hadn't expected. I frowned. Wasn't it obvious? 'The giants could attack at any time, Master,' I responded. 'We must be ready.'

'And you feel that we are not ready to face them?' he asked, peering at me with great intent. I glanced at him, trying to work out his meaning. Were they ready? Yes, I thought they were. But also, no. Would we ever be truly ready to face giants in combat? I didn't answer – I wasn't sure what to say. I wasn't sure what he wanted me to say. Moses continued, 'I believe your troop is ready. They are men of valour, a mighty throng. It is no longer necessary to train them every day; all that is needed now is one day each week, *nu?*'

Only one day a week? Relief flooded my mind at the thought of bringing some balance back into my life, but it was immediately followed by a rush of fear and doubt. 'One day a week? Surely that will not suffice. What if the giants attack?' My thoughts scattered as I thought through the possibilities. I could see Moses studying my face. When he stared at me thus, it was as if he could see into my very soul; I found it unnerving. I looked away, concentrating on the ground ahead of me as we continued walking.

'Joshua, you have done well. You have been obedient in following Yahweh's call, heeding the instructions shown to you by His messengers, *nu*? But never forget that it is Yahweh Himself who gives the victory. *He* will break in pieces the oppressor. Train your men, yes! Clothe yourselves with strength, yes! Be ready to meet them in battle, yes! But never put your trust in the reach of a man's arm. Trust only in Yahweh. It is He, and He alone, who will vanquish our enemies. Hmm?'

I nodded, not trusting myself to speak. My thoughts were jumbled and I struggled to separate the many strands that flailed in my mind. Had I not been doing that? I trusted Yahweh. Didn't I? The giant's mocking voice echoed within the cavities of my mind.

'*You are a weak, pathetic creature.*'

'Joshua,' Moses said, putting his hand out to stop me walking again. He turned to face me. 'To defeat the giant without, you must first defeat the giant within.' *The giant within? What did he mean?* 'All of us must battle against giants at least once in our lives – for some, many times.' He must have seen the bewildered look on my face because he tutted and raised his hand. 'I speak not of the giants that you had sight of in Canaan, or the one I saw in the courts of Pharaoh – no, no. The giants I speak of are those that attack our thoughts, that pursue us in the hidden places of our hearts.'

'Forgive me, Master...' I mumbled, 'but what do these giants look like?'

'What do they look like?' Moses leaned in closer. 'What do they look like?' He scrunched up his eyes. Although I was more than a foot taller than him, and possibly twice as strong, he had always been able to cause my knees to tremble with just one piercing look. 'They look like *fear*, Joshua. They look like *fear*.'

'Fear?'

'Yes. Fear.' He continued to study me, trying to ascertain whether I was grasping his meaning. 'Joshua, what is it that you fear the most?' Another unexpected question. I was growing tired of trying to search out his meaning, of being bombarded with questions I didn't understand, let alone know how to answer. 'What do I fear the most? I don't know!' I thought to myself. I had never asked myself that question before. I frowned at him, confused and not a little frustrated.

'Let me ask you this: do you fear that, when the time comes, your men will not be able to defeat the giants? Do you fear that their skill in warfare will not be great enough?'

I thought about his question. 'There is no way of knowing what will take place, Master, but... no. No, I do not fear that. They are brave warriors, skilled in combat, and I have confidence in them.'

'Then what is it that you fear the most, Joshua? What is it?'

The curse reverberated through the hidden caverns of my thoughts.

'You are a weak, pathetic creature.'

I had the distinct impression that Moses knew the answer to the question he was asking me, but was willing me to find the answer without him having to tell me himself. I searched his eyes for clues, then it hit me with the force of a battering ram, jolting my soul to the point where my head jerked backwards.

'Yes?' His eyes widened in anticipation.

'I...' My breaths came in short, shallow bursts. 'My fear is not that my men will not be equal to the task. My fear is that *I* won't.'

Moses breathed out and leaned back, nodding. 'You fear that you are not sufficient for what lies before you?'

'Yes.' A strong wind had blown the fog from my mind; I could see clearly now. 'Until this moment my fear has been hidden from me. But I know it to be true. My fear is that I will have spent so long training these men to slay giants, when I myself will not be able to conquer the same adversary who I prepared them to meet in battle.' The pain of realising so great a fear was countered by a sense of immense relief, of being able to look at it square in the face and face it. I realised that my fear had been driving me and I, in turn, had been driving the giant slayers.

'Did you know of this?' I asked Moses.

He gave a little chuckle. 'I may have had an inkling.' He gestured to the path ahead and we resumed our walk. 'Your fear is unfounded, Joshua, although it would tell you otherwise. That is what fear does; fear is like a mouse masquerading as a lion. It positions itself in such a way that the rays of the sun cast a shadow, making it look mighty. But it is not. Fears are falsehoods, made of shifting shadows and, in the light of Yahweh's glory, those shadows are dispelled and our true selves can be unveiled.'

He turned to make eye contact with me as we walked. 'You *are* sufficient, Joshua. You are more than able to face the giants and cut them off from this earth. But it is not I who you need to hear that from, it is Yahweh. You can defeat the giant within you, the fear that drives you, by only one means – by coming before Yahweh. Do not let your fear cause you to oppress your troops needlessly. Let it propel you towards Yahweh, to seek His truth. Let understanding be pleasant to your soul. It will guard you. It will serve you well. Seek Him until you know your own heart. Pursue Him until you know, because *He* has told you that you are sufficient, that you are His mighty giant slayer.'

I frowned, wanting with all my heart to believe him.

'But for now,' Moses continued, 'just one day of training each week, yes? And return to your duties as you did before the training began.'

I cocked an eyebrow and gave Moses a lopsided grin. 'You would have me return to scribing?'

He chuckled. 'Among other things, yes.' Glancing at me, he hesitated, then murmured, 'I have felt the loss of your company, Joshua. Your absence has grieved my heart. I would have you return to me.'

I was dumbfounded. He missed me? I wanted to explain how much his words meant to me, to thank him and honour him... but my words were inadequate. Instead, I lowered my gaze and murmured in response, 'And I you, Master.'

24

Stinging Curtain

Rays of sun pierced Yahweh's glory cloud, warming my skin and lulling me into a state of blissful drowsiness. I lay on my back outside my tent, one forearm across my forehead, the other folded over my stomach. Our midday break was nearly over; the sun had moved from its position directly overhead and started its downward journey. I sighed, relishing the sacredness of my last few minutes of rest, when the primal, piercing blast of the shofar shattered the peace. I sat bolt upright and listened; it sounded over and over, relentless in its onslaught. That was not the call to assembly, or the call to break camp; that was the sound of the alarm!

'Giants!' I scrambled to my feet, reaching for my sword belt. Tightening it around my waist, I threw my headscarf around my shoulders and sprinted in the direction of the shofar's call. All around me, men emerged from their tents, drowsy with sleep.

'To me!' I shouted. 'Arm yourselves! Giant slayers to me!'

The call of the shofar was coming from the west side of the camp. Within minutes, I arrived at the west watchman's post, closely followed by a throng of warriors. 'Nosson,' I said, clambering up the rocky pile of stones that formed the base of his watching tower. 'How many are th...' My words petered out as I perused the horizon. Relief hit me, followed swiftly by a strong sense of foreboding. Our giant slayers would not be needed today; there were no giants attacking our camp. Instead, on the horizon, I saw a dirty, swirling curtain sweeping across the desert towards us.

A sandstorm!

Sandstorms were not a new experience for my people; they were part of the life of a desert sojourner and we had encountered many of them over the years. But I had not yet seen one as colossal as this appeared to be. Even though it was still a considerable distance away, already the reach of its dusty claws had begun to block out the light. The sky was turning a dirty ochre colour, the air becoming dull and oppressive.

I turned to the warriors gathered around and instructed them to relay messages throughout the camp, warning the people of the forthcoming storm, and reminding them of what to do. The tents in the middle of the camp would not be so ravaged by the storm; those on the outskirts of the camp would take the brunt of its fury. It was essential that they tied their tents down firmly and moved their belongings inside their tents, along with the smaller animals. They would cover the water vessels, wet their headscarves, bind them tightly around their faces, then take their families into their tents to sit the storm out.

Moses arrived just as I finished instructing the men, who leapt into action, running in all directions to relay the messages. I had just told Moses of the forthcoming danger, and what instructions I had given, when I heard the voice of one of the giant slayers behind me.

'Commander, what of Caleb?'

My heart skipped a beat. I pivoted slowly. 'What of him?'

'He took three units out this morning. They have not yet returned.'

My heart sank and an ominous sense of impending doom covered me. It felt like a huge hand was pushing down on me and squeezing my chest. 'Which units did he take with him?'

'He took Asael's, Modi's and...' I braced myself... 'Yoram's.'

My heart burst into a frantic, disjointed rhythm, my breaths shallow and erratic. 'Where were they headed?' I asked him.

'They went east, into the plains.'

'I must go,' I said, turning to the east. 'I must warn them before the storm reaches them.'

I turned to leave, but Moses put out his hand and stopped me. 'No. You cannot go. It will avail nothing.'

'I must go!' I argued. 'I must try to find them!'

'And what will you do, even if you do find them in time?'

'I will... I will help them prepare for its onslaught,' I cried. Anger and frustration assailed me – we were wasting valuable time. 'The storm is coming from the west. They will not see it until it is close to the camp and, by then, it will be too late. It will cut them off from us, drive them further away.'

'Joshua, you must trust Caleb. He has endured sandstorms before, he knows the ways of the desert wanderer.'

'Does he?' I demanded. I wracked my brains, trying to remember whether Caleb had experienced a sandstorm in the open plains before. 'He knows how to survive a sandstorm here in the camp, but does he know what to do out there, in the open?' I asked, jabbing my finger in the direction of the plains to the east.

In a large campsite, the best way to survive a desert sandstorm was to tie everything down, protect yourselves and stay under shelter, away from the turbulent lashing of the sand. When travelling in the open plains, however, the opposite was true. You had to keep moving. With nothing to shelter you, as soon as you stood still, the sand would gather around you, weighing you down so that you could not move, until all that remained when it was over was a smooth heap of sand. Those who did not continue to move paid the price, dying a slow, agonising death by suffocation. Yes, it was torment to keep going, stumbling headlong into the assault of that stinging curtain, but it was certain death to stand still.

'Joshua, you must trust Caleb.' Seeing the hesitation that still clouded my face, Moses took a deep breath, squared his shoulders, and said, 'I charge you to stay in the camp. You are not to go out into the plains.'

I stared at him, incredulous. Was he actually forbidding me to leave? My face contorted with disbelief. He was. The young giant slayer who stood nearby, with Nosson the watchman, lowered his gaze and stood in awkward silence, unmoving. Everything in me longed to defy Moses, but I could not. As much as I wanted to, I could not do it.

'I will stay at the watchman's tower on the east side of the camp until the storm has passed,' I muttered before stalking off. As soon as I arrived there, I sent the watchman home to his family and took his place, ready to keep a solitary vigil. I could hear the howling of the winds and the sounds of frightened animals behind me in the camp as the storm swept through our ranks, but I didn't look behind me. I scanned the horizon in the east for any sign of Caleb and his men.

Nothing.

I continued to scour the plains until the sandstorm prevented me from seeing further.

It began with a breathless dance of shifting, scurrying grains of sand and tumbleweed; compelling and alluring, moving to the accompaniment of a whistling wind. The closer the storm drew, the louder the noise became. It changed forms, creating a growing sense of trepidation as its swirling curtain moved towards us. The whistling turned to rustling, the rustling to a hissing, then to a resounding roar. The wilderness that we traversed was rocky, so the sand was mixed with large amounts of dirt, stones and debris which lashed at your skin, striking legs, arms and face. Funnels of wind created miniature tornados that sucked up everything in their path and, when the full onslaught of the storm hit, it exploded into a howling plethora of stinging, biting missiles.

I crouched down, taking cover behind the stony walls of the watchtower – much good though it did me. For what felt like hours, I cowered on the floor as the streaming chaos launched the full fury of its assault. When the worst of it was over and the tempest moved past our camp and into the plains to the east, I stood up again, trying to peer into the distance. My eyes stung; tears streamed down my face in an involuntary attempt to wash the dust and sand away. Breathing was no longer instinctual; each breath was laboured and deliberate. My throat was on fire; I choked, gagging on the tiny grains of sand and dust that had managed to filter through the flimsy covering of my headscarf. Sand searches out every weak spot; the finest particles even penetrate the pores of the skin, creating a distressing irritation.

As soon as the storm's wind had passed on, I took out my waterskin, trickled some water over my face, and washed my eyes. Spitting out the particles of sand that lodged in my throat, I drank deeply, then crossed my arms and positioned myself to keeping watching, ignoring the incessant urge to scratch my arms and legs.

'Yahweh, protect them,' I muttered, studying the dirty, swirling curtain as it continued its journey across the desert plains. 'Protect them. Keep them safe.'

The retreating storm left in its wake an eerie silence but, gradually, people started emerging from their tents, wiping their streaming eyes, coughing and shaking their heads in shock at the chaos that surrounded them. I was right, this had been no ordinary sandstorm; we had not experienced one of this magnitude before. The landscape of our camp had changed; things that were not tied down securely were in total disarray, and everything was coated in layers of dust, dirt and sand. The colour and life had been sucked out of the camp; all was now dull ochre or brown, and dust-ridden.

After a short while, the watchman returned to take up his post once again. I was grateful for his sight, and for his company. I toyed with the idea of going to check on my family to see how they had fared, but only for a few seconds. I couldn't leave the watchman's tower until I knew what had become of our warriors, and I could not tolerate the thought of having to tell them that Yoram was missing. No. I would stay here and wait it out.

I felt like a captive chained to the walls of the watchtower. I could do nothing but stare into the distance, squinting in an effort to try to see further. After a while, I climbed down and stood in the area just in front of the tower, hands on my hips, peering at the dirty skyline. A surge of resentment rose up in me, like the bitter taste of bile in my mouth. 'How can he forbid me?' I muttered. 'Why must he stop me from seeking them out?' I started pacing up and down. I had to do something. The danger was past. Surely there was nothing to stop me from going to find them now. I was considering disobeying Moses and going anyway when the watchman's voice interrupted me.

'Joshua!'

'What is it?' I shouted, scaling the steps of the tower two at a time. 'What do you see?'

'Men.'

'How many?' I asked. 'How many do you see? *How many?*'

'Seven...,' he said, counting silently. 'No, nine...'

'Nine? Are you certain?' I demanded. Nine? Why not ten? There should be ten. Who was missing? Please, please don't let it be...

'No, ten! There are ten men, my lord.'

'Yahweh be praised!' I shouted, grabbing him by the shoulders and kissing him soundly on his dusty cheeks. 'They are saved!' Without waiting for further confirmation, I rushed down the jagged steps and started sprinting towards the group of dots on the horizon, headscarf trailing behind me, my feet kicking up a steady stream of dust and sand. I slowed down after a few minutes – my heart was racing, and breathing the thick air was still difficult – so I wrapped my damp headscarf around my face and continued running at a steady pace until they were close enough for me to identify their faces.

They were all there. All of them – safe! Yahweh be praised! But they were walking very slowly, some of them limping or hobbling, and one of them was being led by two of his comrades, his eyes covered by his headscarf. The closer I came, the clearer I could see the expressions on their faces; my elation turned to concern. Their faces were streaked with dirt and all of them, without exception, had bloody gashes on their arms, legs or face. Every now and then, they would stop to retch or vomit, and all of them coughed with monotonous regularity.

I went straight to Caleb, embraced him, and kissed him on each of his hot, dirty cheeks before turning to Yoram. 'Yori,' I said, holding him tightly. 'Are you well?' I asked, noticing a large bloody gash that ran down one side of his forehead to the edge of his eyebrow.

'I am well,' he rasped, before succumbing to a coughing fit and turning to vomit.

I spoke to each one individually, getting the measure of how they had fared, until I came to the young man whose headscarf was wound around his head, covering his eyes. 'Tappuah?' I said, putting my hand on his shoulder.

'Commander,' he rasped, trying to stand to attention.

'Be at peace, please,' I told him. 'Tappuah, your eyes – what took place?'

'The storm tore my headscarf off, Commander. My eyes took the full force of the storm.'

I glanced at Caleb, who signalled to me that Tappuah had lost his sight. Squeezing the young man's shoulder, I told him, 'We will ask the healers to tend to you as soon as we return to camp, *nu?*' Our band of stragglers limped into camp and were seen first by the healers, before being released to go to their families. Tappuah still could not see clearly, but had regained partial sight in one eye. Caleb told me that when his headscarf unwound in the force of the storm, a smattering of stones had struck his eyes. Caleb and I met with Moses, and Caleb told us what happened when the storm had struck. It was as Moses had said – Caleb had led the units onwards in the storm, walking steadily through it.

'How did you know you were walking in the right direction?' Moses asked him.

'I didn't,' he replied. 'I just knew we had to keep walking, or we would meet our end.'

His report was brief – he was exhausted and talking was difficult – so Moses did not prolong the meeting, and sent him back to his family. It was only later that night that I found out what had really happened.

I took Yoram home, broke bread with my family and, while we sat together by the firepit after the children had gone to sleep, Yoram gave us a more detailed account of the afternoon's events. They were still quite far out in the plains to the east when they saw the approaching sandstorm. Caleb knew they would not be able to get back to camp in time, so he ordered the men to pair up and tie themselves together using their belts. They soaked their headscarves with water from their skins and bound them tightly around their heads (although, unfortunately for Tappuah, his scarf had not been tied securely enough). Caleb instructed them to form a column of five sets of pairs, two abreast; he and Iru stood in the front, leading the formation. He told the young men to stand close behind the pair in front of them and grasp the shoulder of the man ahead of him, leaving one hand free to shield their face or attend to their needs. It was when he gave the final instruction, however, that things started to go wrong.

Caleb told the men that they would stay in this formation and march forward at a steady pace. Three of the men retaliated immediately, panicking at the thought of walking directly into the tempestuous storm that was now nearly upon them. They insisted that the best plan was to band together, facing inwards, and hold fast. Their insubordination was fuelled by fear, and a vicious dispute took place but, finally, with the support of some of the other warriors, Caleb talked them down and they agreed to heed his instructions.

Yoram looked at those of us gathered around the fire. 'I know Caleb is a mighty warrior – I have seen him fight. He is bold and fearless and has much skill in warfare.' Mesha lowered his head when his son spoke of Caleb in that manner but, for the first time in my recollection, he didn't make scornful sounds or try to change the topic of conversation. 'But, until today,' Yoram continued, 'I had never heard him speak with such authority, such conviction.' Looking directly at his father, he said, 'Without Caleb's leading, we would have perished in the storm.'

Mesha stared into Yoram's bloodshot eyes for a long while before nodding silently. He reached out to touch the ugly gash on the side of Yoram's brow. In time, the wound would heal, but the scar that it would leave behind would become a constant reminder to him, and to me, of what Yoram endured that day, and of the courage and wisdom of the man who had saved him from an agonising, untimely death.

The following day, Mesha arrived at the training grounds in the middle of the morning. The tribe of Benjamin was not scheduled for training, but when Caleb and I saw him approaching, we knew why he had come. Since the day of the trials, Mesha had avoided Caleb. He was careful to attend training when the tribe of Benjamin was scheduled, and continued to carry out his duties as a captain without reproach. But he never looked at Caleb, or spoke to him directly, unless it was unavoidable.

Now, however, he stood tall and looked directly at Caleb.

'*Shalom*, Caleb, Joshua. I... Yoram told...' He paused to steady himself, taking a deep breath in and breathing it out. 'What you did yesterday... I am indebted to you.' He put his hand on his chest and bowed his head, eyes still fixed on Caleb. Mesha's voice broke with emotion as he said, 'With all my heart, thank you.'

Thankfully, Caleb did not respond with a glib comment or try to dismiss Mesha's words. He responded by placing his hand over his heart and bowed to Mesha in like manner. Mesha stared at him, the set of his face crumbling, his eyes softening. His mouth opened and he appeared to search for words, but was unable to find them. Instead, he nodded, glanced at me, and turned to walk back the way he had come.

25

The Rhythm of Life

The years passed by in a steady rhythm of summer and winter, rain and drought, journeying and settling. We were presently camped at Mithkah, or 'sweetness', so named because of the sweetness of the pastures, and the rivers of water that ran through that land. Indeed, it was a sweet time, a time of peace and contentment. Our family had grown considerably over the years of our sojourning. We escaped Egypt as a family of eleven adults and eight children and now, twenty-five years into our desert wandering, our community had nearly trebled in size. Jesher and Shira's children all had their own children, and their children had given birth to children.

'We are flourishing!' I thought to myself, with immense satisfaction.

Shira had seen nearly ninety winters. She was frail and wrinkled, and her hands were stiff and shrivelled with age. She could do little for herself because of her affliction, and needed help to carry out even the most basic tasks such as dressing, eating and bathing, and yet, owing to the transformation that had taken place in her heart after Jesher's passing, there was a fragile beauty about her. Instead of being bitter and resentful, she expressed gratitude to her daughters and granddaughters when they assisted her. I couldn't help but marvel when I thought back to the self-opinionated, hard-hearted woman she had been when I first became part of Jesher's family. In those days, my sole aim was to try to honour her, if only for Jesher's sake; I avoided conversation with her at all costs. Now, however, I found myself looking for opportunities to sit and talk with her, each time revelling in the miracle that had taken place in her heart.

One night, when we had just finished the evening meal, I settled Shira near the firepit and Alya brought a thick sheepskin to wrap around her shoulders. Winter was fast approaching and she felt the cold more keenly than the rest of us.

'Yahweh bless you, Alya.' Shira gave her a warm smile and settled back to ponder the spurts of flames that danced in the firepit when I stirred the embers. The rest of the family were busy settling children down for the night or doing chores, so I kept Shira company. She looked deep in thought and I saw various emotions flicker over her face as she sat there.

'*Ima?*'

'Yes, my son?'

'You seem much diverted. What do your thoughts dwell on?'

She pondered for a moment. 'I was thinking about the perils of growing old.' She smiled at me and, when I waited for her to explain, she studied the fire and continued. 'When I was young, the thought of growing old filled me with fear. To be dependent upon others, unable to care for yourself, unable to work or be seen as useful... I could not imagine a greater curse. My pride in my ability to cook and sew, to keep a good house and raise children, was such that I grew to believe that the work of my hands was the source of my worth. If I could no longer work or be useful, I was no longer worthy of respect... or love. I was afraid to grow old. I was fearful of dying. I have learned much about the blessing of being able to receive love and care from others; I have gained understanding of what a beautiful thing it is to be in need of help and to receive it.' Shira turned to look at me. 'I'm no longer afraid. I am old and full of days, and ready to leave this world, when Yahweh determines that my time has come.'

I reached out and took hold of her hand. 'Age has not soured you, *Ima*. It has made you beautiful.'

'You speak truth, but it has happened by Yahweh's grace alone. I was filled with such sourness when I was younger – like bitter wine, foul to the taste.' She frowned and shook her head, obviously thinking back to some of the things she had said and done over the years. 'I am so thankful to Yahweh for giving me these years to make things right with those I love, to restore that which I had damaged. He has helped me redeem the years that were eaten away by bitterness and pain.' She glanced at me, blinking back tears. 'These seventeen years without Jesher have been the most astonishing years of my life. I have come to realise and be at peace with who I am, without the need to prove my worth by my works. These years have brought me peace and much joy. But they have also been the cruellest, most heart-wrenching years of my life, because I have had to discover these things by myself, without Jesher. It is a great mystery to me how such pain and such beauty can dwell side by side.'

I squeezed Shira's hand ever so gently. She placed her other hand on top of mine and stroked it. Her hand shook, her fingers deformed and stiff, but her touch was soft and warm. I closed my eyes to capture that moment and store it in my memory, at the same time remembering Jesher's hands clasping mine shortly before he passed away all those years ago. After a little while I heard Shira sigh. I looked up to see her grimacing in pain as she leaned forward, adjusting her position. I pulled the sheepskin tighter around her shoulders – there was nothing else I could do to ease her suffering – and was rewarded with an adoring smile.

'I could never understand why Jesher spent so much time sitting out here, just watching people,' she said with a chuckle. 'It angered me greatly. I thought him lazy, and wondered how he could be so indolent when there was much to be done, so many tasks to be accomplished. That is why I was so vexed when you told us about the new laws of Shabbat.' She grimaced and asked, 'Do you remember that day?'

'I remember it well,' I said, looking at her in amusement.

'Mmm. I was so angry! Not to be allowed to work for a whole day, when there was so much to be done! I could not fathom why Yahweh would have us be idle for a whole day. But now I understand.' She gave a satisfied sigh. 'It is important to sit and be still for a while, *nu*? To have time just to think, just to be. My whole life I had been busy... busy doing this, busy doing that... always busy, always *doing*. But I have found the beauty in *being* – not doing anything, just being. Jesher knew that. That was his secret. He knew how to rest, how to *be*. He was at peace with his own soul.' She glanced at me with a mischievous glint in her eye. 'Now that I know his secret, I can do likewise!'

171

I leaned over to kiss her weather-beaten cheek, and put my arm around her. She leaned against me, snuggling into my embrace like a child tucked under the arm of their parent.

Shira died a few weeks later, not sitting outside watching the world go by, as Jesher had, but lying on her bed surrounded by a family who truly loved her, and would now truly mourn her passing. I was with them, privileged to see the peaceful smile on her face as she breathed her last.

The weeks after Shira's passing seemed to be shadowed with death, some anticipated, but some unexpected. Abidan, elder of our family's tribe of Benjamin, passed away peacefully from old age. He had been known for his wisdom and courage, as well as his passion for the ways of Yahweh, and would be greatly mourned. His sight had diminished over the course of his latter years, so Attai, his grandson, had been his constant companion and helper. Attai seemed to have gleaned much wisdom from the years he had spent assisting his grandfather, and was also well respected.

'There is a young man with favour resting on him,' Moses whispered to me, pointing at Attai. 'He may not be a great warrior, but I have talked with him and found him prudent in speech; counsel and sound judgement are his. His heart is loyal, and faithfulness surrounds him. He will serve you well in times to come.' I wanted to ask Moses what he meant by that, but the moment passed and I didn't get the opportunity. It was only some years later that I would recall his words; he was right, Attai would serve me well.

Abidan's death was expected, as were the deaths of several of our esteemed elders who died around that time. There was one, however, that was unexpected. Hareph had been coughing for many months, but we didn't pay him much heed – not because we didn't care, but because we thought this was just another one of a steady stream of maladies that afflicted Hareph, coming and going over the years. This ailment came but, unlike the others, it never left. Hareph's hacking cough became more frequent, and more severe, until the day came when he could no longer draw breath.

Eglah bore his death just as she faced each day of her life: with a quiet dignity. Their son, Davi, now in his eighteenth year, was a great comfort to his mother during that time. He had inherited his father's inquisitive mind and tender heart, as well as his mother's wisdom and intuitiveness. However, in appearance he was nothing like either of them. Guilt plagued me whenever I thought of it, but I couldn't help but wonder how a homely couple like Hareph and Eglah could have produced such a handsome son. Hareph was many things, but fair of countenance was not one of them and, although Eglah bore herself with grace and dignity, she could not have been called a beauty. Davi had been given the best of both his parents' natures, but none of their physical shortcomings, and yet he was oblivious of that fact. His heart was humble and tender, he cared deeply about others, especially his family, and he had a warmth that caused others to love and trust him.

He stood by Eglah and supported her with such tenderness when Hareph died. Many times over the course of those first few weeks, when I looked at Davi, I felt Hareph was still with us. I felt his gentleness and saw his kindness when I looked into the face of his son; it comforted me greatly. But as I studied Davi, I shivered at the thought which shadowed my mind: how would this kind-hearted young man fare if he were to face a giant one day?

26

Judgment Seat

He loathed it. Sitting for hours on end, listening to a never-ending repertoire of complaints or arguments was Moses' least favourite pastime. The older he grew, the more impatient he seemed to become, especially with those individuals whose only interest seemed to be in picking apart the laws of Yahweh.

Yahweh had given us a set of commandments when we encountered His glory at the foot of Mount Sinai, near the beginning of our nomadic journey – laws about food and health, morality, money, marriage, feasts and celebrations, property and relationships. Moses and I (once I had learned how to scribe sufficiently well) painstakingly recorded these laws on parchment and Moses taught them to the elders so they, in turn, could teach our people the ways of Yahweh. The laws He gave us were good and profitable for walking in the way of righteousness, but there were those who tried to use them for their own ends to exert power over others.

'Why can they not see the heart of Yahweh in His laws?' Moses grumbled after a particularly trying morning. 'They cannot see Yahweh's kindness in giving us these ordinances to guide and protect us. They see only a list of commands that they can use to trap others or prove their own virtue.' He put his head in his hands, rubbing his temples with his thumbs. 'There is time for one more case before our midday break, yes?' he asked me. 'Who is the next supplicant?'

'Pelet ben Amnon,' I replied, reading the parchment in my hand. 'He brings a charge against a man named Shimon, of the tribe of Asher.' Moses groaned. 'Is he known to you, Master?' I asked.

'Yes. I know him well. A more self-righteous, judgemental man you

175

would struggle to find.' I could see the conflict that was raging in Moses' mind; it was written all over his face. He scratched his beard, shook his head from side to side, and muttered under his breath. Then, all of a sudden, he lifted his head and stared at me. 'Mmm.' The look on his face made me increasingly nervous. I didn't ask him what he was thinking – I wasn't sure I wanted to hear the answer. 'Joshua,' he said, still peering at me intently. 'You will judge this case on my behalf.'

'Me?' I was appalled. 'I cannot...'

'Yes, you can. It is decided,' he said, standing to his feet. 'You must learn how to sit in the seat of judgement. Come! Let us inform the court.'

'Master, I cannot do this.' I whispered. Standing to my feet, I grabbed his arm in a panic. 'I am a warrior, not a judge.'

'Yes, you are a warrior,' he said, then his face broke into a smile. 'But you are also a man of much wisdom who knows the ways of Yahweh and loves His commandments with a true heart. I have faith in you, Joshua. You must learn to trust yourself as I trust you, *nu?*'

'I beg of you, do not...'

'Come. It is time.'

Moses told the court in no uncertain terms that the judgements I pronounced and the words I declared were as good as the words that came out of his mouth. Before I knew it, he was gone and I was left standing alone at the front of the Tent of Meeting, my face flushed with a mixture of embarrassment and anger. The elders and onlookers who were in the Tent of Meeting looked as shocked as I was. I was mortified. What must they think of me? Did they think I had pushed my way forward, that this was of my making? They must know, as I did, that I was totally unsuited and unprepared for a task of this importance. Whatever their thoughts, however, I had no option but to do as Moses had instructed; the sooner I heard the case, the sooner I could leave. I perched on the edge of Moses's judgement seat and checked the parchment in my hand to make sure I had the name right.

'Pelet ben Amnon,' I said. 'You have a charge to bring against Shimon ben Omar?'

'I do, my... uh... Joshua,' he said, clearly unimpressed that his case was to be judged by me and not by Moses. He sauntered up to the front, half-dragging an old man behind him. To say that the old man was scrawny would have been kind. His face was gaunt and grey; he looked ill. His eyes darted up at me and he bowed in respect before looking back at the ground. His hands were trembling. I resisted the urge to go to his side to help steady him, and focused instead on Pelet.

'What is the charge?' I asked him. 'What has this man done?'

'I caught him carrying wood on Shabbat, my... Joshua,' Pelet announced in a loud voice. 'We all know the penalty for defying the laws of Shabbat, do we not?' he said, swinging around to make eye contact with the other men standing or sitting around the tent. 'Any man who works on Shabbat must be put to *death*,' he announced with a hiss. His dramatic rhetoric was rewarded with a burst of chattering and mumbling from the congregation. I put my hand up to silence them.

'When did this take place?' I asked Pelet, aware that Shimon's shoulders were starting to sag.

'Last Shabbat, just after the sun had set,' he replied with a self-righteous smirk. 'I saw him walking around the outskirts of the camp, carrying a bundle of wood. He was trying to avoid being seen, but he did not escape my notice,' he said with a flourish.

'So it seems,' I muttered. I was beginning to understand why Moses rolled his eyes at the mention of this man's name. I already had a strong dislike for him, and this was only our first meeting. Turning to Shimon, I asked, 'Your name is Shimon ben Omar, is that true?'

'It is, my lord.'

'Why were you carrying wood on Shabbat?' I asked him gently, fearing that he might soon fall over.

Pelet huffed. 'The laws of Shabbat are clear, are they not?' He glared at me with disdain. 'What does it matter what his reasons are?'

'You have presented your case,' I said, giving Pelet a cold stare. 'You will be silent now while I talk to Shimon.' He balked at my words, then put his nose in the air, crossed his arms and looked the other way. 'Please, continue,' I said to Shimon.

'My lord, it was not in my heart to break our Shabbat laws. I am a true follower of Yahweh; I strive to live by His commandments.' I heard Pelet guffaw at Shimon's words, but chose to ignore his rudeness. 'I went to gather wood so I could make a fire to warm some broth for my *ima*. She is not long for this world, my lord. I only wanted to ease her passing, but I am not a young man any more and it took me longer than I thought it would.'

I looked at Shimon and saw no guile, no deceit. There was purity in his gaze; he was speaking the truth. But the fact remained, he had broken the laws of Shabbat. My heart was much conflicted. 'Yahweh, help me,' I prayed silently, desperate to find a way to nullify the sentence that I knew must stand. I could see concern on many of the faces of the assembly; clearly, they agreed with me, although they also could not voice it.

'What did you do with the wood you had gathered, when Pelet found you?' I asked Shimon.

'He took it from me, my lord.'

'Pelet took the wood away from you?'

'He did, my lord.'

Pelet's haughty tones interrupted our discourse. 'I could not let him continue breaking the law, so I took the wood from him, as evidence of his crime. I have brought it with me – it is over here,' he said, gesturing to a pile of timber and thorny branches on the side of the tent.

'You took the wood away from him?' I questioned.

'I did, so I could bring it to this court as evidence.'

'You carried the wood back to your tent, so you could bring it to this court as evidence of Shimon's crime?'

'I did. I carried it home and kept it...' Pelet's voice dried up in horror-struck realisation. The blood drained from his face. A sense of foreboding filled the tent; all conversation halted; all eyes were focused on the accuser. Everyone held their breath.

'You carried wood on Shabbat?' I asked him.

'I... I...' he stuttered, his eyes distended, gawking in shock.

I leaned forward in my chair and stared into his mean little eyes. 'As you yourself reminded us, Pelet, the penalty for breaking the laws of Shabbat is death.'

'I... no! I didn't...' he gasped, like a fish out of water.

'I will have no choice but to carry out the sentence,' I said, eyes still locked on him, 'unless...'

'Unless... my lord?' I stifled a smile at his pitiful effort to make amends by calling me 'my lord'.

'Unless perhaps you feel you have misunderstood the situation? Made an error of judgement? Perhaps you did not see what you thought you did. Would you prefer to withdraw the charges you brought against Shimon?'

He frowned. 'I... well, I... uh...' Breaking eye contact with me for the first time, he glanced around the tent, but was met with a solid wall of unsympathetic faces. He flushed in anger, looked down and mumbled, 'Very well. I withdraw my charge.'

'So be it,' I said. 'We will strike this case from the records. However, there will be a penalty to pay, as you have taken much of this court's time needlessly. You are to gather ten bundles of wood, tie them securely and bring them here to this Tent of Meeting by sundown this evening.'

'Ten bundles? This evening?' he blustered in anger. 'I cannot...' Seeing the steely expression on my face, he stopped short. 'Yes, my lord,' he simpered, bowing repeatedly. 'Ten bundles. I will bring them before the sun sets.'

'You may take your leave,' I said. Pelet flounced out of the Tent of Meeting as I dismissed the assembly and walked towards Shimon, who stood trembling, still unsure of his fate. 'Shimon, is your *ima* still alive?'

'She is, my lord, but I fear she does not have long,' Shimon whispered. I saw tears fill his eyes and he lowered his head. I took hold of his arm to steady him.

'Have you no other family to help you care for her?'

'No, my lord. I am her only son. My *abba* died when I was but a boy in Egypt and I have always cared for my *ima* on my own. I never married.' My heart constricted with compassion for this man. I knew what it was like to be an only child, forced to watch your parent die in less than ideal circumstances.

'Shimon, would you permit me to come to your tent to meet your *ima*?'

'Permit you...? It would be my honour, my lord, but I have nothing to offer you...'

'I want nothing from you but to meet your *ima*,' I reassured him before sending him home to his *ima* on the arm of one of the elders who was camped nearby. I noticed that Abidan's grandson, Attai, who had been part of the assembly that morning, still lingered at the back of the tent. Once Shimon left, Attai approached me. 'My lord, please permit me to say...' he paused, seeming to search for the right words. 'You showed much wisdom in your judgement of this case.'

I thanked him, then a thought occurred to me. 'Attai, are you needed somewhere?'

'No, my lord. I have been my *saba*'s companion for many years, aiding him when his eyes grew dim. But, as you know, he passed away. Do you have need of me?' he asked.

'I do,' I said, an idea forming in my mind. That afternoon, Attai and I gathered supplies and went together to see Shimon and his *ima*. We took with us warm fleeces, fuel for a fire, some of Helah's freshly made broth, a few of Alya's herbal remedies, grains, fruit and oil, a full skin of water, and two newly formed clay dishes. Attai found two other men to help him collect the ten bundles of wood from the Tent of Meeting that evening, and bring them to Shimon's tent. Tears filled Shimon's eyes as he saw all that we had brought; the firewood alone would last him many days.

Attai and I stayed with Shimon and his *ima*, prayed blessings upon them and made sure they had all that they needed. When Moses heard of my judgement later that evening, he not only agreed with my decision, chuckling as he imagined Pelet's fury at being outwitted, but insisted on coming with me to visit Shimon and his mother the following day. Shimon, overawed at the sudden arrival of our nation's leader in his tiny, shabby tent, could hardly speak. He bowed repeatedly, stuttering a greeting, until Moses stopped him by drawing him into a fatherly embrace. Once Shimon had recovered enough to speak, the two men spoke for hours. I discovered that what Shimon said was true: he was a true follower of Yahweh and he knew, and loved, His commandments.

When Shimon's *ima* passed away a few days later, she was warm and comfortable, with a full belly and a peaceful smile on her face. Shimon told me that, of all the time they had spent together over their lives, their last few days together were the most precious. I looked after

Shimon for many years afterwards, until his own passing, making sure that he wanted for nothing, including company and love.

That was the first time I sat as judge on behalf of Moses, but it would not be the last. Time and time again during the years to come, I found myself sitting in his seat, pronouncing judgements in his name. Although I never relished the task of pronouncing verdicts, and was still uncomfortable having to decide the fate of those who stood before me, I gained much experience in dispensing justice and learned not to spurn such an honourable responsibility.

Of all the cases I judged over the course of time, however, the one that would be forever seared in my memory, and in my heart, was that of Pelet and Shimon.

27

Patriarch

'Azriel's death was as the call of an alarm to Mesha,' Helah explained. 'He knows his time is coming, but does not know how to prepare himself. His heart is empty of ambition, Yoshi. He has no desire to lead this family. It is an honour he would refuse – if he could.' Helah blinked away the tears and gave me a watery smile. 'But he cannot.'

We walked together through the camp on our way to deliver some baskets which Helah had woven. From a young age, she had developed great skill in weaving and still now, in her latter years, whenever we sat around the firepit in the evenings, Helah would have her basket of tender green palm fronds next to her. Her nimble fingers would tear the fronds into precise strips, weaving them into beautiful patterns with great dexterity, and she delighted in teaching the youngsters how to weave baskets, mats or coverings, and paint colourful designs on them.

'What does Mesha fill his days with, now that he no longer serves in the army?' I asked her. 'Is he still tentmaking?'

'He sits with Yoram and Arad when they work but, more often than not, he just watches them. He takes great pleasure in seeing their work. It pleases him that he has passed on his skill in tentmaking to his sons and that they, in turn, are passing it on to their sons.'

I smiled and nodded. 'That is a worthy legacy. He has been a good father to his children, and he is beloved of his grandchildren.'

'He is,' she said, giving a little chuckle. 'It is when he plays with his grandchildren that I see the life return to him. That is when he is once again my Mesha; my headstrong, wild, fun-loving Mesha. They love him for it, as do I. He plays with his grandchildren in the same way he played with our children when they were young. Sometimes I cannot believe he has seen nearly seventy winters.'

'You speak truth; he is still strong and comely, and your sons look to follow in his footsteps, *nu*?' She looked at me with pride, and we walked on in silence until I interrupted her contemplation. 'Helah, Mesha no longer talks to me about matters of the heart. Tell me, is he at peace? Is he at peace with me, with Caleb...?'

The smile fell from Helah's face. She sighed. 'He doesn't talk much about you or Caleb. It is as if that part of his heart has been closed off. He will not tear open that gateway – not because he does not want to – ' she added, watching the expression on my face to make sure her words were not causing me grief, 'but because he doesn't know how to.' She paused for a moment, waiting for me to respond. When I didn't, she continued. 'Mesha has always loved you, Yoshi, you know that. You will always be the brother of his heart. That is why it broke him when he thought he had lost you to Caleb.'

'He did not lose me. He could never lose me,' I protested, frowning at the absurdity of that concept.

'I know that and I think he knows that now, but so much has happened, so many words were spoken which cannot be taken back, and so much time has passed. It is hard to go back, to try to repair that which was broken.'

'Helah, we don't know how long he...' I stopped short. 'Should I say it?' I wondered to myself. I studied the steady trudging of my feet in the dirt as we walked. Should I put voice to the question that I knew haunted both of us, but which we were both unwilling to say out loud? I took a deep breath in and exhaled. Yes. It must be said. 'I would have Mesha be at peace with this world, and with all who dwell in it, before he meets his end.'

There. I had said it.

We had but three years left of our forty years as desert wanderers and, sometime within those three years, Mesha would go the way of all the earth. My greatest desire was that he did not pass away not having reconciled with those he had anything against. Helah just nodded. We walked the rest of the way in silence, both wrestling with our thoughts, both unwilling to say any more on the subject. It was as if, by voicing my fears, some unseen countdown had begun; we were now just marking off the days until Mesha would be taken from us.

Another countdown had started crowding my thoughts in recent weeks. I knew I was also marking off the days until I would have to face the giants of my dreams and confront my deepest fear: was I a victorious, giant vanquishing warrior, or the 'weak, pathetic creature' that they cursed me to be?

28

Speak or Strike

My conversation with Helah replayed in my mind many times over the following months, but the time never seemed right for me to broach the subject with Mesha. During that time, Leora breathed her last and rested with her husband, Azriel, and time moved on. The illusive progression of light and shadow, morning and evening, summer and winter passed by, and still Mesha and I had not spoken of the things that were buried deep in our hearts.

As the time to enter Canaan grew nearer, Yahweh's cloud led us into the Wilderness of Zin, a rocky terrain, and we were confronted with a situation that was all too familiar: insufficient water for a people as great and numerous as ours. The last time this had happened was at Rephidim, in the first year of our sojourning. I thought back to the miracle that had taken place at that time, picturing Moses standing on a huge rock with his staff in hand. The memory was still fresh in my mind, such had been its impact. He had lifted his staff with both hands and struck the rock with all the strength he could muster. An earth-shattering crack had sounded, followed by a mighty rumbling as the earth we stood on began to shake and moan. It was terrifying, but exhilarating at the same time. The result of that cacophonous noise was a torrential outpouring of water which flowed from the midst of that ruptured rock, silencing the rebellious voices that had cried out only moments before, for Moses' death.

Nearly forty years had passed since then and yet, once again, our people raised their voices in uproar at the lack of water, questioning the power of the God of Israel, and challenging His chosen leader. Aaron and I stood with Moses as he surveyed the mass of fearful, defiant people who swarmed below us. We had spent much time that morning in the Tabernacle, praying and seeking Yahweh's face, and He had spoken.

'Gather the people together and go to the rock, you and your brother, Aaron. Speak to that rock in front of the people, and it will bring forth water for them and their livestock.'

Moses scowled at the multitude of hostile faces; he was not in good humour. He had never been a man who suffered fools well but, the older he grew, the more impatient he seemed to become. He was angry. Very angry.

'For nearly forty years we have wandered this wilderness,' he muttered, scrunching his eyes up to protect them from the glare of the sun. '*Forty years*! In all that time, Yahweh has sustained us and provided everything we have need of, and yet still, they do not trust Him. Still, they rebel against Him and do not believe His words.' Aaron, Eleazar and I glanced at each other, but said nothing. We knew all too well that when Moses became zealous for Yahweh, it was best to stay silent. Moses continued glaring at the masses for a while longer, mumbling under his breath. Then he lifted his staff and bellowed, '*Listen to me, you rebellious people! You demand water from our God? Well, then, let it be so!*' He pounded his staff on the rock, and the crowds below gasped. A few screams rippled through the congregation, anticipating a demonstration of Yahweh's might.

But nothing happened.

I glanced at Aaron, who frowned with concern. He started to move towards Moses but, before he could take a step, Moses lifted his staff again and struck the rock with a mighty roar. This time, the earth obeyed his command, shuddering and rumbling in response to his touch. A deluge of water poured out of a massive crack that opened in the rock, flooding the area below us within minutes. It was just as it had been all those years ago; the angry cries of the multitude changed within moments into shouts of joy and celebration.

'Double-souled people,' Moses spat, before turning on his heel, stalking off in the direction of his tent without a backward glance. He had no need of me that afternoon, so it was only the following morning that I saw him. I found him much changed. He hardly spoke a word and, instead of continuing our work of chronicling our people's journeys in the wilderness, Moses went straight to the Tabernacle and spent the rest of the day on his face before Yahweh. The following day repeated the pattern of the first day, and the day after that. On the fourth day, he summoned me early in the morning and asked me to walk with him up into the mountains that surrounded the camp.

We walked in silence until the sun was well risen, before finding a place to sit down. 'Joshua, there is something I must tell you,' he said, staring into the distance. His tone was measured and calm, almost devoid of emotion. I didn't like it. It made me uneasy.

'Master?'

He took a deep breath. 'Joshua, Yahweh has declared that I should not go into the land of Canaan.'

'We are not going into Canaan? But wh...'

'Not we. I.' He turned to look at me. 'I will not enter the land Yahweh has given to us.'

'But... no!' I felt the colour drain from my face. A dizziness swamped my senses. 'Why, Master? I don't understand.'

'It is due to my own disobedience, Joshua. Yahweh commanded me to speak to the rock, and then water would be released.'

I nodded. 'Yes, I remember. You did so, and the rock brought forth water, just as it did at Rephidim.'

'No, Joshua. I did not speak to the rock. I disobeyed the Lord. I struck the rock. I did not speak to it and, because I did not hallow His name, I cannot enter Canaan. He will let me ascend Mount Abarim to see the land He is giving to our people, but I will be gathered to Him there and my feet will not walk that land.'

'No!' I jumped to my feet, wild with panic. The impact of what he was saying was starting to dawn on me. 'No, Master! This cannot be so."

'It is so, Joshua. The Lord has decreed it will be thus.'

'But... you have served Him faithfully all these years. Why is He punishing you like this?'

'Punishing me?' Moses looked at me with raised eyebrows. 'Joshua, Yahweh is not punishing me. To go to be with Him is not a punishment, it is a great honour.'

'Then why will He not let you go into Canaan? That has the look of punishment to me.'

'Hmm.' Moses pondered for a while. 'Come, sit,' he said, gesturing to the rock next to him. I didn't want to. I couldn't just sit placidly while my world collapsed around me. No! This couldn't be happening. Perhaps it was a test. My thoughts darted around like gossamer dragonflies on a hot, sultry afternoon; hovering, fluttering, never still, never alighting in one place for very long. He waited until I looked at him, then gestured to the rock again. I sat down.

'Joshua, when I hit the rock, nothing happened. Do you remember that? No water came out because I had disobeyed Yahweh. I struck the rock instead of speaking to it, as He commanded. But the second time I hit the rock, He caused water to flow from it, just like he did all those years ago at Rephidim.' He turned to me, urging me to understand. 'Joshua, I disobeyed Him, but Yahweh was gracious to me. He did not leave me to face the wrath of our people, or dishonour me in their sight. He gave us water from that rock. Yahweh is faithful and merciful, full of compassion. But I did disobey Him, and every sin has its consequences.'

'But surely it is not such a wrongdoing, to strike a rock instead of speaking to it?' My thoughts were starting to make some sense, my questions aligning. I desperately needed to understand. 'Is that sin worthy of so great a punishment?'

Moses thought carefully before responding.

'Joshua, I am Yahweh's chosen leader. Our people follow me; they watch everything I do. Whatever I do, wherever I am, they are watching me. If they see that I have disobeyed Yahweh and that there are no consequences of that disobedience, they will believe that they too can disobey Him without reaping the consequences of their actions – and we have seen where that can lead to, *nu*?' I snorted and my face contorted. 'Joshua, I have been given great responsibility in the leading of our people up until now, and I have received much blessing in return – talking with Yahweh, seeing His glory and knowing His heart! Seeing His glory and knowing His heart. What greater honour can a mere man ever hope to gain? When a man is given such honour, much is required of him in return. Do you understand this?'

I looked at my mentor. My mind shouted out, 'No! No, I don't understand any of this!' but I heard myself mumble, 'I think so, Master.'

Moses smiled. 'Yahweh is a kind and gracious God, Joshua. He is faithful even to those who fail Him and turn away from Him. My brother is one who experienced His unmerited favour, yes? The idol he formed led many of our people into idolatry and iniquity, but Yahweh forgave him and gave his line a perpetual promise of the priesthood, for generations to come. He is a gracious God, but He is also a just God. He cannot wink His eye at sin, *nu*?'

I looked into his eyes, searching for the fear that I knew must lurk there. I couldn't find it. There was no fear. There was no anger either. I saw only peace. Peace? How could he be at peace about this? I had so many questions to ask, so much I wanted to say, but no words with which to articulate the stirrings of my heart. I looked out over the landscape that stretched before us, and paused for a moment. There was one question I did want to ask. I needed to know the answer.

'Master?'

'Mmm?'

'Why *did* you strike the rock instead of speaking to it?'

Moses sighed. 'I have pondered much on this. In truth, it happened so quickly, I cannot recall my thoughts at the time. The people were shouting at me to strike the rock. That had borne fruit before; it could be that I assumed it would do so again. Perhaps I was unsure what to speak to the rock, so I chose instead to strike it. Or possibly my anger at the people's rebellion overshadowed my diligence to harken to Yahweh's voice. I know not.'

Shock and grief were starting to set in; my head felt fuzzy, my heart sore. I felt sick at the thought of no longer being able to serve Moses. It was too surreal, too absurd to countenance. 'Master? Who will lead us into that land if it cannot be you?' I asked. 'Where will Yahweh find a man to walk the paths that you have trodden? Can there be such a man?'

Moses stared at me with great intensity; it felt intimidating. Was he angry with me for asking such a question? 'Yahweh will choose the man who His favour rests upon. A man strong of soul, who know His will and walks in His ways.'

I started to run through a mental list of our elders, but the idea of one of them taking over from Moses seemed preposterous. All the elders who had come out of Egypt had died over the years of our desert wanderings, and our newly appointed elders were still young men, all younger than me – none of them had seen three score years. But perhaps I could be of service to whoever it was that Yahweh chose to lead our people.

'Whoever Yahweh chooses,' I mumbled, blinking away some errant tears that threatened to overflow, 'I will offer my service to him. I will serve him as I have served you, if he has need of me.'

I looked up to see Moses frowning. He seemed bemused by my words. 'Mmm,' he mumbled, still staring at me intently. 'Yes, you will. You will indeed.'

29

Safe Passage

'They have refused us safe passage through their land.' A stunned silence filled the tent, followed by a barrage of questions that erupted from the mouths of the elders gathered in the Tent of Meeting.

'But why?'

'They cannot do this!'

'What is the reason for their refusal?'

'What did the messenger say?'

Moses lifted his hands to silence them. This news was unexpected, even to him. The Edomites were our kin; their descendant, Esau, was brother to our descendant, Jacob, and both brothers came from the line of our ancestor, Abraham.

We had begun the journey north, readying ourselves to cross over into Canaan in the months to come. The land of Edom lay directly in our pathway, so Moses sent a message to the king of Edom explaining the trials we had endured in Egypt and outlining the reason for our many years of travelling in the wilderness. He asked for permission to pass through their country, giving his word that we would not drink water from their wells, or take of the fruit of their land. Our plan was to travel along the King's Highway through the middle of the land of Edom and not deviate from that path. Moses' request was really only a courtesy on our part; not one of us expected them to refuse. Not only had they refused, but our messengers had been told with great clarity that, if we did enter their land, they would attack.

Our elders were angered by the king of Edom's response and greatly offended at the mention of attack. Moses, however, was not angry; he seemed more bemused than anything. This was not something he had foreseen. After much deliberation with the elders, he decided to appeal to the Edomites. A second message was sent, assuring them that we would only travel along their main highway on foot, and that we would pay for anything we had need of along the way. The second response was even shorter than the first one: 'You may not pass through.'[15] Within hours of receiving that response, our spies reported seeing a great and powerful army amassing on the borders of Edom.

Theirs was no idle threat; they were preparing for war.

'Let me assemble our troops,' I said to the elders who had once again gathered to discuss the situation. 'We will meet the Edomites in battle and show them the fate of those who stand against Yahweh's chosen people!' An outburst of cheers filled the tent, every voice lifted in raucous approval, every man standing to his feet, applauding... except one. Moses sat still, watching our passionate response. He waited until the noise had died down, then slowly stood to his feet.

'I will seek the counsel of the Lord on this matter,' he said, looking around the room. The elders nodded, voicing their agreement of Moses' plan, confident that Yahweh would commission us to show these arrogant Edomites what happened to those who dared oppose us.

He didn't.

Yahweh did not sanction our attack on Edom. Instead, He told Moses to take a long detour around their land. His instructions were clear: 'Do not provoke them to war, for I will not give you any of their land, not even enough to put your foot on. I have given Esau the hill country of Seir as his own.'[16]

I was just as surprised as the elders when Moses told us of Yahweh's decision. When I questioned the reasoning behind it, he took me aside after the meeting and explained. 'Joshua, you are a great warrior. Your instincts will always lead you to fight, to attack, to take ground, yes? This is good; Yahweh made you this way and it is good. But never forget what I am about to tell you; mark my words well.' Moses pointed his finger in my face. '*Never* go to war unless Yahweh has instructed you to do so; for if you do without His blessing, it will not go well for you.'

15 Numbers 20:20.

16 Deuteronomy 2:5.

He waited, giving time for his words to sink in, before continuing, 'You will fight many battles in your lifetime – many, many battles. Yahweh has given you the heart of a lion, but even a lion must apply wisdom in knowing which enemy to attack, and when, and how. Joshua, you *must* seek the Lord's counsel for every battle you fight, every enemy you face. The plans in a man's heart are many, but the Lord knows the way we should go.' He chuckled, his face breaking into an unexpected smile. 'Aah, we make so many plans, *nu?* We think we know best. We think we know what to do, how to do it. But our thoughts are not the thoughts of Yahweh; our ways are not His ways. We are not like the other nations, and we do not make war in the manner that they do. Remember the battle against the Amalekites?'

I nodded. I had just been thinking of that very same battle. Who would have thought that a people like ours, inexperienced in the ways of warfare, with no weapons or training, could defeat a powerful adversary like the Amalekites, simply by Moses holding a wooden staff aloft while our warriors fought? 'Truly, His ways are not our ways,' I pondered in my heart.

Moses stood up and stretched. 'Yahweh does not always move in the same way. He is not predictable like a man, *nu?* Never presume you know what His will is; always ask Him. That is something I have come to realise – and never more so than now,' he said, rubbing his temple. 'Seek His counsel, because sometimes He will tell you to strike the rock, but at other times He will command you to speak to it, mmm?' He looked at me with a wry expression.

I didn't respond, instead choosing to look away. I didn't want to go down that pathway. Not now. Since the day Moses told me that he would not be going into Canaan with us, the thought of being without him had been too overwhelming for me. I couldn't even imagine what my life would be without him. I couldn't countenance the idea of facing giants in battle without him by my side. I couldn't think on it. I *wouldn't* think on it.

So I pushed it to the back of my mind and refused to enter that den of pain.

I was content to delay this final part of our travels. I was happy to take a long detour around Edom instead of passing through its midst. The longer we spent journeying, the more time I would have before I had to face the inevitable torment of saying goodbye to my master, my mentor. My father.

30

High Priest

'When will this take place?' I asked.

'Tomorrow.' Eleazar looked like he was about to pass out. Gesturing to him to sit down, I closed the tent flap before sitting next to him. This would not be a quick conversation, of that I was sure.

'Speak your mind, my friend.'

He shook his head. His breathing came in short gasps. 'I cannot do this!' he blurted.

'Why do you speak thus?' I asked him. 'You have prepared for years to become high priest. You are ready for this great honour.'

He grunted. 'You sound like Phinehas. He cannot stop talking about it. He is even talking of the day he will become high priest after me.'

I shrugged. 'Your son is a righteous man, and a zealous follower of Yahweh. Is it not a good thing that he desires to follow in your footsteps as high priest?'

'Yes, but he sees only the honour of becoming high priest. He does not see the pain of what must happen before that time – the pain of having to lose your *abba* in order to gain that honour. I am not ready to rip the mantle of high priest from my *abba's* hands.' Eleazar's voice was gritty; he spoke with uncharacteristic aggression. Now I understood the conflict that he was grappling with and why he had sought me out. It was usually I who sought him out when I had need of counsel or conversation, but this time, it was he who came to me. I was glad of it.

We left Kadesh Barnea after our dispute with the Edomites and travelled on to Mount Hor, near the border of Edom, being careful not to trespass on the Edomites' land. We made camp near Mount Hor yesterday and, this morning, Moses had called Eleazar and Aaron to tell them that Yahweh had spoken. Moses was to take Aaron and Eleazar up Mount Hor, where he was to remove Aaron's priestly garments and put them on Eleazar. Aaron would die on the mountain and be gathered to his people, and Eleazar was to be anointed as high priest in his place.

I reached out to grasp Eleazar's shoulder. 'It is not an easy thing to lose your *abba*, this I know well. I have endured it twice. But to be anointed as high priest is a very great honour; it is not something to be spurned.'

'What if I do not want this honour? For I do not!' he ranted. 'Not if it means I must be robbed of my *abba*.'

My heart felt his pain; I knew it well. How could I help him prepare himself for what was inevitable? 'Eleazar, it is Aaron's time. I am sure he has come to peace with this.'

'He has!' Eleazar exclaimed. 'That is what I cannot fathom. How is it that he can be at peace with this? How is that possible?'

I thought for a while before responding. 'I cannot answer that question. Only Yahweh can comprehend the mysteries of a man's heart. But I do know that when my *abba*, and Jesher, and even Shira grew old and full of days, they seemed to know that their time had come. They were ready to leave this world. Yahweh's grace was upon them for that time, as I believe it will be for Aaron.'

Eleazar closed his eyes and started rocking gently backwards and forwards. I had no wish to interrupt him, so I waited until he was ready to speak again. 'I have not always thought highly of my *abba*, especially when he... the golden calf – you know that; we spoke of it often. But he brought forth fruit for repentance and has remained faithful to Yahweh since that time. He fathered Ithamar and I with love and care. There is much love in my heart for him and... I am not ready for him to leave us.'

'I know. I was not ready for either of my *abbas* to depart this life. But our times are in Yahweh's hands, and He has decreed that the time is right for your *abba* to rest with his fathers.'

'Mmm.' Eleazar glanced at me, clearly wrestling with some unseen dilemma. 'There is something my *abba* told me which I have never spoken of. It seemed wrong, almost shameful, to speak of it. But now...

I must give voice to these thoughts,' he blurted. 'They have troubled me for too long.' He frowned, gazing at me, as if seeking permission to offload this burden.

'Speak. Your words will not leave this tent; my heart bears witness to that.'

Eleazar nodded and breathed a big sigh. 'After the golden calf... when Moses went back up the mountain, leaving us here, I spent much time with *Abba*. There was a bitterness in his words at that time, a shame that lay heavy on him. He unfurled the contents of his heart, telling me things I had no knowledge of before then.' Eleazar looked at the ground and continued. 'He told me of the conflict that raged within him... towards his brother. He spoke of the time when Moses returned to Egypt, of his joy at being reunited with his brother after so long. They marvelled at the plans of Yahweh to free His people and my *abba* was filled with purpose and passion.

'Yahweh had decreed that He become the spokesman, the voice of the Lord God Himself, because Moses was unable to do so.' Eleazar turned to me, emboldened to speak out the truth that had been hidden within him for decades. 'He told me how he spoke with authority in the courts of Pharoah; he demonstrated the might of Yahweh. It was my *abba* who threw down the staff in Pharoah's court. He watched it transform into a snake, then took hold of the snake's tail and it turned back into a staff. It wasn't Moses who performed that miracle, it was my *abba*. He did it. Moses could not do it; *Abba* said he did not yet have the courage. But *Abba* did. He was filled with zeal for Yahweh and it made him bold.'

I could see wonder on Eleazar's face as he reminisced. 'It was also my *abba* who Yahweh commanded to stretch his staff over the Nile River; he watched it turn to blood. He said Yahweh worked through him to send a plague of frogs on the Egyptians, and it was he who struck the ground with his staff and watched the dust turn into gnats, lifting off the ground in flight. It was my *abba* who performed those miracles. He heard the voice of Yahweh and obeyed Him. His face was alight with passion when he told me how Yahweh had worked wonders through him.'

Eleazar's face fell. He looked away and grunted. 'But our people don't remember that. When they look at him now, they don't see a miracle worker. They just see Moses' brother, the one who sinned. The priest who made an idol.'

Eleazar leaned forward, resting his forearms on his thighs, his head bowed. 'He said he has always walked in Moses's shadow. Even though he was the older brother, Moses was the one that everyone looked to. My *abba* was the spokesman – in the beginning, at least – but he was never the "One". The leader. The miracle worker. The prophet. Moses was. And so the passion in his heart turned sour, like ripe fruit left to ferment.'

Eleazar sat up and made eye contact with me again. 'I love my uncle, you know that. In truth, Moses has been as much of an *abba* to me as my own father, and I have learned the ways of Yahweh through him. But my *abba* is leaving this earth, and... and I would have him remembered for the mighty works he did, not for the golden calf that he made.'

'Eleazar,' I said, grabbing his arm. 'It is within your power to do that. You can tell the stories of what Aaron did, write songs of the mighty ways in which Yahweh moved through him. You can teach our people these stories, write the chronicles of what happened, preserve his memory for generations to come. You can do that! I will help you!'

Light entered Eleazar's eyes as a flicker of hope countered the pain of the loss he knew he would have to endure. We spent the rest of our time together talking and praying, preparing him for the events of the following day and, in the morning, he was pale and strained, but there was an air of peace about him as he walked closely by Aaron's side through the crowds that thronged the pathways. He focused on the path ahead; he looked neither to the left nor to the right. His head was held high and his steps were sure.

I walked with them to the foot of the mountain, then kept watch as the three of them climbed higher and higher, until they were lost to me in the clouds. I stayed there the whole day, praying and fasting, while at the same time fighting the demons that tormented my own mind with thoughts of Moses going up another mountain, at another time, also never to return. Moses and Eleazar returned as twilight fell.

Eleazar spoke not a word, but his body was rigid and, as I held him in a tight embrace, he shuddered with emotion.

Neither Eleazar nor Moses told me what had taken place when they came down the mountain, and I never asked them. I didn't want to know. Not yet.

Some things are better left unsaid.

31

Captured

After the thirty days of mourning for Aaron were completed, we continued on our journey northward, along the Way of Atharim towards Canaan. My senses were on full alert from morning until night, and throughout the watches of the night; this was giant territory.

A curious conflict was taking place within me; a battle between two forces, equally as strong. On the one hand, a passionate desire to enter this land and face the giants who had dominated my thoughts for around forty years. I wanted to be done with the uncertainty and dread that pulled at my mind, stretching my thoughts until they became like animal skins staked out in the sun, straining for release. On the other hand, I had a desperate longing to remain where we were, on the edge of this wilderness, so I wouldn't have to face the agony of losing my master or facing the giants without him.

I hadn't been able to think on who Yahweh might appoint to lead us in Moses' place; I could think of no one who would qualify for that great honour, and I couldn't stomach the thought of someone else taking his place. So I blocked these thoughts from my mind and refused to dwell on them.

We sent teams of spies out into the surrounding areas on a daily basis. Some of our best warriors were among them, although they dressed in ordinary garb and any weapons they carried were carefully concealed. Their instructions were to blend in with the people of the land and glean information about the territory and its rulers. Whenever a team returned, Moses, Caleb and I would meet with them to discuss their findings. The information they shared was always valuable, but even more so today, when a team that had just returned from a five-day foray into the land of Moab, north of Edom, told us their news.

'A giant? Their king is a giant? Are you certain of this?' I asked the leader, my breaths already coming in short, shallow bursts.

'It seems certain, Commander,' he responded. 'We heard it not from one, but from many different sources. The Moabites speak of their king, Og, with great pride. He is heralded as their champion, and is unbeaten in combat.'

'They even told us of the size of King Og's bed!' another of the spies blurted, his eyes widening with fervour. "They say he has an iron bedstead, built by their craftsmen to fit his frame and carry his weight. It measures 13ft long and 6ft wide!'

'Hmm.' My stomach started churning within me, but my face maintained a calm disposition. I would not let these men see the flush of fear and zeal that assailed me at the thought of facing Og in battle.

'Ha!' Caleb shouted. 'The bigger the target, the easier it will be for our weapons to find their mark, *nu?*' We all sniggered and whooped in response – we had heard that many times from Caleb's lips – but I saw Moses watching me. I may have been fooling the rest of them, but I knew he was not taken in by my composed exterior. When the noise had died down a bit, he looked directly at me.

'Their pride in their king could be their downfall.'

'How so?'

'When a people like the Moabites have a leader as formidable as Og, they begin to feel invincible themselves. They start to believe that there is no one who can defeat them, and *that*,' he said, leaning forward with a glint in his eyes, 'is when they are at their weakest. When their defences are down, we will attack, yes? Their overconfidence will become their greatest weakness.'

We discussed Moses' theory for some time afterwards, until our discourse was brought to an abrupt close by the return of another group of spies whose news was equally as ominous, but more urgent in nature. The Canaanite king of Arad had heard that we were journeying along the road to Atharim and would, in all likelihood, want to pass through his territory. Our spies reported that he had amassed a great army and was preparing to attack us. There was no time for further discussions. We sounded the alarm and I assembled the captains, instructing them to gather their best troops. Half of them would stay and guard the camp, the other half would march out within the hour to meet the Canaanite horde.

Everything happened so quickly, it was only the following day that I realised I had completely disregarded what Moses told me after our dispute with the Edomites. I had not sought Yahweh about how to attack them and, indeed, whether to attack them at all.

We marched all that afternoon and made camp when twilight fell. My sleep was fitful and disturbed, once again invaded by images of flawless giants wearing golden crowns on their shining heads. I was half-awake when the jarring call of the watchman's shofar sounded.

They were upon us before the dawn had fully broken – thousands of them, swarming into our camp like flies upon a fresh carcass. Our warriors were trained to sleep with their weapons by their side, so they were able to rally quickly and fight back, but it was some time before we realised that the Canaanites had attacked us from two sides. Our camp lay in an elongated shape; by attacking us from both the north and the south, they succeeded in trapping us. Once we discovered their plan, we rallied the troops and divided them into two divisions; Caleb led one division north-east while I led the other south-west. We fought back with renewed zeal, cutting through our enemy's ranks and quickly gaining the upper hand. Swords hissing and arrows whistling, we pushed them back until it seemed that the enemy troops on the southern edge of the battle were retreating into the surrounding hills.

Our warriors blew the trumpets, sounding the call of victory. A tumultuous roar was raised by our warriors, who brandished their weapons, shouting defiantly at our foes as they disappeared over the ridges. Our two divisions re-grouped and we instructed the men to gather the wounded and tend to their needs. The tribal captains did a head count of their warriors and it was only then that we discovered that a large number of our warriors were unaccounted for.

'What do you mean?' I asked Ishbah and Hanoch, two of our captains of a thousand who had come to report their findings. 'Are they among those slain?'

'No, Commander. The dead have been gathered and accounted for, the wounded along with them. These men are just... missing,' Ishbah replied, glancing at Hanoch before continuing. 'We believe they may have been taken captive by the Canaanites. Some of the men in the north division saw movements on the outskirts of the battle, a large number of our foe moving away in formation. At the time they believed them to be fleeing, but it seemed odd that they were marching, not running, and their shields were raised, creating a barrier.'

'How many are missing?' Caleb asked him.

'To my count, nearly a hundred warriors.'

'A hundred warriors?' Caleb repeated, shocked at that revelation. 'Joshua, we must deliver them from the hands of the Canaanites.'

My head was spinning. A hundred of our warriors, taken captive? How? Why is it we didn't see it take place? What would these heathen idolators do to them? I didn't want to answer that question. I knew the ways of the Moabites and of their pagan god Chemosh, who required human sacrifices to appease his wrath. We all knew of it. We had heard the horrific stories of Moabite children sacrificed by their own fathers on the altars of Chemosh during their cultish ceremonies on feast days and new moons. We also knew of their belief in the ritual torture and sacrifice of their defeated enemies, as an offering to Chemosh to thank him for subduing their adversaries. It was a well-known fact that it was far better to die on the battlefield than be taken captive by those barbarians, to be mutilated and carved up like an animal carcass on the altar of Chemosh for his perverted pleasure. My stomach turned and a wave of nausea hit me.

'Joshua?' Caleb was staring at me, wild with passion. 'We must go now. You know what they do to captured warriors. We must muster the troops and go aft...'

'No.' I realised with horror what I had not done, knowing now what I must do.

'*No*? What is...'

'Thank you, Ishbah, Hanoch, for your report. You may leave us. I will send for you when I have further instructions.'

'Commander.' The two men nodded and, although clearly disturbed, they placed their palms on their chests, gave a curt bow, and took their leave.

'Joshua, I implore you,' Caleb grabbed me by the shoulders. 'We cannot leave them to the mercy of Chemosh, we must rescue them. They are our brothers.'

'That is my desire too, Caleb, but we must first enquire...'

Just then, the tent flap was flung open and Yoram strode into my tent, eyes blazing with passion. 'Yoshi, we must rescue the captured warriors! We cannot leave them to die by the hands of those monsters. They are faithful men, some of them from my division. I know their families – our children play together. We cannot abandon them.'

'Yoram, I cannot...'

'You must! We cannot leave them to die by the hands of the Canaanites and their gods.'

'Yes, but I must first...'

'You cannot forsake them! I beg of you! They are your...'

'Yoram, *stand down!*' I barked. It had the desired effect. Shocked into reflexive action, Yoram stood to attention, clenching his jaw and staring straight ahead. As a captain of a thousand, he was one of my highest-ranking officers. I had never had cause to rebuke him before; this was the first time. I hated it as much as he clearly did. Caleb stared at me in shock. I didn't ask him or Yoram to sit down. There was no discussion to be had. Pausing for a moment to gather myself, I spoke with a calm, clear tone.

'Surely you cannot believe it is in my heart to abandon our men to the Canaanites. This could never be! I would willingly give my life to save theirs. My hesitation is not from fear or apathy. I would leave this very moment and pursue our foes, but I cannot. Before I put my hand to my sword, I must enquire of Yahweh. We must seek His direction.'

I could almost hear the unspoken question that hung heavy in the air between us. 'Why?'

'Do you not see?' My voice cracked with emotion. 'If I had but sought Yahweh before coming out to battle these Canaanites, this might not have happened. It will be my guilt and shame to bear if any evil befalls them. I have disobeyed the Lord and I must repent before Him, and enquire of Him as to His will in this matter.'

I saw Yoram's jaw unclench and his shoulders relax as understanding entered his heart. Within minutes, instructions were issued and the men who were physically able to, assembled. We sought the face of God together. I repented before Him for my disobedience and we enquired of Him as to the rescue of our captured men-in-arms.

Yahweh heard our cries. We were to redeem their lives!

32

Vengeance

Just over an hour later, a new squadron of warriors set out northwards in the direction of Zephath, where the Moabite army was camped. Caleb was by my side, and Yoram, Ishbah and Hanoch were among those chosen for this mission. Although we were not great in number, our troop contained our most skilled warriors. Yahweh had deigned that this quest would not be about strength or numbers, but about stealth and cunning. We made our way towards Zephath using pathways less trodden, keeping to the bushy undergrowth where possible. The sun was setting as we neared the Canaanite camp, so we hid among the hills and waited until darkness fell.

A luminous full moon lit the sky. Caleb jostled my arm, pointed up at the moon and grimaced in frustration. It would not be easy to sneak into their camp with the moon lighting our every step. I gestured to him to wait, and prayed silently to Yahweh to help us.

'Yahweh, we are Your people. This battle is not ours, but Yours. For Your glory, for Your people, make us invisible, or blind our enemies' eyes to us.'

As we waited, a thick band of black clouds moved across the night sky and halted in front of the moon, blocking out the light. Caleb grinned at me and raised his fist in response. The night air was warm, filled with the aroma of meat roasting on the fire and the sound of much laughter. Our enemies were feasting, probably celebrating the capture of a fresh batch of victims for Chemosh, clearly not expecting a counterattack. I sent Yoram and Ishbah to scout out the camp under the cover of cloudy darkness; they returned to report that our captured comrades were bound and corralled in an enclosure on the west side of the camp. Most were wounded but, for the most part, they looked in good spirits. There were but six men guarding them. Moses' words about the Moabites sprung to mind: 'Their overconfidence will become their greatest weakness.'

'Yahweh, let it be so, this very night,' I prayed.

We waited in the darkness through the first watch and into the second watch of the night, until all was quiet and the roaring campfires had disintegrated into glowing piles of embers. We made our way around the outskirts of the camp to the prisoners corral. Caleb, Yoram, myself and three of our captains each targeted one of the guards. The rest of the men spread out and, on my signal, we crept towards our prey. The element of surprise was crucial, so no clashing of swords would suffice; the guards must be silenced and their throats cut so they could not raise the alarm.

It was done with relative ease – four of the six were asleep, and the two who were awake were somewhat stupefied from the after effects of too much wine and feasting. Our men entered the corral and cut the prisoners' bonds, giving each of them a weapon which they had brought with them for that purpose; then we moved through the camp like silent assassins, lurking in the flickering shadows. Yahweh's instructions were clear: 'utterly destroy' them.[17]

Our warriors fanned out through the camp and slipped into tent after tent of snoring bodies, killing swiftly and silently. Most of the Canaanite soldiers were so well oiled with wine that they never awoke, but died in their slumber. Others woke to find themselves greeted by a Hebrew blade and an appointment with death. The plan worked well; our units moved systematically, a curtain of death drawn over our enemy's camp, until the early hours of the morning, when we were surprised by a Canaanite solider who stepped out of his tent to relieve himself. His cries of alarm were silenced when he met a hasty end, but his shouts had woken some of his friends and, all around us, men emerged from their tents, blinking and rubbing their eyes.

The time for silent attack was over.

'For Yahweh! *Attaaaack!*' I shouted, brandishing my sword.

---

17   Numbers 21:2, NKJV.

Issuing blood-curdling shrieks, we ploughed into our enemies, releasing all the pent-up energy that we had suppressed throughout that night. Hearing Caleb's voice, I turned to see him swinging his sword in a frenzied fashion, slashing and hacking at the drowsy soldiers whose eyes bulged in horror at the sight that met them.

'For Yahweh!' he roared, launching himself at the terrified men with unmitigated zeal. He stopped when he saw me, shrugged and grinned, then continued his relentless assault on our adversaries. All around me, warriors exploded into action, leaping and lunging, sparing no man. Yoram's division fought near me and even he was uncharacteristically frenzied in his attack. The zeal of God was in these warriors, and I was amazed by what I beheld.

I paused to catch my breath, panting as I scanned the area, when I saw Attai grappling with a large Canaanite solider. Attai himself was not a man of great stature, although he was undoubtedly a man of great courage, so I watched to see if he had met his match in the Canaanite or needed assistance. Attai's short time as a captive seemed to have lit a fire in him; I had never seen him fight with such fervour. He was more than a match for his opponent. As I watched him finish it, I saw a movement behind him. Another Canaanite soldier had crawled under the curtained wall of his tent and was stalking Attai from behind, dagger in hand. I was too far away to confront the man, and the clamour of battle was so loud, I knew Attai would not hear any warning I shouted to him. Drawing my dagger from its sheath, I narrowed my eyes, took aim, and hurled it at the man, hitting him squarely in the chest.

Attai must have heard the man's cries. He turned, shocked to see his stalker fall to his knees in front of him, still clutching his own dagger, shocked at the foreign blade that protruded from his chest. The man fell to the ground and Attai swung round to find the warrior whose true aim had saved him. Searching the squirming mass of bodies in front of him, he locked onto me where I stood, tall and still, watching him. For just a moment, the noise of the battle dumbed down and the fight raging around us seemed to move in slow motion. Our eyes met, warrior to warrior, in a mutual acknowledgement of valour. Attai put his palm on his chest and bowed his head. I returned his salute, then we continued the fight as if nothing had happened.

But something had happened.

An indefinable shift had taken place; a unique bond had been seared into our souls. A knowing, an honouring that can only be experienced when one warrior saves the life of another.

We routed the enemy that night, executing vengeance in the name of our God. Our losses were minimal, theirs were catastrophic. None were spared. Any survivors were executed, and there was much bounty to be had when it was all over. We plundered their camp, retrieving all their weapons, armour, livestock and supplies, before making our way back to our camp, carrying our dead and wounded on Canaanite carts.

I stood surveying the desolate remains of their camp, wiping their blood from my sword and my hands on a piece of discarded material. War was a bloody business. There was no escaping it, but I did not revel in it. I looked into the cold, vacant, staring eyes of the fallen who littered the ground around me. Each of these men had a family; a wife, children, an *ima* and *abba*, who would never see them again, never share a meal together or feel the warmth of their embrace. I sighed. I took no pleasure in claiming a man's life, even demon-worshipping barbarians like these, but my zeal for Yahweh and His kingdom far overcame my loathing of bloodshed. I did what needed to be done, for my people and my God.

Attai approached me as I stood there, hands caked with dry blood, staring with loathing at the scene of devastation before me.

'Commander?'

'Attai! *Shalom*. It is good to see you strong and well. You fought like a man possessed,' I said, unable to keep my admiration for him from showing on my face.

'Possessed with the zeal of Yahweh, perhaps,' he said with a grin. The smile left his face and a look of immense gratitude clouded his countenance. 'My lord,' he said, putting his palm on his chest in another salute. 'My life is yours. If I can ever be of service to you, it would be my honour.'

'Thank you, Attai. ' I returned his salute and then reached out to grasp his forearm. 'May the Lord increase your days and fill them with honour.' Attai gave me a solemn nod, turned, and went on his way.

At the command of Yahweh, our armies went on to attack and conquer the surrounding Canaanite cities. We vanquished every single one of them, retrieving much spoil for our people before continuing on our journey along the Way of Atharim. The city of Zephath would never be called by that name again. Henceforth, it would be called Hormah, the place of 'Utter Destruction', as a sign and a warning to those who would dare to raise arms against the God of Israel and His chosen people.

33

Cup of His Fury

Word had spread. Our spies reported fear among the nations around us at the mention of the name of the God of Israel who worked mighty wonders on behalf of His people. We were now a force to be reckoned with, a rapidly rising threat, and our enemies knew it.

After defeating the Moabites, we travelled northwards on the King's Highway towards the land of Ammon. The Amorites were descended from Emer, the fourth son of Canaan, and were known for being 'the height of cedar trees', and for their skill in warfare. Although they didn't hold to the practice of human sacrifice, as did the Moabites, they had turned away from Yahweh in days gone by, and now worshipped a moon god, Sin, and a shepherd god, Amur, among many others.

Moses sent messengers to their king, Sihon, just as he had done with the king of Edom, asking for permission to pass through his country. Yet again, Moses pledged to travel on the King's Highway through the land of Ammon and not turn aside to the left or to the right, not to drink water from their well or take of the produce of their land. He received no reply to his message but, within a few short days, our spies reported that Sihon had mustered his whole army, and was marching south, towards us.

'Once again,' Moses muttered on receiving the news, 'our offer of alliance is spurned and they turn instead to make war on us. This is by the design of Yahweh,' he said, glancing at me. 'Their idolatry is as a foul stench in his nostrils; He would rid the land of it. The stories tell of the time when Sihon fought against the former king of Moab and took this land from him.' He grinned at me. 'And now we will take it from Sihon. He gained his land by war, and he will lose it by war. This will be his undoing.'

Moses and I had spent much time before Yahweh enquiring of Him as to His will for this land, and specifically the Amorite territory. The Lord spoke clearly; we knew His will. We also knew that the Amorites were a warring people, fierce and strong, but we had an advantage over them, something they could not know or fully comprehend. Our warriors had been waiting, honing their skills in warfare for nearly forty years with one single goal in mind: to take this land that had been promised to us, for our people and our God. The Amorites would defend their land out of fear, but we fought for conquest.

Throughout each day, at the forefront of my mind was one thought: that of facing the giant, Og. My desire to vanquish this Amorite horde and rid the earth of their idolatry was secondary to my drive, indeed my innate need to face Og in combat. I felt like a horse champing at the bit, full of nervous energy. I couldn't settle or put my hand to anything for very long. I found myself pacing up and down, envisaging what would take place when I faced him across the battle grounds, steeling myself to look into his flawless face and not bow to its allure. The faces of the giants who had taunted me in my dreams for so many years flashed within my consciousness day in and day out, filling me with an obsessive hunger to engage the titan in battle and be done with it, one way or the other.

Our people camped near the Arnon river. We left a sizeable number of our armed forces to guard the camp, and marched out to meet the Ammonites in battle, coming across them at Jahaz, a short distance away from their capital city of Heshbon. Thanks to our victory over the Moabites, our warriors were now all fully armed, and more than ready to engage these heathens in battle. The morning sun reflected off their shields and helmets with a threatening glare as we drew up in battle formation. I stood before them, my heart filled with pride and a bizarre kind of love for these faithful fighters.

'Today we face the Amorites, these idolators who dare to defy the living God,' I shouted. They roared in response and banged their weapons on their shields. 'They are a people mighty in stature, well trained in warfare, but our spies tell us that they fear us – and *so they should!*' I roared at them, pacing up and down in front of the thousands of warriors assembled on the plain.

'Marvel not at my words, for today our enemies do not fight mere men; they fight the God of the armies of Israel! For from the *Lord* comes deliverance. He will come forth as a mighty man of war and cut off all His enemies from before Him. Why should we fear those who trust in their own swords and chariots? Our trust is in the name of our Lord and our enemies will drink the cup of His fury.'

More banging on shields and shouting ensued. I waited until the noise subsided before drawing my sword. 'I charge you now: gird yourselves with strength and let us break in pieces the oppressor. Then all the earth will know that *there is a God in Israel.*' I thrust my sword into the air, which exploded with the tumultuous roar of thousands of voices cheering and shouting. Weapons were brandished aloft, glinting in the bright sun as the Amorites drew near to do battle.

The years of training and preparation rushed to the fore and was released from our warriors with a ferocity not unlike that of captive beasts when they are released from their cages. I knew they were well trained – I had overseen their training myself – but I had not seen the zeal of Yahweh move through them in such a way before now. We charged towards the Amorites, shouting at the tops of our voices, like a colossal wave, smashing through their defences. Most of the Amorites were taller than us, but it made not a bit of difference. Our giant slayers led the way, ducking, twisting, and thrusting their swords into the backs of the Amorites' knees as they had been trained to do. It was a massacre of glorious proportions.

I found myself seeking out the tallest, strongest warriors, charging them with bullish intensity. They were but the training ground for me. The real battle would take place when I faced the giant, Og...and I could hardly wait!

34

Og

Our victory over the Amorite king Sihon was indisputable; we put his army to the sword and went on to capture all the cities and surrounding settlements under Sihon's reign, including their capital, Heshbon. A number of our people settled in each city that we captured, along with Levites to lead their worship, and warriors to defend them. The reach of our influence was spreading fast. As soon as the new cities were established, we turned our sights towards Bashan, where the second Amorite king lived: the giant, Og. My heart pounded within me whenever I thought of the forthcoming confrontation. Fear and anticipation became my constant bedfellows; I lived minute by minute under the tension of their conflict.

'My Lord, permit me to face this monster, I beg of You,' I muttered to Yahweh in prayer. 'Let him meet his end by my sword; I would be done with this agony of waiting.'

Moses, who clearly recognised the conflict that raged in me, accompanied our armies on our journey northwards towards Bashan. I was glad of his company. He brought a much-needed calm, a reassurance to my disquieted soul. We sought the Lord together for His will regarding King Og and, once again, Yahweh spoke clearly.

'Do not be afraid of him, for I have delivered him into your hands, along with his whole army and his land. Do to him what you did to Sihon king of the Amorites, who reigned in Heshbon.'[18]

Our two armies marched along the Way of Bashan, King Og's army marching south, ours marching northwards to meet them. The battlelines were drawn on the open plains near a city called Edrei. As

---

18   Numbers 21:34.

our troops made camp and prepared for the following day's confrontation, Moses and I walked to the creek which ran along the floor of the nearby wadi. The late afternoon sun bathed the plains and nearby hills in pastel shades, and the quiet lapping of the creek brought a calming rhythm to the beating of my heart. It seemed absurd that a place of such tranquillity would soon be host to the clamour and stench of a battle that would see the demise of an empire and the death of its famed king.

I washed my face, neck and hands with water from the creek, drank deeply of its cool sweetness, then stood up to survey the land before me. This was good land, fertile land. This was a land of promise. This was our land. A silent voice told me, 'This is the land where Og, King of Bashan, will make his last futile stand against the children of Israel.'

'My Lord, let it be so, according to Your will,' I responded.

I looked at Yahweh's cloud, which hovered above us, beautiful velvety swirls with glimmers of silver running through it. When I looked carefully, I could see hues of rainbow colours in the cloud's form, and the movement of celestial wings swooping and rising within it. Yahweh was with us. His presence had been my chief joy throughout these years of wandering; my sole source of peace, strength and hope. I gazed up at the billowing canopy, soaking in the beauty of His presence. My soul stirred within me. All was well.

Moses sat down by a tree near the water's edge, leaning his back against the trunk. I joined him and we sat in companionable silence for a while, listening to the chirping of insects in the tall grass. I watched a busy lizard as it darted along a branch of the tree, its tail quivering as it paused to gape at us with beady eyes.

'Joshua.'

I turned to face him. 'Master?'

He looked at me with intensity for a few seconds before speaking with great assurance. 'You are well able to defeat this giant king. Yahweh has delivered him into your hands.'

He said no more. There was nothing more to say. His declaration stood firm. I nodded in acknowledgement and continued gazing at Yahweh's cloud, drawing strength from Him. We stayed there by the creek until the dim fingers of dusk stretched out over the land.

I didn't dream of giants that night. I didn't dream of anything. My sleep was deep and rewarding, and I woke long before the dawn, refreshed and ready for this long-awaited day. A grey, misty dawn greeted us as we prepared for battle. Our troops formed the battlelines and moved into position on the plains, but mist had drifted down from the surrounding hills, blurring our vision. I stood in the frontlines, peering across the plain, eager to see this infamous giant, to find out whether he was all that people said he was. I heard the sounds of men talking across the plain, of stomping feet and the clattering of metal, but could still see nothing. Squinting into the mist, we waited until finally the murky wisps started to dissipate, revealing our adversaries.

The stories were true; Og's army made a striking first impression. Row upon row of rugged warriors, powerfully built and armed to the teeth with an imposing array of weaponry. I searched through the retreating tendrils of mist, looking for Og. Where was he? Where was this renowned warrior? The urge to know what my ill-famed adversary looked like grew until I thought I would burst with anticipation.

Then the mist parted and I saw him.

He would be hard to miss. He stood at least two or three feet taller than his warriors, and they were not short of stature by any means. King Og was every bit as impressive as I had expected him to be. He stood still, head held high, his mane of thick, dark hair blowing in the breeze, as if fully aware of the impact his striking features made, even across the stretches of a battlefield.

I studied Og with a curious eye, but with no sense of foreboding. What I felt was anticipation, impatience and even a surge of excitement. But not fear. The giant within me had been slain over the preceding years and now all that was left to do was deal with the one that stood facing me across the vast plains of Canaan.

When we faced King Sihon's troops, I had smelt fear on them, but King Og's armies smelt only of arrogance. His warriors were cocky and overconfident, just as Moses had foreseen. Their casual posture betrayed their attitude of derision and their laughter rang out across the plains at the sight of us. Our men were not swayed by the Amorites' stature or their mocking laughter. They knew Yahweh's instructions;

there would be no need of a rousing speech by their commander today. I could feel their passion and energy welling up behind me. They were ready – more than ready – to engage this horde in battle. My admiration for them knew no bounds.

I was just about to step forward when I saw a movement on the plains to my right, a glimmer of light like the sun reflecting off a weapon. I gasped.

'They're here!' I said to Caleb, who stood by my side awaiting the word to attack.

'Who?' he said, staring at our adversaries.

'~~No~~ The shining men!' I whispered. 'They are over there.' I gestured to where they stood. The same two messengers who had appeared to me nearly thirty years before to show me how to slay a giant stood before me again, shining with the self-same nobility and glory. They were fully armed, but their weapons were sheathed and they stood, arms by their sides, staring at me with glowing intensity.

'What are they doing?' Caleb asked, still searching the place where I had pointed. 'Do they have a message for you?' The two celestial warriors turned simultaneously to stare at King Og, then focused back on me. They needed speak no words; I knew what they were there to say.

'Yes,' I told Caleb, still staring at these magnificent shimmering men. 'They have brought me a message.'

'Well? What is it?'

I took a deep breath in and exhaled. 'Tell the giant slayers that Og is mine.'

'That is as it should be,' Caleb said. 'Let's take this giant down and wipe that smile off his pretty face!'

'No,' I said, shifting my focus to the titan that stood across from me. 'He is mine. I will face him alone.'

'Alone?' Caleb frowned. 'You would fight him without me?'

I turned to him. 'Do you doubt me?'

Caleb did not waver. 'Not for a moment. But we have trained for this task in units, never in single combat.'

I smiled at this man, this courageous brother-in-arms. I knew he would go with me to the ends of the earth if I asked him to, or fight a horde of giants single-handedly; but this was not that time. Reaching out, I put my hand on his shoulder. 'The shining men are here; this is their message to me. Og will fall by my hand.'

We sent a steward with a message for King Og to say that Joshua ben Nun, commander of the armies of Israel, would challenge him in face-to-face combat. Og and his men burst into raucous laughter on receipt of the message, slapping each other on the back in their mirth and pointing at me in derision. Og threw his helmet to the ground, then dropped his shield after it, posturing and speech-making to his men. He threw down his sword and lifted his weapon of choice, a huge, heavy, spiked mace. Holding it above his head, he shouted at his men, who roared and cheered in response.

I knew that mace; I had seen it many times in my dreams. I had a score to settle with it.

Og lowered his mace and strolled onto the battlefield, still laughing at me where I stood.

I looked at the shining men, who stood unmoving but for an imperceptible nod of their heads. Drawing my sword, I gripped it with both hands, taking a moment to focus on the splendid colossus striding towards me.

'I will not bow to you, today or ever,' I muttered. 'Indeed, you will bow your knees to the God of the armies of Israel, the One True God!'

Drawing a deep breath, I took my sword in my right hand and took off, sprinting across the grassy plain towards Og. My eyes never left him. As I came near, he lifted his mace and started swinging it in anticipation. I measured the length of its reach and, just as I neared the titan, I skidded on my back under the reach of his weapon, coming to a stop just behind him. Before he had time to turn around, my sword found its mark: I slashed the back of his knees, just like the shining men had shown me all those years ago, first one, then the other. I had a strong sense of having done this before, and pictured the straw-filled images of giants that we had trained on for so many years.

Og's knees were the height of my waist.

The giant dropped his mace in shock, staggering and hollering in pain as his knees buckled beneath him, blood gushing out of his wounds.

The roars and cheers which had accompanied Og as he strode onto the battlefield turned into shocked silence. He lashed out at me with his right arm, roaring with rage, but I dodged his arm and my blade found its second target: his armpit. Leaping into the air, I thrust my sword upwards. The blade sliced through his flesh then, while he clutched it in agony, I rammed my whole body hard into him. I heard a thud, like the sound of a huge tree falling to the ground. Og lay there, eyes wide in disbelief and fear, blood spurting out of his mouth. Without hesitation, I lifted my sword and, with a thunderous roar, severed his helmetless head. Moses was right: Og's arrogance and overconfidence had been his downfall.

It was done.

The giant was felled.

It had taken less than a minute.

I stood over Og's crumpled body, listening as the cursed words, '*you weak, pathetic creature*', echoed in the atmosphere around me. The taunting tones of the giant's curse decreased in volume and potency until they disappeared altogether, carried away on the wings of the winds that swept across the plain.

Our warriors burst into tumultuous applause, roaring and whooping, while Og's men stood, frozen in horror at the sight of their hero king laying smitten on the battlefield.

'Giant slayers!' I shouted, raising my sword to our troops. '*Attaaaack!*' They swarmed onto the battlefield, sprinting towards their opponents, cheering and shouting, closely followed by the rest of our warriors. Seeing the men stampeding towards them, Og's men shook themselves free of their stupor and drew their weapons, ready to face the coming onslaught. Not all their warriors were so willing to fight, however. Many of them turned and fled in fear of the Israelites who had slain their champion. Those that stayed put up a half-hearted defence, still reeling with shock.

I watched with pride, revelling in our giant slayers' skill and courage as they took on Og's captains in units of three, just as we had taught them. They struck them down, working together faultlessly, until, by the end of the day, not a single man of the Amorites was left standing. It was an overwhelming victory.

I turned to find the shining men. They were still standing in the same place, surveying the battle taking place. Turning to face them, I placed my hand on my chest in acknowledgement. I could have sworn I saw subtle smiles on their glowing faces as they inclined their heads to me and disappeared.

35

Reconciliation

It was happening! What Yahweh had told us was coming to pass. After our defeat of Og and the vanquishing of all remaining Amorite towns and cities, we continued travelling north. Our spies reported that our exploits, especially the recent slaughter of King Og, had put the fear of our people on all the nations under heaven.

Caleb and I had been summoned to Moses' tent to hear a report from Adiel, one of our most experienced spies. Adiel was fleet of foot, thought to be our fastest runner, and a man of great integrity who we trusted implicitly. But the news he brought us was such that it caused even Moses to question him.

'A prophet? The Moabite king hired a prophet to curse our people?' Moses repeated, obviously wanting to make sure he had the facts clear. 'Adiel, are you certain of this?'

'Yes, my lord. His name is Balaam, son of Beor, and he dwells at Pethor.'

Turning to me, Moses asked, 'Joshua, have you heard of this man before?'

'No, Master. His name is not known to me.'

'And you say this Balaam is a prophet?' he asked Adiel, who frowned and screwed up his face.

'Their people call him a prophet because he interprets dreams and performs signs for them, but I do not believe he is a prophet of Yahweh, my lord. From what the people say, he worships many gods. I believe him to be a diviner.'

'Did you look upon this Balaam?'

'No. King Balak sent a delegation of officials, with much silver and gold, to summon him, but they had not yet returned when I left to bring this news to you. Beerah and Meshullam are still camped in the hills outside the city. They continue to talk with the people in the marketplace and, when they hear more news, one of them will come back to inform you, but we decided it was best to tell you what we have found out so far, before anything further takes place.'

'Yes, you were right to do so.' Moses nodded his head. 'So, King Balak is not willing to engage us in battle, *nu*?' he muttered, scratching his beard. He chuckled. 'Perhaps he is a wise king after all. He seeks instead to curse us, to try to weaken our power.' His eyes glinted with fiery excitement. 'Let him try! We shall see which holds the greatest power: the curses of our enemies, or the blessings of the mighty God of Israel!'

Just then, Davi appeared at the entrance to Moses' tent. '*Shalom*, Moses, *shalom* my brothers,' he greeted us, his countenance respectful but serious. 'Please forgive my intrusion.'

'Davi!' I said, scrambling to my feet. 'Is all well with Eglah? The family?'

'My *ima* is in good health, thank you, but I have been sent to ask you to come without delay.'

My heart skipped a beat; dread filled me. 'Is it...?'

Compassion radiated out of Davi's kind eyes... Hareph's eyes. 'It is my uncle Mesha. He is... unwell.'

I froze. I could feel my heart thumping, but my body refused to respond. His words lay like stones in my gut. There was a strained silence for a few seconds, then Moses said, 'Go. Stay with your family until Mesha is at peace and your mourning is fulfilled.' The honesty of his words was like a blow to my chest, but then, Moses had never been one to mince his words or avoid difficult issues. What would have been the point in saying '... until Mesha recovers...'? He was not going to recover. This was his time. Moses knew it, Davi knew it and I knew it too.

I cleared my throat, trying to get rid of the lump that blocked my words. 'Please tell my family I am on my way,' I rasped to Davi, who nodded at me, bowed to the other men, then backed out of the tent.

'With your permission, I will take my leave,' I said to Moses. My words felt awkward, overly formal, foolish. My mind was in a fog, I couldn't think straight.

Caleb stood up. 'I will walk with you,' he said. We bade Moses and Adiel farewell and walked towards my tent. I gathered some belongings, tied them in a bundle, slung them over my shoulder, and we set off together, walking side by side in silence. When Caleb and I first met as young men he was very rarely silent; thoughts tumbled out of his mouth in a disorderly fashion, like seeds spilling out of a bursting pod. Over the years, however, he had gained much wisdom; his current silence was testimony to that fact. I was glad of it; I could not have endured trivial conversation, not at a time like this. In the end, it was I who spoke first.

'I have been dreading this moment for so long, I hardly know what it is like to live without the fear of being summoned to my brother's deathbed. I would rather face another giant than bear this.' Caleb gave me an understanding smile. We trudged on through the camp, our dusty feet scuffling out a mournful, rhythmic pattern in the dirt. I was desperate to get there quickly, but some hidden internal resistance slowed my feet down, trying to put the moment off for just a little longer.

'I have been thinking much about Canaan in recent weeks. I still remember the expression on Mesha's face when we came back from spying out the land and spoke of the fruits we tasted there.' I turned to Caleb. 'He lit up, especially when we mentioned the pomegranates. He tasted one once, in Egypt, and the desire for more has never left him. It fell off the back of a passing cart and split open.' I chuckled at Caleb. 'Mesha picked it up, washed the dirt off it and devoured it within a few short moments.'

Caleb grinned. 'Pomegranates were my favourite fruit of all the bounty of Canaan. Mesha has good taste.'

'Mmm,' I agreed. 'He has lived so long; I was beginning to think perhaps Yahweh had relented and would spare him. But... it seems not.' I focused on the pathway ahead. 'My heart's desire was for him to taste the fruit of that land, to savour the sweetness of a pomegranate once more before he passes away. But...' my voice cracked, 'it seems it is not to be so.' I steadied myself for what lay ahead. We were getting nearer to home. I had lived on my own in my tent near Moses for so many years now, and yet I still could not call that home. Home was where my family dwelt, whether I was with them or not.

'Joshua,' Caleb said after a while. 'Would you permit me to come with you, to see Mesha? There is much I would say to him; I would make peace with him before he leaves this earth.' I hesitated. Caleb's intentions were good, but I didn't feel this was a decision I alone could make.

'Your thoughts are noble, my friend, and my heart desires the same, but I cannot speak on Mesha's behalf, and I would not see him troubled when he is near his end. I will speak with Helah and Mesha, and send word to you, yes?' Caleb nodded, then stared off into the distant land of Canaan, lost in thought. I wondered if perhaps he was offended by my words, but there was no time to ask him; we had arrived. He grasped both my shoulders, embraced me fiercely, then turned and left, breaking into a jog. He seemed oddly eager to leave.

Alya, Davi and Eglah were sitting outside the family tents watching over the children as they played games. The little ones were trying to build a tent with a pile of sticks and some pieces of cloth, while the older ones played a hopping game, linking one of their bent legs and clapping in time to a beat as they hopped round in a conjoined circle, trying not to be the first to fall over. I listened to the sounds of laughter and chatter and, for a moment, I wondered if perhaps Davi was wrong. The scene before me was so normal, the atmosphere so happy – how could Mesha be nearing his end when they were all so contented?

Alya, Davi and Eglah rose to greet me. Eglah gave me a lasting embrace then drew back. Her hand cupped the side of my face, her face radiating love as she whispered, 'He will be so happy to see you; he has been waiting for you to come.'

The rest of the family were packed into Mesha and Helah's tent. I greeted them, embracing them all individually, and they made room for me at Mesha's bedside. He didn't look like he was dying. To look at him, you wouldn't think he had lived more than seventy years, but then Mesha had always had a youthfulness about him. His mop of curly hair was still full, and only slight tinges of grey could be seen among his dark brown locks and in his beard. He still looked rugged and handsome, as he always had, and my mind could not conceive of his grave illness – until he spoke. I sat by his side and took his hand, greeted him and kissed both his cheeks.

'Are you in pain?' I asked.

'No,' he whispered, 'just very tired.' His breath was laboured and he spoke quietly, although his countenance was peaceful and he still had the same cheeky smile. Helah told me what happened. Over the past couple of weeks, Mesha had been feeling more and more weary but, being the stubborn man he was, he refused to slow down. He had been helping Yoram and Arad stake out a tent they were repairing when Helah heard him cry out and saw him clutching his chest. They caught him as he collapsed and brought him inside to rest; he had been lying on his bed since then.

Yoram, Joel and Helah decided not to call for the healers. They knew it was Mesha's time, and now they knew how he would die; it seemed his heart was failing.

36

Brother of My Heart

Helah needed no healer to tell her that her husband was dying. For my part, I was just grateful that Mesha was not in pain. I could not have borne that well. Helah told me he could eat and drink, albeit it slowly and only small amounts, and I noticed that his bright eyes were still fully aware of who was with him and what was happening around him.

I had been apprehensive about how I would find Helah, but she was unusually composed. Initially, when the death sentence had been proclaimed, Helah had taken the news very badly and, in her anger, had turned on me. She could not understand why I should be allowed to live and enter Canaan, when her beloved husband who, in her eyes had done no wrong, would not. Those were dark days but, as is often the case, in the passing of time balance was restored and Helah once again embraced me as a brother. During the weeks and then months that followed, Helah's grief was slowly replaced by a kind of numbed acceptance. A new understanding of the preciousness of life drew her and Mesha closer together, as they learned the necessity of living each day fully. Over the years, she had learned to find the special moments, storing them up in an unseen treasure chest which she held close in her heart. I realised that she had been preparing for this day for nearly thirty-eight years. She was ready.

I, on the other hand, was not.

Soon after I arrived, Mesha asked to speak to me alone. When the rest of the family left us, he drew me close. 'Yoshi... You have always... been the brother... of my heart,' he gasped, struggling to draw breath.

'As have you,' I assured him.

'Yoshi... forgive me...' he mumbled. I started to protest, but he held up his hand to stop me. 'Forgive me... my stubbornness.' He blinked away tears. 'I wasted... so many years.' I waited while he regulated his breathing. 'I couldn't... take back my words. Forgive me, brother.'

Tears flowed from both our eyes and fell, unhindered. He held out his arms to me so I helped him sit up and held him in my strong arms, supporting his back. All the anguish, the jealousy and anger, the pain of separation, flowed out of us, leaving in its place an immense sense of peace. Drawing back, Mesha whispered, 'Helah... Yoram... the children... look after them ...for me.'

'Of course. You have my word. As the Lord lives, they will want for nothing.'

I lowered Mesha back on his cushions and, when he was settled and his breathing had evened out again, I told him of Caleb's desire to visit him and asked if he would like to see him. Mesha was keen to speak to Caleb; it seemed he had unfinished business that he wanted to resolve with his warrior friend. Helah came to sit by Mesha's bedside while I went to ask Davi to take a message to Caleb.

We sat with Mesha, talking and reminiscing along with the rest of the family, into the afternoon. He was very tired, but said he wanted to stay awake to talk to Caleb when he came. It had been a while and Davi still had not returned. Where was he? He knew that time was of the essence; there was no way of knowing when Mesha would breathe his last. I was pacing up and down outside trying to decide whether to go and find Caleb myself or stay with Mesha, when Davi returned.

'What do you mean, you cannot find him?' I asked the young man, who was panting, wiping away the beads of sweat from his brow.

'I have looked everywhere,' he gasped, before taking a swig of water from his skin. 'He is nowhere to be found. The warriors who are training have not seen him, and Moses says Caleb has not come back to his tent since you both left there this morning. But Caleb's wife, Johanna, said she received a message at midday when she returned from visiting her family, saying that he had gone on a scouting mission, and that he had taken Iru with him.'

A scouting mission? Now? Caleb knew that I was going to send word to him about Mesha. Why did he choose to go on a mission now? And why did he go himself when we had plenty of scouting parties who went out regularly; there was no need for him to go. This made no sense. It was irresponsible and reckless of him. I was thoroughly irritated by his actions, and more than a little frustrated. I had raised Mesha's hopes of reconciling with Caleb, and now he was nowhere to be found. I felt responsible.

'Joshua,' Davi continued, filled with concern. He knew what was at stake. 'I checked with the watchmen. Nosson started his shift at midday, and reported seeing Caleb and Iru leaving the camp, heading northwards, shortly after midday.'

'Did they say where they were going?'

'No. They didn't speak to Nosson at all. He said they left in great haste, running fast across the plains. They wore no armour, and travelled light with just a small bundle each. I left word for a message to be sent to you here as soon as they return.'

I thanked Davi for his help and went inside to speak to Mesha. I explained that Caleb had been delayed, but promised to wake him if Caleb should arrive. Then Helah and I sat with Mesha as he drifted off to sleep. He looked so peaceful, so contented. Every now and then, Helah laid her hand on his chest to check his breathing. The first time she did it, she looked at me and blushed. Helah was now a mother of five and grandmother to many little ones. Her long, dark hair was streaked with grey and her brow was wrinkled with age but, when she blushed, she still had the look of that feisty young woman I met all those years ago.

'I was thinking of the night before we left Egypt,' she whispered. I raised my eyebrows, confused as to why she would be thinking of that now. 'The night of the death of the first-born – the first Passover,' she said. 'I sat up the whole night, watching Yoram, checking his breathing to make sure he had not been smitten in his sleep.' She sighed, looking down at her husband with a look of utter tenderness. 'And now I am doing the same thing again, forty years later, but with my husband.'

We sat together, keeping watch over Mesha, along with other family members, throughout the watches of the night. Caleb still had not come, or sent word. My frustration was fast turning to anger. How could he do this? The new day dawned and Mesha woke, seeming well rested and ready to break his fast. Helah and I looked at each other, surprised and somewhat bemused but, at his insistence, we carried him outside to rest in the shade of the tent overhang. He lay outside watching the children at play and his sons mending the tent; the tranquil look on his face reminded me of when Jesher used to sit outside in the shade and watch the world go by. Tranquillity was not something I would normally have associated with Mesha, but it suited him well.

Davi had gone out at first light, checking to see if Caleb and Iru had returned, but there was no sign of them. The day passed by and still Mesha hung on, breathing slowly but steadily, Helah sitting by his side holding his hand for much of the time. The evening drew in; we had just carried him inside and placed him on his bed roll when I heard a commotion outside, familiar voices. Caleb and Iru had arrived. I strode outside to confront him, but was silenced by what I saw.

Caleb had never been a man who cared much about appearances, but his measure of dishevelment was beyond anything I had seen before, apart from when he had just come off a battlefield. Both he and Iru were filthy, covered with dirt, from their dust-covered sandals to their grubby faces. Their headscarves trailed behind them and they were panting, as if they had been running for hours. They looked exhausted and blurry-eyed, and yet in their countenance was an odd air of triumph.

Before I could say a word, Caleb blurted, 'Mesha, is he...?'

I frowned. 'He is... resting.'

'May we see him?'

My anger dissipated, as did my carefully thought-out rebuke about his irresponsible behaviour, both replaced by curiosity. Wondering whether I should suggest they wash and change their clothes first, I decided against it and led them inside the tent, where Yoram and Helah were keeping Mesha company. Mesha's face lit up when he saw Caleb and Iru.

'You came!' he whispered, holding his hands out to grasp theirs.

'Yes. And we have brought you something,' Caleb grinned back at him, opening a rather dirty-looking linen bag. From it, he withdrew a sizeable bunch of grapes, some plums and oranges. Their fragrance filled the tent with a pungent citrus smell and we gasped at the luscious display before us. Then, with a flourish, Caleb produced not one, but six perfectly formed, huge, blushing red pieces of fruit.

'Pomegranates!' Mesha blurted in delight. 'But... where... where did you get... these from?' he asked.

Caleb and Iru glanced at each other before announcing, 'Canaan.'

'Canaan!' we exclaimed with one voice.

'You went into Canaan?' I asked, incredulous. 'How? When?'

'We left soon after you returned here. We ran through the night, keeping to the hills, until we came upon some vineyards and groves, where we found these treasures. Please,' Caleb said, turning to Helah, 'forgive the state of our apparel. We have not had time to wash or change.'

'That is no matter,' she said, stunned by what she was hearing. 'But... Canaan! Just the two of you? Was that not dangerous?'

'Did you encounter any giants?' I asked.

They grinned at each other like two co-conspirators and Iru replied, 'We did come across some, but it turns out being a lot smaller than them has its advantages.' Glancing around the room, he chuckled and said, 'It makes it much easier to hide!'

'But... how did you know about...' Mesha stuttered.

'Joshua told me of your longing for pomegranates and, since I share a similar passion, I could not have you... leave us... without tasting of the delights of the land that Yahweh has given us.' The laughter in the room ceased. We stood motionless, stunned at the extraordinary act of honour and bravery we were witnessing.

'You did that for me?' Mesha's eyes clouded over.

The two men stared at each other.

'Yes.'

A sob rose in my throat. I swallowed hard and blinked back tears. We left them alone. They spoke for quite some time in the privacy of Mesha's tent. He reconciled with Caleb. Caleb didn't speak much about it, but he did tell me that Mesha made him promise to slay some giants in his name. He also told me that Iru vowed to name his next son Mesha.

Mesha lived for another two days after Caleb and Iru's visit: two days of feasting to his heart's content on the fruits of the promised land. He died with a smile on his face and the taste of pomegranates on his lips.

37

Numbness

An obscure kind of numbness settled upon me following Mesha's death; I couldn't seem to shake it off. At times I found it hard to believe that he was gone. It was like a bad dream, hazy and muddled. He was so youthful and full of life – how could he be dead? It didn't make sense.

A few times, I found myself going into Mesha's tent to check if he was there. Each time that happened, a fresh deluge of memories would flood my mind; images of Mesha and I as young men in Egypt, strong and seemingly invincible. Mesha sparring with me, desperate to win, his shaggy mop of hair slick with sweat as he struggled to escape my grip. Mesha sitting with me day after day when my *abba* died, not really sure what to say or do, but just knowing that he needed to be there. The expression on his face on the day of his betrothal to Helah, and the tears that fell when he held his first-born, Yoram, in his arms.

The memories ripped into me, raw and ragged, but I welcomed the pain. I wanted to grieve. I needed to grieve. I needed to feel the stabbing jabs of anguish tear into me. I needed to get it all out, because, at the back of my mind, a persistent thought throbbed in my subconscious; that of another death that I would have to face soon, possibly sooner than I expected. I pushed the dread of that farewell down and would not let it enter my conscious mind.

'Time enough to face that when I have to,' I muttered to myself. I had enough to contend with right now.

The numbness dissipated over the days and then weeks of my mourning. Although the threat of Moses' departure still hung over me, I was grateful to have that time with my family, to live close to them again, to soak up their love and share in their grief. Watching the children play gave me hope – they seemed to have an innate ability to accept death without wrestling with it like we did. For them, death was part of life. Mesha and Helah's grandchildren missed their *saba* a lot, but they cried and cuddled and then continued living their lives. They embraced their loss and were then able to move on.

I admired their resilience.

During that time, my inspiration came from an unexpected source: Helah. She had always been an emotional woman, given to deep feelings and feisty opinions, but a poignant grace seemed to carry her through her time of mourning. I stood in awe of the peace that had pervaded her being – I had not expected that. Watching her with her grandchildren and great-grandchildren one day, I realised what it was that enabled her to do that. Love. She poured all the love in her heart for her deceased husband into the lives of her many grandchildren and great-grandchildren – and there were many! Over our wandering years, Samina seemed to have been permanently with child; soon after she had weaned a child, her belly would swell with another new life. She had given birth to seven children and was now carrying her eighth. Yoram delighted in the children she bore him, and in the now rather rotund shape of his beautiful wife and, when their older children were wed and started to have their own families, his cup of happiness overflowed.

'You are the joy of my heart,' he told his little flock as they crowded around him, demanding hugs and kisses from their father or grandfather. 'And you,' he said to Samina with unashamed adoration, 'are the queen of my heart, my beloved.'

All of Yoram's brothers and sisters were married, with children of their own, so Helah was constantly surrounded by little ones tugging at her skirts or climbing into her lap. She poured her love out on them and, in return, found healing. It was extraordinary to witness.

I had many opportunities during our time of mourning to talk with my family, to catch up with them and, in some cases, to get to know them afresh. It was a time of enrichment, of stopping and resting, of watching instead of doing. I marvelled at the mystery of family, realising that, especially in the last few months, my life had become so driven. This time of mourning was about drawing breath again and, even though I knew it would not last much longer, I revelled in it while I could. I smiled to myself; Jesher would have liked this. He would have liked to have seen me resting, spending time with my family – his family. Joel had been the patriarch of our family for some time and he was worthy of that honour. With Alya by his side, I knew they would lead with strength and wisdom; once again, our family was in good hands. They had both seen nearly sixty winters, and their children and grandchildren, along with the rest of the family, were flourishing under their care.

Both Caleb and Eleazar visited me from time to time while I was with my family, and updated me with the latest news, especially that which concerned the 'supposed prophet', Balaam.

'He could not curse us?' I said to Caleb as we sat outside in the shade of an awning by the family tents. 'What stopped him?'

Caleb wrinkled his nose. 'He claims to hear from Yahweh. He said Yahweh told him that our people are blessed and that he was not to curse us – although he still went with King Balak's officials to meet the king.' Caleb guffawed. 'The smell of all that gold and silver must have been too strong to resist, *nu?*'

I grunted in derision. 'If he truly was a prophet of Yahweh, He would know not to resist Him or rebel against Him, lest he face His wrath.'

'Well, our spies reported that Balak took Balaam to a high place, Bamoth Baal. He built seven altars – not one, but seven,' he said, grinning. 'He must have been desperate, yes? They sacrificed bulls and rams, but when Balak asked him to curse us, Balaam said, "How can I curse those whom God has not cursed?"'[19] Caleb shook his head, chuckling to himself. 'The king was greatly enraged, but it seems he is a stubborn man. He took Balaam to the top of Mount Pisgah, built more altars, and offered more sacrifices, but when it came time for him to curse us, again Balaam spoke only blessing.'

'What did he prophesy?' I asked, curious to know what this heathen prophet would say about our people.

'The spies said he spoke many words, but the ones they remember

---

19   Numbers 23:8.

most are these: "The LORD their God is with them; the shout of the King is among them."'[20]

I was fascinated. The shout of the King is among us? What did that mean? 'Well, heathen or not,' I muttered, 'this Balaam speaks as the oracles of God. "The shout of the King"? Hmm. Did Balak have him killed?'

'No,' Caleb said, giggling like a naughty child. 'He took him to a *third* high place, this time on the top of Mount Peor, built more altars and offered even more sacrifices!'

'In truth?'

Caleb nodded. 'This time, the words he spoke were not only blessings over our people, but curses over the Moabites – a foretelling of their destruction in the days to come. His predictions brought great fear to King Balak and his people.' Caleb went on to tell me that the king had sent Balaam away, back to his own land, with his life intact, but without the promised silver or gold.

'Moses has expressed a strong desire to meet this Balaam,' Caleb gave me a sly grin. 'Now *that* is an encounter I would very much like to see!'

---

20   Numbers 23:21.

38

Harlotry

Eleazar visited me a day or so after Caleb, but the news he brought was not nearly as diverting or as humorous as the reports of Balaam's inability to curse our nation of Israel.

'Our people are committing harlotry with the Midianite women,' he said, lowering his voice so that the children playing nearby could not hear what he was saying. 'Some of them have even taken part in sacrifices to their gods – pagan gods! They have eaten sacrificial meals and bowed down before these pagan idols,' he whispered. The quietness of his tone could not mask the rage in his voice. 'Did they learn nothing from the iniquity that took place with the golden calf...? So many died needlessly, because of their stubbornness and rebellion. Are they so foolish that they would deign to walk that same path again? To turn their backs on Yahweh? Joshua, I... I cannot...' He put his head in his hands and groaned. Looking up at me, his face filled with anguish, he rasped, 'Zeal for Yahweh lies heavily on me.'

Eleazar's news had shocked me beyond belief. I didn't know what to say, so instead I asked, 'How does Moses fare?'

'As you would imagine. He is filled with rage at the blindness and stupidity of our people. He spends much of his time fasting and praying before the Lord. This has caused much conflict within him.' Seeing the question on my face, he went on to explain. Moses's own wife, Zipporah, was a Midianite, and Moses himself had spent two score years with their tribe after he had run from Egypt. His father-in-law, Jethro, had been instrumental in helping Moses heal from the pain of his past, as well as realise his true self over the time he had lived with them. The Midianites had been allied with our people up until now, but I knew these gross acts of idolatry would change everything. It seemed a rather morbid thought, but I was thankful that Zipporah had passed from this world, purely so Moses would not have to deal with the conflict this could have created in their marriage.

Pausing for a while, Eleazar gathered himself, sat upright and set his shoulders back. 'Joshua, I would not have disturbed your time with the family or spoken to you of this unless I had to; I had to come and warn you. A plague has broken out in some parts of the camp.'

'*Plague*? Here?'

'Yes. Yahweh's judgement on this heinous idolatry.'

Plague? In our camp? Even though many thousands of our people were now settled in the various towns and cities that we had conquered on our journey northward, there were still hundreds and hundreds of thousands of us camped together here, on the plains of Moab. A plague in a camp the size of ours would spread like wildfire.

'Moses will have need of me. I must return with haste,' I said, rising to my feet.

'No!' Eleazar reached out and grabbed my arm. 'Moses knew you would say that. He instructed me to command you not to come back until your time of mourning is completed. He has forbidden it.'

My face contorted in disbelief. 'He forbids me to return?'

'Yes.' Eleazar stood up to face me. 'Those were his words. You are to stay here with your family until your time of mourning is complete. Look after them, protect them. Do not let them leave their tents except of necessity. Tell your women, when they go to get water, to cover themselves fully. They must stay away from the other women and not touch anything. The news will spread fast. We are trying to isolate those who are infected, and Moses has commanded that the bodies of those who die from the plague be burned outside of the camp.'

I nodded. This was a bleak picture that Eleazar was painting. 'Where is the main outbreak?'

'It seems to have started in the Simeonite tribe, but there are outbreaks all over the camp so it is difficult to know how far it reaches or how fast it is spreading. I must take my leave of you now and return to Moses.' Placing his hand on my shoulder, he said, 'Stay here, my friend. Protect your family, yes?'

'I will do as Moses commands but, I beg of you, come back tomorrow and tell me what has come to pass.'

Eleazar wrapped himself in a large, thick cloak and pulled his head-scarf over his head and face, leaving only a slit for his eyes. 'I will come back as soon as I can. *Shalom*, Joshua.'

'*Shalom*, Eleazar. May the Lord bless you and protect you. May no evil come near you or your family and no plague come near your dwelling.'

'Amen!'

Up until now, I had been quite content to stay with my family at their home without the need to go anywhere. But now that I knew I should not, or could not, leave the family home, it was all I wanted to do. I felt like an animal cooped up in a pen and found myself pacing up and down outside Yoram's tent, where I was staying, staring in the direction of the Tabernacle. Moses' tent was pitched right by the Tabernacle, Eleazar's and my tents near his. I wanted to be there with them, not here, stuck fast, unable to do anything to help. I studied the cloud of Yahweh's presence that hung like a glowing canopy over us. The tell-tale flashes of lightning and dark heaviness of the cloud confirmed what Eleazar had told me: Yahweh was angry.

Eleazar didn't return the following day, or the day after that. We stayed huddled in our family tents, trying to keep the children from roaming outside the perimeter of our community, and only going to fetch water from the stream when it was absolutely necessary. The nauseating smell of burning flesh filtered through the camp from the plains surrounding us, a constant reminder of the terrible plight we found ourselves in, and of the blatant sinfulness that had brought it about. From time to time, we heard the sound of screaming, of shouting and voices raised, carried by the warm wind that blew across the length of the camp. I paced up and down, staring into the distance, desperate to know what was taking place.

On the third day, I saw Eleazar striding towards me. I stood up with relief to greet him, and led him to a sunny spot on the outskirts of our family huddle of tents. Eleazar took off his cloak and headscarf and we sat down. Eglah brought us both water to drink, and some olives, then left us alone to talk.

'Tell me, what has happened?' I asked, impatient to receive an update. My close association with Moses meant that I was one of the first to hear any new information, so to be on the outside like this was frustrating and felt very isolating. I wasn't used to not knowing what was going on. I didn't like it.

'There is much to tell,' he said, raising his eyebrows.

'Yes? So...?'

Eleazar spoke for a long time with very little interruption from me. Moses had instructed the elders and judges of the twelve tribes to seek out the idolatrous men who had yoked themselves with these shameless women of Moab, and put them to death. Many of them had already died of the plague, which by now had killed thousands of people in the camp, but the idolators who had survived the plague paid for their sin, nevertheless. It was done. I realised that must have been the sound of screaming and shouting we heard. Eleazar told me that, yesterday, Moses went to the Tent of Meeting with a large assembly of leaders, elders and priests. They were praying to the Lord with much weeping, interceding and repenting on behalf of our people, when a man named Zimri walked nearby, arm-in-arm with a Moabite woman.

'Zimri?' I frowned. 'I have not heard that name.'

'No. His father, Salu, is a leader in the tribe of Simeon, but Zimri himself has done nothing notable or worthy of honour among our people. Until now, he was unknown to us.' Eleazar went on to tell me that Zimri had stopped near the assembled leaders and embraced the Moabite woman in their sight. She was wild and wanton, her face uncovered, with painted eyes and lips, and she had returned his affections with unrestraint.

I was horrified. 'Before all the leaders? Outside the Tent of Meeting, openly for all to see?'

'Yes. Then he led her away in the direction of the Simeonite camping grounds.'

Apparently Moses and the leaders with him were so stunned by

Zimri's actions that it took them a few minutes before they decided to go after them. There was one, however, who had been so incensed by Zimri's blatant display of rebellion that he did not hesitate, but slipped out unseen and followed Zimri and his harlot as they sauntered back to his tent. He watched them enter Zimri's tent and then, looking around, the man saw a spear lying nearby. Taking the spear in his hand, he entered the tent and, finding them lying together, drove the spear without hesitation through Zimri's back and deep into the woman's stomach.

'Who did this deed?' I asked Eleazar. He looked at me with a mixture of pride and sorrow.

'Phinehas.'

'Phinehas? Your son, Phinehas?'

'Yes. When we arrived, we found Zimri and the woman lying together in his tent, the spear still piercing their bodies, the women from his family shrieking and wailing. Yahweh told Moses that since Phinehas was zealous for Him to honour His name, He would turn His anger away from our people. The plague has been stopped.' Eleazar looked at me, tears brimming over. 'My son's zeal for Yahweh has saved our people from much destruction.'

We stayed quiet for a while in recognition of the solemnity of his words. Then I spoke. 'Phinehas is a mighty man of valour, and what he has done will be written in the chronicles of our people. His name will be honoured because he has surpassed his brethren in excellence. He will be fastened as a peg in a secure place and his name will be established for time to come.'

Eleazar nodded and wiped the tears with his sleeve. 'I spoke with Phinehas last night and asked him what made him do it. He reminded me of the stories of when I first raised my sword to slay another man, in zeal for Yahweh.' He glanced at me to see if I knew what he was referring to.

I did. I remembered it only too well.

It was during the beginning of our wanderings in this wilderness, when Yahweh's people had turned to idolatry, just as they had now. A deep darkness had slithered its way into the camp, causing many of them to turn from Yahweh and worship a golden calf which Eleazar's father, Aaron, had crafted for them. It was a dark time for our people and many were infected by the nefarious evil that had poisoned their souls. Eleazar and I were the first to answer Moses' call to make a stand for the Lord, but Eleazar was still a young priest at that time. He had hardly held a weapon before, let alone killed a man. But he did that day. His passion for the ways of Yahweh superseded both his loathing of violence and his love of peace. I could still remember the look of revulsion and anguish on his face as he stood over the dead body of the leader of the rebellion, Shimea, holding a sword still dripping with Shimea's blood.

'I remember it well,' I whispered.

The tribe of Levi had been set aside for service to Yahweh from that time onwards, as a result of the sacrificial stand they had made for the Lord on that day. Now, nearly forty years later, Eleazar's son had stood for righteousness, just like his father before him. And, just like his father, the favour and blessing of Yahweh would rest upon Phinehas' ancestors for generations to come, because he upheld the Lord's cause with courage and righteousness.

The plague stopped on the day Phinehas slew Zimri and his harlot; the smell of burning corpses no longer defiled the air around us. Soon afterwards, when my time of mourning was fulfilled, I returned home to my tent. Moses and I spent much time discussing what had happened.

'The woman Zimri took as his harlot was named Kozbi,' he told me. 'She was the daughter of one of their tribal chiefs. This will cause much discord between our people and theirs. There will be retribution.' He was right. Just a matter of weeks later, the battlelines were drawn and we went to war against the nations who had tried to infiltrate our ranks with the stench of idolatry and harlotry.

Accompanying the warriors who marched out to face them were our high priest, Eleazar, and his valiant son, Phinehas. Both of them had swords tightly grasped in their hands.

39

Fly

'These mountains are indented with the fingerprints of Yahweh. They speak of ancient rhythms,' Moses whispered, looking around at the craggy peaks of Mount Pisgah. 'It was on a summit like this that Yahweh first spoke to me,' The wind whistled around us, blowing our robes until they billowed like sails on a sea vessel, begging to be released.

'What was it like, when Yahweh spoke to you first?' I asked, hanging onto my headscarf with both hands to stop it from taking flight.

'*Ech*!' Moses exhaled and stopped, shaking his head at the recollection. 'It was the most terrifying experience ever – and the most wonderful!' He spoke with such conviction; it caused a thrill to run through me. We continued walking. 'I was tending Jethro's sheep; they were so restless that day, scattering and running away. I was getting frustrated and had just decided to lead them back down the mountainside to safety when it happened.'

'What? What happened?'

'I felt the hairs on the back on my neck bristle – there was something behind me. I thought it was a wolf, so I slowly unsheathed my knife and swung round to face it. But there was nothing there except...'

'Except what?'

'A bush,' said Moses.

'A bush?'

'A bush that was on fire.' Moses wrinkled his nose. 'It doesn't sound very remarkable, does it? But it was, because the bush was covered in flames, glowing yellow, orange, red, even shades of purple and blue – but it did not burn up. The leaves on the bush were still green and glossy. They did not crumble or blacken, but they were on fire.'

'That sounds like what happened on Mount Sinai when Yahweh came down to speak with His people. The mountain was on fire – I saw bushes and plants engulfed in flames – but they did not perish!'

'Yes, it was very much like that,' Moses replied, 'except it was just one bush, not a whole mountain and it was the first time I had encountered the fire of Yahweh's presence.'

'So what did you do?'

'What any red-blooded male would do. I went closer to have a proper look. That is when I heard His voice. He told me to take my sandals off, because the place where I was standing was holy ground. I removed them, threw them aside, and bowed down with my face to the ground. I could not look on the bush, it seemed to burn into my very heart.' Moses' eyes watered. 'That was the moment when this all began. Yahweh told me that He was sending me back to Egypt to confront Pharaoh and bring His people out of bondage in Egypt.'

'What did you say?'

Moses cringed. 'I argued with Him.'

'You argued with Yahweh?'

'I did.' Moses shook his head and pressed his fingers to his forehead. 'The Lord is gracious, Joshua. Not only did He *not* punish me for my insolence, but He told me that I would work miracles with this staff,' he said, looking at it with great fondness. 'When I continued to resist His command, He said that Aaron would go with me and be my spokesman.'

'Why did you need Aaron to speak for you?' I asked, although my mind was already recalling what Eleazar had told me about Aaron working miracles in Egypt.

'Aah, Joshua, you didn't know me then. I could hardly string a sentence together, and speaking in front of large groups of people terrified me. I stuttered and stammered.' He shook his head from side to side. 'It was shameful.'

'Truly, Master?'

'Truly,' Moses nodded, chuckling at the disbelieving expression on my face.

'Oh'. I thought for a bit, then gave a cheeky grin. 'Well, you don't appear to have that problem now!'

We laughed and he pointed to a nearby outcrop of rock. 'Come, let us rest a while.' Moses was surprisingly agile for his age and certainly did not look like a man who had lived for one hundred and twenty years. However, I had noticed he was a lot slower now; we had been climbing the slopes of this mountain for at least an hour, which had left him breathless and wheezing.

'You never told me that story before,' I said as we sat on a rock and looked out over the endless vista of mounds and valleys before us.

'No. But it is good that you hear it today, because this is an important day for you, Joshua.'

My smile froze. A wave of dizziness hit me and my heart started pounding. No! Not now! I glanced at him. He was waiting for me to respond, so I mumbled, 'Today? How so?'

Moses turned to face me and said, 'Because Yahweh has chosen you to take over leadership of His people when I go the way of my fathers. You will lead this great people into their promised land of Canaan.'

I felt the blood drain from my face. I shook my head. 'No! No, Master, that is not possible. I cannot do it. I am not like you, I cannot ...'

'Joshua,' Moses said, putting his hands up to stop further protestations. 'Yahweh has spoken and He has chosen *you*. His choice is true. There is no one else who can take on this mantle.'

'Master, I cannot lead this people, I am not like you. I am your manservant, not a great leader. You must understand, I am not the right choice for this task. Yes, I can lead our warriors into battle, but I cannot lead Yahweh's people.'

He frowned at me. 'Joshua, did you truly not know that you are to lead our people when I leave? Has Yahweh not spoken to you of this?'

'He... I... well, yes, He...' I stuttered, trying to put words to the thoughts that were darting around inside my head. 'He told me long ago that I would perform great wonders and lead our people... but I believed Him to be speaking of my feats in warfare and slaying giants... not...' My voice petered out and I glanced at him helplessly.

'Mmm.' Moses scratched his beard, as he often did when he was deep in thought. 'What you have accomplished is praiseworthy and honourable; you have done all that was asked of you with courage and excellence. But leading our armies and facing giants was only preparing you for what Yahweh would have you do. You *will* lead this people, Joshua.'

'I cannot!' I blurted. Panic rose up, hammering inside of me, demanding a voice. 'You don't understand! I am not like you. I am not a prophet who speaks the oracles of God!'

'I was a stammering, reclusive naysayer when Yahweh called me. But you see, it is not our strengths or abilities that matter, it is *His*. If He calls you, He will be with you, and you will find a strength that you never realised was there – and courage – and wisdom. It is all here within you, Joshua,' Moses said, reaching out to put his hand on my heart.

'Master, do not go. I beg of you, do not leave me. I cannot do this without you. Stay! Stay with me and help me.' My forehead was clammy with sweat.

Moses frowned. 'Joshua, my time is nearly over. It is *your* time now. You must take on this mantle, this great honour.' He searched for a flicker of excitement or resolve, but I knew he saw only fear. He looked away, scanning the panoramic landscape that extended as far as the eye could see, and fell silent. I knew I was disappointing him. I felt ashamed, like the coward that I was, but I could not pretend to be something that I knew I was not. I would not be false. Not even to please him.

A haunting screech interrupted our musings. We looked up to see an eagle gliding across the sky, high above us. Moses grunted and muttered to himself, before asking me, 'Do you know much about the way of the eagle?'

'No, Master.' I squinted, looking at the magnificent creature circling the heavens. I couldn't look at Moses. I couldn't bear to see the disappointment in his eyes.

'Mmm. As a boy in Egypt, I had a tutor whose passion was eagles. He would take me far out into the desert from time to time to study them. He showed me the places where they built their nests, high up on the mountain peaks, and told me how the adult eagles teach their babies to fly.' He leaned back against the rock behind us, studying the eagle's flight.

'When the babies have grown, the parents break the twigs in the nest and throw the soft leaves out to make it uncomfortable for their young one. Then, one day, the parent hovers over the little one and flaps its wings vigorously, beating its chick with its wings, until the baby scurries onto its parents' back to try to escape.' He turned to me with a glint in his eye. 'That is what it had been waiting for!' I looked at him, bemused and sullen. Why was he instructing me about eagles at a time like this? Much though I loved his stories, I was really not in the mood for one now. Moses ignored my disgruntled expression and stood to his feet, acting out his story.

'The parent takes off in flight, the baby clinging onto its back as it flies higher and higher. Then, just when the baby is starting to get used to the feel of the wind rushing by, the parent darts out from underneath it and the baby falls, plummeting down, down, down to the earth below.' He stretched his arms out, flailing dramatically, acting the part of the baby. 'He flaps his wings as hard as he can, but his wings cannot hold him up. Just before he hits the ground, the parent swoops underneath the baby and bears him up again, flying higher and higher. Time and time again they do this, carrying the baby high up into the sky then dropping him. Each time, the baby's wings grow stronger until, finally, his outstretched wings catch the wind, he is lifted up, and the youngling starts soaring in the heavens, as Yahweh created him to do.'

He finished his story and sat down, heaving a deep sigh of satisfaction. I gave him a quick glance, wondering if he was waiting for me to respond in some way, but he seemed content to continue staring up at the eagle gliding overhead, so I stayed silent and watched with him. After a while, he turned to face me. Leaning in, he peered at me.

'Joshua, it is your time to fly.'

40

My Name

'Come, let's eat. You have brought food, yes?' Moses asked, his tone light, as if we were on an enjoyable day out, simply passing the time with nothing pressing to dwell on.

I nodded in response and reached down to open my bag. I always brought food when we ventured out, otherwise we would never eat. Food was not something that featured very highly on Moses' list of priorities. I was surprised he'd thought of it at all – it was usually I who suggested it was time to eat. I pulled out of my bag a linen pouch, which I untied and laid on the rock between us. Inside it were some manna cakes wrapped in cloth, a second parcel containing a lump of cheese with some olives, and a selection of figs and dates that were loose inside the pouch.

We ate in silence. The lump in my throat forbade me to speak. The pain in my chest demanded I stay silent. Even if I could have spoken, what would I have said? There was nothing more to say.

It was done.

Yahweh had spoken and it seemed I had no choice but to take up the mantle and accept the impossible quest of walking in Moses' footsteps.

'Joshua, you will fly.'

'Will I?' I thought to myself, struggling to swallow my mouthful. 'How? My wings are not strong enough. How can I fly without you by my side, teaching me and guiding me?' I removed the stopper from my waterskin and took a few mouthfuls.

'You are not alone,' Moses urged me, as if reading my thoughts. 'Yahweh is with you; you will do mighty exploits in His name.' Seeing the look of doubt and disbelief on my face, he sat up straight and frowned at me. 'You honour me as prophet of the Most High God, so now hear my words: you *will* lead this people into the promised land of Canaan. Yahweh *will* be with you and you will accomplish all that He sets before you.'

He took a swig of water, wiped his mouth, and continued, 'You have good men around you. Listen to them. Eleazar has not been high priest for long, but he has grown in wisdom and stature and displays much grace and strength. He is no longer the timid, clumsy young man he once was. He is a wise, much respected high priest – and he is very perceptive,' Moses said, tapping his finger on the side of his head. 'He can read the thoughts and intents of people's hearts and will be a great help to you in leading this people. You can rely on him. He will not let you down. Draw counsel and strength from him.' He bit into a fig and chewed with vigour.

By now, I realised that objecting would be fruitless, so I sat still, my heart dull and listless, listening as Moses spoke over me what felt like a death sentence. 'The new elders that have been appointed are men of honour and integrity. Yes, they are all younger than you, but they know the ways of Yahweh and they will stand by you. You also have Caleb,' he said, wagging his finger in my face. 'He is no longer the imprudent, impetuous man that he was in his youth. He is brave and loyal, and he follows the ways of Yahweh wholeheartedly. You will do well with a man like Caleb by your side, and there are many others like him – your own nephews, Yoram and Joel, among them.'

Looking into my eyes with a disarming stare, Moses reiterated, 'You are not alone, Joshua. You are not alone. Yes?' I nodded. There was no point in disagreeing or objecting. He sighed and looked around us. 'This mountain is like an old friend to me. Many adventures have I had here. This was the place I first heard His voice, and this is the place where He will call me to Himself. It started on a mountain and it will end on one.'

'It will end here, Master?' I asked, my voice squeaked like the sound of cane scraping on wet leather.

'Yes. This is where Yahweh will take me to be with Him when the appointed time comes.' I didn't say anything. A suffocating sadness engulfed me. 'Come!' Moses said, slapping his knees and standing up. 'Let us make our way down now, *nu*?' I stuffed the last fig in my mouth and shook the remaining crumbs onto the ground. Retying the linen bag, I slung it over my shoulder and we started off down the mountain together. We walked in silence for a while, reflecting on what we had discussed, until Moses broke the quietude.

'Joshua, our people must understand how important Yahweh's presence is.' He stopped and turned to face me. 'You must not let them forget that Yahweh's presence among us is what makes us different from every other nation. His love for us is everlasting, and His presence – they must not turn away from Him. Do not let them turn to other gods.'

'I will do my best, Master.' A numbness was overtaking my senses, replacing panic with a dull sense of resigned acceptance.

'This is what Yahweh wanted, from the beginning of time – to walk with His people, as He did with our first father and mother, Adam and Eve, in the garden. To be their God, and for them to be His special treasure. But time and again, His people reject Him and turn aside to other gods.'

'Not all of them.'

Moses turned to smile at me. 'No. Not all of them.' Just then, we walked through a spacious clearing on the mountainside. The sunshine lit up the landscape and we paused to look out over the distant lands of Canaan. I pointed out some of the landmarks that I had seen all those years ago, when I went to spy out the land.

'You see that flat area, over there,' I pointed far into the distance. 'That is where we first saw a giant. We took refuge in a grove of acacia trees just beyond that point and hid there for hours.'

'Yes, I see it,' Moses replied, concentrating hard.

'You can see it? You can see the grove of trees?' I was astonished.

Moses swung round, amused. 'My eyes are not dim, Joshua. Yahweh has been kind to me. My body is still strong, and my eyes sharp. I am ready to go the way of my fathers when Yahweh calls me, and I go with eyes that see clearly where He is leading me.' Moses saw the look of concern on my face. Putting his hand on my shoulder, he said, 'Do not fear for me. I am not afraid of death. Although,' he chuckled, 'I will admit, I did ask Yahweh if He would change his mind. Not,' he said, lifting up a finger, 'because I was afraid of dying, but because I wanted to see our people enter the land that was promised to them.'

'What did He say?'

'He said no! But He told me to come to the top of this mountain, and look upon the land that He has given to our people. Mmm,' he muttered. 'This is a significant day. I have seen His promises. I have looked... beyond the horizon and it is good. This land is good. Our people will flourish there.' Coming back to reality with a start, he said, 'Come, we must go down, the storm clouds are gathering. We must return to the camp.'

Moses plunged down the mountain path with fresh energy, stopping a few moments later to say, 'Do you know, the eagle is the only bird which flies directly into a thunderstorm. Hmm? Yes, it is true. Other birds fly away from a thunderstorm, seeking refuge and shelter in the safety of a tree or their nest. Not so with the mighty eagle. He flies directly into the thunderclouds.' He regarded me with a look of such pride, it took me by surprise. Was he referring to me? Did he truly see me as being like one of Yahweh's mighty eagles? I brushed it aside. It could not be.

We walked single file down the mountain, silently contemplating the day's events and, as we neared the campsite, he paused and turned to me.

'Joshua, would you do one more thing for me?'

'Of course, Master, anything.'

'I want to hear you call me by my name.'

'Your name? But, Master, I ...'

'Joshua, we have walked together for a long time. You started out as my servant, but you are not my servant now.' Moses placed his hand on my shoulder and looked at me with such tenderness, my heart leapt. 'You have not been my servant for many, many years. You are my *friend*. You know me better than my own family, better than my own blood. I am not your master now and I have not been for quite some time. I am your friend. And I want to hear you say my name, as my friend.'

I looked at him, shocked. Seeing that he was serious, I gulped hard and said, 'Your name... your name is Moses.'

Moses leaned back, grinning. 'This is good, Joshua. Yes, this pleases me. Say it again!' he said. 'I want to hear it again. *Say it again!*'

I looked at him in bewilderment and sighed. 'You are Moses.' Tears pricked the back of my eyes. I could fight them no longer. My voice trembled. 'You are Moses. My master... and my friend.'

'Yes. I am. I am indeed. This is good. Now we are ready! You will call me master no longer! Come my friend, let us go and tell these people who the Lord has chosen to lead them into this land that He has given them!'

41

Chosen

As soon as we arrived back at camp, I sought out Eleazar. We walked a little way out of the camp where we could talk, and I poured out my heart to him about all that had happened on the mountain that day. As always, he listened without interrupting me, occasionally nodding and 'hmm'ing to himself. When at last I was done, I looked to him for a response. None came.

'You don't seem surprised by what I have told you,' I said. 'Did you know of this already?'

'Yes.'

'Who told you? Moses?'

'No one told me. I knew in my heart that you were Yahweh's chosen vessel. I have known for some time that you were the only man worthy of taking on this mantle.' I shook my head in disbelief. 'Joshua,' he said, leaning forward, 'this is a great honour that Yahweh has bestowed on you.'

I snorted. 'It is not an honour I have sought after.'

'I know, and that is why Yahweh has chosen you; because you are not a man who grasps for power, who desires to control others or use them for your own ends. Yahweh has your heart and that is why He has chosen you. He knows He can trust you.'

'Would that He had chosen someone else,' I muttered, kicking the twigs and dry leaves that lay on the dusty ground where we sat.

'Joshua, the man that tends the fig tree will eat of its fruit.'

I snorted. 'I do not wish to eat its fruit. I am content to continue tending the tree.'

Eleazar frowned at me. 'Moses is right. You are ready to take on the mantle of leading this great nation.'

'It is not something I desire.'

'Why?' Eleazar asked, his brow wrinkled with confusion.

'Because...' I huffed. 'Because... if I take on this mantle then he must take it off.' I stared at the pebbles in the sand at my feet. 'He cannot leave.' My voice broke. 'I cannot be without him.' It was said, out in the open. Like the sun breaking through dark clouds, the fog that had clouded my mind lifted and all became clear. I was not fearful of leading our people. I could do that if I had to. I had led thousands of men for many years, I could continue to do that. I was not fearful of taking on the mantle being handed to me; but I was desperately, overwhelmingly afraid of doing it without Moses.

Eleazar nodded and fell silent, rocking slowly backwards and forwards, as was his way. I could find no words to pray. Twilight was falling and, in the mellow calmness of dusk, I became aware of the rhythmic chirping of insects in the tufts of grass nearby. I watched a lizard scurry up a tree, its tail flicking from side to side as it stalked a hapless fly resting on a leaf, oblivious to its impending doom.

I felt like that fly.

The sound of lambs bleating drifted towards us from the pens on the outskirts of the camp, and a firefly floated in front of me, winking lazily in the fading light. The mouthwatering aroma of bread baking on the coals wafted towards us, carried by the evening breeze, and I could hear the voices of families laughing and chattering as they gathered for the evening meal. How could the lives of those around me carry on when the world as we knew it was falling apart? I felt so alone.

No one knew the pain that speared my heart.

No one could understand the immense burden that was about to be placed upon me, or the conflict that ripped my soul apart.

'It was not so long ago when we had this same conversation; only then it was I who longed to turn away from the honour afforded me, not you.' Eleazar's dulcet tones merged with the gentle sounds of dusk, shaking me out of my mirey thoughts. 'That day, when we went up the mountain, Moses took the high priestly garments off my *abba* and put them on me. I wanted to tear them off my body. They felt heavy and alien. They were not mine; they were of my father. He was the high priest. How could I receive these robes that were his very essence, his life, his service before Yahweh? When Moses placed the ephod over my head, I wanted to jerk my head away.' Eleazar closed his eyes, pain shadowing his countenance. 'The material was smooth, softer than any I had felt before, finely twisted linen in colours that jarred in my consciousness – blue, purple, scarlet, gold. They were foreign to me; they were not my colours.'

He looked up, silently daring me to stop his confession. 'He placed the waistband around me and, when he knotted it, I felt it tightening, like the bonds of a prisoner. I was captive to its demands, my life no longer my own.' Eleazar did not blink as he continued his discourse. 'The breastplate... so heavy, so ornate... the precious stones mounted on it, engraved with the names of our twelve tribes. It was *wrong*,' he blurted, an uncharacteristic anger blazing in his eyes. 'All wrong. I knew I should not be wearing it. I could not carry the responsibility of this people.' Eleazar's breaths were shallow and rapid. 'The tassels and woven pomegranates, the bells on the hem of my robe – their jingling was as a discordant clanging in my ears, screaming to me that *I could die*! I could die in the very presence of Yahweh, if I were found unworthy! And I did feel unworthy.' He paused and closed his eyes, trying to regulate his breathing. 'Then he placed the turban on my head and I felt as if the weight of the world had been placed upon me.' He opened his eyes and looked at me. I couldn't speak. There were no words.

I was wrong.

I was not alone.

There was one other who understood the exquisite torment of letting go of one treasure in order to embrace another.

'When it was done,' Eleazar whispered, 'he stood there dressed only in his tunic. He looked naked, exposed. Seeing him stripped of his robes cut into me like a dagger. I couldn't look at him. I couldn't look into the face of the one who had been disrobed on my account.' He exhaled. His shoulders relaxed and a soft smile appeared on his face. 'Then he called my name. I looked into his face and the smile I saw there defied the nakedness of his personage. His smile was one of love, of passion... of pride. He was proud of me. He was glad to be disrobed, greatly desirous that I should accept the honour of being the high priest of Yahweh. He was ready to leave. I was not ready for him to go, but he was ready.' Eleazar wiped the tears away. 'And now, when I put the robes on and minister before the Lord, I feel him with me – my *abba*. The robes that once felt so alien and hostile are now a part of me. They are beauty and righteousness and holiness – the mantle of Yahweh on my person. And when my time has come to leave this world, I will look upon Phinehas with the same love and pride that my *abba* looked upon me, and I will pass the mantle on to him.'

We sat silently side by side. Nothing more was said – at least, not in words.

We watched the flickering flames of Yahweh's presence as His glorious cloud transformed into the pillar of fire that we loved so much. Blurred patches of amber and auburn appeared in the towering cloudy pillar and morphed into burning embers. Fanned by unseen winds, they glowed brighter and brighter until they erupted into blazing bursts of light, dancing and swirling around a magnificent shimmering edifice.

42

Inauguration

The day of my inauguration dawned bright and sparkling, glistening with anticipation. Our people gathered together as one body, solemn yet expectant, to witness the moment when Moses would hand over leadership of our mighty nation to a man such as I.

I felt sick.

I stood before them, looking out over the endless sea of faces before me. Some stared at me curiously, a few looked sullen and doubtful, but many smiled at me, their eyes full of hope. 'My Lord Yahweh, let me not disappoint them,' I prayed. The elders of our people and the captains of thousands stood at the front of the assembly in the places of honour. Caleb caught my eye and grinned at me, and Yoram, who was both an elder and a captain, smiled encouragingly. I knew he could sense the fear that pulsated through my body.

Eleazar stood with me, dressed in his high priestly robes. His words rang in my ears: 'He was proud of me... greatly desirous that I should accept the honour... I was not ready for him to go, but he was ready...' but the painful thumping of my heart would not let me find release.

Moses stood a few feet in front of us, calm and resolute. Raising his voice, he announced, 'The Lord God, who gives breath to all living things, has appointed someone over this community to go out and come in before you, one who will lead you out and bring you in, so the Lord's people will not be like sheep without a shepherd.'[21]

I couldn't look at him in the eyes. I studied his chest, focusing on the uneven weave of his robe, the tiny wisps of thread that had

---

21   Paraphrase of Numbers 27:16-17.

strayed from their place. I could feel my body shaking; I held myself rigid as he continued.

'Joshua, son of Nun, a man in whom is the spirit of leadership, is to stand before Eleazar the priest. At his command he and the entire community of the Israelites will go out, and at his command you will come in.'[22]

I heard Moses's voice echoing, as if far off in the distance, inviting me to step forward.

My feet would not move. I was a tree, rooted to the spot, until I felt Eleazar's hand in the middle of my back, a warm, gentle pressure urging me forward. I took a step and stumbled. Quickly righting myself, I took another step, and another, and two more, until I stood before Moses. Eleazar stood by my side, my faithful helpmate.

I shut my eyes, trying desperately to block out the waves of fear that washed over me as Moses declared, 'Be strong and courageous, for you must go with this people into the land that the LORD swore to their ancestors to give them, and you must divide it among them as their inheritance. The LORD Himself goes before you and will be with you; He will never leave you nor forsake you. Do not be afraid; do not be discouraged.'[23]

I felt Moses' hands on my head. Waves of warmth flooded through my body, igniting within me sparks of life. I felt a flickering, then a quickening, then jolts of energy pulsing through my body. Thoughts of the multitudes gathered there to witness this solemn event faded into the background of my consciousness. The man standing before me and the words that he was declaring blended into a blur; there was nothing except the all-consuming Presence that was invading my being.

I was vaguely aware of Eleazar by my side, calling Caleb and Phinehas to come and stand behind me. They told me afterwards that I started shaking violently when Moses laid his hands on me, and that I would have fallen to the ground had they not supported me.

I have no idea how long it went on for.

When I came to myself, I looked straight into the face of my master,

---

22 Paraphrase of Numbers 27:18,21.

23 Deuteronomy 31:7-8, with capitals for deity added.

my friend. His smile broke me. My chest started heaving, but no sound came forth and no tears fell until he placed his hands on my shoulders. At that very moment, the blast of a hundred trumpets sounded, and the people erupted into a deafening roar. I collapsed to the ground, howling in pain. Moses dropped his staff and knelt by me, gathering me into his arms. As if by some unseen signal, Eleazar, Caleb and my faithful captains of thousands stepped forward. Moving to standing with their backs to me, they created a solid wall of bodies around me, shielding me from sight.

They stood, motionless, staring outwards as the crowds cheered on and the music played, while I sobbed in the arms of my master – my friend – for the last time.

43

Strong and Courageous

'Joshua?' I started and turned around to see Eleazar walking towards me.

'*Shalom*, Eleazar,' I replied, swivelling back to stare at the path that led up the mountainside. He sat down next to me and we remained there for a while, sitting side by side on that lonely mountain in the warm late afternoon sun. After a while, Eleazar cleared his throat.

'Joshua?'

'Hmm?' My gaze never left the pathway.

'It's time to return to the camp.'

'Not yet.'

I could hear him breathing in and out a couple of times, as if steadying his nerves. 'You've been up here for hours. It's time to go back now.'

'*Not yet*,' I muttered through clenched teeth. I could feel anger building in me. More silence. I willed him to go away and leave me in peace, but he didn't. Eleazar was never one to give up easily. He was just like his uncle.

'Joshua,' he murmured. 'What are you waiting for?'

I turned to him, frowning at his stupidity. 'I'm waiting for Moses.'

'Joshua …' Eleazar sighed. Tension lay thick in the air around us. 'He is not coming back.'

'We don't know that.' My voice was tight and raspy. I could feel my heartrate increasing. 'If he comes back, he must not find me gone.'

He put his hand out to touch my shoulder. I flinched. He removed his hand. 'Joshua, he's not coming back. Not this time. You know that; he told us himself. He is gone from this place now. He will not return to us.'

I could not speak. My heart was thumping so hard, I thought it would explode. I shuddered. My throat constricted; I felt like I was about to choke. I couldn't have said anything, even if I had wanted to. I didn't want to. All I wanted to do was lash out at Eleazar, beat my fists into his body over and over again to make him feel some of the pain that besieged me at that moment. My body started to heave as desperate sobs built up inside me, threatening to explode. I closed my eyes, gritted my teeth, and started rocking – short, sharp movements. Then, as if in a dream far off, I heard groaning, gasping, panting. I looked up to see Eleazar's anxious expression as he watched me wrestle with my demons. The noises were coming from my body. Beads of perspiration appeared on my forehead. My breathing came in short, sporadic bursts.

Eleazar watched and waited, saying nothing.

I could stand it no more. A noise like the howling of a wolf erupted out of my mouth and I crumpled face down on the ground, sobbing and wailing in a mire of agony. Eleazar was next to me in an instant, his arms around my shoulders, as grief poured out of me like a dam that had burst its banks. His tears overflowed, unchecked; he didn't even bother wiping them away. My weeping and wailing turned to groaning and travail as I laboured with the birth pains of my grief. Lifting my head to the heavens, I shouted, roaring into the wind in agony.

'Moses!' I howled. 'Moses...!'

Still, Eleazar sat in silence, holding me tight, a solitary sentinel guarding his charge. Desolation swept over me, wave after relentless wave. The wind raged around us, joining me in unspoken partnership, rushing and roaring, until my wrath started to transition into lamentation. As the outpouring of my grief diminished, so too did the wind die down. When all that remained was the sound of my erratic breathing, Eleazar released his hold on me. I sat back, glassy-eyed and spent, on the ground where I had laboured. We stared at one another, as if seeing each other afresh. Then he stood up, held out his arms and lifted me to my feet.

Still, he said nothing.

I looked up at the lonely mountain pathway one last time and heaved a deep, shuddering sigh. Gathering my cloak around me, I pulled my headscarf down to cover my face, and started down the mountain. Eleazar fell in step with me.

Caleb was standing by the entrance to my tent in the darkness, waiting for our return. One look at our faces told him all he needed to know. He led me inside and sat me down. Bringing a bowl of water, he dipped a cloth and began to wash my face. I remember thinking to myself that for a seasoned warrior, he had a very gentle touch. He washed my hands next, tenderly unfurling my fists, which were still tightly balled. Then he untied my sandals, took them off and started washing my feet. I watched him in hollow silence. My thoughts were disjointed. Nothing made sense. I felt as if I were a spectator watching what was happening, and it was only when Eleazar brought me a drink and a dish of broth that I spoke.

'Thank you,' I said, looking at them through swollen eyes. Eleazar smiled at me and squeezed my shoulder. I could only manage a few mouthfuls of broth. 'Forgive me, I can eat no more.' They sat with me, praying, and waiting. 'Waiting for what?' I thought to myself. 'What now?' He was gone. It was all up to me. 'I cannot do this,' I muttered. 'I cannot do this. Not without him. I cannot lead this people!' I cried. 'Without Moses, I am... I am nothing.'

'Those thoughts are falsehood, Joshua,' Eleazar responded in calm certainty. 'Do not listen to the voice of deception. You are Yahweh's chosen one. You alone are His choice. He will speak to you and tell you what to do.'

'Will He?' I asked, panic and confusion choking my heart. 'Why would He choose a man like me? Why?'

Eleazar sat up. 'Yahweh chose you because His favour rests upon you for this time. You are a strong man, Joshua, a courageous man, a man who longs for His presence and walks in His ways. You have spent much time in the Tabernacle seeking His face in prayer. You *know* Him, Joshua. You know Him; that is why He chose you. This was not a mistake; you are the right man to lead this great nation.'

Caleb, who until now had been listening from his seat in the corner, got up and walked across the room to stand before me. 'Do you remember when Moses laid his hands on you at your inauguration? Do you remember what he said to you?' He paused and gave me time to think before continuing. '*I* do. I remember it well. He said, "Be strong and courageous, for the Lord Himself goes before you and will be with you; He will never leave you nor forsake you. Do not be afraid; do not be discouraged."'[24]

Crouching down before me, he spoke with passion, his eyes fired with purpose. 'He will never leave you, Joshua. *Never*! Yahweh is with you. *I* will never leave you, and Eleazar will never leave you. We are for you and we are with you, and you are *well able* to lead this people.' I drew in a deep breath and sat up, lifting my head. Could it be true, or were these just the well-intentioned ramblings of faithful friends?

'"Be strong and courageous". That is what Yahweh commanded you,' Eleazar smiled. '"Do not be afraid; do not be discouraged, for the LORD your God will be with you wherever you go."[25] He is with you.' Looking across at Caleb, Eleazar stretched out and joined his arm with Caleb's. 'And so are we!'

I looked at them, amazed at such loyalty and faith in the face of my weakness. Turning to Caleb, I said, 'I am grateful for your companionship. I will have much need of you. We are surrounded by men much younger than us. It makes me feel old.'

'*Agh*!' Caleb snorted. 'We are not old! We are as young and strong as we've ever been. We will outrun them, outfight them and... outlive them!'

'Moses sowed seed in the springtime,' Eleazar said, 'but you will harvest the first fruits of the autumn – and my hearts tells me there will be much fruit in this harvest.'

I grasped his arm. 'I am so thankful that the Levites were not numbered with our warriors; I would not have wanted to enter Canaan without you and your brethren.'

'We will grow old with you, Joshua. We will go with you into Canaan and stand by your side. We will take this land together.'

'Moses said you would not let me down. He was right.'

'He was usually right,' said Eleazar, raising his eyebrows. He pulled me up and straight into in a bear hug, slapping me on the back.

'*Ech*!' Caleb muttered after a while. 'How long must I wait?'

'Patience, Caleb. All comes to pass in time, yes?' Eleazar replied,

---

24 From the verses mentioned above.

25 Joshua 1:9.

grinning at his friend. He released his hold, and Caleb immediately drew me into another tight embrace, with more back-slapping.

When we had finished, Caleb stepped back and asked, 'So! What is your command, Master?'

'*No!*' I lifted my hands in protest. 'Never call me that. Never. I am no one's master.' Then, recalling my conversation with Moses, I smiled at Caleb and Eleazar in turn. 'I am not your master and I will never be your master. But I will always be your friend.'

44

Thirty Days

I had thirty days. Thirty days to mourn. Thirty days to come to terms with the fact that he was gone, to try to wrap my mind around the immense task that was now my sole responsibility. Thirty days to try to come up with a plan of how to take our people into the land of promise, and displace our enemies.

Thirty days to convince myself that I was able to accomplish it.

The fact that the whole camp was in mourning was a comfort to me. I wasn't the only one grieving the extraordinary man who had freed us from our Egyptian oppressors and faithfully fathered us through forty gruelling years in this arid wilderness. Although our necessary tasks continued, there was no singing or feasting in the camp, no family celebrations, no wearing of fine clothes or playing of joyful music. It was life in its simplest, most basic form, and it suited me well.

Caleb and Eleazar came to my tent every day during the period of mourning. At first our discussions had all been about Moses; they seemed to understand that I needed to talk about him, to place my pain squarely on the ground in front of us and dissect it piece by piece. We reminisced about the time Moses arrived back in Egypt, the miracles we had witnessed by his hand, his passion and zeal for Yahweh, his great humility, his anger when confronting sin, his sense of humour, and even the way he would raise his bushy eyebrows and peer at us when waiting for us to respond to one of his outlandish ideas. He had been terrifying and yet appealing, humble yet mighty.

And he was gone.

I found myself torn between the desire to move on into the new era that lay before me, and a stubborn insistence on clinging to the old.

If I let myself move on into the new, it was tantamount to saying I no longer needed him – and I did. My need for Moses, for his guidance, his wisdom, even his humour and wit, was so strong, it filled me with a constant ache. My days no longer had a rhythm; my routine had left me when he did. I didn't know how to live life without him. I had already said goodbye to two fathers, and Moses was no less a father to me than Nun and Jesher had been. In some ways he had fathered me more – I had spent the majority of my time with him over the years, learned from him and loved him. I missed him so much, sometimes I could feel a physical pain gripping my chest.

The night-times were the worst. I lay on my bed roll listening to the sounds of the camp; the bleating of sheep, the murmur of voices, the cracking of the fiery pillar nearby, the cries of a distressed child. One question haunted me during the night watches, a question which battered my thoughts night after endless night. One question that I knew I would not find an answer to.

The question of Moses' resting place.

I could find no resolution. My mind replayed my parting moments with him over and over again, but it was a story with no ending, and it pleaded with me to be brought to a conclusion. Countless times I visualised Moses walking up that mountain path, staff in hand, head held high, while I stood, captive and helpless, watching him leave. Over and over my heart leapt and then sank, as I recalled him turning to me one last time, not to bid me come with him, but to give me one last joyful, lingering smile before he disappeared into the mist.

It took every shred of self-control that I possessed not to run back to that mountain to search for some sign of life... or death. As painful as it was when my fathers, Nun and Jesher, died, at least I had been able to visit their graves and grieve them there. They had a resting place. They were at peace.

But what about Moses? Where was he now? Was he at peace? How did he fare?

I was bombarded by thoughts of Moses wandering, not able to rest, lost and alone on that mountain. My mind conjured up images of his body being ravaged by wolves, or vultures picking at his rotting corpse.

These gruesome visions drove me to distraction. Sleep eluded me, and night-times became a torturous cycle of drifting, waking, weeping, fearing... Most nights, exhaustion and grief took over in the early hours of the morning, and I would sink into a restless slumber. It was on one such early morning two weeks into my mourning period that Yahweh took pity on me.

I dreamt of walking in a valley, in the cool of the day. The sound of birdsong filled the air and, although I couldn't see it, I could hear the burbling of a nearby brook. The air was warm and peaceful; a gentle breeze teased the strands of hair that hung freely about my shoulders. I walked towards a shaded area, drawn to a large tamarisk tree with outstretched branches. It was in full bloom and its feathery, needle-like leaves were dotted with an abundance of white flowers. As I drew near, my heart leapt; two of Yahweh's shining men were standing under the tree. They didn't speak, but I knew they were welcoming me, beckoning me to come closer.

As I neared the place where they stood, I saw a grave. It was no ordinary grave. Simple in appearance, it was unlike the huge, decadent rock edifices that the great leaders of our time often commissioned for themselves. However, I knew without being told that every part of this grave had been prepared with the utmost care, each stone chosen for its unique colouring and shape, every one placed with precision. It was a thing of rare beauty – if a grave could be described as such?

There was no name carved onto any of the gravestones, and nothing to signpost who had been laid to rest there. But at its head was a bush. The bush was thick and luxurious, it's leaves glossy with life – and it was on fire! The same colours that graced Yahweh's pillar of fire in our midst each night also flickered here – shades of copper, crimson and gold, with threads of azure, cobalt and magenta running through it.

I stood before the grave, overwhelmed by the beauty of Yahweh's presence, which filled the atmosphere. Glancing at one of the shining men, I silently asked for permission to kneel by the grave. He smiled and nodded, so I sank to my knees and shut my eyes. Rocking backwards and forward, like Moses was apt to do, I found I had no words to pray. I didn't need them. The burden of fear and despair that had weighed me down since his death lifted off me as effortlessly as a bird taking flight.

The next moment, I found myself standing in an open field where a group of men and women stood talking in an animated fashion. They laughed together as they spoke and I revelled in the sense of joy and harmony that existed between them. I felt drawn to a man who stood with his back to me, so I walked a little closer. As if sensing my presence, he turned to look at me.

It was Moses!

I gasped in shock. Yes, it was Moses, but this was Moses as I had never seen him before! He was much younger, still bearded but with a mane of flowing dark hair. He stood tall and straight, the stooping of age gone, and was dressed in a simple robe, tied with a belt. His trusty staff was also gone, but his face broke into a playful smile and he laughed as he told me, without saying anything out loud, that he no longer needed it. His eyes twinkled with the same brightness that they always had, but gone were the creases of worry that had so often surrounded them. Instead, he radiated a fiery joy and peace... and love. Love flowed out of him, billowing towards me, catching me up in the exquisite fulfilment of being totally known and unconditionally loved.

Out of the corner of my eye, I saw a shining being walking towards the group. He glowed like the shining men I had encountered in times past, but with a much greater power, and the surge of love and goodness that radiated from him brought me to tears. Moses gave me one last smile and turned to meet the Man.

The dream faded. I woke up sobbing, not with grief or fear, but with relief. He was well! He was at peace! He had come home.

45

A Simple Man

Caleb and Eleazar found me much changed. Most mornings when I awoke, my thoughts had turned without thinking to what Moses would have me do that day. Then I would remember that he was no longer there, and my heart would sink like a rock in a sea of despair. It would take me a while to rouse myself to action, to decide what to do, to actually do anything at all. That morning, however, I woke with a profound sense of peace, which I had not experienced for many, many months.

I trusted Caleb and Eleazar implicitly and wanted to share with them my dream of the previous night. However, try as I might, I could not find the words to adequately describe what I had experienced. I need not have worried. The change they saw in me was enough to satisfy them, and the little I had been able to share enabled them to understand the essence of what I had encountered in my dream.

Over the course of the weeks of mourning, our conversations turned away from discussing Moses, and onto matters pertaining to leadership and what lay ahead. I still felt unnerved by the immensity of the task set before me but, little by little, my anxiety lessened and I started to get a clearer picture of how it might be accomplished. One afternoon near the end of our time of mourning, I noticed Eleazar and Caleb sharing probing glances.

'What?' I asked. 'What is it you are not saying? Speak your mind.'

Eleazar cleared his throat. 'We have been discussing your tent.'

'My tent?' I said, frowning as I glanced around. I had never been one for fine furnishings or a surplus of furniture. My needs were simple. I liked it that way. 'What of it?'

'Well, now that you are... leader of our people... you will need a larger tent.'

'Why? I have no need of more space. This tent serves me well. Besides,' I threw in the clincher, 'Mesha made this tent for me.'

They exchanged glances that seemed to confirm they knew what was coming, then Eleazar spoke up. 'Yes, as your own tent it is sufficient, and obviously well-made, but you will be meeting with larger groups of people now, and you need to be able to host them with... grace and ease.' I didn't like what he was hinting at. There was nothing wrong with my tent. Yes, it was on the small side, but it was functional. I had managed with it for years and I planned to continue in the same way. I didn't like a lot of fuss, and I had a sneaking suspicion that what Eleazar was suggesting would create exactly that.

Caleb spoke next. 'We believe it would be of great benefit if you used Moses' tent.'

'*No!*' The word shot out of my mouth. I paused and gathered myself before continuing. 'No. I cannot do that. No.'

Caleb and Eleazar shared another glance, and Eleazar took over again. 'Moses knew you would say that, which is why he instructed us to tell you that it was his personal request that you move into his tent.'

I couldn't believe what I was hearing. Moses knew about this? It was his idea? 'He spoke to you about this, before he...?' I stammered.

'He did.' Eleazar spoke calmly, but there was a firmness to his tone that I recognised; the same stubbornness that I saw in him had been in his uncle, and I knew that it would be fruitless to resist. I glowered at him. He took my silence as a sign of my agreement. 'Joshua, Moses was right. You need a tent that befits the leader of the nation of Israel.'

'What about his sons? Surely Gershom and Eliezer will have need of their father's tent.'

'No. They are happy with their own tents and are in full agreement with Moses giving you his tent. They like the quiet life that they lead and have no desire to have a larger, more prominent tent or position among our people.' I grunted and looked away. I knew how they felt. Eleazar continued, ignoring my disdainful disapproval. 'You will also need someone – or some people – to help look after your needs.'

'I need no one to look after me,' I barked. 'I have looked after myself my whole life and that need not change now.'

'Your responsibilities have increased significantly,' Eleazar continued smoothly, for all intents and purposes as if I had never spoken. I noticed Caleb was not saying much; he leaned back and watched our interplay with a look of suppressed amusement and what I believed to be a reluctant admiration for Eleazar, for the expert way he handled me. 'You will need someone to cook for you and your guests, to clean and help with...'

'Are you suggesting...?' I was incredulous. How dare he!

Eleazar's brow creased in confusion and then he realised what I was implying. 'Oh! No. No, no, I am not talking about... you... uh... taking a wife. Unless that is your desire.' Peering at me from underneath his furrowed brows, he suppressed a smile and said, 'Moses left no instructions in that regard.'

'So...?' I said, shrugging. What was Eleazar speaking of, then? I glanced over at Caleb who, by now, was openly chuckling and obviously thoroughly enjoying our discourse.

'No, I was not referring to a wife, I was referring to your family. You will have need of your family, Joshua, if you are to do all that is set before you. Yoram and Samina, Joel and Alya, Helah, Eglah, Davi... they will be an invaluable support to you.'

I shook my head in exasperation. 'Eleazar, I see your heart in this matter, but I do not have the time to walk there and back every time I want a meal or need my robes washed, and I cannot move back to live on the other side of the camp with my family. I must dwell here, near the Tent of Meeting and the Tabernacle.'

'Yes,' he interjected without hesitation, 'which is why *they* have agreed to move here to be with you.'

'They...? Move here? How many of them?'

'All of them. We spoke with Joel and Yoram, they discussed it among themselves and they are all in agreement. The day after tomorrow, when our time of mourning is fulfilled, they will pack up their tents and move here, to be with you. We will move your belongings into Moses' tent on the same day – it is all arranged.'

I looked at Eleazar, my mouth gaping in shock. He smiled back at me benevolently, although I detected a definite air of smugness in his demeanour. 'Oh, yes!' Caleb said, raising his pointed hand. 'Yoram asked if you could give your little tent to Shallum and his family – if that meets with your approval. Theirs is getting shabby and is in need of repair.'

'Yori wants my tent for Shallum?' I stood up and walked over to the tent flap, staring out at the surrounding tents, trying to imagine what it would be like to have my family with me again. I swung round to face the triumphant pair, who by now were both grinning openly, enjoying my obvious discomfort. 'Is there anything else that you have organised on my behalf that I should know about?' I asked with open arms and raised eyebrows.

'Well, there is one more thing,' Eleazar said.

I groaned. 'No! No more. Eleazar, I am a simple man with simple needs and I do not like lots of change. This is enough!' Caleb and Eleazar exchanged yet more glances.

'Yes, yes, I know that, but if you are to perform your new duties efficiently, you will need a manservant,' said Eleazar.

'I have no need of a manservant,' I said, frowning at the absurdity of that concept.

'You will. You will have need of a man whose word you can trust, whose heart is for Yahweh – someone who can deliver messages and meet with people on your behalf, just like you did for Moses.'

My shoulders sagged. I knew there was no point in arguing. 'And who did you have in mind for this great honour?' I asked, not bothering to hide the sarcasm in my tone.

'Attai!' Caleb said, standing to his feet. 'A more trustworthy man you would struggle to find. As Abidan's grandson, he already commands respect in the camp, and his wife is a woman of virtue and wisdom who will stand by his side and uphold his good name.'

'Attai?' This was all too much. I felt as though they had stripped me of everything I knew, everything comfortable and familiar. I felt naked and vulnerable. I sank down on a cushion and faced them both, exhausted.

'Mmm,' said Eleazar, looking at me with pity, trying unsuccessfully to hide a smile. 'We must leave you now – you have much to think on.' He nudged Caleb in the side. 'And we have many plans to make, *nu?*' I heard them chuckle as they left.

46

Fraud

It happened just as my two loyal 'advisors' (although, in truth, they felt more like taskmasters than advisors) said it would. I had just one day to ponder the imminent changes to my life, then our time of mourning ended and change was upon me with all the speed and severity of a desert storm.

Eleazar arrived at my tent that morning before the dawn had broken, closely followed by Caleb and Iru. Before the sun had even begun its daily cycle, my meagre belongings were taken to Moses' tent and I found myself standing in a space that was much too large for me, surrounded by furniture that was superfluous to my needs.

I felt ridiculous. I had never had a table, chairs, or benches of any kind while sojourning, let alone the ornate, beautifully carved pieces that now filled my new home. I felt hemmed in by them.

I was a fraud.

Commander of the armies of Israel though I was, I was still just a simple man at heart, and these beautiful furnishings were foreign and unwanted. I walked over to the ornate acacia wood table that Joel had made for Moses and ran my fingers along the grooves of the fruit and foliage he had etched into the tabletop and sturdy legs. I could still remember the day Joel started carving this table for Moses. He had been a young man, not yet married, and one of Bezalel's newest apprentices, when he had been given the great honour of working on such an important piece. It had caused quite a stir among the other apprentices, but Bezalel was unwavering in his choice of Joel for the task, believing in his exceptional skill and the potential he saw in him. Bezalel was right. Joel's skill surpassed that of his peers, as well as most of the older, more experienced carpenters who had worked with Bezalel for years. When the master craftsman had gone to be with his fathers a few years before, he bequeathed his workshop and many of his tools to Joel, who now had his own thriving business and an abundance of apprentices.

Although the elegant table felt out of place in what was now my home, I couldn't deny that it was good to have a physical reminder of Joel and my family with me. Never having married, I had not accumulated the homely trappings and ornaments that most men's wives bring into the home. I picked up a large pitcher and basin which Moses had used for washing. They were beautifully crafted, with matching patterns painted into grooves on their surfaces. They looked strangely familiar. Curious as to their origin, I turned them upside down and was surprised to see the mark of our family's pottery on their base.

'How did Moses come by these?' I mumbled to myself, reluctant to admit that I was pleased to have more reminders of my family in this elaborate new home of mine.

It felt odd to be surrounded by anything more than functional necessities, but I would get used to it. I grunted. I would have to; it seemed I had no choice. I walked the length of the large outer section of my new tent, through the thick goatskin curtain that divided it from my new sleeping quarters. At least my sleeping section was not oversized; I could not abide the thought of sleeping in a large, empty area, much preferring a cosy, closeted space in which to lay my head. I walked back through to the large meeting room and over to the chest where Moses kept his parchment maps and the chronicles of our journeys in the desert. They were mine now. I gave a cryptic laugh, thinking of the hours, days and weeks of anguish I went through learning how to read and write. I wondered if Moses had known, even back then, that I would have need of those skills, that I would one day lead this mighty people in his stead.

I shook myself out of my idle brooding; Attai would soon be arriving, I should prepare. I put my hands on my hips and looked around. Prepare how? What should I do? Eleazar and I had gone to see Attai the day before to ask him if he would be my manservant. I cringed as I said those words to him. Heat rose up my neck and into my face at the awkwardness of it all, but Attai had accepted with unreserved enthusiasm, seeming overcome by 'this great honour' that had been bestowed upon him.

'This great honour.' I snorted, shaking my head. What honour? And now he would soon be here, reporting for duty. What would I do with him? I didn't know how to have a manservant. I only knew how to be one.

I was staring at the scrolls of parchment that lay in neat piles in the chest, when I heard his voice behind me.

'*Shalom*, Master.'

I froze. No! Absolutely not!

Some things I could accept. Some things I *had* to accept, but not this. This I must make clear from the very start. Swinging round to face him, I said, '*Shalom*, Attai, *shalom*. Come in. Thank you for arriving... so early.' I gestured to one of the benches that lined the tent's meeting space, and we sat down facing each other. 'Attai, if you are to serve me, there is something I must insist on.'

'Yes, Master?'

'Attai, I am not your master and I cannot have you call me that. I am no one's master, and I am no one's lord.'

If I had struck him, he could not have looked more shocked. 'Then... what am I to call you?' he asked.

'Joshua,' I said, gesturing with open hands, as if it was obvious. 'That is my name. You can call me Joshua.'

'Forgive me, my...' He looked down and fiddled with his fingers in his lap. 'I... I cannot call you by your name.' He made a helpless gesture and looked up to make eye contact. 'My heart would chastise me... there is no honour... forgive me, but I cannot do it.' He spoke with such conviction, I hadn't the heart to contradict him. I respected his feelings in this matter, but resented the predicament he was placing me in. What could he call me, then? I would not be called 'master' or 'my lord', no matter how much his heart chastised him. So what, then?

'Ah!' I blurted, sitting up, triumphant. 'Commander! You are a warrior in the army of Israel, I am your commander. You will call me Commander, *nu?*'

The tension eased around his eyes. He smiled. 'Commander. Yes. I will call you commander.'

'We are agreed then,' I said gruffly, eager to move on from this awkward, painful discussion.

'How can I serve you, Commander?' he asked, standing to his feet, arms by his side.

I had no idea.

What should I tell him? What could I ask him to do? I looked around, trying desperately to think of something I could instruct him to do, but everything was in its place and nothing seemed amiss; I could think of nothing. 'I have no need of you at this time,' I said, silently berating myself for sounding so formal. 'Go, help your family to settle into their new home. I will call for you when I have need of you.'

A shadow of disappointment flickered across Attai's face, but he bowed his head and said, 'As you wish, commander,' before turning to leave.

'Attai...'

He swung round to face me. 'Commander?'

I stood up, exhaled, and squared my shoulders. 'I have not had a manservant before,' I said, despising the warm flush that I could feel spreading up my neck into my face. 'It may take me some time to... learn... how to walk these paths.'

A look of both understanding and respect came over Attai's face. 'And I have not been a manservant before, Commander. We will walk this path together and trust Yahweh to guide us both.' Nodding to me, he smiled and made his exit.

I sank down on the bench, grateful for the wisdom I sensed in this man who was to serve me. This was only my first official day as leader of the nation of Israel, and already I felt as though I was being pulled along by the current of a fast-flowing river, helpless and totally ill-equipped to direct its flow or navigate my own course.

47

Together Again

My family arrived in droves later that morning, the men pulling strong carts, the women carrying bundles over their shoulders, herding or carrying the little ones.

I must confess to being surprised and, if I'm honest, more than a little apprehensive, when I saw how many of them there were. Whenever I had visited my family, their tents had been laid out in the same communal circle and everything was as it always had been. However, seeing them like this, in a large group with all their belongings, made me realise how large our family had grown. My mind flashed back to our first few weeks as sojourners in the wilderness. Back then, we had just one large, ragged tent, divided into sections by makeshift curtains. That tent housed Jesher and Shira, me, three of their four children (their daughter Zivah lived with her husband, Seled, and his family), and their few grandchildren. Now, forty years later, we were a family of some magnitude.

I rubbed my temple, staring at the throng of humankind winding its way through the scattering of tents towards me. Leading the host was Joel, with Alya close by his side, as always. He put down the shafts of the cart he was pulling and rubbed his sweaty hands on his robe.

'*Shalom*, Joshua,' he said, grinning as he walked towards me. We embraced warmly, then he turned to gesture to the rapidly accumulating mass of bodies and beasts behind him. 'We have come, as requested.'

'Joel, this was not at my request,' I interjected. 'I would not have asked such a thing of my family. It was Eleazar and Caleb who...'

'Joshua, be at peace,' he interrupted, placing his hand on my shoulder. 'We are of one mind. It is both an honour and a blessing for us to be by your side, to stand with you at this time. It is also a joy to be reunited again, to have you share our table and break bread with us – and savour the fine food our women cook, *nu?*' His words warmed my heart. Without further ado, he glanced around the open space near my new home and asked, 'Where would you have us set up our living quarters?

Moses preferred to have an area of open ground around his tent, as he didn't like to be surrounded by tents or too much noise. Clearly it would not be the same for me; I wouldn't have that luxury. But I didn't mind. In fact, I could already feel the stirrings of excitement at the thought of being surrounded by my family again; the chaos, the noise, fun, laughter and tears that was family life. I hadn't realised until that moment just how much I had missed it. All of a sudden I didn't feel so alone, and the task set before me didn't feel quite so overwhelming.

I gestured to the open space around us. 'Here, if this will meet your needs?'

'This will do well, thank you.' Joel turned to the family gathered behind him and started to give instructions about who was to lodge where, and who should carry out which duties. I felt a strange sense of pride as I watched him. I thought back to the insecure, traumatised young man he had been when we first escaped Egypt, and marvelled once again at the incredible transformation that had taken place in his heart.

Yoram strode up to me as soon as Joel had finished his discourse. 'Yoshi!' he said, clasping me to him and slapping me on the back before kissing me on each cheek.

'Yori, it is good to see you,' I replied, blinking away the tears that seemed to have surfaced out of nowhere. Despite the fact that Yoram was one of my celebrated captains of a thousand, when we were away from the rigours of warfare or training, we still called each other by the names we had stumbled on when he was just a toddler.

I watched in amazement as my adopted family burst into a buzz of activity. Everyone seemed to know exactly what to do and they set about erecting their tents, digging firepits and organising their camping site with something akin to military precision. It was impressive, to say the least. Joel led with a firm yet gentle hand and I could see how much the family respected and loved him for it. The stirrings of joy in my heart deepened as I realised what this would mean. No more lonely evenings sitting by the fire on my own. No more eating food donated by well-meaning friends. No more falling asleep to the sounds of silence or rising with a sense of emptiness in my belly.

I had a family and we were all together again!

Helah came over to greet me, two of her great-grandchildren in tow. She gazed at me with undisguised love, cupped my cheek in her hand, and whispered, 'Mesha would have liked this, Yoshi. He would be so happy to know that we all back together again.' An errant tear rolled down her wrinkled cheeks, but her smile confirmed the fact that it was a tear of joy, not sorrow. 'We have planned a feast in your honour tonight,' she said. 'Caleb and his family will join us, and Eleazar and Bathshua's family. Eleazar told us that Attai and his family are to be our neighbours, so we will invite them too. It will be a time of celebration, just like the old days, *nu*?'

I could not speak. The lump in my throat was too big. Instead, I swallowed hard, clasped Helah to me again and held her close, stroking the soft, greying tresses of my adopted sister, while my heart hammered with pent-up emotion.

The rest of the day flew by and, before I knew it, twilight was upon us. I stood in the entrance of my new tent, surveying the bustling community in front of me. Thanks to Mesha's tentmaking skills which he had passed on to his sons and grandsons, nearly each couple in our family had been blessed with their own tent when they married or, at the very least, soon afterwards. It started when Mesha made a tent for Yoram and Samina for their nuptials, and continued on from there. In our culture, when a man took a wife, they lived with his parents in their tent, with a curtained-off section for their sleeping quarters. Only those who were exceptionally wealthy had their own tent – or, it seemed, those whose family included those with the skill of tentmaking!

Staring at the miscellany of people milling around, it dawned on me what an unusual and enterprising family ours was. It was the norm for a father to have a trade or occupation that he passed down to his sons, but our family had no less than *three* different trades in its midst – something very unusual in our culture. Mesha had fallen into tentmaking more by necessity than desire when we started wandering the desert, but pottery had been the family trade passed down from Jesher to Azriel, and then to Naim and his sons. Ethan and his sons, with the help of Eglah's son, Davi, worked with Naim to maintain a thriving family pottery trade.

Joel had found himself thrust into the world of carpentry early on in his life, and his sons were now apprenticed to him, along with a few other talented young men. The strong carts that they used to transport their belongings were all thanks to Joel and his sons, along with an assortment of intricately carved chests, furniture, poles and platters found within our family homes. Having carpenters in the family had been a great blessing for all of us. In addition to that, Joel's wife, Alya, had become well known throughout the camp as a skilled midwife, and her daughters had trained under her.

I had never thought of our family as being anything but ordinary. However, thinking on it now, I realised we were anything but!

After discussing their plans with me, Joel, Yoram and Naim had decided to keep their potter's wheels, carpentry tools and tentmaking provisions packed for now. There was no point in digging ovens for firing the pottery, setting up workshops or staking out skins for tents, if we would be continuing our journey northward in the next few days – and we would!

'There are many more giants waiting to meet their end,' I said under my breath, 'and much territory to conquer.' My spine tingled as I thought about the plans that Caleb, Eleazar and I had made during the last couple of weeks, and I clenched my fists, all of a sudden eager to grasp my sword and make war again. 'This peaceful interlude will not last for much longer, *nu?*' I asked no one in particular. 'But while it does,' I thought, savouring the mouthwatering aroma of roasting meat on the spit, 'I will certainly make the most of it!'

Our celebration feast that evening was sumptuous! An assortment of colourful woven mats was laid in a sequence of circles around the wide communal firepit and we gathered around, sitting in our family groups. I was given the seat of honour, in-between Joel and Yoram, with Helah nearby. Fat from the skewered lamb and goat carcasses dripped into the fire, hissing and smoking, as our women brought out dish after dish of bread cakes, manna raisin cakes, dates, figs and olives. We devoured the roasted goat with unrestraint, the younger men stripping the carcass clean, even sucking all the bones. I ate and laughed and talked until I felt I would burst with the deliciousness of it all. I could not recall the last time I felt such joy, such completeness. Moses was never far from my thoughts, but somehow I knew he would approve of our celebrations that night.

Dinner was followed by a time of singing and dancing, led by Joel and Yoram who, despite their senior years, still played the reed pipe and drum with almost inappropriate abandon. Some of the young-sters joined them with tambors, lyre and more drums and, within moments, our family enclosure was filled with bodies leaping and spinning, dancing and stamping their feet. Shadows from the oil lamps mounted on poles flickered on the tent walls and shouts of joy rang out, echoing into the night.

'So...' Caleb sidled up to me and nudged my arm. 'Were we right to bring your family to you? Yes?' I gave him a disparaging look, which only made him nudge me harder. 'Yeeees?' he said, raising his eyebrows with a cocky smile.

'Yes,' I said, unable to resist any longer. 'You were right.' I stared at the precious people congregating outside my home, laughing, singing and dancing together. 'You were right, my friend. Thank you.' I turned to look at him and coughed, trying to clear my throat. 'Thank you – for all of this.'

Helah wandered over to me. I put my arm around her and she nestled into the crook of my arm, watching the dancing with a contented smile on her face. She looked up at the blazing pillar of fire that towered over us. 'I've never been this close to Yahweh's pillar of fire before. It is magnificent, isn't it?'

'Yahweh's presence is the delight of my heart,' I whispered back, staring up at the object of my desire.

The sound of music and celebration filled the air; all seemed right with the world. I sighed, glowing with contentment. Our little community had grown. From feeling so alone and overwhelmed, I now found myself surrounded by people who embraced me, supported me... and seemed to believe in me – my adopted family, bursting at the seams with children, pregnant mothers and proud fathers. Eleazar and Bathshua's tent was close by, with their family, and Caleb and Johanna had also moved their whole household near us. I chuckled to myself as I recalled Helah's excitement at having her daughter, Serah, living close by again. Iru and Serah had lived with Caleb and his family in the tribe of Judah's allocated camping grounds since their marriage, but now Helah would be able to see more of them and their children.

Attai and his wife, Mara, had settled into their new location with their little family. I had not asked Attai to move his tent to be near me, it was his decision, but I was happy to agree to his request. I looked up to see he and Mara busy chatting to Yoram and Samina, getting to know them better. Attai was also of the tribe of Benjamin; it would be a comfort for him and his wife to have other Benjaminites nearby, and children for their little ones to play with.

Helah went to talk to Iru and Serah, leaving Caleb and I standing alone. I lowered my voice and whispered to him. 'I need your help with something.'

'Anything.'

I leaned in close. 'I need you to help me choose two men. They must be young and strong, brave of heart; men of wisdom who walk in the ways of Yahweh.'

'What will these men be doing that no one can know about?' He cocked an eyebrow in a conspiratorial manner.

I looked up at him, a mischievous smile on my face. 'They are to go and spy out the city of Jericho, and report back to me!'

Caleb's eyebrows shot up in his face. 'Spies? Aah,' he said. 'So,' he said, leaning in further, 'it is not to be us this time, *nu?*'

'Not this time, my friend, not this time. So, will you help me choose them?'

Caleb grinned at me. 'What do you think?'

48

The Taste of My Sword

'Joshua, the spies have returned,' Caleb announced, flinging open my tent flap.

'When? Where are they?' I said, looking behind Caleb to see if they were with him.

'They have just arrived. I told them to go and see their families, wash and eat, and come to your tent after midday.'

'Good! Good!' I muttered. In the weeks that had passed since Moses' death, I had been able to come to terms with his passing, and with the mantle of leadership that had been given to me. Caleb, Eleazar and I had spent much time together, discussing Canaan and strategising about how to conquer the land, and their relief when I started to return to my normal self was tangible.

'What did they say? Did they tell you anything about what they discovered?' I asked, reluctant to wait until after midday to hear their findings.

Caleb lit up with excitement. 'They did! Their journeying was not without danger, but they were able to spy out the land without being detected, and they had a most interesting time in Jericho.' Watching to see my reaction, he said, 'They stayed in the house of a... a harlot.'

'A *harlot*?' I said, horrified. 'Why? Why did they do this? Do they not remember the harlotry of our people with the Midianite women, and Yahweh's judgement on them?'

'They did nothing unworthy. They did not dishonour themselves in any way and it seems that the... uh... woman, Rahab, was used by Yahweh to help them evade capture.' I raised my eyebrows in disbelief, but Caleb continued, 'I don't know all the details, but they will tell us everything when they meet with us later.'

'Hmm.' I frowned. 'Did they say anything about the people who live there? Are they a warring tribe? What do they know of our people?'

Caleb grinned. 'Oh, they have heard of us,' he said. 'The spies said the LORD has surely given the whole land into our hands; the people are melting in fear[26] because of us. Imagine that!' he said, laughing with delight. '*Melting in fear!* Because of *us*?'

'Truly?' I asked. Caleb nodded. I clapped my hands together and started pacing up and down. 'We must put our plans into action, right away. I will ask Attai to send word to the elders – we will meet tomorrow morning straight after breaking our fast.' I sat down, drumming my fingers on the wooden bench, thinking deeply and muttering to myself, but found I couldn't sit still for long. Striding up and down, I said, 'The time has come!' Turning to my friend, I clenched my fist and said, 'Caleb! It is time, *nu*? It is time!'

Caleb laughed at my restlessness. Standing to his feet, he grabbed me, slapping me on the back in a firm embrace.

'*Agh*,' I groaned. 'I cannot just sit here and wait for them. Come! Walk with me. Let us climb the mountain and look out over the land that Yahweh has given us!'

A flood of memories bombarded us as we stood overlooking the land. We had stood in that exact spot all those years ago, looking out on the land that had been promised to us, and now here we were again. For quite some time, no words were spoken. The memories hung around us like waterlogged clouds, dripping with expectation.

I turned to Caleb. 'Do you still remember it?'

'Like it was yesterday,' he replied with a roguish smile.

'We were so young, so strong – so desperate to take this land.'

'We still are!' said Caleb, balling his hands into fists and flexing his biceps. 'We are not much changed.'

The desire for conquest rose up in me again, as fervent as it had been decades ago, perhaps even more so. My thoughts went back to that fateful time, and our entrusted mission to spy out the land of Canaan. I had never seen anything like it. Mile after mile of lush countryside, trees and plants, streams and brooks in abundance, teeming with all

26   See Joshua 2:9.

manner of fish. Pastures full of fat livestock feasting on thick, glossy tufts of grass, trees laden with pungent-smelling fruit, ripening lazily in the sun.

'I still remember the pomegranates,' Caleb said, giving me a mischievous sideways glance.

'*Eish*! Still with the pomegranates?' I rolled my eyes.

Caleb chortled to himself and we sat down, gazing out over the fertile expanse before us. 'Truly, it is a land that flows with milk and honey.' Caleb swung round to face me, passionate tears forming. '*Joshua*! We've waited so long for this moment. Think of it! To walk in that land again, to settle there, build homes and raise our families in the land where our forefathers lived!' He jumped up, yanked me to my feet, and lifted his arms, shouting into the wind, '*Our time has come!*'

We put our heads back, shouting and whooping. Jumping up and down like giddy teenagers, we seized each other, slapping each other on the back.

'We have waited so long,' I gasped, 'but now it is time.'

'And this time, we're ready,' said Caleb, locking eyes with mine. 'There is no going back. This time, we're going *in!*'

A surge of passionate expectation coursed through my body. I started panting, my chest rising and falling, quickening in response to the fire that burned in my belly, begging for release. Turning to face the lush green land set before us, I stepped forward, drew my sword, and yelled, 'Hear me now, people of Canaan! Hear me and tremble! Let your hearts melt with fear!' The sound of my voice echoed, bouncing off the surrounding hills, returning to me as in a reawakening.

'Your day of reckoning has come and your time is *over*! I claim this land in the name of the One True God, the God of Israel! Ready yourselves, giants of Canaan, for you shall surely *taste the edge of my sword!*' I roared, thrusting my sword upwards.

My shouts reverberated back to me, wave after wave. Overshadowing the echoes, I heard a pulsating sound, like thunderous applause, rippling in the heavens overhead.

49

The God of Joshua

'How is this possible?' I mumbled, sinking down onto a bench. 'Yahweh, help me, I beg of you! Let me not be put to shame.' Doubt pulled at me, threatening to overshadow my zealous thoughts of conquest. I raked my hand through my hair. My head was spinning.

The two spies had just left, and with them Caleb and Eleazar, leaving me alone to ponder the seemingly impossible feat of breaching the walls of Jericho. Thanks to the two spies, we now knew that there were not one, but *two* walls encircling that great city – walls so wide and strong that chariots could drive on them. Even if we managed to break through the outer wall, their archers would fell us before we could batter our way through the second one. This was a problem I had not envisaged. The thought of great numbers of our warriors being slain in an attempt to breach the mighty walls of Jericho was not one I relished. The faces of the brave men who fought by my side flashed through my consciousness, driving me to my knees.

'Yahweh, show Yourself faithful,' I whispered. 'Lead me in the path You would have us take.' Realising that I was rocking, I gave a cryptic laugh. 'Moses rocked when he prayed,' I thought, 'and now I find myself doing the same thing.' I sat back, looking around the spacious tent where Moses had spent so much time; the place where he and Yahweh had met and talked on a daily basis.

'He sought Your face right here, in this tent,' I murmured, 'and You answered him. You spoke with him as a man speaks with his friend. You worked miracles through his hands. Would that you would work through mine in the same way.' I looked down at my rough, calloused hands. I shook my head at the incongruity of that thought, longing for one more chance to be able to ask Moses what to do. He would know what to do. But he wasn't there.

This was my space now. My tent. My place of communion with Yahweh.

'You are not alone.' I could hear Moses' voice ringing out as clearly as it had on the day he told me that I was to take over leadership of our people. 'Yahweh is with you; you will do mighty exploits in His name.'

'Mighty exploits?' I grimaced, raising my eyebrows. 'What, like breaking down the unbreakable walls of the city of Jericho? How? Tell me, how?'

'*Be strong and courageous.*' The words reverberated around me, bouncing off the walls of my tent, echoing back and forth. The words were those spoken over me by Moses at my inauguration, but the voice was not my master's.

I stood to my feet. My legs started trembling, the hairs on my arms stood up. Wisps of glimmering mist were forming before my eyes; soft tendrils of velvety swirls that sparkled, flowing through the air unhindered. They grew in volume, thickening into an undulating cloud of shimmering glory.

Yahweh's presence! He was here! In my tent!

A surge of courage coursed through my body. Propelled by a desperate longing to commune with Him, I raised my voice and cried out, 'Prove yourself to me, as you did to Moses! You showed yourself faithful to Moses, now show yourself faithful to me. Let the God of Moses be the God of Joshua!'

Driven by the fierce boldness that burned within me, I shouted, 'You showed me what to do, how to defeat giants. Speak to me again, Lord God! Show me how to take this land in Your name! Open my eyes to see what you would have me do!'

In a split second, a vista opened up in front of me. The walls of my tent were still there, but they faded into insignificance as a clearer, more defined image unfurled before me. A city with huge, towering walls; it could only be Jericho. As I studied its imposing heights, I felt myself being lifted up out of my body, like the eagle that soars the heavens. I circled the city from my lofty perspective, noting the vast dimensions of its walls and the expanse of the metropolis' reach. A seething anger settled on me as I saw the vast temples and altars dedicated to the worship of Ashtaroth, their pagan goddess of the moon, and the obscene activities that were taking place there.

My gaze was drawn downwards to an enormous army that marched towards Jericho. I homed in on the faces of the warriors, faces of men who I knew and esteemed. Each man was silent and serious, focused on the task before him. As I studied their faces, I heard the blast of trumpets echoing all around me, accompanied by the roar of thousands of voices shouting, over and over again, in a cacophonous battle cry. There was a great uproar; the sound of people screaming, cries of terror and the deafening rumbling of stones crashing to the ground. My outlook shifted and I watched, breathless with shock, as the great walls of Jericho crumbled and collapsed amid billowing clouds of dust and debris.

'But how? What caused these walls to topple?' I asked, squinting to try to see through the dusty curtain that obscured my vision.

The vision transformed; the ruinous remains of Jericho dissipated and I found myself standing outside a cave set into the side of a mountain. Before me knelt five rulers, each wearing a crown.

'Who are you?' I muttered, frowning in concentration as I studied their faces. I recognised none of them.

A giant hand reached down from the heavens, took the crowns from their heads and dashed them to pieces before me. The kings were thrust face down on the ground, and five dusty sandal-clad feet were placed upon the back of each ruler's neck. I frowned in confusion but, before I could ponder the meaning of the vision, the mountainside faded and another great city loomed up in front of me.

My eyes alighted on Caleb, surrounded by our valiant warriors and by the dead bodies of our enemies. My heart pounded with excitement as Caleb lifted his sword and roared in triumph, the warriors around him echoing his victory cry.

'*Yes!*' I clenched my fist. The shout of victory was long and loud; I couldn't help but join in. When the roar died down, Caleb's face vanished, and town after town, city after city, flashed before my eyes.

Each time a new settlement appeared, I saw the faces of my trusted captains standing victorious in that conquered land, surrounded by their slain enemies. Dizziness beset me as the visions appeared and disappeared in quick succession, each heralding an irrefutable victory, until finally they stopped, and Eleazar stepped into my line of vision.

He was dressed in his priestly garments and stood before a multitude of our people. Turning to me, he reiterated the words he declared on the day Moses passed away. '"The LORD your God will be with you wherever you go." He is with you ... and so are we ... We will go with you into Canaan and stand by your side. We will take this land together.'

The pounding of my heart diminished; an immense sense of warmth and peace flooded me.

Eleazar's calm smile faded from my vision and my heart skipped with excitement as the faces of the two shining men I had met years before appeared before me: the first dark and handsome, the other blond and burnished. Flashes of light started to spring up all around them as more shining men appeared, then more, and still more, until the landscape was covered with a glittering display of light, like a field full of lamps on a dark, moonless night.

The shining men turned as one towards the form of a Man who appeared in the distance, eclipsed in light, pulsating with goodness. Bowing down, they worshipped the glorious beauty of the Man. Propelled forward as if in flight, I found myself standing before Him. Flinging myself at His feet, a surge of ecstasy flowed through me as a mighty voice billowed across the firmament, like the roaring of many waters.

'Be strong and courageous! I will deliver your enemies into your hands. Now go! Take the land which I have given you!'

Book 3

in the *Wilderness trilogy*

It seemed like an impossible task! How could Joshua possibly hope to walk in the footsteps of the extraordinary man of God who he had had the privilege of serving for the last forty years? As Moses' manservant he had witnessed miracles first-hand. He had seen Yahweh's power move through his prophet master as he led the Israelites through forty gruelling years of wandering in the wilderness. And now, as Yahweh's chosen leader, it seemed Joshua had no choice but to take on the mantle of leading the nation of Israel in Moses' stead.

Joshua's self-doubt and fear would prove to be unfounded; he would see the power of God move through him, just like He did through Moses. Aided by some remarkable 'shining men', Yahweh's celestial messengers, this extraordinary warrior leader would witness the waters of the Jordan River part, see the sun standing still at his command, watch the mighty walls of Jericho crumble and fall at the blast of trumpets and the shouts of his men, and have the kings of the land of Canaan bow their knees in subservience to him.

This book is the exciting conclusion to the inspiring story which tells of the courage, humility, and devotion of the military hero, Joshua ben Nun, as he leads his people into Canaan on a quest to possess their promised land.

> The hairs on my arms stood up, and my legs started to shake. I turned around slowly and put my hand up to shield my eyes from the glare of the sun, which was nearly at its peak. Although I couldn't see clearly, I could just make out the vague outline of a Man standing a few feet away, watching me. The

Man was tall in stature and well-built, and He held in His hand a long sword that glinted in the sunlight. Instinctively, my hands went to pull my sword out of my scabbard but, to my dismay, I realised I was utterly defenceless.

My heartrate increased rapidly as I weighed my options. Should I run? No, the Man was so tall, he would in all likelihood outrun me in no time at all. Should I look for rocks to throw? Not enough time. The Man was so close, by the time I was able to pick some up, He would be upon me. I would certainly not be able to wrestle Him to the ground, that much was certain.

My military training told me to stand my ground and not run, so I stood, ready to move at any moment, my heart in my throat. I stared at Him from behind the cover of my hand, but couldn't see His facial features because of the glare of the sun, so I couldn't read His expression. The weight of silence continued.

'Who are you?' I thought to myself. 'Why don't you move, or say something?'

Still the Man stood.

He didn't attack and He didn't retreat. He just stood, watching me.

'Is he a spy from Jericho?' I wondered. 'Or an assassin hired to kill me?'

Still the Man stood.

Finally, I could bear it no longer. 'Are you for us or our adversaries?' I shouted.

The Man didn't respond immediately but, when He did, my knees went weak and I found myself bowed low on the ground, without even knowing how I had got there.

'No,' the Man said. 'As Commander of the army of the Lord I have now come.'

Available in 2024.